PLAYING DEAD

By the same author

Loverboy

PLAYING DEAD

Richard Belsky

Hodder & Stoughton

First published in Great Britain in 1998 by Hodder and Stoughton
A division of Hodder Headline PLC

10 9 8 7 6 5 4 3 2

British Library Cataloguing in Publication Data

A CIP catalogue record for this title
is available from the British Library

ISBN 0 340 69287 1

Typeset by Hewer Text Ltd, Edinburgh
Printed and bound in Great Britain by
Mackays of Chatham PLC, Chatham, Kent

Hodder and Stoughton
A division of Hodder Headline PLC
338 Euston Road
London NW1 3BH

prologue

From the confession
of David Galvin
(a.k.a. Felix the Cat)
to New York City Police

July 12, 1987

The pretending was always the best part. Even better than the killing.

I remember one of them – it was either the second or the third time – that lasted for two weeks.

She lived in a house that made it so wonderfully easy to spy on her. Every night I'd watch her come home and see how she lived. I knew what she ate, what she wore, what she liked on television, what her favorite music was – even what she wore to bed. Sometimes I'd gaze at her for hours as she slept in her bed – dressed in a sexy nightgown and looking so peaceful and innocent.

I felt incredibly close to her at those times. Just like I was lying there in the bed right next to her.

I suppose I was falling in love with her.

During the day, I'd follow her to work or to the store or when she went to meet a friend for lunch. I rode on the same bus and sat in the same restaurant and found excuses to be around the same building where she worked. We were always together. We were inseparable. We were true soulmates.

Twice, I even made real contact with her. The first time was when her hat blew off in the street on a windy day. I picked it up, handed it to her and smiled. She smiled back and said 'thank you.' The other time was in a department store. I held the door open for her as she left with her arms filled with packages. She mumbled a 'thank you' again this time, but it was perfunctory and she barely looked at me. I was just one of millions of faceless people in New York City to her.

No, she never knew that I was such a big part of her life.

Until the very end.

And the end, when it came, was especially satisfying. Probably because of the long buildup. I think that's true of a lot of things in life. It's why a big meal tastes so good when you're really hungry. Or why it's so much better to wait until Christmas morning to open your presents, instead of giving in to temptation and peeking in the closet early. Well, that's how I felt about her too. Anticipation makes the heart grow fonder.

But, after two weeks, I knew it was time. The truth is I was getting tired of her. It was just like any other relationship. The first time you make love is exciting and passionate. But after awhile it becomes routine. She was becoming routine. I didn't feel the same jolt of excitement anymore that I used to when I'd see her lying in bed or taking off her clothes or making up her face in the mirror.

It was definitely time to move on to someone new.

The best thing about this one though was the way she acted at the end when she finally realized what was happening to her.

They're all different, you know.

Some of them cry. Some get angry. And some become very quiet – as if they could will their way out of it by pretending it was just a terrible dream that they were going to wake up from at any minute.

But she begged.

Oh, did she beg. She told me about her life, her dreams, all her plans for the future. She promised me anything if I would let her go. She offered me money. Sex. She said she'd never tell anyone.

I never saw anybody who wanted to live so badly.

That made me very happy when I killed her . . .

PART ONE

Felix the Cat

ONE

[illegible] I wish you would [illegible]
[illegible] suddenly [illegible]
All right [illegible]
And if [illegible]
[illegible] with [illegible]
[illegible]

The best lack [illegible]
passionate [illegible]

[illegible] for a [illegible]
[illegible] emotionally involved [illegible]
[illegible] between you [illegible]
[illegible] the grizzled vete[illegible]
[illegible] at all, con[illegible]
[illegible]

[illegible] told me [illegible]
[illegible] you and the people [illegible]
[illegible] let them [illegible]
[illegible] terrible [illegible]
[illegible] the time it's wr[illegible]
[illegible] you can't eve[illegible]
[illegible] cases, writ[illegible]
[illegible] every patien[illegible]
[illegible] my life [illegible]
[illegible] they have to [illegible]
[illegible] after all [illegible]

one

• • • • • • • • • • •

'I wish you wouldn't keep appearing and disappearing so suddenly,' Alice told the cat.

'All right,' said the cat.

And this time it disappeared quite slowly, beginning with the tail and ending with its grin, which remained some time after the rest of it had gone.

Lewis Carroll
Alice in Wonderland

The best lack all commitment, and the worst are full of passionate intensity . . .

William Yeats

The first rule for a newspaper reporter is to never get personally involved in a story.

They teach you that right from the very start. All the old-timers, the grizzled veterans, the newsroom pros that you meet. They've seen it all, done it all in this business. They know the pitfalls.

Dougherty, they told me, you've always got to keep a wall up between you and the people you cover. You need to get into their lives, but don't ever let them get into yours. Tragedy, violence, sickness; all sorts of terrible things like that happen to people in this world all the time. It's what you fill a newspaper with, day after day. But you can't ever let any of it touch you.

It's the same, I guess, with a lot of other jobs. I mean, doctors don't grieve over every patient they diagnose with a fatal disease. Or firemen for every life they don't save. Or cops for every murder victim they have to put in a body bag.

It's just a job, after all.

And you should always remember that.

Otherwise, it will eat you up alive.

The second rule a newspaper reporter has to learn is the truth about the first rule. It's all bullshit.

There is no wall that can render reporters invulnerable from the things we cover, no safe zone, no protection for any of us. It can't be done. Sooner or later, we all come face to face with a story we can't just walk away from after the presses start running. The murder victim whose death is so so senseless that it makes us question our most basic beliefs about human decency. The convicted defendant who is sent off to jail even though we're convinced he's really innocent. The memory of a horrible car accident or airplane crash or burn victim that we just can't seem to get out of our system.

Sometimes the line between all this and our other life – the one we have outside the newspaper, if we're lucky – begins to blur.

And, when that happens, we stop being impartial observers at the game – and become a player.

Some people learn this lesson very early in their career. They realize that being a reporter isn't like being Clark Kent at the *Daily Planet*. And it isn't like being Humphrey Bogart or Cary Grant in some old 1940s newspaper movie. These are real people and real lives that we're dealing with here.

Others don't find that out for a long time. Maybe it's the luck of the draw, maybe it has something to do with them – but they can go for years before they come across the story that makes them come face to face with their own feelings and fears and inner demons.

And then there's the reporter who thinks that he's got it all figured out. That he's got everything under control.

Except it's all a lie.

Because – in the end, when he finally learns the truth – he realizes he's already been in way over his head for a long time.

Like me.

two

• • • • • • • • • • •

Ossining State Prison – which used to be called Sing, Sing – is in a tiny, peaceful town nestled along the banks of the Hudson River, about thirty-five miles north of New York City.

Ossining looks like a rustic hamlet, not the home of one of the country's most notorious penitentiaries. There are antique stores, landmark historical sights and comfortable restaurants. But the prison itself is anything but rustic. It is grim and grey and forbidding. A series of spiraling towers and walls and barred windows overlooking the Hudson, which houses murderers, rapists, drug dealers, armed robbers and others of the worst of society's misfits.

The guard who met me at the front entrance of the prison was a woman.

She was about thirty-five, with blonde hair rolled up into a bun behind her head, and a face that looked very hard. She wore a uniform that clung a bit too tight to her breasts and thighs. There was a gun on her hip. When I used to cover stories, I hardly ever ran into women law enforcement officers. Now I see them around all the time. It just shows how long I've been away.

'Your name?' the woman guard asked me.

'Joe Dougherty.'

'Where are you from?'

'The *New York Banner*.'

'And your business here?'

'I'm supposed to see David Galvin for an interview.'

She looked surprised.

'Felix the Cat?'

'That's what everybody used to call him.'

'He's our most famous prisoner.'

'You must be very proud.'

I flashed her a smile when I said it. The same kind of smile that used to open up doors all over New York. That used to charm people into talking to me. That got me so many exclusive Page One stories back in the old days.

Of course that was a long time ago.

'Are you a crime reporter at the *Banner*, Mr Dougherty?' she asked.

'Something like that.'

'What exactly does a crime reporter do?'

'Oh, I look for clues, chase bad guys – all sorts of neat stuff like that.'

'Are you any good at it?'

'Sure, I've already found two clues this morning. Ten more and I get to send away for my Dick Tracy secret decoder crimestopper's ring.'

I smiled again. The guard laughed this time. Her face didn't look so hard when she laughed. I revised my estimate of her age downward a bit. Maybe barely only thirty. Maybe a job like this just aged you very quickly.

'Galvin's in the prison infirmary,' she said. 'He's got cancer, you know. A real pisser of a cancer that's eating up his insides. They say he's only got a few days left. The sonavabitch is dying.'

'It couldn't happen to a nicer guy.'

'Yeah, no one here's too broken up about it.'

David Galvin was a monster. He was pure evil. The devil. The anti-Christ.

Eleven years ago, Galvin had murdered nine women in New York City. Later, he said he picked his victims at random and then stalked them – for days, sometimes for weeks – watching everything they did without any of them suspecting a thing. Then he struck, and the terror was unspeakable. Some of the deaths were mercifully quick. Others he lingered over – playing out his sick fantasies in the victim's dying hours. Two other women survived. One was in a wheelchair, the other in a mental hospital.

Unlike many serial killers, he came from a privileged background. His father was a high-powered corporate attorney, his mother an advertising executive. They lived in a big house in a posh suburb of New Jersey, and vacationed each year in Martha's Vineyard. Until David Galvin was arrested, he was a student at New York University, where his major was pre-med. He put down on his application to the program that he wanted to become a doctor to help people.

Maybe the most frightening thing about the killings though, was his motive. There was none. None at all. He said he just did it for thrills. For kicks. Everyone has a passion for something. Sex. Food. Alcohol. His passion was killing.

He began writing to the media after each body turned up. The notes were done in poetry; bizarre rhymes in which he talked about his victims and their suffering and his excitement in a detached way, that sent chills through the people of New York City who read them in the newspapers.

Every woman was terrified that she might be his next target.

Until he was captured, most people thought he got the idea for his nickname – Felix the Cat – from Son of Sam, the infamous 1970s serial killer. Son of Sam always claimed that he coined his name because of a barking dog that used to keep him awake.

But Galvin later insisted Felix the Cat was his own creation. He said cats – unlike dogs – were intelligent, mysterious and moved quietly through the night, just like him. And, he said, they had nine lives. Even if you took away one of them, he still had plenty to go.

But now he was dying a painful death.

God works in wondrous ways.

'Galvin's in the prison infirmary,' the guard was saying. 'He's pretty weak. But he's still got restraints on. There's a twenty-four-hour guard on his door too. No one wants to take any chances with this guy. I'll walk you down there myself. The guard will only be a few feet away if you need help or anything. Okay?'

I nodded.

'You got some identification?' she asked. 'How about a press card?'

My press card. Christ, when's the last time someone asked me for one of those. I rummaged around in my wallet and somehow found it. My old New York City press card from the last time I worked for the *Banner*. I took it out and handed it to her.

'I think it may have expired,' I said.

She looked at the date and whistled softly in amazement. 'Yeah, it sure has.'

'I keep meaning to have the thing renewed,' I said. 'But I've been kinda busy.'

'This press card isn't just the wrong year,' she said. 'It's the wrong decade.'

'I've been real busy.'

The guard shook her head and handed the card back to me.

'It looks to me like it's been a long time between assignments for you, Scoop,' she said.

'Yeah,' I told her, 'a very long time.'

three

• • • • • • • • • • •

It had been eight years.

That was how long ago that the *New York Banner* fired me.

So I was more than a little surprised when I got a phone call at home on a Sunday afternoon in early May from Andrew J. Kramer. Of course, when I used to know him he was just Andy – a struggling young cub reporter at the *Banner*. I was a big newspaper star in those days. Now he was managing editor, the No. 2 man on the paper, and I worked at a public relations firm in Princeton, New Jersey. It's funny the way life works out sometimes.

'Hi, buddy,' he said now. 'Long time, no talk, huh?'

'How've you been, Andy.'

No way I was going to call him Andrew.

'Great. Just great. You should see my office, man. It's the size of a battleship. I've got a corner window, a wet bar and a secretary with a body like Pam Anderson. Who'd have ever thought I'd be here back when I was sitting at the end of the night rewrite bank, huh?'

Nice of you to call up and rub your good fortune in my face, I thought.

But I didn't say that.

'I'm real happy for you, Andy,' I told him. 'I always figured you were going to be a big success.'

'Listen, I hear you landed a big job too.'

'I guess so.'

'Some kind of public relations firm?'

'Lyman, Stiller and Nash.'

Whenever I said that, it sounded like a '70s singing group.

'And you're getting married?'

'This fall. Her name is Carolyn Nash. She's a lawyer from Princeton. She works for one of the big pharmaceutical firms down here. And she also happens to be the daughter of Paul Nash, senior partner of Lyman, Stiller and Nash. Just a coincidence, of course.'

Kramer laughed. Now I hadn't talked to Andy Kramer in years. When I got fired from the *Banner* and my life was falling apart, some of the people there tried to help me. They kept in contact with me, offered support and gave me encouragement. Andy wasn't one of them. I remembered going into a bar one time about six months after it happened. Andy was there, but left in a hurry as soon as he saw me. I knew why. He didn't want to be seen with me. I was damaged goods, I was yesterday's news. I couldn't help him any more. There was no reason for him to be my friend.

So why was he calling me now?

'Actually we were just talking about you the other day,' he said. 'How you used to be one of the best reporters this paper ever had. You were really something, Joe.'

I realized he was talking about me in the past tense – as if I was dead.

'Everyone said you had an unerring reporter's instinct. You had a real nose for news. You were aggressive. You opened doors that no one else could get past. And when you got your teeth into a big story, you never let go.'

'That's what they all said, huh?'

'Absolutely.'

'Did anyone also happen to mention that if I didn't have all the facts of a story, I sometimes just made it up?'

'C'mon, Joe – that happened a long time ago.'

I figured if I waited him out long enough, he'd eventually get around to the real reason for this phone call.

'How come you never drop by the office to say hello?' Kramer asked.

'I was fired. Remember?'

'Well, sure, but . . .'

'When you're fired, it's kind of a message that the company doesn't want you around anymore. It's not exactly a social invitation to keep in touch. I figured I was *persona non grata*.'

'You? You're a friend. We go back a long way, you and me, Joe.'

I sighed. 'What do you want from me, Andy?'

'Do I need a reason to call up an old friend?'

'Yes.'

'What makes you think that.'

'My unerring reporter's instinct.'

Kramer laughed. 'You're right, Joe. I do need something from you.'

Then he told me the latest news about Felix the Cat.

'It's an easy gig, Joe. You'll get paid; you'll get some nice publicity for it, which should be good for your public relations business; and then you can go back to your job there and your house in New Jersey and your pretty new fiancée and live happily ever after. What do you say?'

'It would be just this one assignment, right?' I said. 'I'd go see Felix the Cat in jail, interview him for the *Banner*, then write up the story – and that would be it.'

'Absolutely,' Andy Kramer said. 'In and out. No problem.'

'In and out,' I repeated.

four

Andy said the letter had arrived in the mail three days earlier. It was addressed to 'Letters to the Editor, *New York Banner*', and came from Ossining State Prison. Inside the envelope was a piece of paper with a typewritten message, written in simplistic verse – just the way Felix the Cat used to send his notes to the media. At first, the *Banner* editors thought it might be a hoax. But there was a handwritten signature at the bottom, so they checked it out. It was from David Galvin.

I sat in Andy's office and read it:

Dear Editor:

I've been away in prison for eleven long years,
Now there's lots of regrets, lots of tears

It's finally time to do the right thing,
Send me a reporter, and I promise to sing

I know secrets about those old days,
when I was big news on the front page
Now I want to tell the truth behind it all,
the terrible deeds, the blood and the rage

You've got a newsroom full of reporters,
but I don't want anyone new
Joe Dougherty's my choice
He's the only one that will do.

Dougherty, Dougherty, he's my man
If he can't save my soul, no one can!

David Galvin
(Felix the Cat)

'Why me?' I asked Andy after I finished.

'I don't have the answer to that.'

'I mean, it doesn't make sense. Sure, I was working at the *Banner* during the Felix the Cat murders, but I didn't have any kind of a big role in it. I didn't break any exclusives. I didn't get any personal notes from the killer. I never wrote public appeals for him to turn himself in like some reporters did. I was just one of a very large pack of reporters covering the case.'

'Your byline was on the story of Galvin's arrest,' Andy said. 'I pulled it from the library.'

He handed me a story across the desk. I looked down at the clipping:

FELIX THE CAT CAPTURED!

Cops Swoop Down
On Killer of Nine,
Rescue Woman Captive

By Joe Dougherty

'So what?'

'Maybe he's been obsessing about that article – and about you – all these years in prison' he said. 'Pinned it up to the wall of his jail cell and reads it every day until he thinks you're his pal or something. I don't know – the guy's crazy, man.'

'On one level, yes. But he's also very smart. I remember reading somewhere once how he had an IQ of 161. I figure there has to be some other reason.'

'So you'll ask him when you go to see him. Are you up for this or not, Joe?'

Before I could answer, an editor came in to run down the day's front page stories. The biggest one was about the murder of a wealthy Wall Street investment banker, who had been found shot to death with a pretty young call girl in his Upper East Side apartment a few weeks earlier. Authorities were now zeroing in on a jealous girlfriend as the main suspect – who also happened to be the daughter of one of the city's most prominent businessmen and political movers and shakers. The story had everything: violence, sex, money, power. It had been in the headlines ever since the shooting happened. There was also a building collapse in Washington Heights, a massive drug bust in Queens, a fiscal crisis at City Hall and a $36 million winner in the lottery.

I remembered when I used to live and die with the news like that, each day of my life. Every story, every assignment; they all seemed so important. Now I barely listened to the news. I didn't care anymore about investment bankers getting murdered or car crashes on the Long Island Expressway or four-alarm fires or shootouts in Times Square or sanitation strikes. I didn't have time for that stuff anymore. I was all grown-up. I had a life now.

I told that to Andy Kramer.

'I guess I can understand what you're saying.' he said. 'You've been through a lot over the past few years. The mess here at the *Banner*. Then the way your wife and son died right after that. It looks you're finally getting things together again. You don't want to do anything to mess it up, right?'

'Something like that.'

He cleared his throat nervously. 'By the way, Joe, I know this is awfully belated – and I'm sorry I never called or dropped you a note at the time – but I was really sorry when I heard about the deaths of Susan and your son . . . what was his name?'

'Joseph. His name was Joseph Jr, and he was a year and half old.'

Kramer shook his head. 'That's tough.'

'I survived.'

And now I was all the way back. I was just about to marry a lovely woman, and soon we would have our own children. Another little boy just like the one I lost and maybe a daughter too. I'd go to work every day at a real grown-up job, with my own office and normal hours and three-martini lunches. No more living on coffee and junk food and spending hours staking out crime scenes like I used to. Then, at night, I'd go home to our big, beautiful house in the suburbs of New Jersey and enjoy the new life I had for myself.

All I had to do was say that to Andy Kramer, and tell him to take this job of his and shove it. Then I could leave here and never think about him or the *New York Banner* or David Galvin again.

Yep, that was the thing to do, all right. Just stand up and walk right out the door.

'I've got a city room full of reporters out there, Joe,' Andy said. 'Most of them are eager, ambitious young guns – just like you used to be – who would love to do this interview. But Felix the Cat asked for you in the letter. So do you want to do the story or not?'

'Yeah, I want to do the story,' I heard myself say.

Raymond Chandler said it best a long time ago: There is no trap so deadly as the trap you set for yourself.

five

David Galvin had changed a lot in eleven years. The last time I'd seen him was on the day of his sentencing. He was a dark, good-looking youth of twenty-two then, with a smug, arrogant look on his face. Even as he was leaving the courthouse after the judge gave him a life sentence, with no possibility of parole, he proudly flashed a thumbs-up sign to the press and curious onlookers outside. There was never a hint of remorse for the unspeakable atrocities he had committed.

But now he looked like he'd aged thirty years.

He was thin and emaciated, his hair was mostly gone and his eyes had that vacant, hopeless look that people have when they know they're going to die.

Despite his condition, Galvin was still kept restrained by heavy wrist and ankle cuffs that were attached to his hospital bed, just like the woman at the front gate had said. A guard was posted outside the door, only a few feet away from me. Every five minutes, he looked in to see what Galvin was doing. Even in death, this man was going to suffer the indignities of being deprived of even the smallest of life's freedoms.

Just like his victims had.

Above Galvin's bed was a portrait of Jesus and the Twelve Disciples at the Last Supper. On the table next to him was a Bible. I remembered reading somewhere how he had become religious after being diagnosed with cancer a year earlier. He said he prayed to the Lord every day now for forgiveness for the things he had done. All he wanted now was to go to Heaven.

'Hello, Galvin,' I said. 'I'm Joe Dougherty. From the *New York Banner*.'

He turned on his side in the hospital bed and looked across the room at me.

'They really did send you.'

'That was what you asked for.'

'I didn't think they would. I didn't know if they could find you. I wasn't even sure you were still alive.'

'I sometimes wondered about that myself.'

'Yeah, me too. I wake up every morning now and thank the Lord I still have one more day where I can draw a breath. It's funny how precious all the little things are that we used to just take for granted. Do you know what I'm saying, Joe?'

I pulled up a chair and sat down next to the bed. I took out a notebook and pen and set my tape recorder on the table next to the Bible. I was nervous. I wasn't sure exactly what to say to him next. Or how to get the interview started. It had been a long time since I'd done anything like this.

'So how are you doing?' I asked him. 'Hanging in there?'

When in doubt, go for the cliché.

'As well as can be expected. I've got cancer. The worst kind too. It started in the colon, then it spread to my liver and my pancreas. They figure it's probably in the bone marrow, lungs and even my brain by now too. Or if it isn't, it's headed there very soon. I'm fucked, my man. Totally fucked.'

'I'm sorry – I guess,' I said. 'I really don't know what to say, except . . .'

'Except no one's going to mourn me very much when I'm gone, huh?'

I nodded. 'You did a lot of bad stuff.'

'That I did.'

I looked around the room. At the picture of Jesus on the wall. The Bible next to his bed. There was even a copy of the 23rd Psalm pinned to the wall next to him. 'Yea, though I walk through the Valley of Death, I fear no evil . . .'

'So now you've decided to make peace with God, huh? Say "I'm sorry" and hope all is forgiven. March right up to the heavenly gates with your head held high, just like you were a normal human being. Instead of a murdering son of a bitch.'

'God is all-forgiving,' Galvin said. 'The scriptures tell us this.'

'Well, if he really is, then you're going to be the ultimate test of that theory.'

He smiled weakly.

'What am I doing here, Galvin?' I asked. 'I haven't been a reporter at the *Banner* for eight years. I haven't even worked for any kind of a newspaper for awhile. Why did you ask for me?'

'It's not important,' he said.

'Yes, it is,' I said to him. 'I need to know why.'

'You'll find out.' Galvin smiled weakly. 'Soon enough.'

He looked down at the tape recorder next to him.

'You better make sure that thing's on,' he said. 'I don't have much time. I fall asleep a lot. And, if I don't, the drugs for the cancer make me hallucinate and lose concentration. But I have to take them. It's the only way I can stand the pain. So let's just get going, Dougherty. I have a story to tell.'

He told it then. The whole thing, from the first murder to the last. He recounted the details of the killings, the terror his victims felt, the pleasure he got from his acts. He talked about the dead ones. The two who lived, too. The one that was with him when he was captured. And another victim a few months earlier that police had found barely alive. The cops had come very close to catching him that time, Galvin remembered. He said he wanted to contact the woman now – to tell her how sorry he was for what he'd done to her – but the prison officials wouldn't let him.

'It doesn't matter,' I said. 'She couldn't have heard you anyway.'

I remembered the woman lying in the hospital after the police found her. The way she looked. The fear in her eyes. The way she cringed in terror when anyone, even the nurses, touched her. It never got any better either. They say she just retreated into her own private little world. A world far away from terrible people like David Galvin. But far away from the rest of us too. The doctors didn't think she'd ever recover her sanity.

'That's too bad,' Galvin said when I told him about her.

I wasn't sure if he meant it was too bad about her problems or too bad he'd never had a chance to finish the job of killing her.

'So what's the point of all this?' I asked. 'Now that you're dying, you suddenly feel compassion for all your victims? And you want to say you're sorry?'

'Yes, I'm sorry.'

It reminded me of an old Steve Martin comedy routine. One he used to do on *Saturday Night Live*. Whatever the trouble, Martin used to tell the audience, there's two magic little words that can make everything all right again: 'I forgot.' I forgot to pay my taxes. I forgot I was married to you when you caught me in bed with that other woman. Gee, judge, I forgot armed robbery was supposed to be a crime.

And now David Galvin was saying 'I'm sorry' – I just forgot murdering innocent young women was wrong.

'And that's it?' I asked him impatiently.

'No, there's more.'

'What is it?'

'There's more,' he repeated.

I stared at him. For a few seconds I didn't get what he was telling me. Then it suddenly hit me. 'More victims?' I asked.

'Uh-huh.'

'More than the nine dead people we already know about?'

'We were very busy.'

'And that's what you called me here to confess?'

'I had to tell someone before it's too late.'

I tried to let the enormity of what he was saying sink in. More victims. For eleven years, we'd known that David Galvin – the man who called himself Felix the Cat – was a monster. But we thought we knew the boundary lines of his evil. Now – in his dying moments – he was telling me that it was even worse than we had ever imagined.

There was something else bothering me too. He'd said we.

We were very busy.

'What do you mean "we,"?' I asked. 'You and the cops. You and the press. I don't understand.'

'We murderers,' he said.

That's when I realized what he really wanted to confess to me before he died.

'I didn't do it alone, Joe,' he said.

six

'We called ourselves The Great Pretenders,' David Galvin said. 'There were four of us. All students at New York University. All from good families, well-to-do backgrounds, excellent grades. The best and the brightest. The stuff the American dream is supposed to be made of. Only I guess we became the American nightmare.'

Then he told me about the games.

The fantasy games.

'In the beginning,' he said, 'that's all we were doing. Playing a game. But it turned into much more than that. It became our lives. I guess you'd say things got out of hand.'

He told me about games with names like Dungeons and Dragons, Goth and Realm of the Gods. I'd heard about them before. They'd been a hot fad at high schools and colleges for years; turning campus geeks into imaginary netherworld heroes with extraordinary powers.

The players in these kinds of games took on alter egos. They then became that person, living in their fantasy world for hours as mythical gods, whose powers were enhanced by cutting off people's heads or killing their opponents or otherwise spilling someone's blood.

All this emphasis on violence worried some people. Critics warned that kids became so obsessed with the games that they lost touch with reality. Others called them a satanic tool. And fantasy games had even been linked to a number of teen suicides and other violence.

But, to most people, it was all just a game.

That's what I thought too. Until David Galvin told his story.

'Looking back on it all now, if I had to come up with a reason for what happened – well, I guess it would be boredom,' Galvin said. 'All four of us were looking for excitement. Thrills. The ultimate high. We were the first group of students who grew up in the MTV generation, and we craved instant gratification.

'Oh, we tried all the usual things: sex, drugs, drinking. But it was never enough. Everyone else had already done those things. We wanted to do something new. Something bold, something dangerous, something so mind-boggling that the world would sit up and take notice of us. Like Captain Kirk used to say on *Star Trek*, we wanted to go boldly where no one had ever gone before.

'I don't remember exactly how it started. I think it was late at night, and we were all sitting around somewhere – maybe in one of the dorms, maybe in a bar, maybe even on the grass at Washington Square Park under the moonlight. And we started talking about killing.

'At first it was still a fantasy kind of thing, you know, like slaying a dragon or your opponent on the field of battle in some mythical kingdom. We were just playing the game. Like we always did.

'But then one of us – I'm not sure who, maybe it was me – said that they thought the ultimate thrill would be to really take another person's life. For real. That it would make us stronger. Make us god-like. Turn us into true immortals.

'Well, no one said anything for a long time. But then, slowly at first and after awhile with a growing excitement, we all began talking about the idea.

'It was a fascinating concept. To kill another person. To simply snuff out their existence. To just remove them from this earth. To make them vanish – in a single instant of violence – as if they had never existed. Poof – and they were gone. What an amazing thing that must be to feel that kind of power. What a high. What a thrill. It really would almost be like being God himself.

'We talked that night about people who had killed for thrills, like Charles Manson and Theodore Bundy. These were intelligent men. There must have been a reason for what they did. But what was it? Did they know something that the rest of the world didn't know? A delicious secret that only a few select people would ever be able to share? That murder – the ultimate crime, the ultimate sin, the ultimate taboo of society – could also be the ultimate pleasure?

'Anyway, somewhere along the line, it stopped being a fantasy. The game became a reality. We were actually going to do this. We were going to kill people. Not for anything they did or for personal profit or for any real motive at all. Just because we wanted to see what it felt like.

'And you want to know something, Joe? It felt great. It truly did. I know it sounds terrible – and I hate to admit this now because God has made me realize the enormity of the sins I have committed – but I enjoyed it.

'It's an incredible experience at the end. The fear in their eyes, the violence, the sexual thrill of it all; everything coming together in one glorious burst. At that moment, I used to feel such passion. An all-consuming passion. A passion like I never felt for anything else in life. And I knew this was something I had to do – because God, in his infinite wisdom, made me like that. I could fight it, I could resist it, but I could never stop it. Have you ever felt passion like that, Joe?

'Anyway, we decided to give our secret society a name. The Great Pretenders. It came from the old song by the Platters. Do you remember it: "Oh, yes I'm the great pretender." Well, we heard it one night on a jukebox, and it seemed perfect for us. Totally appropriate.

'Then, within The Great Pretenders, each of us had individual names and characters. Me, of course, I was Felix the Cat. We all had different ways of carrying out the murders too. As you know I liked to linger over mine – to watch them for a long time and even spend some quality time with them at the end. The others did their work a lot quicker.

'We also had different ways of picking our victims. I know you think the victims were all women, because that's what I did. But there were other people murdered in our dark little game. Men. Children. Families. The Great Pretenders were an equal-opportunity killing machine.

'It really did become a game for us. An incredible game, while it lasted. We competed against each other. Not only to see who could kill the most people, but also which one of us could come up with the most creative ways of doing it.

'I always led in the numbers. I was very busy. But the others – well, let's just say they were much more imaginative about murder than I could ever dream of being.

'I was the only one who went public though. Sometime, early on in my spree, I realized something was missing. I was killing people – making them disappear off the face of the earth through the sheer power of my will – but no one realized I was doing it. No one had put the different murders together. They were just isolated crimes.

'So I decided to write the letters to the papers so that the whole world would see what I was doing. I thought that it would make the thrill of the kill even more delicious than it already was. I was right too. I truly felt like a god.

'In the end, I suppose that was what did me in. The publicity. It enraged the public, the police – even the other members of our little group were upset with me over it.

'And then I was caught. A lucky break for the police actually. Otherwise, I might have gone on for years. But all good things must come to an end. And my life really ended eleven years ago. Until I was reborn again last year when I discovered Jesus.

'As for the others, well – they just went on with their lives. No one knew about them, only about Felix the Cat. The police, the public, the press – they thought Felix the Cat was the monster. They didn't know that the monster had more than one head. That the evil was worse than they ever knew.

'I never told their secret to anyone until today. I mean I'd taken an oath with the others. We were The Great Pretenders. And that's what those people are doing now. The three of them are still out there – still pretending. Pretending they're just normal people that are living normal lives.

'You'd never recognize them now. They have careers, families, money – they've become what our parents used to be. They became respectable, successful members of society – nobody ever knew about the deadly secrets in their past. Ironic, huh? The rest of the Great Pretenders all disappeared just like the people we all murdered. Poof – and they were gone.

'I've followed the news about them from here in prison. I don't think they think about me too much.

'In fact, I figured they'd all forgotten about The Great Pretenders and what we did back at NYU. Tried to put it out of their minds forever.

'Or at least I used to think that.

'Until . . .'

David Galvin's voice had been fading as he talked. A couple of times his eyes closed, then opened again. I assumed the drugs he was taking for the cancer were the reason. Or maybe it was the cancer itself. He didn't seem like he had much time left.

'I need to tell the truth,' he said now. 'I need to do the right thing before I die. God told me to confess everything. God told me he would forgive me.' He seemed delirious. 'I must stop it!' he said. Then his eyes closed again.

'Stop what?' I asked.

There was no answer.

I moved over closer to the bed, until I was only a few inches away from his ear. 'Stop what, David?' I shouted. 'What is it you're trying to tell me?'

Still nothing.

'Wake up, you son of a bitch!' I was screaming at him now. I had so many other questions I needed him to answer. Who were the other three people in The Great Pretenders? Where were they now? How many other victims were there that we didn't know about?

A nurse came running into the room. The guard was behind her. The nurse looked down at Galvin lying on the bed next to me.

'I'm sorry, you'll have to leave now, Mr Dougherty,' she said.

'Just a few more questions.'

'He can't hear you.'

I looked down at the sleeping figure on the bed. I knew she was right.

David Galvin was a monster who a long time ago destroyed a lot of people's lives, and now dreamed of doing something that would somehow still allow him to get into Heaven. He'd revealed a lot of secrets to me. There were many more secrets still locked inside the dark recesses of his soul.

But David Galvin was going to tell me no more secrets today.

seven

There's nothing better than being in the city room of a New York City newspaper when you have a big story. It's the ultimate high. A real jolt of adrenalin. An incredible sense of exhilaration that you feel when it seems like everything is breaking your way.

I used to love it so much.

Later, after things started to go bad, I tried to find that same excitement from other things in life besides newspapers.

But I never could.

The only thing that ever came close was gambling. When I was riding a lucky streak at the tables – and the cards were coming up aces, the dice throws were all winners, the wheel was rolling for me – it was almost like being back in the *New York Banner* newsroom again with a front page story.

Almost.

There was a downside, of course. At a newspaper, they pay you for what you do. At the gambling table, you pay them. Oh, sometimes you win for awhile, but in the end you generally come out on the short end. That's the way it works. It's a game you can't ever win. So why do people play it? Well, it's a helluva trip until you get to the last stop.

But now I was back in a bigtime New York City newsroom – home again after a long, long time. At least temporarily. Kramer had given me a desk in the middle of the office that belonged to the paper's chief diplomatic reporter, who was on assignment in London. A few people I used to know stopped by to offer an awkward greeting. But I was surprised how many new faces were there. Newspapers are not long-term organizations, I guess. People burn out very quickly.

'So you're Joe Dougherty, huh?' someone said.

I looked up. There was a woman, maybe about thirty or so, standing next to the desk. She was smiling. She was small and thin, with red-hair that was cut very short. She wasn't pretty and she wasn't homely, but the smile made her seem more attractive than she really was. She also looked really wired. The kind of person who's always filled with energy.

'I'm Bonnie Kerns,' she said. 'Maybe you've seen my byline. Page One today.'

She pointed to the story that I'd heard Andy talking about in his office; the murder of the investment banker and the hooker. The dead man's name was William Franze. Her story said the chief suspect was a woman named Lisa Montero, whose father, John Montero, was a legendary Wall Street wheeler-dealer.

'That's the sixth Page One byline I've had this month, but then who's counting? So anyway, I wake up this morning, and the first thing I do is check out my horoscope. It tells me my Aries is rising and my Virgo is in some fuckin' house somewhere – and it's going to be a really cool day. I figure that just means I'll get another big story or win a Pulitzer or something. But then I walk into the newsroom and see you sitting here. The famous Joe Dougherty himself. Whoa . . .'

She stuck out her hand.

I shook it. 'Do I know you?' I asked.

'No, you were before my time. Hell, I probably was still in high school when you were a big star around here.'

She didn't look that young. I told her that.

'Okay, maybe college,' she laughed. 'I know all about you though. You're a legend. Andy told us all the whole story the other night in the bar. Boy, talk about an up and down career. You've been up, and you've been down bigtime, haven't you? So where the hell are you now?'

'Somewhere in the middle, I guess,' I told her. 'What exactly did Andy say about me?'

'That you were one of the greatest reporters who ever worked here. Of course, I already knew that. I sometimes go through old *Banner* clips in my spare time, trying to learn about the paper and get ideas and make myself a better reporter. I'm a little obsessive about this job – I don't know if you've noticed. So I'd seen your name a lot. Anyway, Andy says you would do anything for a story. That you once posed as a waiter to cover a secret dinner meeting by the mayor. That you went into a bear cage at the zoo to show how lax the safety regulations were there. That you parachuted into an exclusive celebrity wedding in the Hamptons. That you even used to go through people's garbage looking for news tips. He said you treated every story you did like it was Watergate.'

'Andy said that, huh?'

'Yeah. Is he a friend of yours or what?'

'He used to be. A long time ago. I guess he's changed quite a bit since then though.'

I looked across the city room into Andy Kramer's office, which was enclosed in glass and took up much of one wall. Andy was holding an editorial meeting. He looked very impressive. He looked like an executive.

'Do you like working with him?' I asked Bonnie.

'You mean Zig Zag?'

'Zig Zag?'

'That's what we call him. Behind his back, of course.'

'Why Zig Zag?'

'Because he always changes his mind on everything, depending on which way the wind is blowing. He doesn't really have any opinions of his own. He just does whatever he has to do to get ahead. If you're riding high, he's your friend. But if you screw up, he doesn't want to know you. He goes with the flow. Zig Zag. Understand?'

I nodded. 'Maybe Andy hasn't changed so much, after all.'

'What about you?' she asked. 'How come a hotshot reporter like you wound up getting fired?'

'Didn't Andy tell you?'

'No.'

'Well, I guess I just zigged when I should have zagged,' I smiled.

I always thought of the newspaper business as a noble calling.

A mission.

A public service the way John and Robert Kennedy used to make politics sound back in the days when people were idealistic and trusting and still believed they could make the world better.

I devoured newspaper movies when I was growing up. I've probably seen every one that was ever made. *The Front Page. His Girl Friday. Deadline USA. Ace in the Hole.* And, of course, *All the President's Men.* Especially *All the President's Men.*

Watergate was the one thing that inspired me more than any other to become a newspaper reporter. I wanted to be like Bob Woodward and Carl Bernstein. I wanted to change the world the way they did. I must have seen that movie a hundred times. I'd sit in a darkened theater, mouthing Robert Redford and Dustin Hoffman's lines even before they said them. I knew them all by heart.

I never broke anything as big as Watergate in my days as a reporter, but I did some pretty good things. I got politicians indicted for graft and fraud. I did an investigation that uncovered widespread patient abuse in nursing homes. I wrote a series that led to a reform of laws that protect battered women from their husbands.

I cared a lot about things like that back then. I guess I still do. People at the paper always used to tell me that I needed to be more impartial about the things that I covered.

'I've accomplished a lot here by not always being impartial,' I remember pointing out to one cynical editor.

'Like what?'

I ran through some of my big stories.

He shook his head.

'No matter how many politicians you put away or nursing homes you get cleaned up or beaten-up women you save from their husbands, it's all just a drop in the bucket,' he said. 'This city's a cesspool. Hell, the world's a cesspool. There's a million more cases out there even worse than that.'

'I do what I can do,' I said stubbornly.

'What's the point?'

'Maybe someday I'll expose them all.'

'You're a dreamer, Dougherty,' he laughed. 'But you're young. You'll outgrow it.'

'I hope that never happens,' I said.

'Why?'

'The world needs dreamers.'

I wrote my story about Felix the Cat's new confession quickly. It had been a long time since I'd been a reporter, but this story practically wrote itself. It just poured out of me.

Of course, I didn't have any proof for any of it. Galvin might have just made it up for a joke, I suppose. Or been delirious from the pain or the drugs. But I didn't think that it wasn't true. He was a dying man, and dying men generally don't tell lies. Besides, I believed him. And so did Andy.

Andy told me the story was going to be all over Page One.

After I was finished writing it and turned it into the city desk, I could have gone straight home. But I didn't. I did what I used to do whenever I had a big story. First, I waited around until it was cleared by the copy desk and sent upstairs to the composing room. Then I went upstairs to watch it being laid out on the front page. After that, I went to Lanigan's – a bar next door to the *Banner* where the reporters hang out – until the presses started rolling at about 9 p.m. I was in the press room when the first copies of the *Banner* rolled off. I picked one up and looked at it.

FELIX THE CAT: I
DIDN'T KILL ALONE!

Serial killer reveals in
deathbed confession
he had accomplices
during terror spree

Exclusive Special Report
By Joe Dougherty

I read the article from beginning to end. Then I read it a second time. And a third. It felt good. After that, I went back to Lanigan's to have some more beers with the reporters there – basking in the glory of my big moment and happy to be a player again – even for a little while.

It was a great night. Until Jack Rollins showed up.

Rollins was the executive editor of the *Banner*. Eight years ago, when I'd left, he'd been the city editor. My boss. He was one of the people who pushed the hardest to have me fired.

'Well, well, well,' Rollins said, walking over to the table where I was sitting. He was dressed in a tuxedo, and he looked like he'd already had a few drinks somewhere else. 'Look who's back – the Gambler. Kramer told me he put you on this Galvin story. I told him he must be out of his mind.'

I didn't say anything.

'I have an idea how we can pay you though,' Rollins said. 'Instead of giving you the money, we'll just give it directly to your bookie. Cut out the middle man entirely. What do you think, Gambler?'

'I don't bet anymore,' I told him.

'Yeah, right,' he said sarcastically. 'Sorry, but I don't believe that for a second. Of course, I don't believe anything you say. You always did have a bit of a problem telling the truth, didn't you? Or have you forgotten about that already?'

Rollins was a real asshole, a bean counter who loved to slash reporters' expense accounts, while at the same time using his position to wangle invitations to the best parties, social events and freebie travel junkets in town. I didn't really have to take any shit from him now, since I wasn't actually working at the *Banner* anymore. On the other hand, I didn't want to do anything that would get me taken off the David Galvin confession story. It was a great story. It was my story.

I looked at the tuxedo he was wearing. 'So what was on the social schedule tonight, Jack? Dinner at the Mayor's mansion? Drinks with the Trumps?'

'I gave a speech at Columbia Journalism School,' he said.

Beautiful.

'Well, you know what they say,' I told him. 'Those who can – do. Those who can't – talk about it to journalism students.'

Rollins glared at me.

'This is a big story you're working on, Dougherty,' he said. 'Don't screw it up.'

'I've worked on big stories before,' I told him.

'Yeah, that's right. You have. And the last time you did, somebody wound up dead.'

eight

• • • • • • • • • • •

It was nearly 2:30 a.m. by the time I got home to New Jersey. Carolyn was asleep, of course. But she stirred slowly as I crawled into bed. Then she rolled over and pressed her body close to mine. She opened her eyes.

'What time is it?' she asked.

'It's the middle of the night.'

'I waited up for you for a long time.'

'The story suddenly got a lot bigger.'

I told her about David Galvin's confession. The excitement back at the *Banner* when I told them. My byline on Page One in today's editions. The way everyone wanted to talk to me and buy me drinks at Lanigan's afterwards. Carolyn was quiet for a long time after I'd finished.

'So it's not over, is it?' she said.

'I have to go back to see Galvin again tomorrow.'

'Why?'

'To get the rest of the story. Who were his accomplices? Where are they now? What about the victims we don't know? And why did he pick me to tell all this to?'

'You said it would only take one day.'

'I didn't know the guy was going to pick this moment to bare his soul. But he's dying. He wants to clear his conscience. I'm the guy that's helping him do it.'

I leaned over and kissed her on the cheek. She was very beautiful. Some women don't look pretty until they get up and put on their makeup. But Carolyn had a kind of natural, clean-scrubbed beauty that was always there. I nestled my head against the side of her neck and buried my face in her blonde hair. I hugged her tightly.

I'd met Carolyn eighteen months ago. I was sitting in a coffee shop of a Holiday Inn in Harrisburg, Pa., where I worked for a small local paper. I was supposed to interview the motel's manager for a Chamber of Commerce feature on leading area businessmen. For me, it was the last stop in a journalistic (and life) freefall that had taken me from New York City to Newark to Westchester County to Trenton and then finally to Pennsylvania.

Along the way, I'd taken time to grieve for my dead wife and infant son; indulge in a serious gambling habit that left me deep in debt and dodging loansharks everytime I left the house; and come as close to hitting rock bottom in my life as a man can.

I was a mess.

So you can see that on that day in the Harrisburg Holiday Inn when I met Carolyn Nash . . . well, it was like a desperate horse player who suddenly hits the supertrifecta at the track with the last $20 in his pocket.

Carolyn saved my life.

She was my salvation.

I owe her everything.

I just started up a conversation with her in the coffee shop. I always had a good line of patter. I could charm people with superficial talk from the minute I first met them. It was one of my tricks as a reporter. I never lost it. Even in those days – in the depths of my despair – it wasn't until people got to know me better that they realized how empty I was inside.

But Carolyn was different.

She told me that she lived in Princeton, NJ. She said she was a lawyer for a big drug firm in New Jersey. She said she was in Harrisburg to attend an executive seminar and had a long day of meetings with corporate types ahead of her. I told her about my life. All of it. Even the deepest, darkest secrets. She never made it to her executive seminar, and I never did the Chamber of Commerce interview. We spent the rest of the day, that night and the following day together.

After she got home, she called and asked me to visit her in Princeton the next weekend. Pretty soon, I was there every weekend and during all my other free time too. Finally, she convinced me to quit my job at the Harrisburg paper and move to Princeton to live with her. I tried doing some magazine feature freelance writing for awhile, and then Carolyn's father offered me the job with his public relations firm. Everyone says I'm a natural in the public relations business. That I have a real knack for it. A few months ago, I proposed to Carolyn, and she accepted. Now we're going to be married in September.

Looking back on it now, I realize how much I needed someone like Carolyn in my life. Someone who could put me back on course. She's everything a man could want. She's pretty. She's smart. She's loyal. She's truly a good person.

Joe Dougherty finally wins one in life.

I hugged her again now. Then we made love. After it was over, she fell asleep in my arms.

I didn't fall asleep for a long time though. I had too much to think about. I couldn't get David Galvin out of my mind. All his talk about other victims and accomplices and his desperate quest for forgiveness for all his sins. He scared me. I wasn't scared in a physical sense. I was scared because he had somehow touched me emotionally. On some weird level, I had connected with him in that hospital room.

'It's an incredible experience,' Galvin had said. 'The fear in their eyes, the kiss, the sex, the violence – everything coming together in one glorious burst. At that moment, I used to feel such passion. An all-consuming passion. A passion like I never felt for anything else in life. And I knew this was something I had to do, because God, in his infinite wisdom, made me like that. I could fight it, I could resist it, but I could never stop it. Have you ever felt passion like that, Joe?'

Yeah, David, I have. Tonight. When I was back in the *Banner* city room again – and writing your story.

We all want passion in our lives. Some of us just look for it in different places.

What about me, David? If I'd been on the NYU campus with you and those three other students eleven years ago, would I have joined in your sick, deadly game? Would I have been one of The Great Pretenders?

No, of course not. But I understand what you were looking for. I think I might even understand why you did what you did. That's why I'm so frightened.

I looked over at Carolyn. She had rolled over to the other side of the bed. She was sleeping peacefully, with strands of her blonde hair falling over her face. I could reach out and touch her if I wanted. She was still only a few feet across the bed from me.

But – at that moment – she seemed a million miles away.

nine

'David Galvin is dead,' they told me at the prison the next day. At first I didn't believe it.

'That can't be,' I said.

'He was very sick.'

'But I just talked to him yesterday. I was here for several hours. Only I didn't have time to finish my interview. They said if I came back this morning . . .'

'He died during the night, Mr Dougherty.'

Did I want to talk to any of the other prison officials about this?

I started to ask for the warden. But then I had a sudden inspiration. All the warden was going to do was read me the official press statement about the death. He wasn't going to know the answers to any of my questions. I needed to find somebody that David Galvin might have confided in before his death. Okay, he probably wouldn't have confided in the warden. But then who?

I want to get into Heaven, he told me, that's the most important thing to me now.

Galvin had turned to religion in his dying days.

'Do you have a prison chaplain?' I asked.

'Yes. The Rev. Harold Campanella.'

'I want to talk to him.'

The Rev. Harold Campanella was a pudgy man in his sixties, with thin, grey hair and a rumpled suit that looked as if he'd slept in it for several nights. I wondered how being a chaplain at a prison like this ranked in the hierarchy of minister success stories. Was it at the top of the ladder or the bottom? Looking at Rev. Campanella, I opted for the bottom.

'Tell me about David Galvin,' I said.

Campanella seemed uncomfortable at the mention of Galvin's name. He looked over at a Bible on the corner of his desk, as if maybe it could give him inspiration.

'He murdered many people.'

'I know that.'

'But, at the end, he sought forgiveness for his sins in the eyes of the Lord.'

'I know that too.'

'And you would be. . . ?'

'My name is Joe Dougherty.'

'Oh, the newspaper reporter.'

'Galvin mentioned me to you?'

'Several times.'

'Do you have any idea why he specifically asked to see me?'

'No, I don't.'

'Did he tell you about our conversation yesterday?'

'Unfortunately, I never got a chance to talk with him at the end. He slipped into a coma. My last meeting with him was yesterday morning. I knew he didn't have much time left.'

He shook his head sadly. 'I must tell you, Mr Dougherty, David Galvin presented me with perhaps the most vexing moral dilemma I have ever faced in my long years of service to the Church. On the one hand, the man epitomized true evil – he did horrible, Satan-like deeds during his short lifetime.

'But yet, during my conversations with him, Galvin truly tried to embrace Jesus Christ. Maybe he finally saw the light, or maybe he was just afraid of dying. I'm not sure. But if we accept the concept of God as all-forgiving, then we must offer the hand of forgiveness to the David Galvins of the world too.

'Anyway, that's what I decided to do. I'm afraid it wasn't a very popular decision in some circles around here. But I work for God, not the New York State prison system.'

'That sounds very noble, reverend,' I said.

'Are you a church-going man, Mr Dougherty?'

'No.'

'But you do believe in God?'

'Yes, I do.'

'So did David Galvin.'

He reached into his desk and took out a white envelope. He handed it to me. My name was on the front. That's when I knew my old reporting instincts were still there.

The reverend, not the warden. Of course.

'David wrote three letters in the days before he died,' Campanella was saying. 'He left them with me to distribute after he was gone. One was to his parents, who I'm afraid weren't very pleased to receive it. I think they wanted to just forget their son ever existed. The second one was to me. And the third one, the third letter, was supposed to go to you. There it is, Mr Dougherty.'

I tore open the envelope and read Felix the Cat's last words . . .

'It's a list,' I told Andy Kramer on the phone after I left Campanella. 'A fucking list of victims.'

'How many names are there on the list?'

'Twenty-one,' I said.

'Galvin was responsible for eleven, right? Nine dead and two hospital jobs. That leaves ten other killings.'

'I already checked them with the *Banner* library before I called you. Eight of the names are from unsolved murders or deaths. Most of them awhile ago, a few very recent. Cases where no one was ever caught, no motive was ever found. They're not all women, but Galvin said they wouldn't be. Otherwise, it fits the Felix the Cat pattern, Andy.'

'And the other two names on the list?'

'They're still alive.'

It took a second for the impact of that to sink in on him.

'These are murders that haven't happened yet,' I told him.

'Jesus Christ!' Kramer said.

'There's one more thing here that I think's going to blow your mind. I heard you talking about a big murder story when I was in your office. The one that's been all over the front pages. About the Wall Street bigshot who got blown away a few weeks ago in his East Side townhouse.

'William Franze,' Andy said.

'William Franze is on the list too,' I told him.

ten

There was more. But I needed a little time to think it all through, before I talked about it with anyone else. After I left the prison, I walked around the town of Ossining aimlessly for awhile. Eventually, I found myself where you could look out over the Hudson River. The Hudson this far north was truly a majestic sight, stretching across more than two miles at some points as it wound its way from New York City all the way up to the St Lawrence Seaway.

As I stood there watching the water lap up along the shore in the soft spring breeze, I though about what a strange business death can be.

I mean, we hear about people dying all the time. Murders. Accidents. Disease. If you're a newspaperman, death is as much a part of your daily life as breathing. And yet none of it means very much. Just names in an obituary or a news story.

Unless it's someone who matters to you.

I remembered how I felt when I found out that Susan and Joe Jr had died. I used to think there was nothing more important to me in the world than a big newspaper story. But, without my wife and son, newspaper stories didn't matter to me anymore. Nothing mattered. I didn't matter.

If he had lived, my son would be nine years old now. He'd be in the third grade; probably starting to play Little League baseball or soccer; and – with a little boy's astonishment and wonder – discovering the world the same way I did when I was his age.

I never got a chance to hear his first words; never got to see him walk; never got to read bedtime stories to him; never got to teach him how to throw a baseball or shoot a basket or fly a kite. You want to hear something really sad? I even had a crazy dream – I remember first thinking about it at the hospital on the night Joe Jr was born – that he would someday grow up to be a great newspaperman just like his dad.

And Susan . . . well, Susan was the love of my life. I'd never admit that to anyone now, certainly not to Carolyn, but it was true. Susan and me were more than just husband and wife. We were lovers for life. Best friends. Soulmates. I'd never met anyone like her before, and I've never met anyone since who could take her place. I just never imagined growing old without her.

Someone once asked me when I knew that she was the one for me.

I just did. Right from the very start.

I asked her to marry me on our first date. We were sitting at this trendy East Side restaurant that had been written up in *New York Magazine*. I'd taken her there to try and impress her. The magazine said it had terrific food, terrific service and terrific ambiance. But I hated the restaurant. I hated the food. I hated our waiter. And most of all I hated the ambience.

'So what do you think of this place?' I asked Susan, after we'd finished our salads and were starting on the main course.

'It's fine.'

'No, really. I want you to be honest.'

'Okay,' she said slowly, 'it's not fine. The truth is I think it's overrated, overpriced and I have this overwhelming desire to slap that arrogant smirk off the face of our asshole waiter.' She smiled at me across the table. 'You know, Joe, you didn't have to spend all this money on me. I wanted to go out with you. We could have gone to a McDonald's, and I'd have been happy.'

'Will you marry me?' I blurted out.

She stared at me in amazement. 'You don't waste any time, do you?'

'Well, I was going to wait until we got to the dessert, but then I figured what the hell . . . I'll just go ahead and ask the question now. So what do you think?'

Susan laughed. 'I haven't even decided whether I'm going to let you kiss me goodnight yet.

'Actually that was my second question.'

'Well, I think if I say yes to the first question, that pretty much answers the second one too.'

'Will you?' I asked.

'Kiss you or marry you?'

'Either one.'

'I'll think about it,' she said.

She did kiss me when I took her home that night. Then we made love. Passionate love. When it was over, she held onto me for a long time. Finally we fell asleep in each other's arms. Sometime during the night, she woke me up with a kiss.

'Yes,' she told me.

'The marriage question?' I asked sleepily.

'Absolutely,' she said.

I loved her so much. The kind of all-encompassing, no-questions-asked love you think will never die or grow old or go bad. I've only felt that way about two other things in my life besides Susan: newspapers and New York City. The first time that I walked into a newspaper city room I knew that was where I belonged. And I felt the same way when I got off a bus at the Port Authority on a hot summer night a long time ago and began walking around New York. It was love at first sight.

Of course, none of the three worked out the way I hoped. I don't work at a newspaper anymore, I live in New Jersey and Susan has been dead for a long time. But I don't regret any of it. As the old saying goes, it's better to have loved and lost than never to have loved at all. That's the way I felt. And I'd finally come to peace with the way everything turned out. Or so I thought anyway, until the letter from Felix the Cat.

I looked down now at the letter I was holding in my hand.

I had wondered why Felix the Cat wanted to tell his story to me – a burned out, disgraced reporter who hadn't worked at the *Banner* for years – instead of picking some young hotshot journalist who was getting bylines on the front page today.

Now I knew.

I didn't have a lot of other answers I needed yet, but at least I had that one.

I read through the names on Galvin's list one more time.

Twenty-one names. Twenty-one victims of a group of thrill seekers. Four rich, spoiled kids on a college campus, all from wholesome American upstanding families, who just thought it would be a real kick to go out and murder a lot of people.

Simply snuff out their lives.

Make them vanish.

Poof – and they're gone.

David Galvin said he wanted to do something right at the end. And I guess maybe he had. But he never had time to finish. So now I was left with a lot of questions that I couldn't answer. And Galvin – the only person who knew the answers – was gone for good.

I remembered the story of the Cheshire Cat from Lewis Carroll's *Alice in Wonderland*. I hadn't read that book in a long time, but Alice's encounter with the bizarre cat, who appeared and disappeared at the most inopportune times, always stuck in my mind.

I thought about it now:

> 'I wish you wouldn't keep appearing and disappearing so suddenly,' Alice told the cat.
>
> 'All right,' said the cat.
>
> And this time it disappeared quite slowly, beginning with the tail, and ending with its grin, which remained some time after the rest of it had gone.

Just like Felix the Cat.

Was David Galvin grinning at us all now from wherever he was?

I shook my head sadly and looked down at his list in my hand one more time. I still couldn't believe it.

Twenty-one names. Women. Men. Children. But it was two of those names – two of the innocent victims who were on that list – that had suddenly turned my world upside down again.

Susan and Joseph Dougherty.

My wife and son.

PART TWO

The Great Pretenders

eleven

I needed a place to start. No matter how complicated a story is, no matter how impossible it seems, no matter how confusing, a reporter has to begin somewhere if he he hopes to have any chance of unraveling it. Watergate started with a second-rate burglary that nobody paid any attention to for a long time. Son of Sam – maybe the most notorious serial killer of our time – was finally caught because of a parking ticket. Nothing is too small, nothing too insignificant in this business.

A tangled story is a lot like a tangled piece of string. You have to pull on one piece of it first, then another and hope the whole thing eventually unravels. Pull on the right thread first, and it's easy. Pull on the wrong thread, and you just get more and more frustrated.

I needed to find the right thread to pull on this story.

I had checked into a hotel in Gramercy Park after filing a long piece to the *Banner* on Galvin's death and his list of victims.

Kramer said he was putting me on special assignment for the paper until the story was over. So there was no way I could deal with the long commute back and forth to Princeton anymore. I had a lot of work to do. I needed all the time I could get.

There were six new murder cases – a total of eight more mysterious deaths – on the list Galvin had left me.

That first night, sitting in my hotel room, I took out a pen and yellow legal pad and wrote down all the information I had:

1. Thomas Macklin
   Married white male, aged 28
   Lawyer for Park Avenue law firm
   Cause of death: stabbing
   Body found in men's room of notorious gay bar in Greenwich Village on 10/04/86. Victim had no history of gay involvement. In fact, several girlfriends were located and questioned as well as his wife. All were cleared.
   CASE UNSOLVED

2. Marilyn Dupree
   Divorced white female, aged 32
   Waitress at posh East Side restaurant/aspiring actress and dancer
   Cause of death: Gunshot wound
   Body found in apartment on 11/26/86 by restaurant manager, who became concerned when she didn't show up for work. Found in dancer's outfit at time of death, although no evidence she had participated in either dance class or performance recently.
   CASE UNSOLVED

3. Judith Curran
   Single black female, aged 21
   Student at Fordham University
   Cause of death: strangulation
   Body found floating in Hudson River on 3/28/87

Victim last seen two weeks earlier leaving
class on Fordham University campus. Time of
death estimated as several days before
body was found. Whereabouts during unaccounted
for time never established.
CASE UNSOLVED

4. Toni Aiello, Rockville Centre, Long Island.
Single white female, aged 18
Student at Rockville Centre HS
Cause of death: Gunshot wound
Body found in Washington Square Park
during the early morning hours of 6/13/87.
Victim was still dressed in same formal gown
she'd worn to senior prom the night before.
Her date and friends all cleared by cops.
CASE UNSOLVED

5. Susan and Joseph Dougherty
Married white female, aged 26, young
white child, aged 1½
Cause of death: Boating accident
in Sag Harbor, Long Island
Died on 7/28/90.
CASE LISTED AS ACCIDENTAL DEATH

6. William Franze and Whitney Martin
Married white male aged 45; single white
female aged 24
Cause of death: Multiple gunshot wounds
Died on 4/26 of this year in bed together at
Franze's townhouse. Appeared to be having
sexual encounter at time of death.
Woman had been hired by Franze from the
Elite Escort Agency.
CASE UNSOLVED

None of them, at first glance anyway, seemed to have happened the same way as the original Felix the Cat killings. For one thing,

David Galvin had used a gun, the same gun – a .40 caliber semi-automatic – in all of his killings. The new victims had died in a variety of ways.

Some of them, like the high school girl in her prom dress and the waitress in her dance outfit, now appeared like they certainly could be more of the sick fantasies from the man who called himself Felix the Cat. But, until Galvin put them on his list, no one ever suspected a connection between any of the deaths. And a couple of them, William Franze, for one, and my family too, seemed to bear no resemblance at all to the rest of the murder chain.

Then there were the two living people on Galvin's list who seemed to be the next targets. The police were trying to contact them now to offer them special protection.

One of them was a woman named Linda Hiller. She was thirty-two years old and managed a theatrical agency in midtown Manhattan. The only clip I could find about her in the *Banner* library was a small piece in *New York Magazine* from a few years ago in which she was listed as one of the magazine's Hot 100 up and coming new business women in Manhattan. I couldn't see anything she'd done to make someone want to kill her.

The other target was an accountant named Arthur Dodson. Dodson was thirty-four years old, and had just been named a senior partner in his firm. He lived in Westchester County with his wife and two young children, coached a Little League team and belonged to the Kiwanis Club and Chamber of Commerce. Nothing that seemed particularly controversial in his life either.

Of course, maybe Linda Hiller and Arthur Dodson had some deep dark secrets in their lives that I knew nothing about.

On the other hand, it was much more likely they were just picked at random like the rest of the victims appeared to have been. So they were not likely to know the reason they were on Felix the Cat's death list.

It all seemed hopeless.

Galvin said he had three secret accomplices. But, as far as I could see, he didn't leave behind any pertinent information which might help me track them down.

Maybe there were some clues to their identity on the NYU campus. I could go there and investigate Galvin's college years: what he did, where he lived, who his friends were, etc. Except it all happened eleven years ago. The people at NYU I needed to talk to were long gone. The trail was going to be very cold.

My best hope for a lead seemed to be William Franze, the recently murdered Wall Street executive who somehow turned up on Galvin's list of victims.

Authorities had been going in another direction in that murder investigation, zeroing in on Franze's ex-girlfriend Lisa Montero, the daughter of wealthy businessman and longtime political mover and shaker John Montero. Was Galvin mistaken? Or have the cops been on a wild goose chase, while the real killer of William Franze sits back and laughs at them? I wasn't sure.

There was one thing I was sure of though.

Unlike the other deaths, the Franze murder trail wasn't cold yet. This trail was definitely fresh; the clues in the case new; the murder investigation still very much alive. If Galvin was right, and everything he had told me so far had checked out, then maybe the death of William Franze was connected to the long-ago killing spree at NYU.

I drew a big circle with my pen around the name of William Franze.

That was one string I could definitely pull on.

Of course, I knew there was another aspect of this whole thing that I hadn't even dealt with yet. My wife Susan and son Joe were on Galvin's list too. Sooner or later, I needed to find out why. They'd died years ago. But now they couldn't rest in peace, and neither could I, until I got some answers.

Except that would have to wait.

If I opened up those wounds now, I knew I would become consumed by it. It would eat me up alive. I would become immobilized. All my reporting skills, my perception, my professionalism would go out the window in a rush of emotional frenzy.

I needed to take this one step at a time.

I'd solve the mystery of the rest of the names on Felix the Cat's death list and that would lead me to the answers I needed about Susan and Joe. That was my theory anyway.

I was getting sleepy. I put down the pen and legal pad, switched off the light and closed my eyes. I wondered if I should call Carolyn. I decided not to. It was late, she was probably already asleep. Besides, it hadn't gone well when I told her I was going to be staying in the city while I worked on the story. But I'd assured her that I'd be home again soon, that this was only temporary.

When I finally fell asleep, I dreamed about being back in Princeton and lying in bed next to Carolyn. She leaned over and woke me up with a kiss. It was wonderful. I suddenly felt a passion, an excitement I hadn't felt in years. 'I love you,' I told Carolyn. 'I really do love you.'

Then I opened my eyes.

Except it wasn't Carolyn there with me.

It was Susan.

twelve

The cop who had arrested Felix the Cat eleven years ago was a homicide lieutenant named Dennis Righetti.

The last time I'd talked to Righetti was when I was a reporter, and we used to drink together sometimes at a place in Little Italy after we got off work. He'd feed me tips about cases I was covering. In return, I put his name in the paper when he did something good and kept it out if he screwed up. It was a nice little arrangement, as I recall. We became pretty good friends. I even went to a family barbecue at his house on Long Island one Fourth of July.

Now Righetti had been promoted to captain and worked out of the commissioner's office; he was a rising star in the department.

A lot of stuff changes when you've been away for eight years. Righetti didn't seem that different though.

'Boy, you are a sight for sore eyes,' he boomed in a loud voice, pumping my hand when I went to see him at his office in police headquarters in downtown Manhattan. 'I wondered what happened to you. Then I heard they ran you out of town. How long have you been back at the *Banner*?'

'Well, I'm not really back.'

'But you said on the phone . . .'

I gave him an abridged version of everything that had happened to me over the past few days.

'Yeah, I read your story,' he said when I was finished. 'Felix the Cat returns. Now he had people helping him too. Not that I necessarily buy any of it.'

'Galvin said it was true.'

'And, of course, you believed the murdering son of a bitch?'

'He was dying. I think he wanted to tell the truth before the end.'

Righetti shrugged. 'All I know is that I spent hours interviewing this guy after his arrest. And he never said anything about anybody else or any other murders. Not that he was reluctant to boast about his exploits either. I mean he seemed to enjoy it. So if your story is true, it sure makes me look like a horse's ass after all these years.'

'Galvin said he took an oath with the other members of this secret group – which he called the Great Pretenders – to never reveal anything about them. And he kept his word. That's why he never talked about them. Until the day he died.'

'A sense of honor from a mass murderer?' Righetti asked incredulously.

'It happens,' I said.

Righetti still didn't seem convinced.

'Tell me everything you remember about the Felix the Cat case,' I said.

There had never been another serial killer quite like him.

Not Son of Sam. Not the Zodiac killer. They just murdered their victims. It was over in a matter of seconds. But the full horror of Felix the Cat wasn't known until he was finally captured and he delivered his shocking confession to police.

That's when he revealed how he had stretched his own special nightmare for his victims out for days, sometimes even weeks.

First he stalked them. According to what he told cops, he would follow a woman target to work or school or out on dates.

Watch her in her house as she did exercises; got dressed; ate meals; watched TV; talked on the telephone; and prepared for bed. He learned the unsuspecting victim's innermost secrets.

Then – when he finally tired of the game – he struck.

He always found a way to get into the house. Maybe he posed as a TV cable repairman or a salesman or someone who needed a phone to report an accident. Maybe he met them on the street or at a singles bar or in the grocery story, and somehow convinced them to invite him back to their house. By all accounts, he could be very charming and persuasive. If all else failed, he'd simply break in and be waiting for them when they got home.

That's when the real horror began. And it was't over quickly. I suppose you could compare it to someone like Jeffery Dahmer who held his victims captive and tortured them for a long time before they died. Galvin didn't just torture them in the physical sense. What he did was worse.

He played a sick game with them. Pretended they were lovers, sweethearts or husband and wife – and made the captive woman play out this bizarre sex fantasy with him. He talked to her about her hopes, her dreams, her plans for the future. He stroked her hair and caressed her cheeks and held her hand. He made her dress up in her prettiest clothes and put on a fashion show for him.

Until it was finally time to say goodbye.

The fascinating thing, Galvin said in his long rambling confession more than a decade ago, was the victim's reaction.

Most of them fought for awhile. They cried, they begged, they threatened him with all sort of things. But, in the end, they all played the game with him. Trying to be the perfect woman he was seeking, trying to please him, trying to make him fall in love with them. Because they thought, if they could, maybe they could convince him not to kill them.

Of course, it was a game they could never win. But none of them knew that. They all clung to the thin glimmer of hope – of life – until the very end.

He killed a total of nine women before he was stopped. While he carried out his terrible spree, Galvin made only two missteps along the way.

The first was Becky Spangler, who somehow managed to get

out of the house before he killed her. She was the only eyewitness police had until he was caught. But she was never of much use. After forty-eight hours of captivity by Felix the Cat, she had become pretty much a basket case. She never really recovered and was still in a hospital.

The other mistake was Janet Parsons, the one he was with when police SWAT teams burst into her house and captured him. She was in pretty bad shape, physically and emotionally, when they got to her. She recovered enough to testify against Galvin at his trial. But she would spend the rest of her life in a wheelchair.

'I don't think I've ever met anybody quite as scary as Galvin,' Righetti said.

'What do you mean?'

'Well, I've interrogated a lot of bad people over the years: rapists, killers, terrorists. But none of them ever affected me like Galvin did. I spent days questioning him after the arrest, taking his confession for all those murders. It really got to me. I used to have nightmares about this case. Sometime I still do.

'There was something else too. His eyes. Galvin's eyes were just so cold and piercing and terrifying. I'll never forget those eyes. I saw them close up for all that time I spent with him. I looked directly in them.' He shuddered involuntarily even now at the memory. 'They were evil, Joe.'

'So what's the department doing about my story?' I asked Righetti when he was finished.

'Well, of course, we want to make sure nothing happens to the two live people on Galvin's list. Linda Hiller and Arthur Dodson. We've already put a twenty-four-hour guard on Hiller. We're still trying to locate Dodson. We're also looking into whether there's any obvious links between Galvin and any of the other deaths he told you about. But, except for the Franze case, it's been a long time since these people died. It's going to be really difficult to find out anything new. The bottom line is, Joe, that we may never know the answers.'

I understood what he was saying, of course. But I couldn't accept that.

'The difference between you and me,' I told Righetti, 'is that I have to know those answers. This is more than just a job or another story to me. It's very personal.'

He knew what I meant.

'Listen, I was really sorry to see that your wife and son were on that list,' he said. 'I mean it's tough enough to lose your family. But to find out that their deaths might be part of some sick asshole's fantasy . . .'

Righetti shook his head.

'I want to to help you, Joe. I really do. But after all this time . . . hell, I don't even know where you start looking to try to find some answers. None of it makes any sense.'

He was right, of course. It didn't make sense.

Eleven years ago, this madman David Galvin – who called himself Felix the Cat – had gone on a terrifying murder spree. Then he was caught and sent to jail for the rest of his life.

We all thought it was over. We put the nightmare behind us. We got on with our lives.

And, according to Galvin, the rest of The Great Pretenders did too.

They graduated from college. They got good jobs. They became pillars of society. And now, eleven years later, they'd all come a long way from the secret society of bored, rich kids who got their kicks by playing a deadly game of make-believe.

That's what Galvin had told me in those last desperate hours as he tried to make his peace with God.

I didn't do it alone, Galvin said. There were three other killers. Three people who got away with murder.

And they were out there now.

Or at least someone was.

Starting it up all over again.

Still pretending after all these years.

thirteen

The campus of New York University is located downtown at the end of Fifth Avenue, all around Washington Square Park.

It's very unique; the kind of college campus you'd find only in New York City. There's the famous arch at the north entrance. The park itself with its eclectic mix of students, street people and ageless hippies still reliving the '60s. Walk a block west and you're in the center of Greenwich Village, with all its character, energy and zaniness. The university's classrooms and offices are dotted all around the area.

I found the administration building, walked up the steps and into the lobby. There was a receptionist sitting at a desk. She was young – probably still a teenager – and I figured she was a coed at the school working a part-time job. I told her what I was doing there. She was very impressed. Probably never met a big-time reporter before. I wondered if she'd run right home afterward to tell all the other kids in the dormitory.

She said the person I needed to talk to was Dean Gerald Hynes.

Hynes was the dean of student affairs. He looked maybe ten years older than me, with surprisingly long light brown hair which hung down over his ears. He was wearing a button-down dress shirt, open at the collar, and faded blue denim jeans. I pegged him as a guy waging a valiant battle to look hip, but losing the war. He didn't seem nearly as impressed to see me as the receptionist.

'I'm looking for information on some students,' I told him.

'Current students?'

'No, they would have been on campus about eleven years ago.'

'What are their names?'

'I don't know.'

'Then what are you looking for?'

'I'm not sure.'

'Well, do you know anything at all about them?'

'They're all from nice, affluent family backgrounds. They've probably since gone on to successful – maybe even high-profile – jobs in their chosen professions. Oh, and they murdered a lot of people while they were students at this institute of higher learning. I don't think that last thing would be in their record files.'

Dean Hynes looked at me as if I'd just dropped in from the planet Neptune.

'I'm telling this very badly,' I said.

So I went through the entire story for him. He knew about Galvin. Everyone there knew the story of David Galvin, he said, who, he pointed out, was not exactly an example of the kind of future leaders the school turned out. But he said that was all before his time. He'd been dean of student affairs there for six years.

'Now what do you want from me?' he asked.

'I'd like you to let me see the records of all of the former students who would have been on campus at the same time Galvin was here.'

'That's a big job.'

'I know.'

'What exactly are you looking for?'

'I'm not sure. Something that jumps out at me. Some clue. Some connection to Galvin that everyone else has missed all these years. I'm hoping I'll know the clue when I find it.'

I knew he wasn't going to go for my idea. It would have meant making a decision, putting himself on the line, doing something he really didn't have to do. Dean Hynes didn't seem to me like a person who did that very often. He wasn't a put-yourself-on-the-line kind of guy.

'Why don't you just try the library,' he said impatiently. 'They have old yearbooks there. You can go through them.'

'That's not good enough. Not everybody's picture is in a yearbook. Maybe they didn't graduate or they were sick on photo op day or they were just camera shy. Maybe some of the yearbooks are missing. I need to have access to your entire student personnel file.'

'I'm not opening up those records to you.'

'Why not?'

'Because I don't have to,' he said smugly.

'Look, I'm trying to catch a murderer here.'

'You're not the police. You're just a newpaper reporter. If the police ask to go through my records, I'll let them. But not you.'

He stood up behind his desk.

'Good day, Mr Dougherty. Our business is finished.'

I walked back outside into Washington Square Park. It was midmorning, and there were lots of people around. I started talking to some of them, asking if they were here when David Galvin was a student. Did they know anyone who was? Did they ever hear about him having any friends? I showed people a picture of Galvin from the *Banner*'s old files the way he would have looked eleven years ago.

Everybody knew who David Galvin was.

Nobody revealed anything new to me about him.

Nobody gave me any clues.

Nobody confessed to me that they were a secret member of The Great Pretenders.

I walked over to the NYU library and asked the woman behind the reference desk where I could find school yearbooks from the mid-80s. She said the old yearbooks were kept in storage in a different building. If I wanted to see them, she said, I'd need to get approval from someone in the university's adminstration office. I asked her for a name to contact. She suggested Dean Hynes. Terrific.

I had another idea. I asked her to show me any information they had about fantasy role-playing games. The kind of games David Galvin said he and his friends used to play.

I'd heard of the fantasy role-playing phenomenon before, but I thought it was just another game like Mario Brothers or Space Invaders or PacMan. I never realized it was such serious business.

I spent the rest of the morning reading newspaper and magazine articles, from places like the *Washington Post*, *Newsweek* and *USA Today*, about how it became an obsession to some people.

The most popular of the games, Dungeons and Dragons, had been invented in the 1970s. Now an estimated four million Americans – primarily high school and college students, most of them extremely intelligent – played it and similar role-playing games.

There were stories about young people who played as much as forty hours a week. Some of them totally lost touch with reality, taking on the personality of their imaginary game character in real life.

At least fifty deaths – some of them teenage suicides, others senseless thrill killings – had already been linked to these fantasy games, according to critics.

The game itself was incredibly complicated which was why it attracted mostly bright, gifted young people with vivid imaginations. There was no game board; no real rules; and the games themselves could go on indefinitely, spinning out more and more elaborate fantasies. Players assume the identity of sorcerers and gods and demons – and then must use incredible violence and treachery to reach their goals. Characters are killed, resurrected and reincarnated.

'This is a very intense, very violent game,' according to one critic. 'It's full of human sacrifice, eating babies, drinking blood, rape, murder of every variety and curses of insanity. It's extremely fascinating, just talk to people that have played it. But when you have fun with murder, that's dangerous. The game causes young people to kill themselves and others. Kids start living in the fantasy . . . and they can't find their way out of the dungeon.'

I made notes as I went through some of the horror stories I found in the news clippings:

News item: A 16-year-old boy – taking his high school finals in Montpelier, Va. – wrote on the test sheet, 'This is the last paper I will ever write, GOODBYE.'

That night, he went home and shot himself in the chest with his father's pistol.

His parents say they are convinced his suicide resulted from a 'curse' put on him in school earlier that day while he was playing the fantasy game of Dungeons and Dragons. He was so distraught over the curse, they say, that he killed himself.

News item: A family of four was brutally murdered in Bellevue, Wash. by two teenagers obsessed with playing fantasy games. Prosecutors said their only motive was the the 'sheer thrill of killing.'

The teens are said to have played fantasy games so zealously that they were kicked out of one game by the other participants for overdoing it.

'You just can't make sense out of it,' the mayor of the city said after the pair were arrested for the slayings. 'Something like this where you lose touch with reality and say, "I've got to kill somebody just for the hell of it . . ."

News item: The family of a 16-year-old boy in Castle Rock, Colo. say they knew something was wrong when he took down his Sports Illustrated swimsuit model posters and replaced them with pictures of demons.

A short time later, he killed himself with carbon monoxide from his parents' car.

Family members blamed the suicide on his obsession with fantasy role-playing games.

'He opened a door to the occult,' his sister said.

News item: The bodies of two little second-grade boys were found brutally stabbed to death and hidden under a pile of leaves in a wooded area near Virginia Beach, Va.

When a clean-cut, gentle-looking 16-year-old was arrested for the murder, everyone wondered why he did it. They soon found the horrifying answer: His obsession with the fantasy role-playing game had become pathological.

The headline on the article in the Norfolk Virginian-Pilot said:

FANTASY TURNS TO NIGHTMARE
For accused Teen, Life, Games, Merged

There were a lot more articles like this, but the pattern was always the same. A bright, imaginative young person. A cleancut, wholesome, all-American kid from a nice respectable family. Looking for some excitement in life. Who instead plunges into a bizarre world of make-believe – and then can't get out again.

I read one of the quotes I'd written down from a psychologist who counseled teenagers with behavioral problems.

'Games like this give these kids something they don't have in their normal lives,' the pyschologist explained. 'Control. Total control.

'Players get to command vast armies, make life and death decisions on people, obliterate all their enemies. They cannot possibly ever experience this as a real life situtation. So they turn to these fantasy role-playing games and escape into a pretend world.

'For kids who feel they have no power over their own lives, these games can be like handing them a pack of matches. The players become so wrapped up in the seductive fantasies of their make-believe world that they lose touch with reality.'

Is that what happened to David Galvin?

And the rest of The Great Pretenders too?

At lunch time, I walked back to the administration building and took a seat on a park bench across the street. I bought a hot dog and a soda from a street vendor and waited until Dean Hynes came out and headed away in the opposite direction. On his way to a well-deserved lunch break, no doubt. Then I went inside and talked to the receptionist again.

'Does Dean Hynes have them ready yet?' I asked her.

She looked confused. 'Have what ready?'

'The personnel records. The ones of all the students from when David Galvin was here. He promised me you would print them out for me.'

'I'm sorry, but he never told me anything about it.'

'Can you do it now then? I'll wait.'

'I – I don't know. Dean Hynes just went to lunch. Maybe I should ask him when . . .'

'I'm on deadline,' I smiled. 'I really need them in a hurry.'

'Well, I suppose if Dean Hynes said it was all right . . .'

It took awhile for her to make all the printouts. There were thousands of students who had passed through through the campus during the nearly four years that Galvin was a student here. It was a race against time whether she'd finish before Hynes came back from lunch. I was betting that he was the kind of guy who took a long lunch. I won the bet.

That night I stayed up late in my hotel room going over the printouts. I was looking for any name that I recognized. Any possible connection to David Galvin. Anything that looked like it might mean something to me.

I didn't get very far. Dean Hynes was right about that. It was a lot of work.

But I did find one name that I recognized.

Lisa Montero.

The daughter of Wall Street tycoon John Montero – the same woman who was also the leading suspect in the most recent of the murders on Galvin's list – had gone to NYU. She'd majored in business administration, arriving as a freshman coed during Galvin's junior year on campus. After that, she'd moved on to Harvard, earned an MBA and now was a vice president in her father's business.

Not that it proved anything, of course. I mean thousands of people went to NYU, and the odds were pretty good that a lot of people I'd heard of would turn up on the lists.

But it was, at the very least, an intriguing coincidence.

And she did fit the pattern. The one Galvin had told me about. He said The Great Pretenders all came from affluent, upwardly mobile families, just like he did. And he said, while he languished in jail, the others had gone on to become big successes and prominent names.

I was very proud of myself. I'd found a clue. A goddamned clue. Of course, I wasn't quite sure what to do with my clue. Or if it even meant anything at all.

But I sure as hell had one.

Lisa Montero.

Cool.

fourteen

• • • • • • • • • • •

Someone once said that the acorn never falls very far from the tree. They meant that parents generally produce offspring a lot like themselves. Or like father, like son. I wasn't sure if this was true or not. But I wanted to find out what kind of tree had produced David Galvin.

Galvin's parents lived in Tenafly, NJ, a quiet suburb about fifteen miles north of New York City. The house was a large Tudor located on a quiet cul-de-sac a few miles from the main shopping area. It had two cars in the driveway, a dog sleeping on the front porch and a basketball hoop hanging from the garage.

There was no skull and crossbones on the door.

No image of Satan burned into the lawn.

No sign in front that warned: 'Beware – Birthplace of Felix the Cat.'

Just the house of an affluent family on an affluent street in an affluent American suburb.

Norman Galvin, the father, was in his fifties with short, almost crewcut greying hair. His wife, Barbara, was tiny, blonde and thin. There were framed pictures of their two other children on the walls inside. A girl in a high school cheerleader's outfit; then later all grown up as a young mother posing happily with her two tiny children. Another girl in a high school graduation cap and gown. There were no pictures of David on any of the walls.

'I understand you were one of the last people to see David,' Norman Galvin said as we sat in their spacious living room. A copy of the *Banner*, with my article about their son and the new revelations on the front page, was on the coffee table beside us. 'Thank you. I'm sure that meant something to him.'

'I wasn't doing him any favors,' I said. 'I was doing my job.'

'Well, I'm just glad that he wasn't completely alone at the end.'

The dog had come inside and fallen asleep on my foot. It was a collie mix of some sort, not too old and very friendly. I reached down and scratched it behind the ear. The dog's tail thumped on the floor. I remembered how David Galvin had once said he took the name Felix the Cat because he admired cats more than dogs. I looked around to see if there was a cat in the house too. But then I remembered that had all been a long time ago. If there had been a real life Felix the Cat, the animal was probably long dead by now. And this dog wasn't even born when Galvin went to jail.

'You didn't visit him much in prison?' I asked his parents.

'No,' Norman Galvin said. 'Neither of us had seen or talked to David in more than ten years.'

'Why not?'

'It was just too painful.'

He looked over at his wife, who seemed to be getting very uncomfortable by the whole conversation.

'Barbara and I could have gone at the end, I suppose, when we knew he was sick and dying,' he said. 'But we didn't. We didn't think it was the thing to do. It would have been . . . well, hypocritical.'

Mrs Galvin spoke now for the first time.

'Look around this house, Mr Dougherty. You won't see any evidence that David was ever a part of this family. After . . . after what happened eleven years ago – when we found out what he did – we decided that David had to be cut out of our family like a cancer. Otherwise it would kill us all. We had to do that to survive: me, my husband, our two other children.

'You see, I created that monster that once was my son. I brought him into this world. He grew in my body and I nursed him and I watched him grow up and once – a long, long time ago – I loved him. Do you have any idea what that feels like now? Well, that's what I had to get over.'

I nodded. I understood why she was so upset. She had spent more than a decade trying to forget David Galvin was her son. Now this was all happening to them all over again. Like a horrible nightmare they could never wake up from.

'It was terrible at first after David was arrested,' Norman Galvin told me. 'People called us names, threw things at our house, threatened us. My business suffered too. But the worst part were the people we thought were our friends. It was as if . . . well, as if Barbara and I had done those terrible things. But we hadn't. We didn't kill those people. David did.'

'But you never moved.'

'No.'

'How come?'

'I didn't think that running away was the answer.'

He looked around the house. The house where David Galvin – who would become Felix the Cat, one of the country's most notorious serial killers – once grew up a million years ago. At the pictures of his other children on the wall; the ones who grew up to live decent lives. This house was filled with memories for him. Some were good, but many of them were very, very bad.

'Did you ever have any idea . . . any suspicions?' I asked.

'About David?' He shook his head. 'No, he was our first born, our pride and joy, the genius in the family. David was a brilliant boy. The psychiatrists all said that after he was arrested. They told us his IQ was off the charts. He was good looking too. Popular. Charming. He was going to go on to medical school after NYU. David could have done anything he wanted with his life, he had so many things going for him. So why did he do what he did? I'm afraid I don't know the answer to that. And I gave up trying to figure that one out a long time ago.'

I nodded. I felt sorry for them. I could feel their pain. It was a pain they had lived with for a long time, but they had survived and it had gotten better in recent years. Now the pain was back with a vengeance. And I was one of the reasons. I felt bad about that.

I asked about the letter David had sent them before he died. My letter had contained the list of new victims. There weren't any secrets in the one he'd left for Rev. Campanella at the prison, just thanks for his kindness during the last days of the illness, according to the minister. Maybe he'd told something to his parents. Something else he'd kept hidden all these years.

Norman Galvin shook his head no.

'There was nothing,' he said. 'Just telling us he was sorry for all the problems he had caused – and a lot of religion talk about finding God and being at peace with himself and hoping he still had a chance to get into Heaven.'

'Can I see the letter?' I asked.

'No,' Mrs Galvin said.

I was surprised. The Galvins had been totally cooperative with me up until this point.

'Why not?'

'Because I threw the damn thing away after I read it,' she said. 'It was just too painful to hold on to.'

Like everything else about their son, I thought.

'Mr and Mrs Galvin, when David was a student at NYU, do you ever remember him mentioning a group called The Great Pretenders?' I asked.

'No. I read your article,' the father said. 'I know what he told you. But that's the first time I ever heard of anything like that. He was very specific when he was arrested – he said he'd done it all alone. Now . . . now I just don't know what to believe anymore.'

'David talked in that last interview with me about his obsession with role-playing fantasy games. He said that's what The Great Pretenders was all about. Did he ever talk with either of you about this?'

They both said no.

'Did he play any games like that when he was in high school?'

Mrs Galvin shrugged. 'Oh, he played some video games, I guess. They weren't nearly as sophisticated as they are now. But he loved them. He'd lock himself up in his room for hours on end in front of the screen. It was like he was in his own little world. He was always very compulsive about anything he did. If he liked something, he never knew when it was time to stop.

'But he was that way about everything. One summer he fell in love with basketball. He'd be out out there shooting a ball,' she said, looking through a window at the basketball hoop hanging from the garage, 'until it was too dark for him to even see it. I used to tell him moderation was the key to everything in life. He never listened.'

'So you never thought anything was really wrong with him?'

'No. I just figured it was the normal stuff a teenage boy goes though when he's growing up.'

I nodded.

'How about his friends? Did either of you know the people he hung around with at NYU?'

'Not really,' Norman Galvin said. 'In high school, we did. But they never lasted too long. You see, he never had much use for any of his high school friends. He got bored with them very quickly. David was kind of a loner, I guess. But he said at NYU he'd finally found some people smart enough to understand him, that he could relate to on the same level. He seemed happier in college than he did in high school. That's why I was so surprised when the horrible truth came out about what he was doing.'

'Was there anyone specific at NYU that you can remember?'

'There was one girl. We met her a couple of times. She and David hung out together, he said, but I don't know if there was anything going on between them. He didn't seem interested in her that way. I think they were just friends.'

'But you don't know her name?'

'Well, I didn't until today.'

'What do you mean?'

'Her picture's in your newspaper.'

I stared at him. I didn't know what he was talking about. 'You mean with my article.'

'No,' he said, 'it's on a different page. I just read it before you came. That's when I remembered who she was.'

He picked up the newspaper and and showed me another article. It was written by Bonnie Kerns. The latest story about the murders of William Franze and the call girl. There were pictures of the two victims. And also a picture of Lisa Montero. Underneath it was a quote from an assistant district attorney named Greg Ackerman calling her the prime suspect in the case.

'That's her,' he said, pointing to the picture of Montero.

'Lisa Montero and your son were friends?'

'Weird, huh?' Norman Galvin said.

Lisa Montero had been there all along – drifting through this case right from the very beginning.

I'd heard about her and the Franze murder case that first day in Andy Kramer's office. Then Franze and the call girl wound up on David Galvin's hit list. Bonnie wrote that the authorities thought the Montero woman did it. After that, I discovered she had gone to NYU at the same time as Galvin and The Great Pretenders. And now this from his parents. Lisa Montero knew David Galvin.

She was somehow a part of this story.

All I had to do was find out how.

fifteen

'I'm looking for information,' I told Bonnie Kerns.

'So what do I look like – a 411 operator?'

'You seem to know an awful lot of stuff about an awful lot of things,' I said. 'Everybody at the paper says you're a terrific reporter. And for the past few weeks you've been covering the William Franze murder, which now appears to be connected to my story. I thought you might have some ideas.'

'So that's why I'm getting the five-star restaurant treatment for lunch, huh?'

We were eating at a very trendy place on Park Avenue South, not far from the hotel where I was staying. It had beautiful waitresses, beautiful customers and not so beautiful prices.

'Is this your standard procedure for getting information out of a woman?' Bonnie asked, looking around the place. 'You take her out to a fancy restaurant, bat your big brown eyes at her – and the woman just falls to pieces right in front of you?'

'It has been known to happen,' I said.

A waitress came over to take our orders. She smiled at us. She was tall and athletic looking and pretty, probably an aspiring dancer or a model. She was wearing a pair of skin-tight designer jeans and a low cut sweater with a tag on the front that said her name was Amanda. She continued to smile while she wrote down what we wanted; pasta for me, a fish dish for Bonnie. She was still smiling when she left.

Bonnie rolled her eyes, put her finger down her mouth and made a gagging sound after she was gone.

'Let me tell you something, Joe,' she said. 'You're wasting your time with this whole seduction bit on me. I'm not a seductive kind of girl. Now Amanda there, she is. You could probably seduce Amanda right out of her Calvin Kleins. Me, I'm more the functional type. I mean I know you think you're cute and charming and all that but I'm immune to it. I really am. You want to know a secret? I'm really not even interested in men.'

'Are you. . . ?'

'Into women? Am I a lesbian? Is that your question?'

'Well, yes . . .'

'I thought I was. I tried it for awhile. Now I don't have much to do with either sex, romantically speaking. I just don't date. My choice. Well, no one's exactly beating down the door to change my mind. That's probably because I don't look like Amanda back there. But it works out nice. I'm totally committed to my work right now. I don't need a personal life. Does that sound weird to you? Probably, huh? Hey, what am I telling you all this stuff for anyway? It's just that when I start talking, sometimes I can't stop. I'm kind of intense. I don't know if you noticed.'

I smiled.

'Tell me what you know about the William Franze murder,' I said.

'William Franze was a high roller in the world of big finance. Wild Bill, they called him on Wall Street because he was so volatile and unpredictable. Franze was the kind of guy who could make a fortune on Monday and then be broke by Friday. Do you know what I mean?'

Yeah, I knew what she meant. When that happens on Wall Street, they put you on the cover of *Fortune Magazine*. Try it in Atlantic City or Vegas like I used to, and they call it a disease.

'Franze lived in a lavish townhouse on East 61st Street,' Bonnie said. 'He was married, but no one ever saw him with his wife. He went out with lots of women. One of them was Lisa Montero, the daughter of business mogul John Montero – one of the richest men in the country and a very big force on Wall Street and in New York City politics for years.

'On the night he was killed, Franze and the Montero woman had gone out to dinner and then back to his place. After that they began arguing and she stormed out. Neighbors heard them fighting and saw her leave in a rage. Another witness saw her return awhile later.

'Montero admitted to cops afterward that they'd fought. She said it was because Franze wanted her to have sex with him – and another woman. A *ménage à trois*. He called up an escort agency and ordered a girl to be sent over to join them. She says that when she said no, Franze ordered two hookers then instead of one. That's when she stormed out.

'When cops got to the scene, they found Franze dead in bed. The body of a girl named Whitney Martin, who worked for the Elite Escort Agency, was also in the bed. They'd both been shot several times. Both Franze and the Martin woman were naked, and it appeared as if they had been in the throes of lovemaking just prior to their deaths.'

'He ordered two hookers?' I asked Bonnie when she was finished telling me the story.

'That's why they called him Wild Bill, I guess.'

'So what happened to the other hooker?'

'No one knows.'

The waitress brought our food. She smiled again as she put it down. I looked over at Bonnie. She crossed her eyes and made a face at me across the table. I tried hard not to laugh. I liked Bonnie. I loved her energy, her drive, her absolute conviction that she knew more about anything in the world than everybody else. I remembered when I used to feel that way too.

'And Lisa Montero claims she didn't do it?' I said.

'Right. But the cops and the DA's office don't believe her. Especially this young hotshot named Greg Ackerman in the DA's office. I think he sees a career-making case here. Of course, they all have to tread kind of carefully because of her father's money and political influence. But the word I hear is that they're going to arrest the lady for murder very soon.'

'What's Lisa Montero like?' I asked.

'Very successful. She's a vice president in the Montero Corporation, which is run by her father John and who – the last time I looked – was right up there in the Fortune 500 listings along with Ron Perelman and Rupert Murdoch and some of those Japanese computer guys. She's smart. She's pretty. She's also a bit of a nut case. She dates all kinds of playboy types. The lady likes to party. They say she uses men, flirts with them, charms them – until she gets what she wants. I assume you've already tried to reach her at her office?'

'They told me she was on a leave of absence.'

'You've left her messages?

'Lots of them.'

'Home?'

'Unlisted number.'

'I know a guy at the phone company who can . . .'

'So do I. No good. The DA's office has red-flagged her number and pulled her whole information file. No one can get at it.'

'Just a thought.'

'I have been a reporter before, Bonnie.'

'Oh yeah? Well, if you're such hotshit, Dougherty, how come you're sitting here begging me to help you?'

I laughed.

'If you want to talk to Lisa Montero, it seems to me the best place to catch her is in a social setting,' Bonnie said as she ate. 'At a business office or official function, she's going to have people around her running interference. But when she goes out, she's more vulnerable. She also likes to drink a lot, which shouldn't hurt either.'

'Where does she go socially?' I asked.

'Broadway plays. The movies. Madison Square Garden sometimes for Knicks or Rangers games. Her favorite restaurants are LeCirque and Lutece and the Union Square Cafe. Later at night, she hangs out sometimes at Elaine's on the Upper East side. Hey, try them all. I did. It didn't get me anywhere. But maybe you'll get lucky.'

'Thanks, Bonnie. I appreciate this.'

'It's the least I can do,' she laughed, 'since you bought me this expensive meal – and I won't have sex with you.'

Bonnie looked down at her plate. She picked up a piece of fish with her fork and chewed it on thoughtfully. There was something else on her mind.

'Are you ever going to talk about it?' she asked.

'What?'

'You. The *Banner*. The big scandal eight years ago. What exactly happened anyway?'

'Don't you know?'

'Just some of the basic details. You did a story about some big shot city official, linking him to a sex scandal. There was a big lawsuit, the newspaper printed a retraction and the city official committed suicide. The upshot was that you got fired. After that you had some personal problems, and no one heard from you in years – until you suddenly showed up in the *Banner* newsroom the other day. That's really all I know.'

'That's a pretty good highlights package,' I said.

'You want to talk about it?'

'Not now.'

'Some other time then?'

'Maybe.'

'Okay, let's talk about Nancy Kelleher then.'

'Where did you hear about that?'

'I asked around about you with some of the *Banner* old-timers at Lanigan's the other night,' Bonnie said. 'They told me how you were a legend around here. That you were the most tenacious reporter they'd ever seen. That you never gave up on a story. One guy said I should ask you about the Kelleher story.'

'Nancy Kelleher,' I said slowly. 'She was a hooker who worked on Park Avenue. Came here on a bus from Wisconsin, thought she was going to break into show business and wound up on the street. Her pimp was a creep named Johnny Sanchez. According to the cops, she goes home one night, gets into a fight with Sanchez and shoots him dead in her bed. The story gets a lot of press coverage. Everybody in town is writing about the innocent girl who came here from the Midwest and turned into a murderer. The DA's office figures it has a slam-dunk case – Sanchez was murdered in her bed, she's got no alibi, the murder gun was found in her apartment – and they're right. The jury took about thirty seconds to come back with a guilty verdict.'

'So what's the story?' Bonnie asked.

'There was just something about it that didn't feel right to me. A few loose strands. So I decided to do some more checking. Once I began to pull on a few of the loose ends, the whole thing began to unravel. I finally tracked down a woman who worked as a prostitute for a rival pimp. She said he bragged to her he killed Sanchez as part of a turf war, then tried to make it look like one of Sanchez's own girls did it. I wrote the story, the pimp eventually confessed to cops and Nancy Kelleher was freed.'

'Awesome.'

'There's more. It turns out that the woman who broke the story to me had tried to contact the DA's office during the trial to tell them what she knew. But the ADA handling the case – a young ambitious guy who was looking to make a name for himself – never followed up on it. He liked Nancy Kelleher for the murder better, because she was front page news. One pimp killing the other would hardly make the paper. I wrote about that too. Got him fired from the DA's office and brought up on charges. He finally copped a plea for obstruction of justice.'

'Wow!' Bonnie shook her head in amazement. 'So what happened to Nancy Kelleher?'

'She runs a school for runaway girls in the Bronx now. I knew a guy in social services, I put her in touch with him and he helped her get started. Now she's a big success. She's married too, got two kids of her own. I still talk to her sometimes. We kept in touch.'

'God, I'd love to do a story like that,' Bonnie said.

'She was more than just a story,' I said. 'It was one time when I felt I was really able to accomplish something as a newspaper reporter. To make a difference. When that happens, it's a really good feeling.'

'That's very noble. But you did get a front page story out of it. That's really what it's all about, isn't it?'

'Sometimes,' I said, 'you can break a big story and do the right thing too.'

'But not always.'

'No,' I said, 'not always.'

Bonnie shook her head.

'Let me tell you something, Joe, I'm a pretty perceptive person. I have to be, I'm a reporter. I get paid to figure out what people are all about. Now you, I read you right now as a guy with serious confusion. I know about your family, how they turned up on Galvin's list. And I'm sorry about that wound opening up again. But I don't think that's the only reason you're on this story. I figure you've got something else to prove. To the *Banner*. To the world. To yourself. Am I right or am I right?'

I smiled. 'Like you said, Bonnie, you're a very perceptive person.'

sixteen

Carolyn woke me up with a phone call the next morning.

'You haven't called,' she said.

'Sorry, I've been busy.'

I pulled myself out of bed, still holding the phone to my ear, and looked at the clock. 8:15. I needed to get going. There were computer printouts from NYU scattered over the bed. I'd fallen asleep reading more of them the night before. Outside, the sky was a bright blue and the sun was shining in through the open window. It was going to be a beautiful spring day. I needed to get out there and enjoy it.

'How about I drive down to Princeton later?' I said to Carolyn.

'Do you think you can get away?'

'Sure. I'm supposed to have a meeting with Andy this morning to go over some stuff on the story. As soon as that's over, I'll hit the turnpike. If there's no traffic, I can be walking in the front door an hour later. Maybe an hour and a half tops.'

'Are you sure you remember the way, Joe?' she asked. 'It's been a long time.'

'I'll buy a map.'

'How about finding your way around the bedroom?' Carolyn asked teasingly. 'It's been awhile since you've been there too.'

'I'll buy a map for that too.'

'There are no maps in the bedroom, big guy. You're on your own in that department.' She giggled. 'I guess you'll just have to feel your way until you get where you're going.'

'Maybe I'll ask a friendly face for directions,' I said.

Carolyn laughed. A terrific laugh. She was a terrific person. I sure was a lucky guy to have a woman like her walk into my life. The first good thing to happen to me in a long, long time. Now all I had to do was make sure I didn't do anything to screw it up.

There was only one thing wrong with Carolyn.

I knew what it was, but I couldn't do anything about it.

She wasn't Susan.

After all this time, I still missed Susan. I'd never really stopped thinking about her. But now – ever since I'd found her and Joey's name on Felix the Cat's list of victims – I just couldn't get her out of my mind.

The thing I remember most about Susan was that she was always exciting.

She got excited about everything in life – even the smallest things – and it made life exciting for the people around her too.

Like me.

I remember the first time we flew anywhere together. She was like a kid with a new toy. Everything on the plane made her happy: the takeoff, the landing, the in-flight movie, the airline food, watching the other passengers and making up stories about where they were going. She kept clapping her hands and laughing and just having a great time. It was infectious. I've been on more planes than I care to remember, but I was having as much fun as she was.

It was the same way at the movies. She cheered when the lights in the theatre went down, she cheered for the upcoming previews, she cheered when the main feature came on. Like we were at a baseball game or something. Everything she did was an adventure.

Susan's favorite time of the year was Christmas. Nobody did Christmas like she did. There was always a big tree, decorations everywhere, Christmas cards to everyone she ever met, all sorts of holiday food, Christmas caroling – the whole works. After Joey was born, she got even more caught up in the holiday spirit. She wanted to make Christmas special for him, even if he was too young yet to really appreciate it. I just didn't know it would be the only Christmas the three of us would ever have together.

God, she had such a passion for living.

I guess that's what I really miss about her the most.

'Joe, are you okay?' Carolyn asked over the phone.

'Sorry, I was just thinking about some stuff I have to do before I have to drive down there.'

'But you definitely are coming?'

'Absolutely.'

'I love you, Joe,' Carolyn said.

I couldn't think of anything else to say, so I told her: 'I love you too.'

But I never did see Carolyn that day.

Too many things were happening.

That morning, after I hung up with her, I spent some more time going through the NYU computer printouts. It was an impossible job. There were thousands of names. Even if I found a name that meant something to me – and there was no reason I should – I might very easily miss it because of the sheer volume of the material I was dealing with.

I got lucky though.

I did find two more names that I recognized.

Not that it proved anything, of course. Like I kept telling myself, a lot of students went to NYU and the odds were pretty good that people I knew – or who would go on to bigger things – would turn up on the lists.

The two names I found though were very intriguing, to say the least.

Just like Lisa Montero's had been.

One of them was my old friend Andy Kramer. That really surprised me. I remembered now though that when he first came to the *Banner* as a copyboy, he was still taking classes at some college. I just never realized it was NYU. And he once told me his family had a lot of money – and was disappointed that he hadn't gone into a higher paying profession than newspapers.

The second name was even more interesting.

Once again, the entire pattern was there. The one Galvin had told me about. He said The Great Pretenders all came from affluent, upwardly mobile families, just like he did. And, he said, while he languished in jail, the other three had gone on to become big successes and prominent names.

Well, this third name certainly held a very high-profile, prominent public post.

And, according to the computer records, he'd been at NYU during all of the years Galvin was there.

What was it Galvin had said about The Great Pretenders?

'They all became respectable, successful members of society. Nobody ever knew about the deadly secrets in their past. Ironic, huh? The Great Pretenders disappeared just like the people they once murdered. Poof – and they were gone.'

Except someone was still out there killing people.

I looked at the names on the piece of paper in front of me.

Especially the third name.

It was Greg Ackerman.

The Assistant District Attorney in charge of the William Franze investigation.

I was getting ready to leave for the office with this new information when Captain Righetti, my old friend at police headquarters, called and changed everything.

A big story was breaking.

The Great Pretenders had just struck again.

seventeen

It was President John F. Kennedy who said that anyone can murder another person if they really want to.

There is no amount of protection, no precaution, no safeguard that will ever be enough to stop a truly determined adversary from killing his intended target, JFK said.

Sooner or later, the odds are always against the victim.

That person will die.

President Kennedy made these comments in Houston on the night before his own assassination – which I guess gives them a particular ring of authenticity.

Anyway, it's good theory. A theory that most law enforcement experts agree with, even if they never admit it publicly. But it didn't have much to do with the death of Linda Hiller. Because the killer didn't have to get through any elaborate net of protection to get to her. The cops and the DA's office screwed this one up.

This is how it happened.

After I got David Galvin's list – with Linda Hiller's name on it – the police put her under special guard. She was moved out of her house to a safe place where she was under surveillance twenty-four hours a day. She didn't go to work, she didn't go out, she didn't even tell her close friends and relatives where she was. It wasn't foolproof, but it was about as good as a security plan can be.

Except it got boring.

After a few days of this, everyone got tired of it. The cops and the DA's office didn't really believe Linda Hiller was on some serial killer's list anyway. It had to be a mistake. Who would want to kill her?

They never bought David Galvin's story either. A band of Felix the Cat accomplices still running loose out there? Captain Righetti had told me that first day in his office he didn't think it was for real. A lot of people agreed with him. They figured Galvin had just left the list for me as some sort of sick joke and that he'd made the whole thing up.

So the authorities decided to switch to a lower level of security. Linda Hiller could go back to work. Cops would escort her to and from her job, and keep a squad car outside her house at night. Everyone agreed this was a good compromise solution.

The last time anyone saw her alive was when she left the office of her theatrical agency at 2:15 in the afternoon. The office was on the tenth floor of a midtown high rise. She told her secretary she'd only be away for a few minutes – she was just going to talk to somebody in another office on the first floor about a client she wanted to audition for a Broadway show.

When she didn't return by five o'clock, the secretary went looking for her. She discovered that Linda Hiller had never showed up in the first floor office. The police were called. They searched the building first, then the neighborhood – and finally went back to her house in the hope that she'd just gone home for some reason in the middle of the afternoon. But there was no sign of her anywhere.

Then, the next day, the owner of a shop that sold wedding dresses in a nearby building called the police in a panic. He told them that when he came to work that morning, one of his mannequins was missing. In its place was the body of a dead woman – dressed from head to toe in one of his wedding gowns.

It was Linda Hiller.

I stood outside the wedding gown shop now with Captain Righetti and watched the Medical Examiner's people get ready to carry her body out to a waiting morgue truck.

'Well, this proves it, doesn't it?'

'Proves what?'

'That Galvin was telling me the truth. His friends are still out there playing this sick game. At least one of them is anyway. That's who did this.'

'Maybe.'

'What do you mean maybe?'

'The big boys downtown don't necessarily see it that way.'

'They're the ones who screwed this whole thing up in the first place by letting her out of their sight without any protection . . .'

'Joe, in all the time you've been a reporter, have you ever heard of public officials taking responsibility when they made a mistake?'

'No.'

'Well, then you're not going to be surprised by what I have to tell you. The commissioner and the DA say anyone could have done this. That you guys at the *Banner* printed all the names on the list in your paper. They figure it would have been easy for some copycat nut to knock off Linda Hiller and then make it look like one of Galvin's weird fantasies.'

'Do you buy that?'

Righetti shrugged. He was too smart to answer.

'By the way, everyone blames you for the Hiller woman's death,' he told me. 'I thought you might want to know. They say that printing her name in the paper was irresponsible journalism.'

'Kill the messenger, huh?'

'Something like that.'

'Oh, that's beautiful.'

I tried to sound indignant, but the truth is he had a point. I'd said the same thing to Andy Kramer when I filed the story. I suggested we leave out the names of the potential victims. Say we were withholding them at the request of the authorities. But Andy said no, he wanted to use them. He gave me a big speech about the public's right to know, but we both knew the real reason he was doing it. There's always a fine line you walk at a newspaper between telling people the whole story and stooping to sensationalism. Most of the time you wind up on the sensationalism side.

'What about the other name on the list?' I asked. 'Arthur Dodson?'

'That's a really weird one. Nobody knows where Dodson is. He disappeared right after you published the stuff about the list. We haven't been able to locate him.'

'You think he's dead too?'

Righetti shook his head. 'He left some sort of tearful message for his wife and kids on his answering machine the other day,' he said. 'Told them how much he missed them, but he had to go away for awhile. He said he'd talk to them soon. That's the only thing we've heard from him.'

'It sounds like he's scared and on the run.'

'We'll find him. It's just a matter of time.'

'I think Galvin's list is for real,' I said, as I watched them put Linda Hiller's body into the morgue wagon. 'I think whoever did this is the same person that killed William Franze and the call girl. The same person who's responsible for all the other unsolved killings Galvin talked about too. And I'm going to prove it.'

'Well, if what you say is true, then Lisa Montero would have to be leading suspect.'

'Everyone figures she's the one that killed Franze and the girl, huh?'

Righetti nodded. 'From what I hear, the DA's office is really close to bringing in a double murder indictment against her. This guy Ackerman over there has turned this into a personal vendetta. He says he's going to nail her. I think Ackerman's got some real hard on about her father, John Montero. Not that a lot of people in this town don't. Except John Montero has always been pretty invulnerable. But his daughter – well, maybe she's an easier target. And all the evidence seems to point toward her. Ackerman's had her in his sights for the Franze killings ever since they first happened.'

Greg Ackerman.

Lisa Montero.
David Galvin.
All of them had gone to NYU at the same time.
There had to be some sort of connection.

I followed the same routine as I did before. I wrote up the story, turned it into the city desk and then went next door to Lanigan's to have a few beers with some of the other reporters while I waited for the early editions of the *Banner* to come off the presses. They put it on Page One, of course. The headline said:

NEW FELIX THE CAT KILLING

Woman's Bizarre Murder Linked
to Infamous Serial Killer's Pals

By Joe Dougherty

I read the story one more time, then walked back to Lanigan's for a nightcap. Andy Kramer was there, and he gave me a big greeting. He bought me a drink too. Andy was my friend again. Funny how much difference a big story can make in your life.

'This stuff is dynamite,' he said, pointing to my story on the front page. 'It really does look like those nuts that Felix the Cat went to school with are still out there doing their thing. You're really kicking ass on this story, Joe.'

'I just report the facts, Andy.'

'Well, you couldn't have done better with this one if you'd made them up.'

He suddenly realized what he'd just said.

'Jeez, I'm sorry, Joe – I didn't mean it the way it came out.'

'No problem.'

'What happened, happened. It was a long time ago. That's all water under the bridge now.'

'I've learned to live with it.'

Andy nodded. 'What else have you got?'

I told him everything I'd done. My trip to NYU. The visit to David Galvin's parents. Finding out about the NYU connection to Lisa Montero. The NYU link to Greg Ackerman. All the other leads I was following. He seemed pleased. Everything I did sounded great to Andy these days. I was aces in his book.

'By the way,' I said, when I was finished, trying to make it sound as casual as possible, 'you went to NYU, didn't you?'

'Sure did.'

'About the same time as David Galvin?'

'Yeah, I think I was there during one of those years.'

'But you never knew him?'

'No, I didn't.'

'How about Lisa Montero or Greg Ackerman?'

I guess he suddenly realized where this was headed.

'You're not asking me if I was one of The Great Pretenders, are you, Joe?' he said. 'If I hung out with Galvin and his nutty friends? If I killed a bunch of people just for kicks at my old alma mater before I graduated with honors in journalism and came to the *Banner*?'

Well, Andy Kramer did fit the pattern.

'Of course not,' I laughed. 'I was just hoping you might have remembered something about him.'

Andy took a swig of his beer.

'It sounds like Lisa Montero is your best bet as a suspect,' he said.

'That's what the cops and the DA think.'

'I wonder what her story is.'

'She's not talking.'

'You've tried?'

'Everybody has.'

'She'd make a helluva interview.'

'Yeah, I know.'

'So?'

'I'm working on it,' I said.

eighteen

I found Lisa Montero at Elaine's two days later.

It was a little after eleven at night when she walked in. I was at the bar nursing a beer in what they call the tourist section. There's a real class distinction at Elaine's, which became famous over the years as the 'in' hangout for everyone from Woody Allen to Norman Mailer to Liza Minelli. Anybody – even the tourists from Ohio or Nebraska – can get a seat at the bar. But if you want a table, you wind up back next to the kitchen, so far from the action and celebrities you might as well have stayed home. It's better in the middle of the room. And the front tables are kept for the important people. Lisa Montero got one of the front tables.

She was in a group of six people, three men and two other women. I couldn't tell if she was specifically paired up with one of the men. All of them were laughing and talking loudly; with each other and with people who stopped by their table. They seemed to be very friendly. Everyone was having a good time.

I finished my beer and walked over to her chair.

'Hello, Ms Montero,' I said.

She turned around and stared at me blankly. 'Do I know you?'

I saw her face up close for the first time. She was a real looker, all right. Not a Pamela Anderson type glamour girl beauty, but the real deal. Like Liz Taylor or Joan Collins when they were young. Early thirties, kind of petite, but muscular too – like she worked out. Maybe the best part of her was her hair, jet black and long, cascading down over her shoulders. Her eyes were big and dark, almost black like her hair; she had a nice face; and a terrific body. She was wearing an expensive-looking designer dress that showed off all the crucial curves. There was something else too. There was something very familiar about her. I had this real feeling of *déjà vu* meeting Lisa Montero up close for the first time. Like I once knew her. Or someone a lot like her. I suddenly realized I was staring at her.

'I'm Joe Dougherty,' I said.

'Why does that name sound familiar?'

'I've been leaving you messages.'

'Oh, you're the persistent reporter.'

'You didn't answer any of them.'

She put her finger to her lips and made a shushing sound. 'I'm not allowed to talk to anyone about it,' she said.

Now there's a line you're not supposed to cross at Elaine's. That line is between the tourist section at the bar and all the important people sitting where Lisa Montero was. I'd crossed that line. A burly waiter hurried over to the table.

'Is this man bothering you, Miss Montero?'

She seemed amused by the whole situation.

'I don't know, Bobby,' she said. She turned toward me. 'Are you bothering me, Joe?'

I took a deep breath. I didn't have much time.

'I wrote a story for the *Banner* – maybe you read it – that links William Franze's murder to a series of serial killings by a group of college students associated with the infamous Felix the Cat. If you're really innocent, this might help you to prove it. That's why I want to talk to you. If you help me, maybe I can help you.' I looked over at Bobby who was flexing his muscles next to me. 'It's your move, Ms Montero.'

I wasn't exactly sure what was going to happen next. Bobby looked like he could pick me up and throw me out of the place without any problem. Someone might have already called the cops. Or maybe Lisa Montero would give me an interview.

She looked at me thoughtfully.

'What's your sign, Joe?' she asked.

'Excuse me?'

'Your sign. You know . . .' She began to sing: 'When you wish upon a star . . .'

'I–I don't understand.'

'I'm a Capricorn.'

I nodded. Now I got it.

'Taurus,' I said.

'Neat.'

'Taurus is good?'

'Hey, Taurus and Capricorn are fan-fucking-tastic together!'

She smiled at the waiter. 'Joe the Reporter here's not bothering me, Bobby. Didn't you hear what Joe the Reporter just said? Joe the Reporter is going to help me.'

Bobby looked disappointed, but nodded and shuffled back toward the kitchen.

I sat down. She introduced me to the other people at the table. I didn't get all the names, but then they didn't seem very interested in me either. I was okay with that. I didn't need any new friends. Lisa Montero was the only person I wanted to talk to.

'So what do you want to know?' she asked.

'Did you kill William Franze?'

She looked startled, but only for a second. Then she got her composure back.

'You get right to the point, don't you?'

'I'm a newspaperman. I always like to put the lead in the first paragraph.'

She looked me directly in the eye.

'No,' she said evenly, 'I didn't kill him.'

Thinking back on it now, I realize that was the exact moment I became convinced she was innocent. I believed her. Of course, I would have believed anything she told me right then. The truth is I was having a lot of trouble concentrating because I had developed a serious case of the hots for Lisa Montero. Not that I wasn't used to being around beautiful women. But she was different. There was something incredibly sensual to me about the way she talked, the way she moved, the way she reached over and touched my arm or leg to make a point.

'What exactly was your relationship with Franze?' I asked her.

'He was a business associate of my father's.'

'The cops say you went out to dinner with him on the night he was killed.'

'That's right.'

'Did you have sex with him?'

'No.'

'But he wanted to?'

'He was drunk. He called up this escort agency and ordered a hooker to be sent over. He had this crazy idea about getting us both in bed together.'

'You said no?'

'Of course I said no. That's when he told me he was going to make another call asking for a second girl.'

I nodded. 'Is that why people heard you arguing with him?'

'Billy could be very unreasonable when he was drinking.'

'So what did you do after you left?'

'I walked around for awhile. Then I went back to try to talk to him again. But when I got there, I saw a girl going into his place.'

'And it wasn't the girl they found dead with him? Whitney Martin?'

'No.'

'So it could have been the killer?'

'Yes.'

'Or a witness? Maybe the second hooker he called for?'

'I suppose so.'

'What did you do after you left his place?'

'I decided it would be a really embarrassing scene, so I went home.'

'Alone?'

She shrugged. 'No alibi.'

We talked for awhile longer about the case and also about the Assistant District Attorney, Greg Ackerman, who wanted to indict her for the murder. She said he had been harassing both her and her father. She gave me a lot of good quotes. Plenty of stuff to write a story.

I didn't ask her whether she'd ever known Ackerman when they both went to NYU in the' 80s. And I didn't ask her if she knew David Galvin. I didn't want to push her too hard. I didn't want to scare her away.

After awhile, the other people at the table got ready to leave. Someone offered to take her home, but she told them no. She said I would.

Me, I just sat there and went with the flow. It seemed like the thing to do. I was only doing my job, of course. Sure, she was beautiful and sexy and definitely desirable. But all I cared about was the exclusive interview. No one else had gotten her to talk, and now I had. Joe Dougherty, the consummate professional. So why was I having fantasies right now about leaning over and kissing her?

A few minutes later, we walked out of Elaine's together onto Second Avenue and hailed a cab.

'I did read your story, Joe,' she said as we rode across town to her place on Central Park West. 'You're right. If I help you, I think you can help me. Then you'll find your gang of killers, and I'll be innocent. A happy ending for everyone.'

She reached over and touched my hand.

'And kind of romantic too, huh?'

'What do you mean?'

'You and me,' she smiled. 'Think about it, Joe: dogged reporter helps person from going to jail for a crime they didn't commit. It's like something out of one of those old newspaper movies.'

'Northside 777,' I said.

She laughed. 'Exactly. A great movie. Jimmy Stewart clears a guy who's been in prison for nine years for murder. Right?'

'That's right.'

The taxi pulled up in front of her building.

'Do me one favor, huh?' she said as she got out. 'Try to clear me for the Billy Franze murder before I have to spend nine years in prison.'

Then she reached into her purse and took out a piece of paper. She wrote something down and handed it to me.

'My home phone number,' she said. 'Call me.'

I watched her walk away. She had a terrific walk. Across the sidewalk, up some steps and to the front door of her building. Just before she got there, she turned around and smiled at me one more time.

A terrific smile too.

'Thanks, Joe,' she yelled out. 'It was fun.'

Then she went inside.

I told the taxi driver to take me down to the *Banner* building. I had a story to write. A front page story. I'd gotten an exclusive interview with Lisa Montero. No other reporter in town had been able to pull that off. Except me.

Only I wasn't thinking about a front page story right then. I was still thinking about Lisa Montero.

Who might be a cold-blooded murderer who killed William Franze and the call girl with him.

Who might have killed a lot of other people with David Galvin a long time ago.

Who might even be responsible for the death of my wife and young son.

Or who might be innocent.

There was only one thing I was sure about. I realized now who it was that Lisa Montero reminded me of. Someone I used to know a long time ago.

Susan.

God, it was just like the first time I met Susan.

nineteen

They say there are defining moments in every person's life. Turning points. Milestones. Crucial crossroads. Times of decision that dramatically change us and shape us and put us on an irrevocable path in our lives from which there is no turning back. Robert Frost wrote about them in his famous poem, *The Road Not Taken*:

Two roads diverged in a yellow wood
And sorry I could not travel both . . .

I kept the first for another day
Yet knowing how way leads on to way
I doubted if I should ever come back . . .

I took the one less travelled by
And that has made all the difference.

Me, I like Kevin Costner's description in the movie *Tin Cup* even better.

He's the one who called them defining moments.

When a defining moment comes your way, Costner's character explains, you only have two choices.

You can either . . .

a) Define the moment, or
b) The moment defines you.

They arrested Lisa Montero for the killings of William Franze and Whitney Martin not long after that first night I met her at Elaine's.

I'd written a story for the *Banner* the next day under the headline:

I DIDN'T DO IT!

Exclusive: Montero's Daughter
Denies All to *Banner*
in Tearful, First Interview

Now I watched a videotape of Lisa on the six o'clock news being led out of the police station in handcuffs and taken to court to be arraigned for murder. She looked frightened and confused; like a deer suddenly caught in the headlights.

Afterward, there was an interview with Greg Ackerman – the ADA who seemed to be taking such a personal interest in this case – about why he had arrested her.

He told reporters that Lisa Montero had killed both Franze and the Martin girl in a jealous rage. He said he had more than enough evidence to convict her. And he added that his office had found no connection between the Franze murders and any of the other names on David Galvin's list – which he suspected was just a figment of a dying psychopath's sick imagination. Linda Hiller's death, he said, was probably the work of a copycat killer, who had been spurred to act by the actions of an irresponsible and sensationalistic press.

I've always had a lot of trouble with the hallowed tradition of the reporter as an impartial observer.

I know that's the way it's supposed to work. I'm supposed to be above it all. To be fair to both sides. To never let my personal feelings interfere with my work.

But sometimes it doesn't work out that way.

When I find something that I believe is wrong, I'll go to any lengths to try to make it right. Most of the time I can do that by following the rules. Sometimes I've had to bend the rules a bit. And, on a few occasions, I've done even more than that.

You see, the line between right and wrong can get a bit blurred on some stories.

The problem with crossing that line is you can't just cross over it a little bit. Once you're over the line, you're in dangerous, uncharted territory. You can lose your perspective. Lose your judgement. Lose sight of the noble goal that you set out to accomplish at the beginning.

Me, I'd crossed that dangerous line a few times in my newspaper career.

Now I was about to do it again . . .

I'd made a decision.

My decision was that Lisa Montero was telling the truth. She did not kill William Franze or anybody else. She was innocent. She was being set up by somebody. And that same somebody must be the one responsible for all the other new killings on Galvin's list too.

All I had to do was help Lisa Montero prove that she wasn't guilty.

Then I'd find out who really killed William Franze and his call girl friend.

And that would lead me to The Great Pretenders.

I felt a surge of excitement as I thought about all this. The same kind of thrill and passionate intensity I used to get when I walked into the newsroom with an exclusive front page story that had my byline on it. Or when the cards were falling right or the crap tables were hot – and I was winning big in Atlantic City or Las Vegas. I hadn't felt that way in a long time. I missed it.

Of course, it was a longshot that I could pull this off . . .

But then I've always liked longshots.
So I decided to take the gamble.
My defining moment.

PART THREE

You Bet Your Life

twenty

Andy Kramer called a meeting in his office the morning after Lisa Montero's arrest. It was barely 9 a.m. when I walked in, still bleary-eyed with a cup of coffee from the deli downstairs in my hand, but there were already at least a dozen people sitting there. Some I remembered from my old days at the *Banner*, others I didn't.

There was Jack Rollins, the managing editor I never got along with. Bonnie Kerns and a few other reporters that had worked on the William Franze murder story in recent weeks. A lot of young assistant city editor and assistant managing editor types – both men and women – who eyed me curiously as I sat down, making me feel a bit uncomfortable. I guess they'd heard the stories.

And Spencer Blackwood.

Spencer Blackwood was the editor of the *New York Banner*. He had been a legendary newspaperman in his time, but he was close to seventy now and due to retire very soon. The word was that Rollins and Kramer were the two top candidates vying to take over his job. Blackwood almost never came to news meetings or took part in the daily news coverage planning anymore. This was really a big deal.

'The reason we're here,' Andy said, 'is to talk about our plan of action in light of the recent developments.'

He quickly ran through everything that had happened during the last few hours. Lisa Montero's indictment for murder. Her arrest by police at her Manhattan apartment. An arraignment overnight in Criminal Court, where she'd been sent to the Rikers Island Prison for Women.

Then he talked about the David Galvin story.

'We've been operating so far on the theory that these two cases – Lisa Montero and David Galvin – were linked, that one person or group of persons was responsible for all the crimes. That was Joe's theory anyway. Now there's some doubt about that. Lisa Montero's arrest changes everything. This is going to be front page news for a long time. So we need to decide who's going to work on what.'

Everyone around the room nodded in agreement.

Except me.

'It's my story,' I said.

Andy smiled. 'You're already doing the David Galvin story, Joe' he said. 'Remember?'

'Yeah, and I'm doing Lisa Montero too.'

'You can't do both.'

'Why not?'

'Because, like I just said, we've got two big stories going here, Joe – and you're only one person.'

He looked around the room for support. Several of them murmured their agreement.

'It's not two stories,' I reminded everyone. 'It's really only one. William Franze and the hooker that died with him – the people Lisa Montero is accused of killing – were on Galvin's list. If Lisa Montero did them – and I don't think she did – then she did the others too. If not, then the real killer is still out there. All of these murders are connected.'

'Greg Ackerman doesn't think so,' one of the assistant managing editors pointed out.

'He's wrong.'

I saw Rollins shaking his head in dismay. He looked very unhappy. Jack Rollins was going to be trouble. I should have known that from the minute I walked into the room.

One of the young woman assistant city editors said, 'I think Ackerman may be right. The Franze killing was not like any of the others.'

'It was on Galvin's list,' I said again.

'But the details were different.'

I knew what she meant.

'All the others were preceded by some sort of sick, elaborate fantasy,' she continued. 'Even this last one, Linda Hiller, with the dressing up of the body in the wedding gown. But Franze and the girl from the escort service were murdered in bed while they were having sex. There was no fantasy there. Except maybe for them.'

'How do you know that?' I asked her.

'What do you mean?'

'Maybe Franze and the girl weren't having sex. Maybe they weren't even undressed. Maybe the killer made them undress and forced them into bed in that position. Maybe that was the fantasy. Don't forget, all we saw was the final result.'

The woman nodded. 'I never thought about that,' she said.

'It's just a theory,' I shrugged.

'A good theory though,' someone else said.

Rollins made a snorting sound now and rolled his eyes.

'You got a problem?' I asked him.

'Jesus, Dougherty,' he said disgustedly, 'you don't even work at the *Banner* anymore. I still can't figure out why you're here.' He shot a disapproving glance over at Andy. 'Let's get some real reporters on this before we blow both stories.'

Andy ignored him. I could sense the growing tension between them. They both wanted to make the other one look bad. So the more Rollins turned against me, the more Andy was going to be on my side in this argument. It's funny how things work out sometimes. Me and Andy were becoming allies again. Office politics sure makes strange bedfellows.

'Look, Joe,' Andy said soothingly. 'No one wants to steal your story away from you. We just want to put together a team of people to work on it. You'd be part of that team. An important part. But we've got a lot of people sitting around out there in that city room who can help. Good people.'

'Sitting around is right,' I said. 'If they're so good, how come I'm the only one that got an interview with Lisa Montero?'

'All I'm saying is . . .'

'It's my story,' I said. 'The whole thing. End of discussion.'

Rollins' face darkened with rage. 'I don't have to sit here and listen to this crap,' he said, turning to Spencer Blackwood who hadn't said anything yet. 'Let's just pay this guy off for his time and be finished with him. We'll put our own people on this. Then Dougherty can crawl back under whatever rock he turned over to get here.'

I guess Rollins was trying to make me mad. But I didn't get mad. Instead I just laughed. That surprised him.

'How exactly are you going to do that, Jack?' I asked.

'What do you mean?'

'Well, you can't do this story without me.'

'Why?'

'Because I'm the only reporter in town that Lisa Montero talks to. And I'm also the only one that David Galvin confessed to before he died. You can fire me again if you want, but I'll just take my story over to the *Daily News* or the *Post* or one of the TV stations. Then you can read all about it in the competition, while you and your high-powered team try to catch up with me. Like you said, Jack, I don't even work at the *Banner* anymore. I have no loyalty to you guys. So here's the deal. Either I do the story my way for you – or I walk out the door right now. It's your move.'

No one said anything for a long time. Finally Spencer Blackwood spoke for the first time.

'Maybe we can compromise,' Blackwood said.

'How?' I asked.

'We'll give you someone to work with. Another reporter to help out – unless you decide at some point you need more. You'll call all the shots. You'll tell the reporter what to do and what not to do. In return, you work exclusively for the *Banner* on this until it's over. Anything you find out belongs to us. Okay?'

Rollins started to argue, but Blackwood gave him a look that stopped him in his tracks.

'Who's the reporter?' I wanted to know.

Blackwood looked over to Andy for help. Andy thought about it for a second.

'How about Bonnie?' he said.

I was surprised. I figured he'd go for someone older. One of his pals in the city room. Even though we were uneasy allies at the moment, I figured he'd want someone who could keep an eye on me – and then secretly report back to him on what I was doing.

That didn't sound like Bonnie. According to Bonnie, she didn't even get along with Andy Kramer.

'You like Bonnie, right?' he asked.

I looked over at Bonnie across the room. She hadn't said anything yet during the discussion.

'Yeah, I like Bonnie,' I said.

'And you trust her?'

I smiled at her now. 'Sure, I trust her.'

The truth is I didn't really know Bonnie well enough to trust her. For all I knew even that stuff she'd told me about Andy and her not getting along could have been made up. Maybe he put her up to it just to see what I'd say about him. I didn't really think that was true, but you never know.

On the other hand, I didn't figure I was going to do any better than Bonnie.

So I said yes.

'Now, Joe, I want you to make a complete report to Andy each day on everything you've found out, whether you write a story or not,' Blackwood told me.

'What's the point in that?' Rollins asked sarcastically. 'He'll just make it up. Like he did the last time when . . .'

Blackwood cut him off. 'All right, Jack, I think we all know your feelings on this matter.'

The old editor looked across the room at me.

'That whole incident eight years ago was a very embarrassing and very expensive one for this paper. Nothing like that can ever happen again. I hope you realize that. If you do and things work out well on this story, well . . . who knows? Maybe you'll even have a future again at the *Banner*. Stranger things have happened.'

I didn't say anything.

'They tell me you've really cleaned up your life since the last time you were here, Joe.'

'I'm older,' I said. 'I guess I've learned a few lessons along the way.'

'And you're getting married?'

'Yes, in a few months.'

'What about your gambling?'

'I don't do it anymore.'

'Ever?'

'I belong to Gamblers' Anonymous. I paid off all my old debts. And I haven't put a bet down on anything in nearly two years.'

Blackwood nodded. I was giving him all the right answers. Telling him what he wanted to hear. I had to in order to do this story for the *Banner*. And that was the only thing that mattered right now.

'We're going to give you another chance, Joe,' he said. 'But it's your last chance. You won't get another.'

He didn't have to tell me that.

twenty one

'Here's the way I figure it,' Bonnie said as she drove us through midtown traffic toward lower Manhattan.

She was going to drop me off at the District Attorney's office, where I'd set up an interview with Greg Ackerman.

'We split this up between us. You concentrate for the time being on the stuff about the Montero woman, while I look into the other killings on Galvin's list. That way if it turns out somehow you're wrong – and the two stories aren't connected – we're still covered on both bases. And if they are, then maybe one of us can find the link to prove it.'

'How come I'm on Lisa Montero and you're doing the rest of it?' I asked. 'Why not the other way around?'

'Because this way you can be a big hero to your girlfriend when you prove she's innocent,' Bonnie said, as she swerved suddenly to avoid a double-parked car.

'What do you mean – my girlfriend?'

'Jesus, Joe, I'm not stupid. I see that look on your face when you talk about her.'

'I'm engaged, Bonnie. I'm going to be married in a few months. Carolyn's a terrific woman. I love her very much. I'm interested in Lisa Montero right now because it's my job. Period. That's all there is to it.'

'Yeah, whatever,' Bonnie said casually.

The truth is that Bonnie's idea of how to work on the story was the way I thought we should do it too.

Bonnie honked her horn at a taxi letting off people in front of us, then turned the wheel sharply and sped past him. 'Asshole,' she muttered. She drove just like she talked: fast, frantic and full of energy. I just hoped I survived the ride in one piece.

'Have you heard anything more about Arthur Dodson?' I asked her.

Dodson was the last name still alive on David Galvin's list of The Great Pretenders' victims.

'Somebody killed Linda Hiller,' I said. 'Whether it's one of Galvin's old college pals or a copycat – either way, the next target has to be Arthur Dodson.'

'Yeah. My cop sources tell me, as soon as they find Dodson they'll probably move him to a special safe house with twenty-four hour guards, sharpshooters outside, the works. The guy won't be able to take a shit without some cop wiping his ass for him. No one wants to be embarrassed again.'

'Well, you can never be too careful,' I said.

'Technically, that's not true.'

'Huh?'

'I mean people say that all the time. But it's not true. The truth is that sometimes you can be too careful.'

'Bonnie, what are you talking about?'

'Okay, let's take the President of the United States, for example. If you accept the premise that you can never be too careful, then that means no security precautions to protect the President are ever too extreme. So, if you take that concept to the utmost degree, your only concern then becomes the security itself. You lose sight of the big picture. Ergo, you devote all your time to increasing security instead of actually letting him preside over the country. Which is the purpose of all the security in the first place. Understand?'

I looked at her strangely.

'Just an idle thought passing through my mind,' she said.

The light at the intersection ahead of us turned red. Bonnie floored the accelerator and made it through just before a van almost clipped us coming in the other direction.

'Do you notice anything interesting about the new cases on Galvin's list?' Bonnie asked. 'The ones we didn't know about until he left you the note?'

I thought about it. 'Well, they're different methods of death. Shooting. Stabbing. Strangulation. Felix the Cat shot all his victims. Also Felix the Cat's original victims were all women. There's men on this list too. That sure sounds like different people did the murders. Galvin said there were three other people besides him in the group. So maybe they each had their own style and taste in victims. That makes sense, doesn't it?'

'Maybe. Or maybe Galvin did them all himself – at least the ones that happened before he was caught – and then just tried to make them look different to throw the police off?'

'Why lie about it now? And I've read his confession from eleven years ago too. He was proud of his victims even back then. If he'd killed them, he would have bragged about it. No, the ones we didn't know about at the time of his arrest were the work of other people. And he kept quiet about it for eleven years. Right up until the end.'

'I suppose,' she said.

I looked out the window. We were getting close to Foley Square, where the Manhattan courts and the DA's office were located.

'There's something else,' Bonnie said. 'That business we talked about in the meeting, about how most of the new killings look like they could be the result of that weird fantasy stuff Galvin and these creeps were into; the prom dress, dancer's outfit, etc. And how William Franze and the hooker don't seem to fit the pattern.'

She hesitated for a second before continuing.

'Well, there's another one that doesn't fit either, Joe. I didn't want to bring it up during the meeting, but . . .'

I knew what she was talking about.

'My wife and son,' I said softly.

'Yes,' she answered. 'Look, I'm sorry, Joe. But we have to talk about it sooner or later.'

'It's okay. It's just that I haven't dealt with that part of it yet. Believe me, I know I'll have to do it before this thing is over. And you're right. Susan and Joe Jr died in a boating accident. There was no fantasy involved there. No games. No Great Pretenders, as far as I can see. They don't fit the pattern either.'

'How do you know that for sure?' Bonnie asked.

'What do you mean?'

'Maybe there was some kind of fantasy going on there too,' she said. 'Think about what you said in the meeting about Franze and the Martin woman. About how no one can be certain what the killer did or didn't do before they died. How maybe there really was a fantasy in the Franze murders – and we just don't know what it was yet. Well, the same thing could be true about your family. From what I understand, they were alone out on the water when it happened. I mean we don't really know what happened to them before they died, do we? The point I'm trying to make here is that we can't be sure there was no fantasy in your wife and son's deaths – or in the Franze murder either. I'm sorry to be so blunt about this, Joe but I really think it's something we have to consider.'

She was right, of course.

I guess I was just too close to this one to see it as clearly as she did.

'I'm curious, Joe,' Bonnie said. 'That story Rollins was needling you about today at the meeting. The one that got you fired. Did you really make it up?'

'Let's just say I screwed up very badly.'

'And it was your fault?'

'My name was on the story.'

'And the stuff he said about your gambling?'

'I used to have a gambling problem.'

'And now?'

'I don't anymore.'

'A lot of people gamble, Joe.'

'Not like me.'

'Was it really that bad?' she asked.

twenty two

• • • • • • • • • • •

On the day after I got fired from the *Banner* eight years ago, I went to Atlantic City. I had a severance check for $23,000 from the paper in my pocket. It was the most money I ever had in my life at one time. I cashed the check, took the money in $100s and checked into the Bally's Park Place Hotel on the boardwalk. It was the middle of the week on a cold day in early March, and the place wasn't very busy. The woman at the front desk upgraded my room, at no extra cost, to a big one bedroom suite, with a view overlooking the Atlantic. I took that as a good omen.

I started small. I played the slot machines for the first few hours. There was an incredible selection to choose from. They stretched from one end of the huge casino to the other; endless rows of flashing lights, casino sounds and clanging coins. You could play straight slots, progressive slots, video poker, video blackjack – you name it. There were 25-cent machines, 50-cent machines, $1 machines, and then even more expensive ones that cost all the way up to $100 per spin. I played them all. By the end of four hours, I was up $2600. I took that as a good omen too.

Next came blackjack. There's a lot of systems you can use in a casino to try to beat the house in blackjack. But I didn't try anything like that. I just played steadily – almost conservatively – for several hours. By the time I got up from the table, I had won another $6000. I knew I was really on a roll now.

The real big money for me came at the roulette and craps tables. I couldn't do anything wrong there. Every roll of the dice, every spin of the wheel – I was a winner. After three days of this, I'd turned my $23,000 into $120,000. The way I figured it I was now turning a profit of about $30,000 a day. Screw the *Banner*. I mean, who needed a job anyway? This paid better than newspapers, it was more exciting and the hours were a lot better too.

When I wasn't in the casino, I hung out at the bar. Not that I had any problem with the booze. Gambling has always been my particular addiction, not alcoholism. I just kept a pleasant buzz on pretty much all the time I was there. The experts tell you not to do that, they say it dulls your judgement. But they tell you you can't beat the casinos either. So what was I doing with all this money? I'd figured out how to beat the odds in record time. I felt like I'd discovered this huge secret that no one else knew about except me. And Jesus, it was so much fun!

One night in the bar, I met a young blonde woman named Connie who was a dealer at one of the blackjack tables. She remembered me from all my winnings and I offered to buy her a drink to celebrate. She told me about her ex-husband, the three-year-old daughter she'd lost in a custody battle and how she'd gone to college in Montclair with the idea of being a school teacher, but decided she could make a lot more money working the tables in Atlantic City than as a teacher. I told her about the *Banner* and all the developments in my life. Then we went up to my room and, with the lights of Atlantic City and the boardwalk flicking below us, we made love.

The next morning I woke up and decided I felt like playing poker.

They offer several varations of it in Atlantic City, but no straight poker. You have to go to Las Vegas to play straight poker. Connie said she'd been thinking of going to Las Vegas anyway, because the payoffs at the casinos there were a lot bigger for the dealers.

'Do you want to go with me?' I asked.

'When?'

'Today.'

'Why not?' she said.

When we got to Las Vegas, I concentrated most of my gambling on poker and betting sports. Nothing fancy at the poker table; just the old-fashioned draw and seven card stud games. At the sports book, I bet on college basketball, pro basketball, hockey and even exhibition baseball. I'd always bet on sports back in New York, both informally and with bookies I knew from the *Banner* but this was the real thing. You just walked in, plopped down your money and watched the game on TV right there until it was time to collect your money.

It was all so easy.

And, of course, it couldn't last.

By the end of my second week in Vegas, I'd lost everything I had won. I was down to the original $23,000 or so I'd gotten as severance pay from the *Banner*. I had a choice to make. I could take this money, lick my wounds and take it back to New York City to live on while I tried to find another newspaper job. Or I could try to parlay it into big winnings and go home in style.

They were playing the semi-finals of the NCAA college basketball tournament, and the big story that year was a small school that had come out of nowhere to upset a string of powerful teams. I'd bet on them each time. Even in my downward spiral, they'd continued to make me money. This was my lucky team. I had to back them. That afternoon, they were going to play the defending national champions, who were favored by eighteen points. I knew it would be closer than that. This was another omen.

I bet the entire $23,000 on the underdog small school to beat the eighteen-point spread. All they had to do was get within eighteen, for chrissakes. It was a cinch. Hell, they might even win the game outright.

The game was close most of the way. But, late in the second half, the defending champions started to pull away. It still didn't look like they would go more than eighteen points ahead until they put on a furious finish at the end of the game. With ten seconds to go, the score was 81–62. Then, with time running out, they fouled the best shooter on my team as he drove to the basket. There was only time for two foul shots. If my guy made both of them, I won the bet. Even if he made only one, it was still a push, which meant everybody got their money back. That was OK too.

The first foul shot hit the rim of the basket, rolled around it for a few seconds and then bounced off.

The second one was an air ball – it didn't even come close.

As the crowd spilled out onto the court to congratulate the winners, the announcers were talking about what a gutsy performance the little school had put on during the tournament. They talked about their heart. Their hustle. Their spirit. They said everyone could go back home with their heads held high.

Me, I didn't really listen to any of it.

I ordered a double bourbon and drank it down in a hurry. Then I ordered another – and did the same thing. After that, I walked around the city for a long time, wondering what I was going to do next. I didn't even have enough money for an airline ticket home now. Eventually, I wound up back in my hotel room which was paid up until the end of the week. I told Connie what had happened. When I woke up the next morning, she was gone too. I never saw her again.

I had a wristwatch that Susan had given me for Christmas one year. I pawned it to get enough money to buy a bus ticket. I then spent several days traveling cross country before I finally made it back to New York City.

I was flat broke.

I didn't have a job.

I had no prospects.

I'd thrown away a small fortune in a very short period of time.

And the worst part of it – the absolute rock bottom realization – was that I still desperately wanted to make a bet on something.

That's when I first started to think I might have a gambling problem.

twenty three

Greg Ackerman looked like a man on the way up.

I could tell that after spending just a few minutes with him. He sat behind his desk – dressed in a dark pin-striped suit, starched white shirt, red suspenders and an Ivy League tie – and talked to me confidently about Franze, the dead call girl found with him and Lisa Montero. He made it very clear that he thought he could convict her for the killings.

I'd found out from people at the paper that Ackerman was a real political comer. During the past year, he'd made headlines by successfully prosecuting a longtime Mafia boss, a wealthy drug lord and a scandal-ridden city councilman. He won spectacular jury convictions in the first two cases and got the councilman to plead guilty in return for reduced jail time.

People were already talking about him as a candidate for District Attorney – the incumbent was nearing retirement age and expected to step down – or maybe even for Mayor or Governor somewhere down the line.

That was why he'd gotten handed such a high-profile case like the William Franze murder.

'How can you be sure Lisa Montero did it?' I asked him.

'I'm sure, believe me. I've got witnesses who put the lady at the scene of the crime. And I've got a dead bang motive – she caught him in bed with another woman.' He laughed. 'Poor little Lisa Montero. She's got all that money and she's got all that power, but what she doesn't have is an alibi. Too bad for Lisa, huh?'

'What about the second woman she says she saw at Franze's house the night of the murders?'

'There was no second woman,' Ackerman snapped.

'How do you know?'

'We checked the escort agency – they only sent one girl. We even went through Franze's phone records, every friggin' call he made on the day he died. Just in case he called some other agency or girl. Almost all the calls were to business associates.'

'And the others?'

'There was one to the escort agency – and five to a plumber.'

'A plumber?'

'Yeah, he was trying to get his toilet fixed,' Ackerman said.

I stared at him.

'The toilet next to Franze's bedroom, where the bodies were found, was broken. It had been apparently been out of order since that morning. Franze kept trying the plumber, but the plumber was busy. He wasn't able to get there until the following morning. When he did, he walked in and found the two bodies.'

'A busted toilet,' I repeated. I shook my head. 'Jesus, ol' Billy Franze really had himself a bad day, didn't he?'

Ackerman leaned across his desk and smiled confidently at me.

'Look, there's no question about it, Dougherty,' he said. 'Lisa Montero was the only other woman who was there the night Billy Franze was killed. She did it, my friend. She fought with him, she got jealous, she came back with a gun – and bang, bang, bang! Now she's going down for it. End of story.'

He looked down at a front page of the *Banner* that was on his desk. My story was there. The interview with Lisa Montero where she had proclaimed her innocence.

'You don't really believe any of this stuff she told you, do you?' he asked.

'I think both cases are related,' I said. 'The Franze murders and David Galvin's death list.'

'Yeah, I read some of your other stories,' Ackerman said. 'All about how Billy Franze might have been the victim of a sinister gang of ex-college assassins. How a repentant David Galvin confessed all this to you on his death bed. Sorry, I don't buy it.'

'Why not?'

'David Galvin was a nut.'

'Galvin seemed very sane to me at the end. He was afraid of dying without cleansing his soul. He was getting ready to meet his maker. I believed him.'

Ackerman shook his head.

'Where the hell did you come from anyway, Dougherty?' he said. 'I mean I know all the other reporters at the *Banner* who've been working on the Franze murder, but I never heard of a Joe Dougherty. So I decided to check up on you. I found out they brought you back to life to do the David Galvin confession business. And now you show up here in my office with this wild theory about conspiracies and death bed confessions and killer college students from more than a decade ago. What's the deal with you anyway?'

'I just think that the same person who killed William Franze and the call girl is also responsible for all the new murders on the list that David Galvin gave me,' I repeated.

'Then that would be Lisa Montero.'

'If she really killed Franze.'

'Oh, she did it all right.'

'But what if she didn't? Then there's another very dangerous person out there that we don't know about.'

'She did it,' he repeated. 'I don't know anything about all this Galvin stuff, but Lisa Montero shot William Franze and the hooker as sure as we're sitting here, my friend.'

'How can you be so certain?'

Ackerman sighed. 'Let me tell you some things about Lisa Montero and her family,' he said. 'The Monteros are not very nice people. They've been getting away with stuff like this all their lives. They think they're above the law. Did you ever meet her father?'

'No, tell me about him.'

'Okay,' Ackerman said. 'For twenty-five years, John Montero has been a big man in this town. He rules people with an iron fist. Cross him, and he'll destroy you. Stand up to him, and he'll knock you down. Threaten him, and he'll get rid of you. There's a lot of bodies piled up in the graveyard because of Montero.'

'You're speaking figuratively, of course.'

'Not necessarily.'

'What are you telling me? That Montero has people killed?'

'No one's ever been able to prove that.'

'C'mon, Montero's a businessman, he's not an underworld boss. We're not talking about John Gotti here.'

'Let me tell you a couple of stories about John Montero,' Ackerman said.

'Story #1: A long time ago, there's an idealistic guy in the Department of Justice – a young, ambitious prosecutor, a lot like me – who does an investigation of one of Montero's businesses and uncovers a massive federal kickback and tax fraud scandal. He thinks he's got Montero nailed. He sweats one of Montero's top people, a guy named Louis Archer. The prosecutor threatens Archer with hard jail time and convinces him to turn state's evidence. Only when it comes time for Archer to testify, he mysteriously changes his story. Says he doesn't know anything about any Montero business at all. Convenient, huh? Montero somehow got to this guy and scared him, scared him so bad that he was even willing to go to jail rather than tell the truth. Anyway, Montero beats the rap, he goes back to business as usual and the idealistic federal prosecutor . . . well, he's so disheartened by the whole process that he quits the department.'

'Story #2: Another time Montero tries to engineer a takeover of a small, but extemely profitable business. Except one of the partners won't sell out to him. The word is Montero offers this guy all sorts of money to get him on side – but nothing works. He tells Montero he'll never change his mind. Then one day this guy doesn't show up for work and his wife and little ten-year-old daughter go to the police station to report him missing. The wife says he'd been scared ever since the business with Montero started, that he was convinced someone was following him and she wants Montero arrested. But the cops can't do anything, because they have no proof. A few days later, the guy's body is found floating in the East River. In the end, Montero buys the business from the dead man's partners, the guy's wife winds up a widow and the little girl has to grow up without a father. The case is still unsolved.'

I let my breath out slowly.

'You think the same thing happened to William Franze?' I asked.

'Well, he sure didn't die in his sleep, did he?'

'But we're talking about Lisa Montero here, not John.'

'Like father, like daughter,' Ackerman smiled.

That afternoon, when I got back to the *Banner* office, there was a note waiting for me. It had been delivered in the regular mail, and it was postmarked from the Bronx. There was no return address. It said:

To Joseph Dougherty:

New York, New York,
It's a helluva town
The Bronx is up,
Wall Street is down.

If you're looking for answers about the Wall Street murder and the Great Pretenders, the Bronx is the place to look. Take it from someone who knows – it's a great place to drop out of sight!

A Banner reader

I read the note over several times. The poem at the beginning was written in the same kind of poetic verse that Felix the Cat used to put in his letters to the media. Other than that, I had no idea what it meant. The Bronx is a big place. I couldn't go looking for someone in the Bronx any easier than I could find one of David Galvin's accomplices among all the people who'd gone to NYU.

Maybe it was just a crank letter. Or maybe it was another clue. I wasn't sure. I wasn't sure about anything with this story anymore.

I kept looking for answers.

But everywhere I went, all I found were more questions.

twenty four

Lisa Montero was being held in a cell on Rikers Island.

Rikers Island is a grim city prison that's on an island in the middle of the East River. To get there, you had to take a special bus across a bridge from Queens to the main entrance of the jail. It wasn't quite as remote as a place like Alcatraz, but the geography definitely made escape very difficult. Every once in awhile you'd read about some inmate making a break and trying to swim for either the Manhattan or Queens shorelines. Most of them didn't make it. I didn't figure Lisa Montero as the type to try anything like that.

When I finally got to see her, she was wearing a prison outfit that looked a size or two too big for her. She looked tired. And scared too. She knew she was in trouble. She knew what was at stake here. And she knew how much she had to lose. A little time in a place like Rikers Island can do that to you.

There were dark circles under her eyes, and her hand trembled slightly as she tried to light a cigarette. We were talking on a phone in the visitors' area, where a plexiglass window separated the prisoners from their friends and relatives.

She told me how they had come to get her in the middle of the night.

There were a half dozen cops – four uniforms and two homicide detectives – along with someone from the DA's office. They woke her up at two a.m., told her they had a warrant for her arrest and then put handcuffs on her. After that, she was taken to a precinct house downtown, where she was fingerprinted and had her mugshot taken. They questioned her throughout the night. No one gave her anything to eat or drink, no one let her get any sleep.

By morning, she was exhausted. But she still had to go to court. This was a real photo opportunity for the District Attorney's office, and Greg Ackerman took every advantage of it. He made sure Lisa was marched into the Criminal Courts Building through the front door – wearing handcuffs again – where an army of photographers and TV crews was waiting to record the big moment. It led every news show that night.

Greg Ackerman was a real piece of work.

'My father thinks he can get me out of here,' she told me.

'That's not going to be easy,' I said. 'It's a murder charge.'

'Dad knows some judges. They owe him favors. He figures one of them will come through and set bail. He'll put up whatever amount it takes to convince them that I won't flee the country or anything – and I'm not exactly a threat to society if I'm out on the street, am I? Anyway, that's what he says is going to happen. I hope he's right. I'm in a cell with a 300-pound lesbian named Bertha. I think Bertha is falling in love with me. I may have to get married if I stay in here much longer.'

She tried to smile, but I could tell it was a real effort.

Bertha was more of Greg Ackerman's doing, no doubt. Make it as uncomfortable for her as possible. Make her squirm.

'Ackerman will fight the bail request,' I told her.

'No kidding.'

'What's the deal with him anyway? How come he hates you so much?'

'He hates my father.'

'Why?'

'He's never been able to get at my father before. He's wanted to hurt him for a long time, but he never could because dad's too powerful. Now he can finally hurt him. Through me.'

'It has nothing to do with you?'

'Why would an Assistant DA like Greg Ackerman have a vendetta against me?'

I told her how I'd found out that she and Ackerman had gone to NYU together at the same time.

Just like David Galvin.

'So?' she asked.

'So did you know Greg Ackerman back then?'

'I never even heard of this clown Ackerman until Billy was murdered a few weeks ago.'

I decided this was the time to press the point. 'You're sure he didn't used to carry your books for you across campus at NYU?'

'No.'

'He didn't ask you out in school?'

'No.'

'He didn't buy you a corsage for the big fraternity dance?'

'No.'

'What about David Galvin? Did you know him back at NYU?'

I was waiting for her to lie about this one. I, of course, already had the answer to the question. She had known David Galvin when they were NYU students. His parents told me that. So, if she denied it now, I would pounce on it. Make her admit the truth. Then maybe I could get her to tell me the truth about everything.

'Yes, I knew David,' she said.

I was stunned. 'You did?'

'We were in some classes together my freshman year. We studied at the library a few times. I never went out with him or anything; there was no romance. We just hung out together. After my freshman year, we kind of drifted apart and I hardly ever saw him on campus anymore. I was as surprised as anyone when he was arrested for all those murders. I guess you never can tell what some people are really like.'

'Did you ever meet his parents?'

'Yeah, once or twice. They came down to campus to visit David, and he introduced me. I felt really bad when I saw pictures of them on the news afterward. They seemed like really nice people.'

Okay, so much for all my great detective work. All I had to do was ask her. Brilliant, Dougherty.

I decided to change topics.

'What do you think happened on the night William Franze was murdered?' I asked her.

'Someone was waiting outside when I left his place. Maybe they were planning to kill us both. Or maybe my leaving so suddenly gave them the chance to go ahead with the killing right then. Or maybe one thing had nothing to do with another; it was all a coincidence that I was there and had the argument with Billy. But, whatever happened, someone went upstairs after I left and did the murders. It wasn't me.'

'And the only person you saw was this mystery woman going into the house when you tried to go back?'

'Yes.'

'You figure maybe she was the killer.'

'Or a witness,' Lisa said.

I shook my head. It didn't make sense. 'If she was there, and saw the whole thing, then why wasn't she murdered too? Like the woman from the escort agency.'

'I don't know.'

'Or why hasn't she gone to the police?'

'Maybe she's afraid.'

'We have to find her,' I said.

Then I asked her a lot of questions about her father. His friends. His enemies. His business dealings. His reputation for ruthlessness. I was looking for a reason that someone might want to get back at John Montero by setting his daughter up for murder.

'He's a businessman, who's made a lot of money in his lifetime,' she sighed. 'People who make money make enemies too. It happens. On Wall Street, in government . . . everywhere. Look, my father's done a lot of things I'm not proud of. OK? He comes from a different world and a different generation and a different set of rules. But a lot of what they say about him isn't true. It's just myth and exaggeration.'

I nodded. 'What about you?' I asked.

'Me, I'm from today's world,' she said. 'I went to college – my father is a high school dropout, you know, so that was really important to him – and I got a Masters Degree in Business

Administration. I work with my father now. Some day I even hope to take over for him. Or at least I did, until all this happened to me.'

'What does he think about that?'

'Not much. The truth is he's really doesn't let me do very much. I'm listed as a vice president in the company, but I'm just a figurehead. Like I say, he's old-fashioned. And, of course, I'm a woman. He thinks I should get married and have babies.'

'Do you have any brothers?'

'I had one. He died. My mother's gone too. I'm all my father's got. I figure that sooner or later he'll change his mind about me and the business. Someday.'

'So what do you do with your life until then?'

She looked across the table at me and smiled. A sort of a sad smile. It was one of those moments I'll always remember. Frozen in time forever. Because, right then, I saw the real Lisa Montero. All her defenses, all her protection, all her New York City cool disappeared for just an instant. And, during those few seconds, I knew her for what she really was. A lost soul, trying to make sense out of her life. Just like me.

Or so I thought then, anyway.

'Mostly I wind up with people like Billy Franze,' she said.

twenty five

• • • • • • • • • • •

Bonnie had made some real progress.

Even though it didn't seem like it at first.

'I checked out all the all the new names of victims on David Galvin's list,' she told me. 'First the cases that took place eleven years ago, but no one ever connected to him until now. I went through all the old police reports about these deaths, I talked to some relatives of the victims, I even tracked down a few of the cops who handled the investigations at the time. I'm telling you, Joe, I didn't leave one stone unturned.'

'And?'

'Nothing.'

'What do you mean, nothing?'

'Nothing. There's absolutely no connection – no common denominator – between any of the new victims. Different kinds of victims, different ways they died, absolutely nothing that ties them together. And nothing that links them to any of the other people that we're sure Felix the Cat killed during the same time period. Not that I can see, anyway.'

We were sitting at Bonnie's desk in the *Banner* newsroom. I was drinking a cup of coffee. She was eating a big piece of lemon custard pie from the cafeteria downstairs and washing it down with a Coca-Cola. Everytime I saw Bonnie, she seemed to be eating something, but she still probably only weighed about 100 pounds dripping wet. I figured she burned off most of the calories with her non-stop energy.

'So then I decided to look at the two other new names, the ones that were both still alive when Galvin talked to you. Linda Hiller and Arthur Dodson. I did the Hiller woman first. That's when I hit paydirt.'

She took a bite of her pie.

'The category is US colleges,' she said, doing a pretty good imitation of Alex Trebeck on *Jeopardy*. 'And the clue is "New York University." Please make sure to give me your answer in the form of a question.'

I stared at her. 'Where did Linda Hiller go to school?' I said.

'That is correct.'

Damn.

'Now guess when she went to NYU,' Bonnie said.

I tried to remember the story about the Hiller woman's murder. She was thirty-two at the time of her death, I think it said. I did some quick math, subtracting eleven years from that, which put her at somewhere around twenty-one in 1987 when Felix the Cat was on his rampage. Just the right age for a college coed.

'Linda Hiller was at NYU at the same time David Galvin was there!'

Bonnie drank some of the coke and gave me a big smile. She was very pleased with herself.

'Yeah. Of course, she wasn't Linda Hiller then. She was Linda Kolchak. She got divorced a few years ago, but kept her married name.'

'And you checked out Arthur Dodson too, right?' I asked.

'Gee, no, Joe,' she said sarcastically, 'I never thought of that.'

'Dodson went to NYU too, in 1987?'

'That's right. I talked to his wife and family. They're really upset. Say they have no idea where he's gone. But they were really cooperative. They want us all to help look for him. So the wife gave me the whole life story. She even showed me his college yearbook. He started at NYU in 1984, graduated in the class of 1988. Majored in business administration. Kind of interesting, huh?'

Business administration.

The same thing Lisa Montero majored in.

Yeah, it was interesting. I was mad at myself though. I wouldn't have recognized Linda Hiller's maiden name when I was going through all the alumni records. But I should have caught Dodson's name. Except there were so many names in the files. Thousands of them. It was hard to check all of them out. Now I made a note to go back and do it again. Maybe there was somebody else I was missing too.

The bottom line was that an awful lot of people connected with this case had gone to NYU at the same time. Galvin. Lisa. Ackerman. Andy. And now Linda Hiller and Arthur Dodson too.

'Okay, so let's assume Dodson is still alive,' Bonnie was saying. 'I figure maybe he knows something we don't know. And that's why he's running. Like he once got David Galvin or one of Galvin's friends mad at him in school or something. Some reason why he'd be on a hit list after all this time. Of course, we have to find him to find out what it is. And my police sources say they have zilch on his whereabouts at the moment. But I'm still working on it.'

I told Bonnie about my interview at the jail with Lisa Montero.

'Listen, I'm sorry about that crack I made in the car about you and the Montero woman,' she said. 'I was out of line.'

'No, it was an astute observation.'

'What's the deal with you and her anyway?'

'She reminds me of someone.'

'Who?'

'My dead wife.'

'You mean she looks like her?'

'Not really. Oh, Susan had dark black hair too. And she was very pretty, just like Lisa. But it's more than that. There's just something about her that takes my breath away. I felt the same way when I met Susan too. I guess I just haven't felt that way in a long time.'

Bonnie nodded.

'Do you still think about Susan a lot?' Bonnie asked.

'Yeah, all the time.'

'What do you remember?'

'Little stuff mostly. The way she held a cigarette. The things she liked to drink and eat. Snatches of conversations we had together.' The memories were all coming back now. 'Susan smoked Marlboros. One right after another, she was a real chain smoker. She'd take the cigarette out, then tap it three times on the side of the Marlboro pack. Never twice, not four or five. Always three times. She was precise like that about everything she did. When she drank, it was always Bombay and tonic. Not just gin and tonic, it had to be Bombay and tonic. She never got drunk though. She'd take two drinks – three at the most – and then stop. She had amazing willpower. When she got pregnant, I thought she'd have a lot of trouble giving up the Marlboros and the Bombay and tonics. But she didn't. She never touched either for all those months until Joey was born, then went right back to them again afterward. One day I asked her how she could do that so easily. She just smiled and told me: "I'm full of surprises."'

I shook my head sadly.

'Susan and me, I just always felt we were destined to be together,' I said. 'I met her in this little place where she was tending bar. I'd never been in there before in my life. I just went on a whim. And it wasn't even her regular night to work. She switched shifts with someone at the last minute.

'Did you ever see that movie *Sleepless in Seattle*?' I asked Bonnie. 'It's all about a couple who have never met, but are destined to be in love with each other. I always felt that was like me and Susan. I remember one scene where a woman talks about the first time she touched the hand of her future husband. She said she could feel the magic. And she knew right then they would be together forever. That's the way I felt about Susan. I always felt the magic.'

Bonnie nodded in understanding. 'How about with Carolyn?' she asked.

'What do you mean?'

'Do you feel the magic with Carolyn?'

'It's different with Carolyn . . .'

'Uh-oh,' Bonnie said.

'C'mon, I'm a lot older now. So is Carolyn. We're not kids. I love her very much. She's been great for me. She's turned my whole life around again. We're going to be very happy together. Sure, there's magic. There's plenty of magic. It's just a different kind of magic.'

'Whatever you say, Joe,' Bonnie smiled.

I said I'd write up a story about the interview with Lisa Montero, and she could do her own piece on the mysterious NYU connections she'd uncovered. I figured the *Banner* could run the two stories side by side.

'Which editor do we talk to about all this, Kramer or Rollins?' she asked.

'Kramer, I guess.'

Bonnie grunted.

'You don't like that?'

'It really doesn't make much difference either way.'

'Rollins is an asshole.'

'They're both assholes. Rollins is just a lot more obvious about it than Kramer is.'

There was one piece of pie left on the plate in front of her. Bonnie started to pick it up on her fork, then looked across the desk at me. I guess maybe she felt guilty.

'Hey, do you want a bite?' she asked.

I shook my head no. She quickly popped it into her mouth.

'Let me tell you something about the politics that are going on in this office,' Bonnie said. 'You got a little taste of it in that meeting we were all at with Spencer Blackwood. Blackwood is nearly seventy. The word is he's going to retire in probably six months, maybe a year tops. Rollins and Kramer both desperately want his job. Do you see the picture?'

'Who decides on a new editor? Blackwood?'

She shook her head no. 'The guy that's going to make the call is Jimmy Richmond.'

'Jimmy?'

Walter Richmond was the owner and publisher of the *Banner*. He'd been there during my first tour of duty too. His family had owned the paper for generations.

'Do you remember Jimmy?' Bonnie asked.

'Yeah, I do. I think he was a copyboy the last summer I was here. Everyone was afraid to ask him even to get a cup of coffee. He knew it too. He was kind of arrogant, as I remember. And the kid's running the whole show at the *Banner* now?'

'Pretty much so. The old man spends most of his time on his yacht. No one knows for sure who Jimmy likes for the editor's job; Kramer or Rollins. He and Rollins rub elbows with a lot of the same people at social events. But he and Andy are friends too. They're about the same age. They both worked together here as copyboys while they were still in college.'

The same age.

'What college did he go to?' I asked.

'Who?'

'Richmond.'

She saw the look on my face. 'Joe, I know what you're thinking,' she laughed. 'NYU. The Great Pretenders. Galvin said they'd all gone on to be successful in their chosen fields. Maybe one of them is right under your nose, huh?'

'It's possible.'

'Well, you can forget about Jimmy Richmond. He went to Columbia, not NYU. Graduated from the School of Journalism there. I've seen the diploma on the wall of his office. And about six months ago. he got honored at a fancy dinner up at Columbia for being an outstanding alumni contributor to his alma mater.'

'Hey, you never know.'

I stood up and looked at my watch. Only a few hours until deadline. It was time to go back to my own desk and write up my jailhouse interview with Lisa Montero.

'Oh, by the way, Joe,' Bonnie said as I started to leave, 'it was Clarion State.'

I turned around.

'What?'

'That's where I went to college. Clarion State. Not NYU. It's a little school in Ohio.'

'Jesus, I don't care, Bonnie.'

'Sure, you do. You're obsessed by the fact that so many people involved in this story were students at NYU at the same time during the 1980s. You think there's got to be some sort of connection. Me, I'm basically the same age group as Galvin and Lisa Montero and all the rest, in my early thirties. You were going to check me out sooner or later. I just figured I'd save you the trouble.'

'That's ridiculous,' I told her.

She was right though.

I would have checked.

twenty six

Sometimes late at night – when I still had the dreams about Susan – I'd wake up and be surprised to see Carolyn lying in the bed next to me.

And I'd think: 'What in the hell am I doing here?'

Actually, the question wasn't so much why I was with Carolyn. It was really why she was with me.

She was this classy, ice-cool blonde beauty with a great-looking face and a terrific body. When she walked down the street or came into a room, people turned their heads to look at her. Lots of guys wanted to go out with her. She could have anyone she wanted. So why did she pick me? A guy with 'burned-out loser' written all over him on that first day we met.

I asked her that once.

'You were funny,' she said. 'You made me laugh.'

Okay.

'And you're cute.'

Cute.

'Plus, and this a really big plus, you and I are great in bed together.'

Maybe.

But the truth was I wasn't all that great in bed when we met. I hadn't had a real relationship with a woman in a very long time, and I was out of practice. I didn't even care that much about sex during those dark days. I was too busy feeling sorry for myself. It took a lot of time and considerable patience on Carolyn's part before we were up to speed in the bedroom department.

There was another possible explanation about why she was attracted to me. Carolyn was a do-gooder. A patron of lost causes. The kind of person who gave money to the homeless on the street and took in stray animals and cheered up patients in nursing homes and hospitals. I don't mean to make fun of this, because she's truly a good-hearted person. She's always there for somebody in need. Only sometimes I wondered if I was just another one of Carolyn's charity cases.

Or maybe the clue to our relationship was in a story she once told me about her high school senior prom.

Her date for the prom was the son of a close friend of her father's. He was president of the senior class, head of the debating team and had a scholarship to Harvard. But Carolyn didn't want to go to the prom with him. She wanted to go with someone else; a boy from the wrong part of town who rode around on a Harley motorcycle, wore a black leather jacket and had a small-time police record. She thought it would be really cool to drive up to the dance – wearing her prom dress – on the back of the Harley. But her father made her go with the other guy.

'Did you have a good time?' I asked.

'It was okay.'

'What went wrong?'

'I really wanted to ride on that motorcycle.'

When she met me, Carolyn was practically engaged to an executive vice president at the drug firm where she worked. She dumped him right away. Again, her father was not pleased with her choice in men. He told her I sounded like trouble. I wasn't good enough for her. But this time she was too old for him to do anything about it. In the end, once we knew each other better, her father and I got along fine. He's my boss at the public relations company now. But I still can't help thinking that I'm the guy from the wrong part of town with the black leather jacket and the Harley that Carolyn was never allowed to go to her prom with.

But the bottom line here is that she's a helluva woman for a guy like me. A helluva woman for anyone. So why did I have this feeling that something was missing in my life? Why was I still dreaming about Susan? Why did I think about Susan every time I saw Lisa Montero?

Maybe I was just having a minor case of cold feet, the usual pre-wedding jitters every prospective groom went through.

Maybe I expected too much out of a relationship.

Or maybe it was like the old Groucho Marx joke – the one that Woody Allen told at the beginning of *Annie Hall* – about not wanting to join any club that would admit someone like him as a member.

Yeah, maybe that was me.

How could I ever marry a woman who'd fall in love with a guy like Joe Dougherty?

twenty seven

They found Arthur Dodson's car at 5 a.m. in the morning sitting empty on the Tappen Zee Bridge, about thirty miles north of New York City.

The motor was running, Dodson's wallet was left on the front seat and someone had called police to say that they had seen a person go off the bridge into the waters of the Hudson River below.

'So what do you think happened?' I said to Captain Righetti as I stood on the bridge, watching police go over the car for clues and search the water for any sign of a body.

'Well, the way I see it,' he said, 'there's three possibilities. First, someone caught up with him here, forced him out of his car and threw him off the bridge, leaving his wallet behind to make sure we know what happened.

'Second, he committed suicide. He decided to end it all because the pressure just got to be too much for him. He's on some wacko's death list – God knows why – he's scared and he just can't deal with it anymore. So he drives up here, gets out of his car and does a swan dive down into the water.

'Or option number three – he's not dead at all. He leaves the car, the wallet and makes an anonymous call to police about a man going off the bridge. Maybe he thought it would be better if people thought he was dead. Maybe he thought it would help buy him some time to get far away.'

Bonnie walked over to us. She'd gotten to the scene before I had. The way she drove it was no surprise. I told Righetti what Bonnie had found out about Dodson and Hiller both going to school at NYU at the same time as Galvin.

'There's got to be a connection,' I told him. 'Some reason, some kind of grudge, some motive.'

'Christ, that was eleven years ago,' Righetti said. 'Who carries a grudge for eleven years?'

'Hiller and Dodson both were on Galvin's hit list,' I pointed out. 'Hiller and Dodson both went to NYU at the same time he did. One's dead already and the other one may be. That's more than a coincidence, Captain.'

Righetti looked over at Dodson's empty car sitting on the bridge in front of us.

'Did Mrs Dodson or the rest of his family have any idea at all why he was on that list?' I asked him. 'Or why he disappeared?'

Righetti shook his head. 'They seemed just as mystified as the rest of us.'

'What about when you talked to them, Bonnie?'

'Same thing,' she said. 'They told me he seemed fine that last morning when he went off to work. Then Dodson's wife heard about his name turning up on Galvin's list. She tried to call him at work, but the people there said he'd never showed up. No one's seen him since. His co-workers. Family. It's like he disappeared off the face of the earth until this morning.'

Yeah, Righetti was right; it had to be scenario Number Three.

This didn't seem like a Great Pretender murder. There was no fantasy, no imagination, nothing that seemed even remotely to link it to any of the other killings.

And I didn't buy the suicide scenario either. Why would Dodson kill himself? A man who's afraid of dying doesn't solve the problem by doing it to himself. That just didn't make sense.

No, Arthur Dodson was running.
I was pretty sure of that.
But that, of course, still left one big question.
Who was he running from?

A new contingent of cars arrived on the bridge. Greg Ackerman got out of one of them. He looked first over at the cops who were going through Dodson's BMW, then saw Righetti, me and Bonnie. He started walking toward us.

'Uh-oh,' Bonnie said.

'Be nice,' Righetti told me.

'I don't like him.'

'No one does.'

Ackerman was standing in front of us now.

'Well, you can't blame this one on Lisa Montero,' I said brightly. 'She's in jail.'

'It's a copycat,' he said grimly. 'A Felix the Cat copycat. That's what we're dealing with here.'

'I don't think so,' I told him. 'I think Galvin was telling the truth. He did have accomplices. Everything on that list he gave me has checked out. William Franze, Hiller and Dodson; it's all connected to when he was at NYU. Now we just have to figure out how.'

Ackerman ignored me and started to walk toward Dodson's car.

'By the way, how come you never told me you went to NYU with David Galvin?' I yelled out after him.

That stopped him in his tracks.

'You were a student at New York University eleven years ago, weren't you?' I said.

'Yeah,' Ackerman said. He came back to a few feet from where I was standing. 'So what?'

'So not only was the late Felix the Cat – David Galvin – there at the same time, but so was Lisa Montero. The woman you're so eager to blame for all of this. I find that a very interesting coincidence. Did you know either of them when you were students, Greg?'

I thought Ackerman would get mad at the question, but he didn't. He just laughed.

'Jesus, Dougherty, you really are something. Yes, I guess we all were on campus at the same time. No, I never knew either of them. Just like I never knew thousands of other people that went to NYU with me at the same time. It's a very big campus. I can see where you're going with this one though. You figure that maybe me and Lisa Montero were really secret members of this mysterious Great Pretenders group that Galvin filled your head with before he died. What a great story that would be for you, huh? But why stop there, Dougherty? Why not just arrest everybody who ever went to school at the same time as Galvin – and put them in jail too?' He shook his head. 'Is this what you call being a reporter? My god, you are really reaching on this one.'

He was right. I had nothing.

'Anyway, there is one thing I am very sure of, and that's who killed William Franze.'

'Lisa Montero?'

'Yes.'

'I'm not so sure about that.'

'Oh really? Well do you know what I think, Dougherty? I think maybe you've got a personal interest in Ms Montero. I figure maybe the reason you're not making much sense is because you're thinking with your dick instead of your brain. Hey, I understand that. Lisa Montero's a very attractive woman. She's rich. Smart. A real knockout. On a scale of one to ten, she's probably a fifteen. There's one little problem with her though. You gotta watch her temper. That's the trouble with dating a murderer. Breaking up is so hard to do. Just ask Billy Franze.'

I kept my story about Dodson's disappearance pretty straight. Just the facts along with the possibilities Righetti had laid out. I didn't speculate. I didn't editorialize. I only wrote what I knew. Andy gave me the thumbs up sign after he read it. Another front page story. This one carried a double byline though. Me and Bonnie. That was okay.

It wasn't until after I was finished – and Bonnie and I were about ready to leave the office – that I noticed the letter on my desk.

It was just like the first note. The same plain white envelope. The same postmark from the Bronx. The same block lettering used to write all the words on the page. And the message was in crude verse again, like Felix the Cat used to use.

This one said:

Dear Joe Dougherty:

Roses are red violets are blue
I'd look at El Domingo
If I were a betting man – like you!

There's too many bodies, too many clues
But don't let them get you all confused

There's something no one else sees
They can't see the forest for the trees

Billy Franze, he's the key
Go to El Domingo, and you'll see

There's someone there
who knows it all
If she won't talk,
the rich girl takes the fall!

twenty eight

Lisa Montero was freed on $1 million bail. The bail decision generated a lot of controversy. Victims rights groups assailed it as a license to commit murder. Editorial writers compared Lisa to hundreds of other accused murderers forced to wait in jail for their trial as the wheels of justice turned slowly. Opponents of John Montero talked about influence peddling and favoritism and an abuse of power.

But, in the end, Lisa was a free woman again – at least for the time being.

I guess some judge really did owe her father a big time favor.

On the morning Lisa got out of jail, she called me from Rikers Island. She asked if I was going to be there. Of course, I said. This was going to be a giant media event. When she walked out of that prison, there'd be reporters all over and flashbulbs popping and video cameras recording the whole event for the six o'clock news.

Lisa seemed nervous about that. She told me that her father didn't even want to come because of all the reporters and publicity. She said she wanted someone with her she could trust to get through the whole ordeal. She asked me if I would take her home.

Now if I did that, I was definitely crossing the line between being a reporter and a participant in this story. But that was okay. I think.

I mean I was getting the inside beat on the biggest story in town. All the other reporters would be on the outside, looking in at me. Any good reporter would have done the same thing. That's what I told myself anyway.

Her father sent a limo that was waiting for her outside the prison.

Lisa and I managed to run through the gauntlet of press – I saw Bonnie standing there giving me a funny look from the crowd – and got into the back seat. Then we roared across the bridge and into Manhattan. After a few minutes, I looked around. We'd managed to lose everyone.

'God, I hate the press,' Lisa said.

'I'm the press,' I reminded her.

'You're different,' she smiled. 'You're special.'

Special.

'Do you want to go home?' I asked her.

'Not right away.'

'Where do you want to go?'

'Anywhere.'

'That's a big place.'

'I don't want to be alone,' she said.

'I'm here,' I reminded her.

'I need a drink,' she said.

She said she wanted to go someplace quiet, someplace out of the way where she wouldn't be recognized. I told her about a bar I'd been to a few times down in Union Square, not far from my hotel. It wasn't a celebrity hangout. Just a little place with good beer, dark booths to sit in and a big old jukebox that played a lot of old '50s stuff like the Everly Brothers and Jimmy Clanton and Roy Orbison. She told me that sounded perfect.

I called my story in from a pay phone at the bar, giving a rewriteman all the details of her release from prison.

Afterward, Andy Kramer came on the phone. He was very excited when I told him I was still with her.

'I think I can get even more access to her,' I told him.

'What kind of access are we talking about here?' he wanted to know.

'Enough to do something really in-depth. Some long interviews. Maybe even a diary about her emotions. The *Banner* could start it now and run it through the trial. I might also be able to get an interview with her father. Big John Montero. He never talks to the press. But I'm going to ask her if she can get him to talk to me.'

There was a long silence on the other end of the line.

'Are you doing this broad, Joe?' Andy asked finally.

'No,' I sighed, 'I'm not doing her.'

'You know,' he said slowly, 'I'm on your side here. You don't have to prove anything to me. I'm not Jack Rollins. I never blamed you for what happened to Walter Billings. I always figured you got a raw deal.'

I wasn't sure that was exactly true, but I decided to let it pass.

'That's not what this is all about,' I told him.

'Sure it is,' he said.

Of course, we both knew he was right.

'She's just another story, Joe,' he said.

'I know that.'

'Let me tell you about my all-time favorite newspaper movie,' I told Lisa. 'It's *Deadline USA* with Humphrey Bogart. Bogart is the managing editor of a paper that's just about to go out of business. On its last day ever, a young guy who just graduated from journalism school comes into the paper looking for his first job as a reporter. Bogart looks around the dying newsroom and says to him: "Kid, I'll tell you something about this business. It may not be the world's oldest profession, but it's the best."'

She smiled. 'You make working at a newspaper sound like such a noble calling,' she said.

'It is.'

'How long have you been at the *Banner?*'

'Uh, only since this story started. I'm not actually a fulltime reporter anymore.'

'I don't understand . . .'

'Well, it's kind of complicated.'

'But you used to work there, right?'

'A long time ago.'

'What happened?'

'I got fired.'

'Why?'

I shrugged. 'Sometimes we reporters aren't always so noble,' I said.

We sat there drinking in that little bar for a long time. She told me about everything that had happened to her in prison. She seemed really shaken up by the whole experience, like a scared little girl talking about a nightmare she'd just woken up from.

'Who do you think murdered Billy Franze?' I asked her.

'I don't have the slightest idea,' she said. 'All I know is that I didn't do it.'

'That's good. But someone killed him. Someone who wanted him dead. Someone who had a motive for murder besides you.'

She shrugged. 'I didn't care if Billy lived or died.'

'So who did?'

She thought about it. 'A lot of people probably wanted him dead. Both in his business and personal lives. Billy cut a lot of corners, lied a lot and burned a lot of people. He was really pushing the envelope. He definitely was not one of the good guys.'

'Tell me about his business dealings,' I said.

'Well, I don't know a lot about that. My father does. They worked together on some deals, although I know they didn't like each other very much. My father didn't want me to go out with him. Maybe that's why I did, I don't know. Maybe he knew a lot of stuff about Billy he never told me.'

'Can I talk to him?'

'My father?'

'Yeah, everyone keeps telling me about him. I hear a lot of good things and a lot of bad things. I'd like to find out for myself what kind of person he really is.'

'My father doesn't talk to the press anymore.'

'Yeah, but I'm special,' I said. 'Remember?'

She laughed.

'Will you ask him, Lisa?'

'I'll try.'

I thought about some of the other stuff I'd heard about Billy Franze.

'What about Franze's women?' I said.

'Well, he never exactly provided me with a list of all the other women he was seeing, but there were quite a few. He thought of himself as quite a ladies man. I guess you can tell that from the way he died. It would take quite awhile to go through all Billy's women. It's a very long list, but I'll bet a lot of them would have plenty of motive for killing him. Of course, that's not even counting his wife.'

His wife. Of course. Billy Franze was married. I'd forgotten all about that.

'How did Franze's wife feel about all the other women in his life?' I asked Lisa.

'Well,' she smiled, 'I guess they had an open marriage.'

I decided to ask her about something else that had been on my mind.

'How about the woman you saw going into Franze's town-house the night of the murder?' I said. 'The one that you think might have seen what really happened?'

'What about her?'

'Tell me what she looked like.'

Lisa shrugged. 'She was very pretty. She had dark features. Dark black hair . . .

'Like you,' I said.

'I guess so. Why?'

I ignored the question.

'Could she have been Hispanic?' I asked.

'Maybe.'

'Have you ever heard of a place called El Domingo?'

'No,' she said. 'What's that?'

'El Domingo is a club in the Bronx. It's in a Puerto Rican neighborhood.'

I'd looked it up in the phone book after getting the second anonymous note.

Lisa looked confused. 'Have you been there?'

'No,' I said, 'not yet.'

* * *

At some point in the conversation I told Lisa about me and Carolyn. I'm still not sure why I did that. I guess I just thought it was important that she know. Suddenly her whole mood changed. She looked annoyed.

She was getting a bit drunk now, anyway. Fine, I didn't care. She was entitled to tie one on. I figure I would have too, after spending time in jail. Maybe I'd had too much to drink too. We'd been drinking ever since we left Rikers Island.

'So is that where you're headed after me?' she asked. 'Back to New Jersey?'

'Eventually.'

'My goodness, the old wifey really keeps you on a short leash, doesn't she?' she said.

'She's not my wife, she's my fiancée.'

'Whatever.'

She took a big gulp of her drink and threw her hair back. Yep, she was definitely annoyed.

'So what do you do in New Jersey, Joe?' she asked.

She pronounced New Jersey with a rural accent like she was talking to one of the Beverly Hillbillies.

'I mean, do you slop the hogs?' she said. 'Milk the cows? Plow the fields?'

I looked down at the beer in front of me.

'And then at night you gather around the table in the kitchen for some good vittles, I'll bet. On Saturday nights, you go square dancing. Or maybe just stay home and listen to the Grand Ole Opry or some farm prices on the radio. Assuming you have a radio. Do they have electricity in New Jersey yet?'

'Are you finished?' I asked.

She smiled across the table at me. 'Sorry to be so bitchy, Joe. But you just don't seem like a New Jersey kind of guy to me. You definitely strike me as a New York City kind of guy. How the hell did you wind up in New Jersey anyway?'

'I wanted to see the country,' I said.

'Or maybe someone else decided that for you.'

'What do you mean?'

'My guess is that it's all part of that story you told me before about why you got fired from the *Banner*. Are you sure you don't want to tell me about that?'

'Maybe some other time,' I said.

She nodded and finished off her drink.

'You and me – we really live in different worlds, don't we, Joe?' she said.

'I guess so.'

'But we're a lot alike too.'

I didn't say anything.

'So what do you think?' she asked. 'You figure that two people like us could ever get involved with each other?'

I stared at her. I'm hardly ever at a loss for words, but I sure was this time. I stood there, struggling to think of something witty, something clever, something appropriate to say back. But I couldn't come up with a damn thing.

'Probably not,' I finally stammered.

'I guess it's lucky then we're not getting involved, huh?' she laughed.

twenty nine

I was lying in bed with Carolyn back in Princeton, trying to make up for all the time I'd been away. It was the middle of the afternoon. I'd taken the day off from work, and so had Carolyn. We didn't waste a lot of time on idle chitchat. We just jumped right into bed as soon as I got there.

Only something was wrong.

Not with Carolyn. She seemed fine. In fact, she was the one who suggested we skip all the polite preliminaries and get right into the sack. No, the problem was mine.

At first, I couldn't figure it out. It was like I was making love to a stranger, not my fiancee. No, that wasn't right either. Making love to a stranger is usually exciting. This seemed . . . well, it seemed routine. Like we were an old married couple just going through the motions of a tired ritual. Even though we weren't even married yet. There was no excitement. No thrills. No passion.

Then something happened.

I thought about Lisa sitting in her jail cell.

And suddenly everything changed.

I started making wild love to Carolyn. I kissed her passionately, I explored every part of her body, I made animal sounds and groans of pleasure. She moaned too, softly at first, then louder and louder until she was screaming at the top of her lungs. She wrapped her legs around my body, she clawed desperately at my back. But, of course, it wasn't Carolyn that was in bed with me anymore. It was Lisa. I could see her face in front of me, taste her lips, smell her perfume, run my hands through her long dark hair. 'I love you, I love you, I love you,' I repeated over and over again as we came together in an explosion of lust like I hadn't experienced for a long, long time.

The two of us lay there spent and exhausted afterward.

'Whew!' Carolyn finally said. 'That was something else.'

'Yeah, it was.'

'I guess absence really does make the heart grow fonder,' she laughed.

That night, Carolyn said she didn't want to go out to dinner. Instead, she cooked a big meal for the two of us. Roast beef with gravy, potatoes, biscuits and salad – the works. She was a terrific cook.

While we ate, I told her about the David Galvin story. I talked a lot about The Great Pretenders part of it, and not very much about Lisa Montero. She listened intently as if it was the most important thing in the world to her. And then she told me stories about her job, while I pretended like I was interested.

'When are you coming home for good, Joe?' Carolyn asked.

It was the question I'd been dreading.

'As soon as the story's over,' I said.

'When will that be?'

'I'm not sure,' I told her. 'Maybe a few more days, maybe a few weeks.'

'And that's the end of it?' she asked. 'I mean you'll be finished with the job at the *Banner* then. You can come back to Princeton, work for my father's company again and we'll be married in the fall. That's still what you want, isn't it, Joe?'

'Absolutely,' I lied.

I cut off a piece of the roast beef and chewed on it slowly.

'Do you like the roast beef?' Carolyn asked. 'I bought it from that new butcher on Nassau Street.'

'The one that opened last month,' I said.

'Yes, that one.'

I thought about Lisa again. Sitting in that jail cell. I wondered what she was eating for dinner. I wanted to be there with her. I wanted to talk to her. To comfort her. To hold her.

'Joe, is everything all right?' Carolyn asked me.

'I'm sorry,' I said. I realized I'd drifted off. 'I was just thinking about my story.'

'So what's the verdict?'

'The verdict about what?'

'My roast beef,' she laughed. 'Do you like it or not?'

I wanted to tell her right then about everything.

All the passion, the excitement, the thrills that I'd felt since I'd gone back to the *Banner*.

David Galvin.

The Great Pretenders.

Lisa Montero.

How they'd made me feel alive again.

How I didn't want to go through the rest of my life without feeling that way again.

But, of course, I didn't say that.

'The roast beef really is good,' is what I said.

thirty

John Montero wasn't what I expected. I was figuring on meeting a combination of Joseph P. Kennedy and Howard Hughes and Donald Trump. Some larger than life figure who puffed on a big cigar and had a stock market ticker going next to him and kept getting calls from around the world telling him about the price of the dollar in Japan and Europe. The kind of guy who never went a day without making or losing a million dollars or so. Who was ruthless and merciless and would do anything to make money.

But John Montero didn't look like that at all.

He seemed like a nice guy.

Lisa Montero had called to tell me that her father agreed to talk to me at his house on Long Island. The phone call came in through the city desk at the *Banner*. When someone called out her name for me to pick up on my extension, everyone in the office looked up. I liked that. I was hot. I was happening. I was a star again. She said there was a big pre-trial hearing scheduled in her case for later in the week. She would have to be in court for it. She was very nervous. I told her not to worry, that everything was going to turn out all right.

Her father lived in a huge house on Shelter Island, which is off the north shore of Long Island – facing Long Island Sound and Connecticut in the distance.

A butler wearing a red jacket led me into the living room where Montero was watching a baseball game on TV. It was a huge projection TV with a screen that took up much of the wall. The New York Mets were playing the Atlanta Braves. All of the players looked like giants.

He was a big man, with striking features. You could see where Lisa got her good looks from. I figured he was maybe in his early sixties and still in pretty good shape, even though his black hair was now specked with patches of gray. I remembered Lisa telling me that both his wife and only other child, her brother, had died. Since Lisa had an apartment in the city, I wondered if Montero lived here by himself. It seemed like a very big house for just one person. But then when you had his money and power, you could do whatever the hell you wanted, I guess.

'You want a beer?' Montero asked me after we'd shaken hands.

'Yeah, I'd love one,' I said. 'It was a long, hot ride out here from the city.'

'Good. I never trust a man who doesn't say yes to a cold beer on a hot day.'

He dispatched the red-coated butler to get beers for both of us.

I looked down at a table next to where Montero had been sitting. There were Xerox copies of newspaper clippings on it. They were stories by me. Murders I'd covered. Trials I'd written about. There were maybe a dozen of my biggest stories. The Nancy Kelleher story was one of them.

A loud cheer came from the television. One of the Mets had just gotten a basehit.

'Do you like baseball?' Montero asked me.

'I used to watch a lot of games. Not so much anymore.'

'Who do you root for?'

'Either the Mets or the Yankees, depending on how they're doing at the moment.'

'Sort of a fair-weather fan, huh?'

'Actually, I never used to root in the traditional sense. I guess I wasn't really a fan either. I used to like to bet a lot on baseball. That was the fun part of it for me. Baseball's a tough game to bet on, but you can do it. Hell, you can bet on anything.'

He seemed fascinated by that.

The butler brought out drinks.

'I made a bet of $100 on this game,' he told me. 'Just a friendly wager with a business associate. Well, not that friendly actually. It's not a lot of money, but I want to win. Me and this business associate are very . . . well, competitive. I don't like to lose to him. I don't like to lose to anybody. Anyway, he's got the Braves, I have the Mets. The Braves have won six games in a row, and the Mets have lost four straight. I figured they were due. I've got 5–3 odds. What do you think?'

I looked at the screen. The game was 0–0 in the third inning. The Braves had their best pitcher on the mound, while the Mets were going with a guy they'd just called up from the minors a few days before.

'That's a sucker bet,' I said.

'What do you mean?'

'You never bet on a team to end a streak,' I said. 'You bet on them to continue it. If they're winning, you just keep betting on them until they lose. If they're on a losing streak, you go against them until they win. You've got a better chance of coming out ahead that way.'

Montero nodded. 'Anything else?'

'Yeah, the game is 70 per cent pitching. The pitcher is the most important part of your bet. The guy on the mound for Atlanta is a 20-game winner with a lopsided career-winning percentage against the Mets. The other guy pitching for the Mets is horse manure. Never bet on horse manure.'

'But the odds . . .'

'Forget the odds. The bookmakers set the odds. They know exactly what they're doing. The odds are not meant to be fair, they're meant to get money from suckers.'

'Like me?' Montero smiled.

I shrugged.

'It sounds a little like Wall Street,' he smiled. 'So let me get this straight. If I figure out the odds and go along with your streak theory and work on the theory that pitching is 70 per cent of the game, does that give me a pretty good chance of winning my bets?'

'Not really.'

'But you just said . . .'

'Baseball is a tough game to bet on, Mr Montero. It's just too unpredictable. Football's better, but the odds are stacked against you there too. The best sport to put your money on is basketball; either college or pros. Me, I give a bit of an edge to the college game but even there it's tough to come out ahead on a long-term basis.'

'So how DO I win?'

'If you really want to make serious money gambling, forget about sports betting all together. You're better off going to one of the casinos. Down in Atlantic City or Las Vegas. You can beat the house in either place – if you really know what you're doing. Of course, you can also lose your shirt. The roulette wheel is for suckers. So is the craps table – unless you're an expert. The place you've got your best chance is at the blackjack table, where the odds aren't stacked so much against you. Even there though, you're generally lucky to break even. The only way to win consistently at blackjack is to use a technique called card counting. But the hotels will bar you from their casinos if they find out you're doing it.'

'You mean it's cheating?'

'Not exactly,' I said. 'Well, maybe. I'd call it borderline cheating.'

'And that's the only way to make real money at the game?'

'Pretty much so.'

Montero smiled. 'Actually it is a lot like Wall Street.'

On the TV screen one of the Atlanta players had just hit a grandslam homerun off the Mets pitcher. The score was now 4–0 Atlanta. Just like I predicted. Of course, the odds had been in my favor.

'So tell me some more,' he said.

'Well, there's two classic stories that pretty much sum up all you need to know about gambling, Mr Montero,' I said.

'The first is about a guy who likes betting on baseball games. He's spectacularly unsuccessful. In fact, at one point he loses twenty-two bets in a row. But he's convinced he's due for a hot streak. So he calls his bookie – desperate for some action. The bookie tells him there's no baseball games being played that night. The only action going down is on a hockey game. Does he want to make a bet? "Hockey?" the guy snorts with disdain. "What the hell do I know about hockey?"'

Montero laughed.

'The second story is the classic gambling anecdote of all time. One bettor asks another bettor how he did. "I had a great day," the guy replies. "I broke even." '

He laughed again. On the TV screen, one of the Braves had just hit another home run. The score was now 6–0. The Mets were changing pitchers.

I looked down again at the newspaper clippings of my stories on the table next to him.

'You've been reading up on me?' I asked.

'I always believe in being prepared when I meet someone.'

'So what did you find out?'

'You appear to be quite a paradox, Mr Dougherty. A dedicated reporter. A man of integrity. A man who will go to any lengths to find the truth when he believes in a cause. On the other hand, you once got fired from your job for making up a story. Fascinating. So which one is the real Joe Dougherty?'

'Sometimes things aren't as black and white as they seem,' I said.

I picked up the story about Nancy Kelleher. There was a picture of her hugging me on the courthouse steps after her murder conviction was overturned. It was on Page One of the *Banner* under the headline: 'FREED AT LAST – THANKS TO OUR REPORTER!'

'You think maybe I can do the same thing for your daughter, don't you?' I said to Montero. 'Figure out a way to get her off.'

'The thought did cross my mind,' he smiled.

'The circumstances might be different,' I said. 'I knew that Nancy Kelleher was innocent.'

'And you don't think my daughter is?'

'I'm not sure yet. If she is innocent, I'll do everything in my power to make sure that a miscarriage of justice doesn't take place. But if I find out evidence that she did kill Franze and the girl in bed with him, I'll write the truth about that too. That's what I do. I write the truth. I want you to understand that, Mr Montero.'

Montero looked back at the baseball game on the giant TV. He stared at the screen for a long time. I had the feeling that he was trying to decide something.

'Are you interested in some lunch, Joe?' he asked finally.

'Sure.'

'Is seafood okay?'

'Absolutely.'

He drank the last of his beer and put the glass down on a table in front of him. Then he stood up.

'Okay, let's go then.'

'What are we having?'

'I don't know. We have to catch it first.'

It had been a long time since I'd gone fishing. Of course, even then I just used to sit with a rod and reel in a rowboat or on a pier on a lazy afternoon and hope to get lucky. The way John Montero went fishing was a lot different. The boat we went out on looked as big as a yacht to me. It had a captain and crew, complete equipment for deep sea fishing and even a sophisticated radar system to help track down schools of fish.

It hardly seemed fair to the fish.

'Do you like my daughter?' Montero asked once we were out on the water.

'Sure.'

'Because she likes you very much.'

She does, huh? How about that? I wanted to ask him exactly what she had told him about me. But I didn't.

'Lisa seems really nice,' is what I said instead.

'She's a good kid. A little wild, but she's been through a lot. She lost her mother – and then her brother last year. I'm all she's got left, and she has to deal with all the bad stuff people say about me. Now I think somebody's trying to set her up for this murder. I'm afraid it's somebody who's really out to hurt me. That's why they're going after my daughter.'

I chose my next words very carefully.

'Off the record, Mr Montero,' I said, 'just between you and me, is there any possibility at all that Lisa really could have killed Franze and the call girl?'

He first gave me a look of astonishment, then shook his head and laughed.

'Boy, you've got balls, kid.'

'Thank you. I think.'

'Of course not,' he said to me, answering my question. 'There's no way that Lisa could have ever done something like that.'

'So why did Greg Ackerman arrest her?'

'He's out to get me.'

'He doesn't like you very much,' I agreed. 'He says you're a criminal. He says you should be in jail, except you always figure out some way to beat the rap.'

'I've never been convicted by a jury for anything I ever did in my career,' Montero said evenly. 'So I'm not guilty of anything. That's still the American system, the last time I looked. Don't you agree?'

'Absolutely.'

We sat there and fished for an hour or so together. Sitting side by side there on his big boat, our shirts off, with the late spring sun beating down on us. Talking. And bonding. Me and Big John Montero. Like I said, I didn't think he was a bad guy at all. In fact, I liked him. And he liked me. Even more importantly, so did his daughter.

I never caught any fish, but that was all right. He did, and we ate them back at the house. We talked about Wall Street, the newspaper business and all the murders that had happened. And, of course, most of all we talked about his daughter Lisa and the charges against her.

'Let me ask you the same question you asked me before, Joe,' he said at one point. 'Do you think Lisa could have done it?'

'Off the record?'

'Sure.'

'No,' I told him. 'I think somebody's trying to set her up too, Mr Montero.'

thirty one

• • • • • • • • • • •

The next person I went to see was William Franze's wife.

'I guess they have an open marriage,' Lisa had said.

Maybe. But I figured William Franze's wife couldn't have been too happy with the way he died in bed with a prostitute. Or the way he lived either.

Deborah Franze's house was in Saddlebrook, NJ, a rich suburb of Bergen County where Richard Nixon used to live. It was a big house. Not as big as Montero's, but still damn big. There was a swimming pool, a tennis court, a garage full of fancy cars – and all the other status symbols that showed she was married to a man who had hit it big.

The house was about a half mile from the road. There was a long, winding driveway that led past a duck pond and up to the front door. I drove up it now, parked my car and rang the bell. I told the maid who answered what I was there for. She said that Mrs Franze was playing tennis, then led me to the courts.

I'd expected to find a bitter wife. Aging badly, maybe drinking a lot and definitely angry at her husband for the social embarrassment that the circumstances of his death had caused her. But I was wrong.

Deborah Franze was probably about forty – but a very good forty. She had long, blonde hair; a tanned, attractive face; and a body that looked like she took very good care of it. Whether it was all for real or the result of several trips to the plastic surgeon, I wasn't sure. But the finished package definitely worked.

She was wearing a tight, white tennis outfit, and I could see the muscles ripple in her legs and arms when she swung the racquet. The person she was playing was in good shape too; a dark-haired, handsome young guy in his early twenties who played good enough to make me think he was probably her tennis instructor.

'Deborah Franze?' I yelled out to her on the court.

She didn't stop playing.

'What do you want?' she yelled over her shoulder.

'I'm Joe Dougherty of the *Banner*. I'd like to talk to you.'

She returned a serve.

'I'm busy. Can it wait?'

'It's about your husband.'

'Then it definitely can wait,' she laughed.

Mrs Franze told me to go into the living room and have a drink. She said she'd be there in a little while. When she did come in, she'd changed her clothes. She was wearing a summer dress now that was low cut in the front and had a slit up the side. She toweled her hair off, poured herself a drink and sat down in a chair across from me. When she crossed her legs, I got a nice view. Then she took a big gulp of her drink and shook her hair dry. She was definitely a sexy woman.

'You don't seem too broken up over your husband's murder,' I said.

'Actually, I'm quite the merry widow.'

'I take it you and he didn't get along?'

'I hated him. He detested me. I think that pretty much summed up our relationship.'

'Why didn't you get divorced?'

'No reason to. He didn't want to give me a big divorce settlement. And there were certain financial advantages for me in remaining Mrs William Franze.'

She looked around the beautiful home.

'I'm not doing too badly,' she said.

'And now you get all his money.'

'Yeah, I do. A lucky break for me, huh?'

'That gives you a real motive for killing him.'

Deborah Franze laughed. 'The world is filled with people who had a motive for killing my husband.'

'I guess he wasn't a very nice man, huh?'

'Let me tell you about the kind of man Billy was. One time, early on in our marriage, I was pregnant. It was going to be a little girl. God, I really wanted that baby. But I lost it. Something went wrong at the hospital during childbirth and they just weren't able to save her. Afterward, my doctor told me I could never have any more children. I was devastated. Now the whole time this was going on, there was no sign of Billy. He didn't visit me, call me, tell me where he was – absolutely nothing. I was all alone. I even had to take a taxicab home. When I got there, I found Billy in bed with a naked stewardess.' Deborah Franze finished off what was left of her drink and poured herself another. 'That is the kind of man my husband was.'

I wasn't quite sure what to say to her. 'What about as a businessman?' I finally asked.

'Worse. Oh, he made a lot of money. But Billy never did it the old-fashioned way, he didn't earn it. He conned people. He lied. He stole. Most of the time the people he stole from were as crooked as he was. But not always. I remember one time he met this old woman at a dinner party. Her husband had died six months earlier and left her with a comfortable inheritance for her old age – about $5 million. My husband talked this woman into letting him run the estate for her. He convinced her he could turn her $5 million into $10 million. Well, he lost it all – at least that's what he told her. But the truth was he'd invested it in some dummy corporations that were really just fronts for him. So the money eventually wound up in his pocket. The old woman lost her house too and wound up dying in a nursing home.' Mrs Franze sighed. 'I think that was the one that convinced me I didn't want to live with Bill anymore.'

I realized they were the same kinds of stories I'd heard about John Montero.

'Did your husband have many business dealings with John Montero?' I asked her.

'A few.'

'Do you remember anything about them?'

She shrugged. 'Not really.'

'Montero didn't like your husband much,' I said, remembering what Lisa had told me. 'He didn't want him dating Lisa either. He was very worried about that. He said your husband was a very disreputable, shady character. I guess from what you've told me he was right about that.'

'That's funny,' Mrs Franze grunted.

'What do you mean?'

'Well, I mean it's sort of like the pot calling the kettle black, isn't it?' she said.

We talked for another half hour or so about William Franze. Everything she told me confirmed my image of the man. A rich, arrogant, despicable son of a bitch. No one deserves to be murdered, but if someone had to be a victim, well, it sounded like he would be high on the list of a lot of people who knew him.

Especially his wife.

'So where were you the night that your husband was murdered?' I asked her.

She shook her head. 'I have an alibi.'

'That wasn't exactly my question . . .'

'I know what your question was, Joe. That's my answer. I was here. All night. And I was with someone the entire time. A man.'

I looked out the window. The good looking guy she was playing tennis with was swimming laps in the pool now. 'You mean him?' I asked her.

'No, not Tony,' she said. 'I just play games with Tony.'

'And this guy you were with – he's more than games?'

'A girl's gotta keep her options open,' she said.

'Will you tell me who it was?'

'No.'

'The police are going to want to know.'

'I've already told them.'

'And they believe your story?'

'I'm not the one they arrested, am I?'

I wasn't sure if Mrs Franze was telling me everything she knew or not. But one thing was for sure, she wasn't going to spill any secrets she did hold very easily. She was a smooth operator. Just like her husband. Probably even smoother. I mean here he was dead – and she's left sitting in this big mansion with all his money.

Was that just luck? Maybe.

I needed an angle to crack her though. A way to get close to her. Some weakness in her character I could exploit to get the answers I was looking for. Did she have a weakness?

Well, she liked men.

And I was a man.

Maybe that was the way to go.

I glanced outside at the tennis courts again.

'I play tennis,' I said casually.

'Good for you.'

'If you need a partner sometimes . . .'

'I've got a partner.'

She nodded over toward the young tennis instructor swimming laps in the pool.

'Well, then maybe we could have lunch one day soon. Just you and me. I'd love to . . .'

Deborah Franze laughed and shook her head.

'Don't even think about it,' she told me.

'What?'

'The seduction routine.'

'I just . . .'

'You can't afford me, Joe,' she said.

A few minutes later, Deborah Franze walked me out to my car. The tennis instructor was sunning himself by the pool now. I wondered what else he did besides give her tennis lessons. I decided I had nothing to lose so I asked her one last question.

'Did you kill your husband, Mrs Franze?' I asked.

'Of course not.'

'You had plenty of motive.'

'Sure I did.'

'And you're glad he's dead.'

'Sure I am. But I didn't have to kill him.'

'Why not?'

'Because,' she said with a big smile, 'Lisa Montero did it for me.'

thirty two

• • • • • • • • • • •

'The facts of the matter are pretty clear,' I said. 'There is a very long list of potential suspects who could very well have murdered William Franze besides Lisa Montero.'

I was sitting in another news meeting in Andy's office, along with Blackwood, Rollins and the others; telling them everything I'd managed to find out.

'Franze was not a very nice man,' I continued. 'He cheated people, he lied to them, he stole from them. There's a lot of people with empty pockets after business dealings with this jerk that must have had a grudge against him.

'And then there's his personal life. He's got a wife who's so happy he's dead that she's practically dancing on his grave. She gets everything by the way – the house, the estate, the cars and all the money. There's a lot of girlfriends too. Most of them liked Franze even less than his wife. He went through women extremely quickly – and very badly. Basically, he treated them like all the other people in his life – he screwed them and then dumped them. He was not exactly a sensitive, caring '90s type of guy.

'I don't necessarily think it was any of them that did it. I believe Franze's death is connected to all the other deaths on the list that Galvin wrote out. I think it's someone who went to school with Galvin a decade ago, killed with him and now has started up again.

'I'm simply making the point that there's a lot of people besides Lisa Montero that had a reason for wanting Franze dead.'

Rollins said he still wasn't convinced that anything I'd found out changed anything.

'The DA says that Lisa Montero did it,' he pointed out.

'I think the DA is wrong.'

'Why?' Blackwood asked.

'He's got some sort of vendetta against the Montero family.'

'Well, maybe he knows something we don't. Lisa Montero went to school with Galvin. According to your theory, that makes her a suspect in all of the new killings. Right?'

'Ackerman went to school at NYU at the same time. He could be a suspect too.'

Rollins made a snorting sound. 'Oh, that's beautiful,' he said. 'You think the prosecutor did it?'

'Maybe.'

'Listen, Dougherty,' he said, 'no one wants to hear your theories. Our job is to report the news, not to make it.'

'Oh really? Who told you that? One of your friends up at the Columbia School of Journalism? Well, newspapers DO make news sometimes, Jack. It's called crusading journalism. Sometimes they even give out a prize to the paper that does it the best. They call it the Pulitzer Prize. Did you ever hear of it?'

'Don't lecture me about journalism . . .'

'Why? Am I going too fast for you?'

Andy Kramer put his fingers in his mouth and whistled loudly. 'Guys, guys,' he shouted, 'can we give this a rest, huh?'

Jack Rollins glared at him. Technically, Rollins outranked him, and I don't think he liked Andy talking to him like that. I thought there might be a power confrontation between the two of them right there.

But then Spencer Blackwood stepped in.

'Let's concentrate right now on the business at hand,' Blackwood said. 'There's supposed to be a court hearing this week for Lisa Montero on the William Franze murder case. How are we planning on covering it? Is Dougherty going to be there?'

'Yes,' said Andy.

'No,' Jack Rollins answered at the same time.

'Well, I guess that just about covers all the possibilities,' Blackwood smiled.

'I've already assigned Issacs to do the story,' Rollins told him.

'What about Joe?' Andy asked.

'Rick Issacs is the best court reporter in the city.'

'This isn't just a court story, Jack,' Andy said. 'It's a personality story. Lisa Montero is the personality – and so is her father. And no one is closer to the Montero family right now than Joe.'

Blackwood gave them both a 'what's the problem' shrug.

'So Issacs handles the friggin' courtroom story and Dougherty can do the sidebar personality stuff,' he said. 'OK?'

He looked at both of them and over at me.

We all nodded.

'Anything else?'

'Yeah, I'm still worried about Dougherty,' Rollins said, glaring across the room at me. 'I think he's too close to this story. I think he's too close to the Montero woman. We all remember what happened the last time he worked for us. I don't want to see the *Banner* get embarrassed again.'

'Has he done anything wrong yet?' Blackwood asked.

Rollins shook his head. 'Not yet.'

'Well, Jack, you've got to learn to trust your reporters,' Blackwood told him.

After the meeting was over and everyone else had left, I showed Andy the first two notes I'd gotten in the mail.

'If this isn't a joke,' I said after he read them, 'they could be from someone who knows something about this case.'

'One of Galvin's friends?' he asked.

'Maybe.'

'And now one of them has suddenly got himself a conscience, huh?'

'Or else trying to save their own ass by pointing me in the direction of the other two.'

Andy shook his head. 'That doesn't make any sense. If we found the other two, they'd likely give up the third member too. Our letter writer would just be cutting his own throat.'

I shrugged. 'It's all guesswork, anyway.'

He looked down at the second letter. 'Do you know what El Domingo is?'

I told him it was a club in the Bronx.

'I haven't been there,' I said. 'I'm not sure if I should go until I know more. I'm not exactly going to blend into the crowd at a place like that.'

'We could send a Hispanic reporter,' Andy suggested.

'Except we don't know what to tell him to look for.'

'So what do we do?'

'Wait until our pen pal writes again,' I said.

The next note, when it came, was very brief. It said simply:

There is no more time
for playing games,
The woman you're looking
for is Connie James . . .

I checked with the *Banner* library first. They'd never heard of a Connie James. Then I called Capt. Righetti at police headquarters.

'You got anything on a woman named Connie James in your computer?' I asked him.

'Let me check.'

He put me on hold, then came back on the line a few minutes later.

'Connie James is an alias. Her real name is Connie Reyes. She's been busted six times for prostitution. Once for drugs. She sounds like a lovely girl. You thinking of dating her?'

'Yeah. We met on Love Connection. You got an address?'

'Last known address was 555 Grand Concourse. The Bronx. It's no good anymore though.'

The Bronx. Interesting. And she was a prostitute. William Franze had told Lisa he was bringing over a second call girl just before he died. Maybe she was the missing witness. Maybe she was the woman Lisa saw that night. Maybe she was the key to the case.

I had one other hunch that I decided to try.

'You wouldn't have any other address for her in the computer, would you?' I asked. 'Like a mailing address. A post office drop. A place of work.'

'Yeah,' Righetti said. 'There's something here called El Domingo. She worked at a club called El Domingo.'

thirty three

There was an Off-Track Betting parlor a few blocks away from my hotel. I'd passed by it maybe a dozen times since I'd been back in the city. But I never went in. Until now.

As gambling establishments go, New York City Off-Track Betting parlors are pretty tame stuff. They rank somewhere just above lottery tickets and office football pools on the danger factor for a gambling addict. Most of the people who go to them are just small time horse players. No problem there for me. No problem at all.

But I was kidding myself, and I knew it.

You see, I'd lied to Blackwood and Andy and Jack Rollins that day in the meeting at the *Banner* when I said I wasn't gambling anymore. The truth is I'd slipped a few times along the way on my path to redemption. Nothing major. A friendly card game here and there. Some trips to the track; twice to Belmont, and once to Monmouth Park in New Jersey on a Saturday afternoon when I was living in Princeton and lied to Carolyn that I had a new client. Even a quick run down to Atlantic City for a little blackjack and slots one weekend when she was out of town. But everything was still fine. There was no big time betting. No huge money losses. No sleepless nights. No loan sharks at my door threatening me to pay up or else.

I could handle it, I told myself.

I'd discovered it was possible for me to bet a little – have some fun gambling like everyone else – and not let the disease destroy my life. It was really an incredible discovery. I only wished I'd figured it out a few years ago. It would have saved me a lot of grief. Now I could gamble whenever I felt like it, only I'd do it in moderation.

That was the key. Moderation. Just like everything else in life. It was simple.

Or so I told myself anyway.

But that was all bullshit too.

I knew the truth. The truth was that I was like some alcoholic who convinces himself that it's okay for him to drink socially. He'll do it too. For awhile. Maybe a few days, a few weeks, a few months – even years. But then one night he'll just keep drinking. He'll fall off the wagon big time and then he'll be right back where he started again. A hopeless drunk. Well, that was like me with gambling. Either I gambled or I didn't gamble. There was no middle ground. My gambling was a sickness, and I had to beat it. If I didn't, then it would destroy me.

The first time I ever gambled was with my father. When I was eleven, he took me to a race track, where I bet $1 on each of the nine races. I won them all. My father won too, which made him very happy. That made me happy too because I knew he didn't have a very happy life. All in all, it was just a great day. I felt as if I had found a home.

By the time I was a teenager, I was using the money from my paper route and allowance to bet on pro football and basketball with a bookmaker who lived in a very bad neighborhood. I had to pedal my bike over there to pay off my losses and collect my winnings. Every time I did, I was convinced someone was going to mug me for my money. They never did, but one day someone stole my bicycle from where it was parked. I had to walk five miles to get home.

In college, I would cut classes and hitchhike to Atlantic City for the weekend. I had spent weeks perfecting a system to win at blackjack when I was supposed to be studying. I tried out the system in small increments at first, winning between $50 and $100 each time. By Friday night, I was up $10,000. Sometime during the early morning hours of Saturday, I lost almost everything I had won. On Saturday afternoon, I was flat broke. I called my parents and asked them for money to take a bus home. They wired it to me, and I gambled that away too. Then I tried my college roommate. After that, an ex-girlfriend. I bet everything they sent me and kept losing. Eventually, I ran out of people to call. On my way back, a man who picked me up hitchhiking tried to touch my leg and I fled his car at a rest stop on the New Jersey Turnpike. I had to wait an hour and a half before I could find another ride. It was a cold night in February, and at some point it began to snow. I got back to my college on early Monday morning, where everyone was mad at me because I owed them money. I still believed in my blackjack system though. I knew if I tried it just one more time, I'd be a winner.

I never minded the losing. The winning more than made up for it.

And for a lot of years I managed to keep my head above water.

Toward the end – after Susan and Joey died and I plunged even deeper into gambling to try to forget about my pain – the stakes got higher and higher.

My sports betting by then basically consisted of desperate longshots. Four-team parleys that I'd play for thousands of dollars in the hopes of getting one big score. My average bet on a four-team parley was $2000. If all four teams covered their respective spreads, I'd walk away with $22,000. It happened a few times. But not enough.

At the race track, my wager of choice was a $40 exacta bet. That meant I put $40 down on each of the six combinations that three horses can do if they're bet to finish first or second. If I hit one of these, I was set for the day. But on a bad day, I'd be out at least $1000. A bad week meant I was $5000 in the hole.

Looking back on it all now, the thing I remember the most is that first day at the track with my father and the simple joy I felt when our horses won.

We are all our parents' children. What they do while we're growing up – whether it's intentional or not – sometimes stays with us through our entire lives. My father liked to gamble. Not the way I did, just in a small, very controlled way. He played the lottery, he went to the track once in awhile, he enjoyed a neighborhood poker game with friends. For him it was an escape.

My parents' marriage wasn't a very happy one. I never knew exactly why. I do know my father felt cheated by life. He never got to do the things he wanted to do. He was a very intelligent man, but his family never had enough money to send him to college. So he joined the Army instead. When he came out, he wanted to go to school on the GI bill and become an electrical engineer. But then he got my mother pregnant with me, so he had to get married and find a job instead. That was what you did when you got somebody pregnant in those days. I don't think the two of them ever really got along. My mother was a good person, but she was very high-strung and demanding. Eventually she just wore my father out. The biggest fights they had were about his job. He worked as an inspector at a factory that made automobile parts. He was bored by the work, and still dreamed of someday becoming an electrical engineer. Early on when I was growing up – I guess I was maybe eight or nine – he got accepted into an engineering program at the University of Washington in Seattle that would allow him to go to school at night and have an apprentice engineering job during the day. He told my mother he wanted to move there. He said it was what he'd wanted to do all his life. I'd never seen my father so excited and hopeful and optimistic.

She refused.

After that, I think he just gave up. Years later, after he'd suffered his first heart attack, I went to see him in the hospital. I had just started working at the *Blade* and I was full of excitement about my job and the newspaper business and New York City. He smiled as I sat there next to his bed, letting it all spill out of me. He seemed very pleased.

'Whatever you do, Joe,' he said to me in a weak, raspy voice, grasping my hand in his, 'make sure you enjoy life. Have fun. Have some excitement. Enjoy the ride. I never did. But it's not too late for you.'

My father's gone. My mother's dead too.

But I still think about them a lot.

Maybe that's why it's so important to me that my life is filled with passion and excitement. Because their lives never were. So far, I've found that kind of passion and excitement in three things: newspapers, my marriage to Susan and gambling. When things were going good in my newspaper career and when I was head over heels in love with Susan, I never got too out of control in my gambling. I didn't need it as much. But once those things were gone, I plunged deeper and deeper into gambling until it nearly destroyed me.

Of course, that was a long time ago. Things were different now. I had Carolyn; she was a great woman. I had a great job at the public relations agency. I had a great life. So what was my problem anyway? Why was I thinking about gambling? And Susan. And those things my father had said to me from his hospital bed before he died.

Well, the truth is, I was still looking for excitement.

And I hadn't found any in a long time.

Until The Great Pretenders.

So here I was now, standing in an Off-Track Betting parlor ready to put down money on a horse race.

I put my money back in my pocket, turned around and walked out the door.

Okay. That was easy.

I was able to handle that crisis just fine. I knew why too. I had a job to do. I was going to prove that Lisa Montero was innocent. Then I was going to catch the last of The Great Pretenders. That was my passion right now. As long as I had that, I'd stay away from Off-Track Betting parlors. And the even worse temptations that were out there. I didn't need anything else until this story was over.

I just wasn't sure what was going to happen after that.

thirty four

Lisa called me at my hotel on the night before she was supposed to appear in court for her hearing.

'I'm scared,' she said.

'Everything's going to be fine,' I told her.

'Can you come over and see me?'

'Now?'

'Yes, I'm feeling very alone.'

I remembered what Rollins had said about me getting too close to this case. Ackerman too. Even Andy Kramer seemed worried about my relationship with Lisa.

'I'm not sure if that's such a good idea,' I said.

'Please.'

'Don't you have anybody else you can call?'

'I want you!'

Lisa was wearing a red silk blouse and a pair of tight jeans when I got to her apartment. Her long black hair was piled up on top of her head. She looked terrific. She poured me a drink, then got one for herself and sat down on the couch next to me. She seemed very upset. Close to tears.

'I'm sorry I had to make you come over here and babysit me like this tonight,' she said.

'Don't worry about it.'

'I guess everything just caught up with me all at once. I'm . . . I'm worried.'

'You have nothing to be afraid of,' I told her soothingly. 'You're innocent.'

She looked over at me and smiled gratefully.

'Well, at least I've managed to convince one person of that.'

'You'll convince a jury too.'

'I don't know . . . ' She began to cry. 'I don't know anything anymore . . .'

I moved closer to her and put my arm around her. I could smell her perfume. I could feel the warmth of her body. It took all my willpower not to just take this gorgeous woman in my arms and kiss her right there. It would have been so easy.

'It's going to be fine, Lisa,' I said. 'You'll see. Everything will work out okay.'

She leaned closer to me now and buried her face in the front of my shirt.

'I'm really not a bad person,' she sniffled.

'You're a terrific person.'

'Honest?'

'Honest.'

She looked up at me and our eyes met. I was only inches away from her lips now.

In all the time I'd been with Carolyn, I really tried hard to love her.

I knew she was good for me.

By the time I met Carolyn, I was about as close to rock bottom as a person can get. I'd lost a half dozen jobs, I was in gambling debts up to my ears and I hadn't had a real relationship with a woman since Susan died. I was out of control. I was a mess. And, most of all, I was scared. Scared about what was going to happen next. I don't think it's an exaggeration to say that Carolyn saved me.

That day I met her in the coffeeshop in Harrisburg changed everything. I was all the way back now. I had a job. I had a relationship. I had a life. Carolyn was responsible for all of it. I could never have done it without her.

And so – even though I kept having the flickers of secret doubt, these feelings that something was missing – I said yes to everything she wanted.

The move to Princeton.

Working for her father's public relations company.

The wedding plans.

I tried. I really tried.

But, you see, that was the thing that was different about Lisa. I didn't have to try at all. I knew from the first minute I talked to her that she was the right one. That had only happened to me once before. With Susan.

Holding Lisa in my arms now, I tried to rationalize as best I could what I was about to do. It wouldn't be fair to Carolyn to marry her if I didn't really love her. We'd be living a lie. Sooner or later, she'd find out the truth and then it would be even worse. I couldn't do that to a fine person like Carolyn. This was really the best thing for her.

Of course, that was all an excuse. It wasn't Carolyn that I was thinking about. It was Lisa.

I knew what I was going to do.

I had no choice.

I was all out of willpower.

I leaned down and kissed her.

Lisa seemed surprised. She hesitated for just a second. Then she kissed me back. Cautiously. Tentatively. Like a swimmer trying out the water for the first time.

'We shouldn't be doing this, should we?' she said.

I answered by kissing her for a second time.

She seemed flustered.

'Are you going to do that again?' she asked.

I nodded. Our lips were together now as we talked.

'Is that all right with you?' I asked.

'Uh-huh . . .'

We were locked in an embrace now. This was the real thing. All of her hesitation was gone.

I maneuvered myself down onto the couch on top of her. I kissed her gently at first, then more and more passionately. My hands stroked her hair and began to explore her body. She dug her nails into my back and began to moan softly.

'Do you want to go into the bedroom?' she asked.

Later that night, we sat up in her bed into the early morning hours, eating takeout sandwiches we'd ordered from a deli downstairs and telling each other about our lives in that excited, non-stop way two people do when they've just made love for the first time.

'Well, at least you haven't lost your appetite,' I said.

'Sex always makes me really hungry.'

She took a big bite out of her sandwich. A huge gob of mayonnaise squirted out and onto her cheek. She wiped some of it away, but there was still some left.

I leaned over and kissed her there softly until it was gone.

'We'll have a big victory party when you're acquitted,' I whispered into her ear.

She smiled and hugged me tightly.

'No more secrets, okay?' she said.

'You're keeping secrets from me?' I asked.

'No. You are.'

'What do you mean?'

'Tell me what happened to you at the *Banner*,' she said. 'Why did you get fired?'

I sighed. I knew I was going to have to talk about this with her sooner or later. Now was as good a time as any.

'Did you ever hear of a man named Walter Billings?' I asked her.

'Should I?'

'He was a councilman back then. A big Bible-quoting, family values kind of guy. A real crusader. Well, he organized a crack-down against prostitutes. Put a lot of them in jail.'

She nodded.

'Anyway, I got this tip that he was seeing a call girl himself. I staked him out and sure enough, I caught him going into this hotel with a blonde. I told my editor I needed more time to check it out. But the editor went with it anyway. It was a mistake.'

'She wasn't a call girl?'

'No. She turned out to be some Bible student Billings was trying to recruit for his campaign. The paper had to run a big correction, and Billings threatened a lawsuit. But then he committed suicide. No one ever found out why.'

'Maybe he really did have something to hide,' Lisa suggested.

'Yeah, I've always wondered about that myself.'

'What happened to the editor who made you run the story?' Lisa asked.

'He got promoted. He claimed I'd told him I checked the story out and that it was fine. Everyone believed it. Everyone that mattered anyway. Hell, I think even he believes it now.'

'Who is he?'

'His name is Jack Rollins. He's the executive editor at the *Banner*.'

Lisa was snuggled up close to me in bed. Her head was lying on my chest. We'd just made love again.

'Were you ever married?' she asked.

'A long time ago.'

'What happened.'

'She died.'

'I'm sorry.'

I shrugged.

'Sometimes you remind me of her,' I said.

'Why?'

'You just do.'

'Did you love her very much?'

'Yes.'

'Good,' she smiled.

I thought about my marriage to Susan. But I was remembering another part of it this time. Lots of times our memories play tricks on us. We talk about all the good times, and forget about the bad. Sure, there were good times with Susan. But there were plenty of bad times too.

The arguments. The crying. The endless complaints that I was never around.

It was all coming back to me now.

The whole thing became a vicious cycle for us. We fought about me not being home enough to spend time with her and Joey. And the more we fought, the less I wanted to be there. I began looking for the passion in my life in other places.

By the end, I was hardly ever there for her. I'd work long hours at the *Banner*, hang out at bars all night and spend whatever time I had left over gambling somewhere. I still loved Susan. I always loved Susan. But I thought I could have it all. All the passion and thrills I craved out of life, then her waiting for me at home whenever I was ready. Looking back on it now, I guess I was a disaster waiting to happen.

And when the disaster did strike – and I lost my job – I blamed everyone else. The *Banner*. The editors there. Other reporters who I thought didn't stick up for me. Everyone but myself.

I still think I got a raw deal back then on the Walter Billings story.

But maybe I was at fault too. Maybe my judgement was skewered. I didn't have much of a grip on my personal life, and maybe I let things slip a bit in my professional one too. Maybe this one was someone else's fault. But maybe I would have screwed up the next time. I was pushing the envelope too much. Living too close to the edge. The odds were bound to catch up with me, sooner or later. They always do. At the gambling table and in life.

But I'll tell you a secret.

Something I never admitted to anyone. Not to Carolyn. Not to any of the shrinks I saw after Susan and Joey died. Not even to myself, for a long time anyway. But here it is. Despite everything that happened in my life back then – all the disasters, all the problems, all the turmoil – there is one kernel of truth that I have come to realize.

I miss it.

I miss the excitement.

'What's going to happen to me tomorrow?' Lisa asked, looking up at me in bed with an anxious expression.

'It's called a pre-trial hearing,' I said. 'The prosecution will present the reasons why they believe you should be charged with murder. Your lawyer will move for a dismissal, claiming there's not enough evidence. The whole thing will only take a few days. Then a judge will make the decision.'

'So there's a chance I could get off after this hearing?' she said.

I shook my head. 'It's not likely. Pre-trial hearings are generally pretty cut and dried. The judge goes along with the prosecution and orders a full trial. Unless there's some overwhelming evidence that shows the defendant is innocent. You don't have that yet.'

'What about the woman I saw on the night of the murders?' she asked.

I thought about the description she'd given of the second woman she said she'd seen going into William Franze's house that night. Dark complexion. Dark hair. Maybe she was Italian like Lisa. Or maybe Puerto Rican.

'And the police have no leads on her?' I asked.

'I don't think they're looking too hard.'

'Why not?'

'Because they like me too much for the murders.' Lisa shook her head sadly. 'Maybe she could exonerate me,' she said. 'Maybe she saw the real killer. Maybe she knows what really happened that night. She could be a terrific witness for me at this hearing. But I have to find her first. And I don't even know where to begin looking.'

I leaned over and kissed her.

Passionately.

'I do,' I said.

PART FOUR

Passionate Kisses

thirty five

There was no Connie Reyes or Connie James in the Bronx telephone book. There were a lot of listings for people with the last name of James. Even more for Reyes.

I started calling them all.

'Mr Reyes?' I said to the man who answered the first number that I dialed.

The person on the other end said something in Spanish I couldn't understand.

'Does a Connie Reyes live there?' I asked.

More Spanish. 'Have you ever heard of a Connie Reyes?'

I still couldn't make sense out of his answer.

'Uh . . . *se hable* English?' I asked.

He hung up the phone.

'*Gracias,*' I said into the dead line.

This was going to be even tougher than I expected. A lot of the people I reached didn't speak English. And I didn't speak very much Spanish. I should have thought of that earlier.

I found a copyboy in the city room who spoke Spanish pretty well. I asked him to sit next to me while I made the phone calls. Whenever I found someone who only spoke Spanish, he did the translating for me. It didn't help though. No one I talked to knew anything about a woman named Connie Reyes or Connie James.

So I went to El Domingo. It turned out to be a sort of combination social club/strip joint. The waitresses wore sexy outfits; there were scantily clad women dancing on a stage; and other women came around offering 'lap dances' – which meant they'd sit on your lap and move around suggestively for a few minutes – at $25 a pop. It seemed like one step away from prostitution. I figured there was prostitution going on behind the scenes too.

On the ride out there, I'd come up with what I thought was a pretty good line in case anyone was suspicious about why I was asking so many questions. I said I was with the Plymouth Rock Insurance Agency in Boston. Somebody had just died and left Connie Reyes/James a big inheritance. Now I was trying to track her down to give it to her. I figured if I found anyone that knew her, maybe they'd tell her the good news. Then she'd want to talk to me. But I still got nowhere. Even though I spent a good deal of the *Banner*'s money talking to women in the place. I was starting to get discouraged.

I'd moved over to the bar, and was sitting there trying to figure out what to do next, when a bartender came over and refilled my drink.

'Your name's Dougherty, huh?' he said with a heavy Spanish accent.

'That's right. How . . . ?'

'The girls told me. They say you've been asking a lot of questions.'

'I'm looking for somebody.'

I gave him my whole rap about being an insurance investigator looking for a woman my company owned money to.

'A little bit out of your own neighborhood, aren't you Senõr Dougherty?' the bartender asked.

He smiled when he said it.

'Gee, you mean this isn't an Irish bar?' I said.

Then I wearily started to go through my questions again.

'Did you ever hear of this woman named Connie Reyes?' I asked. 'Or she may use the name Connie James. She's a . . .'

'Nope.'

There was something wrong.

'You answered that pretty quickly,' I said.

'That's because I told the same thing to the other guy a couple of days ago.'

'The other guy?'

'Yeah. The big one with the flowered shirt. Doesn't he work with you?'

'Oh, sure,' I said, thinking quickly.

'You guys ought to get your act together,' the waiter said.

'We sort of lost touch,' I told him. 'Do you have any idea where he is now?'

'Sure. He gave me his card. Said I should contact him if I heard anything about the woman.'

The waiter reached into his pocket, pulled out the card and handed it to me.

It was a printed business card which said:

Victor Granville

Private Investigator

200 Broadway, Suite 610

New York City

The building turned out to be a rundown walkup downtown, a few blocks away from City Hall. I walked inside, took the stairs up to the sixth floor and found a grimy office door marked 610. I knocked on it, then quickly ducked out of sight around a corner at the end of the hall. A man opened the door. He was very big and wearing a flowered shirt. He looked around with a confused expression for a second, saw no one and closed the door.

Now, at least, I knew what Victor Granville looked like.

I went downstairs, got in my car and parked it in a spot close to the front door of the building. Then I waited. Stakeouts were one part of being a reporter that I always hated. You sat around for hours, sometimes for days, waiting for something to happen. Sometimes it never did. I always figured there must to be a better way to get information like this for a story. Only I never figured it out.

Two hours later, Victor Granville came out of the building, walked to a car parked on the street and got inside. Then he drove away. I started up my car and followed him. He drove out of Manhattan, over the Willis Avenue Bridge and onto the Bruckner Expressway. I followed him for about ten minutes or so until he turned off at the exit for Orchard Beach, which is an ocean boardwalk and park in the Bronx. He parked his car in the lot, then walked down to the boardwalk. I watched from a distance as he stood there for awhile looking out at the water. Then a woman walked up and began talking with him.

She looked young and very pretty, probably still in her twenties. They talked for maybe ten minutes or so. Then she walked away down the boardwalk. He went in the opposite direction, headed back toward me and his car. I looked at the woman one more time as she left, trying to decide what to do. I decided it was time to introduce myself to Granville.

'You're Victor Granville, right?' I said when I stopped him on the boardwalk.

'Who are you?'

'My name's Joe Dougherty. I'm a reporter with the *New York Banner*.'

He looked like he was going to have a heart attack.

'Let's talk about Connie Reyes,' I said.

'Who sent you here?' I asked Granville.

'I can't tell you that.'

We were walking alongside the ocean on the beach, comparing notes about the case. Or at least I was. He didn't want to talk much. I had a hunch though who he might be working for. John Montero. Montero had a lot of money. Why wouldn't he hire his own private investigator to try to find the witness who might be able clear his daughter of murder charges? It made a lot of sense.

'Was it John Montero?' I asked.

Granville laughed. 'No way,' he said.

I was confused. 'It's got to be Montero. There's only two people I can think of that would want to talk to this woman as a witness. Either Montero or the authorities. Someone like Greg Ackerman or . . .'

Granville gave me a look of surprise. I suddenly realized what I'd just said.

'You're working for Ackerman?'

He nodded.

Jesus Christ!

'Why you? Why wouldn't he just send one of the investigators from his own office?'

'I don't know,' Granville said. 'He came to see me himself at my office. I thought that was kind of strange too, but as long as he paid I didn't care. Anyway, he told me he'd gotten a tip that a witness to a big murder was hiding out here in the Bronx. He said he'd gotten some anonymous notes in the mail, and he needed to check them out. He hired me to come out here and try to find her. He said he wanted it all done quietly.'

'And you did find her?'

'Yes.'

The woman on the boardwalk.

'What did she say?'

'She said she was working for an escort agency. This guy Franze called up and asked for a girl to be sent over. So she went. She says she was in the bathroom when all the shooting started. She hid in there and saw the whole thing. She says it wasn't Lisa Montero that did it. It was some guy. She doesn't know who . . .'

'And you told all that to Ackerman?' I asked.

Granville nodded. 'He asked me if she planned to come back to tell her story. I told him she said she wouldn't. She was too scared. She didn't want to get involved.'

'What did Ackerman say when you told him that?'

'He said I'd done a good job,' Granville said.

I stared out at the blue-green expanse of the ocean in front of me and tried to make sense out of everything he had just told me. Greg Ackerman, the assistant district attorney in charge of the

Franze murder case, knew the location of a key witness who could exonerate Lisa Montero. But he was keeping it a secret. Why? Well, it had to be for one of two reasons: 1) he'd do anything in his zeal to hurt the Montero family, even send an innocent woman to prison or 2) he had something of his own to hide. Maybe it was even both.

'I want to talk to the Reyes woman,' I said.

'She won't testify. I told you that.'

'She doesn't have to.'

Granville was confused.

'Look, all I need to do is write a story about it,' I explained to him. 'I won't use her name or say where she is. I'll just identify her as a confidential source. Do you think she'll go for that?'

'Maybe.'

'Help me convince her.'

Granville shook his head. 'I don't think so. I don't know what's going on here, but I don't want to get involved.'

'You're already involved,' I said.

'You've got to promise to keep me out of it too – just like with Connie Reyes.'

'Okay.'

'Because if Ackerman finds out it came from me, I could lose my license.'

'All I care about is Connie Reyes saying that Lisa Montero didn't murder anybody,' I said.

thirty six

• • • • • • • • • • •

'Andy, I think I've found the missing witness,' I told him when I got back to the office.

'You mean the woman Lisa Montero says she saw on the night of the murders?'

'Yes. I've just been in the Bronx with someone who has talked to her. He's going to take me to see her. He's setting up the meeting now.'

'What does she say?'

I looked down at the notes I'd made from my conversation with Granville.

'That she was at William Franze's house. She was the second hooker that had been hired for the night. She was hiding in the bathroom during the shooting. She saw who killed Franze and the girl. And she says it wasn't Lisa Montero.'

I told him how reluctant she was to testify. How I couldn't put her name in the story. About making the deal to use her only as a confidential source.

I also told him how Greg Ackerman had this same information, but was trying to cover it up so it wouldn't jeopardize his case against Lisa.

'Jesus,' Andy said, 'this is really hot. Are you sure this woman is for real?'

'I think so. But I know one way to check for sure.'

'How?'

'There are two bathrooms in William Franze's townhouse. One downstairs and one upstairs next to the bedroom where he died. The upstairs toilet was broken on the day Franze died. Ackerman told me that. He said Franze had spent all day trying to reach a plumber. All I have to do is ask her which bathroom she was in while the shooting was going on. If she was in the bedroom, the obvious place for her to go was the upstairs bathroom. Except, that one was broken. She couldn't have used it. She would have had to go downstairs.'

'And if Connie Reyes gives you the right answer to that question, then we've got our story,' Andy said.

Andy had some news for me too.

'Richmond wants to talk to you,' he said.

'Old man Richmond? The publisher?'

'His son Jimmy.'

I rememembered what Bonnie had told me about Richmond's son taking over most of his duties.

'Why does he want to see me?' I asked.

'Jimmy likes to know his reporters.'

'But I . . .'

'We've been talking about bringing you back full time, Joe. Between you and me, I think if you pull this story off . . . well, it's a cinch we'll make you a big offer. That is, if you're interested.'

I said I was interested.

'So go meet Jimmy,' Andy smiled. 'You'll like him. Everybody likes Jimmy.'

I really wanted to like Jimmy Richmond. Honest. Especially because he seemed to be trying so hard to be likeable. His whole office had a real homey feel to it. Pictures of him on on the wall playing softball at a company picnic. Another of him on a sailboat with his family; a fresh-faced, wholesome looking woman and three young children who smiled for the camera. There were a lot of trophies too, for bowling and tennis and golf tournaments. And I saw the diploma from the Columbia School of Journalism. The one Bonnie had told me about.

'Do you play golf, Joe?' Richmond asked, noticing me looking at one of the trophies.

'Not really, Mr Richmond.'

'Call me Jimmy.' He smiled at me.

I smiled back.

Friendly.

'Sure, Jimmy,' I said. 'I used to play a long time ago. But I haven't had a club in my hand in years.'

'You should take it up again. We could go out to my course together sometime. I play with Andy Kramer. Jack Rollins too. If you joined us, it would be a fun foursome.'

'I don't think Jack Rollins wants to play golf with me,' I said.

'Oh, I know you and Jack had a bit of a tiff in Spencer's office the other day. But don't worry about that. You keep doing Page One stories like you've been doing, and you can fight with anyone you want.'

He smiled again. I wasn't sure exactly what to make of Jimmy Richmond. I'd met guys like him before. They seemed like your best friend at first, but then they turned into the Boss from Hell when you least expected it. I wondered if Jimmy Richmond was like that. I know he sure caught me off guard with his next question.

'Did you sleep with her?' Richmond asked.

'Who?'

'Lisa Montero.'

'I – I don't understand . . .'

'Did you sleep with her?' he asked. He wasn't smiling anymore. 'Did you nail her? Did you do the dirty deed with her? Did you bang her like an out-house door in a thunderstorm? Did you play hide the salami under the silken sheets in her penthouse? Am I making myself clear now, Joe?'

'Yes,' I said slowly, 'very clear.'

'So? Did you?'

'No,' I told him, 'I didn't sleep with Lisa Montero.'

He stared at me for a second. I wasn't sure what was going to happen next. But all he did then was laugh. 'Why not?' he told me. 'I sure would have. She is one fine piece of woman.'

I thought about his wholesome-faced wife and their three smiling little children.

'I wanted to,' I said. 'She's very beautiful. I was extremely attracted to her. But it would be wrong. I'm a reporter working on a story. A reporter can't get personally involved in the stories he's doing,' I said, invoking the time-honored First Rule of Journalism in my effort to convince him. 'There's nothing more important to me right now than being a reporter again. I would never do anything to jeopardize that.'

Richmond nodded solemly. 'Did she tell you anything?' he asked.

'You mean about the murders?'

'About anything. Her business. Her father. Her personal life. I mean I read the stuff you wrote for the *Banner*. But I just wondered if you left anything out.'

I wasn't sure what he meant, but I told him all about my conversations with her. The stuff on her personal life. Her relationship with her father. Her hopes to take over his business someday. Then he asked me some of the same questions about David Galvin. I went through my interviews with him at the prison hospital.

After that, we made some small talk about people at the paper. Eventually we got around to Andy Kramer and Jack Rollins again.

'I've only been in this job for less than a year,' he was saying. 'I worked on Madison Avenue most of that time – ran my own advertising firm. But my father's health hasn't been so great, and the paper's always been owned by the Richmond family. So I decided to come back and help see us through this transition period. As you know, Spencer is getting very near retirement. The choice of the next editor is very crucial. We're very lucky though. I'm impressed by both Andy Kramer and Jack Rollins. They're fine men, fine leaders, fine journalists. Of course, I haven't been here long enough to get to know Jack as well as I know Andy. Andy and I go way back . . .'

It really shouldn't have been important, but I asked the question anyway. I was curious. Reporters are like that.

'How did you know Andy?' I asked.

'We went to college together.'

A warning bell went off in my head.

'You went to Columbia,' I said, looking over at the diploma on his wall. 'Andy didn't go to Columbia, did he?'

'I only went to graduate school at Columbia,' Richmond said. 'Got a masters in journalism. Figured it might come in handy someday, what with my father owning a newspaper like the *Banner*. But I did my undergraduate work in political science. That's where I met Andy.'

He didn't say what school he'd done his undergraduate work at, but then he didn't have to. I already knew. David Galvin went there. So did Lisa Montero. Andy Kramer. And Greg Ackerman. Now I could add Jimmy Richmond to that list too. Everything and everyone in this story always led back to the same place.

NYU.

I told Bonnie all about the missing witness when I got back to my desk.

She said she had a lead too.

'Do you remember that picture we ran of Arthur Dodson on the front page the day after his car was found on the Tappan Zee Bridge?' she said. 'Well, it got picked up by TV and the wires and sent around the country. We got a call from some woman in a little town called Hillsdale, Pa. She says she thinks she saw him shopping at a store there. She followed him to a local motel. She says she'll show me where it is. I checked the map. I can drive over there in about three hours.'

I made a face. 'It's sounds to me like it's probably going to be a wild goose chase, Bonnie,' I said.

'Me too,' she said. 'If this turns out to be nothing and I miss out on my big date with Brad Pitt tonight, I'm going to be really pissed.'

There were lots of messages waiting for me at my desk and on my voice mail. Mostly from one person. Carolyn. It had been days since I'd called her. At first, it had just slipped my mind because I was so busy. Now, after what happened between Lisa and me, I realized I was consciously avoiding Carolyn. I knew I had to talk to her sooner or later. But I just couldn't bring myself to do it.

The first messages on the voice mail sounded curious, rather than angry. Where was I? Why hadn't I called? Later, she must have thought about it and realized I was avoiding her. On the last few calls she sounded as angry as I had ever heard her. I'd never seen that side of Carolyn before. And I really wasn't prepared to deal with it now.

Anyway, there was no way I had time to call her now.

I had a big story to do.

And the truth is that by the time Granville and I were on our way to meet Connie Reyes, I'd already pretty much forgotten all about Carolyn again.

thirty seven

Up close, Connie Reyes didn't look as good as I thought she did when I first saw her. She was young and attractive, but she looked aged beyond her years. The kind of woman who'd packed a lot of living into her twenty-five years or so. Twenty-five going on fifty is is the way one cop I used to know described women like her. Or sometimes even twenty-five with one foot in the grave.

The three of us – her, me and Granville – were back at the same spot on Orchard Beach, sitting on a bench overlooking the ocean.

'You got my money?' she asked.

'There is no money.'

She gave a puzzled look to Granville. So did I. Obviously he had not told me everything about what he had to promise Connie Reyes to get her to meet with me.

'I can't pay you anything,' I said, turning back to the woman. 'If I pay you money, it would corrupt the validity of your story. People would say that you only told me what I wanted to hear so that you could get paid. Everything you said would then become worthless. I'm sure you understand.'

She didn't.

'If I don't get paid, why should I talk to you?'

'Because it's the right thing to do.'

Connie Reyes didn't say anything.

'Look, Ms Reyes, an innocent woman's life is at stake here. She's charged with murder. Two murders that you know that she didn't commit. All you have to do is tell me the truth. Please. I need your help. So does Lisa Montero.'

I wasn't sure what was going to happen next. It could have gone either way.

'I won't testify in court,' she said.

'I know that.'

'And you can't use my name.'

'I'll write a story quoting you as a secret source. Nothing more. That's a promise.'

'How do I know I can believe you?'

'I'm a newspaperman. We always protect our sources. It's a sacred oath.'

'You mean like a doctor?' she asked.

'Something like that.'

She thought about it for a little while.

'I've got immigration problems,' she said finally.

'I understand.'

'Problems with the law too. I can't get involved.'

'I won't involve you by name,' I said again. 'I don't have to. The First Amendment to the US Constitution protects me. If a reporter writes a story like this using a confidential source, no one can ever force him to give up that source to any court or law enforcement authorities. So you don't have to worry. You're totally covered by the Constitution.'

That wasn't totally true, of course. The right of a reporter to withhold the identity of confidential sources in a court of law is still a matter of great debate. Sometimes reporters go to jail for refusing to divulge who their source is. Most of the time though reporters wind up turning over the name of a source before it ever gets to that point. Not everybody's a hero. And not every source stays as secret as Deep Throat. But I didn't tell Connie Reyes any of that. The bottom line was I had no intention of telling anyone who she was.

She took a deep breath. 'Okay, let's go,' she said.

The story was pretty much the same one Granville had told me. It totally cleared Lisa Montero. She said the killer was a man. She said she'd never seen him before, but might recognize him again now.

I went over all the details with her several times. Then it was time for the final question. The one about the bathroom.

'I'm thirsty,' she said suddenly, just as I was about to ask her. She looked over at a guy selling soft drinks not far from where we were sitting. 'Do you guys want something?'

We both said yes. I gave her some money, and she walked over to the vendor's cart.

'You believe her story, right?' I said, turning to Granville after she was out of earshot.

'Sure. Why would she lie?'

'Well, I've got to make sure she's telling the truth.'

'How are you going to do that?'

'I'm going to ask her something. Something she could only know if she was in William Franze's townhouse on the night of the murders. If she gives me the right answer, then we'll be sure.'

I looked over toward the soft drink vendor to see if she was headed back yet.

She wasn't there.

I looked all around the beach.

Connie Reyes was nowhere to be found.

She was gone.

Andy was holding Page One for my story.

'Did you get it?' he asked eagerly, when I called him.

'Something happened, Andy,' I said.

'Did you meet the girl?'

'Yes.'

'And she told you all about seeing someone else – not Lisa Montero – kill Franze and the other prostitute, right?'

'That's right. She said it was a man who did it. Not Lisa.'

'All right!' he shouted. 'You got it, Joe. The story of a lifetime. I told Rollins about all it and I told Spencer Blackwood too. We're holding Page One. Now you did confirm it, right? You asked the Reyes woman the question about the broken bathroom? And she gave you the proof we needed to know that she's totally on the level?'

I thought about what to do now.

I knew what I was supposed to do. I was supposed to tell Andy everything. I was supposed to tell him that my exclusive source had taken a powder before I could ask her the crucial question. I was supposed to tell him I didn't have enough yet to go with the story. That's what I was supposed to do. But I wasn't sure if it was what I should do.

I thought about the Walter Billings case too.

I hadn't told Lisa everything about that story.

I'd never told anyone.

You see, at some point after Billings killed himself and I got fired from the paper, I decided I needed to find out for myself what really happened between him and that young blonde girl. Sure, Jack Rollins went with the story too soon, he should have held it until I checked it out more. But I always believed the story. Even after everything that happened. I never bought the line about Billings trying to convert the girl and help her find religion. I still thought he brought her to that hotel to have sex with her.

Of course, I never knew that for sure.

Until I found the girl.

Her name was Judy Pearson. I tracked her down about six months later at a restaurant on the Jersey Shore where she was working as a cocktail waitress. I bought her some drinks when she got off work and – after she got kind of drunk – she admitted to me that Billings tried to have sex with her. She said his people had paid her afterwards to back up his version of the events that night. She'd gone through most of the money. But there was no way, she said, that she would ever go public now with the real story. She was going out with a rich lawyer from a prominent local family, and a scandal might ruin everything before she could marry him. Besides, she was worried about getting in trouble with the law for perjury. No, she decided, there was no percentage for her in telling the truth just to help me. It didn't matter anyway. I wasn't sure that anyone would believe her now anyway if she changed her story after all this time.

But I believed her.

I was convinced my story was right.

That was important to me.

There's a line in *All the President's Men* where a journalist talks about being criticized for messing up a story. 'Everybody says to me, "you fucked up, you got it wrong,"' he says. 'Well, I fucked up all right, but I didn't get it wrong.'

That's the way I felt too.

My instincts on the Billings story were right. Tbey were right about Nancy Kelleher too. And now my instincts were crying out to me that Lisa Montero was innocent, that she was being set up by someone.

Only if I played this one by the rules I couldn't help her.

There's all sorts of people in this world. The ones who always play it safe. The conservative risk-takers. The middle-of-the-roaders, who'll sometimes take a chance and see how it turns out. And then there's the gamblers. The people who just can't say no to any chance for a big score. No matter what the risk.

Me, I always was a gambler.

So at that moment I decided to take the biggest gamble of my life.

'Joe, you do have the story, don't you?' Andy Kramer was saying impatiently over the phone.

'Yes,' I told him. 'I've got it all.'

He put me on with a rewriteman and I began to dictate my story into the phone:

> A secret witness has been found who backs up Lisa Montero's claim that she is innocent of the murders of William Franze and Whitney Martin.
>
> The witness – whose identity is being withheld by the *Banner* – told this reporter in an exclusive interview . . .

Another defining moment.

thirty eight

• • • • • • • • • • •

The judge presiding over Lisa's pre-trial hearing was Robert Maddox. He sat behind a desk in his chambers now, reading the front page of the *New York Banner*. My story. There was a big headline that said: 'EXCLUSIVE: SECRET WITNESS SAYS LISA MONTERO DIDN'T DO IT!' Judge Maddox did not look happy.

'Everybody read the paper this morning?' he asked.

I was there. So was Greg Ackerman. He did not look happy either. But Lisa's lawyer did. He was smiling broadly. His name was Michael Conroy and he was about forty, with blond hair and good lucks that made him look a little like a younger Robert Redford. Conroy was from one of the prestigious Park Avenue law firms in the city. John Montero had spared no expense to defend his daughter. But then you didn't have to be Perry Mason to figure out that I had blasted a rather large hole in the prosecution's case.

'Yes,' said Conroy, answering Maddox's question.

'I read it,' Ackerman told the judge.

'Helluva story, isn't it?' Maddox asked.

He turned toward Ackerman. 'You realize, of course, that if what Mr Dougherty here has written is true, then it raises serious questions about the validity of your prosecution.'

'I'm going to move for a dismissal of all charges against my client,' Conroy said quickly.

'This is all lies,' Ackerman said, gesturing toward my story. 'The whole thing is based on the account of a single source. An unnamed source. I demand to know – and this court has a right to know – who that source is.'

Everyone looked at me.

'Who is your source, Mr Dougherty?' Judge Maddox asked.

'I can't tell you that.'

'Why not?'

'Because, as a reporter, I claim a First Amendment right to protect the identity of my confidential sources.'

That was my out in this whole business. My safety net. My get out of jail free card.

All I had to do was scream 'freedom of the press' and I could keep my big secret about Connie Reyes. No one would ever find out what really happened when I talked to her. Not the judge. Not Greg Ackerman. Not the police. None of them would ever even know Connie Reyes' name, unless I gave it to them. And I wasn't going to do that. So the police could never go back and check out the details of my story. She was my confidential source. Just like Deep Throat. It was beautiful.

Of course, I believed I was doing the right thing. I mean I knew that Connie Reyes' story was true. I knew that because I knew Lisa Montero was innocent.

Judge Maddox looked wearily now over at Greg Ackerman.

'Well, Counselor, it seems to be that we're at an impasse here. Does the District Attorney's office have any ideas on how it wishes to proceed on this matter?'

'Yes,' Ackerman said. 'We request that you order this reporter to reveal the identity of his confidential source in open court – or else face contempt of court charges.'

'I refuse,' I told him.

* * *

Lisa and I walked through Central Park, then sat by the lake holding hands.

'What's going to happen now?' she asked, as she watched the people out on the lake on boats.

'The judge will have to make a ruling on whether or not I have to give up my source.'

'What if he says you do?'

'I won't.'

'You mean you'll go to jail for me.'

'If I have to.'

She squeezed my hand. 'How romantic.'

'But if Judge Maddox rules in my favor, Ackerman's whole case against you falls apart. And then you and I can be together and get married and live happily ever after.'

I leaned over and kissed her.

'I love you, Lisa.'

'Wow!' she laughed. 'Like I said that first night we met, you get right to the point, don't you?'

'I still like to put the lead in the first paragraph,' I said.

The next day Judge Maddox issued his ruling from the bench.

'A very delicate balance exists between the workings of the government and the press' right to keep the public informed,' he said. 'It's not always an easy decision to determine which is most important in any particular case. That's the situation here.

'Therefore, I'm not going to take any contempt action against Joseph Dougherty for refusing to reveal his source.'

Maddox also said that – based on the new evidence that had emerged in the case – he was granting the defense motion for a dismissal of both of the murder charges against Lisa Montero.

She was a free woman.

I'll never forget making love to Lisa that night.

It was like something had been released from deep inside her. She was wild, she was passionate, she practically devoured me with her heat. As I held her tight, as we moved together as one, as I buried my face in her long, black hair, I realized this was what I had been waiting for ever since Susan had died.

It had been an incredible day.

My story, of course, was Page One of the *Banner*:

MONTERO MURDER
CHARGES DROPPED!

Crusading *Banner* Reporter's
Story Breaks Case Wide Open

District Attorney's Office
Now Under Heavy Fire
In Wake of Dismissal

I'd been interviewed by everybody. *People* magazine. *USA Today*. The Associated Press. The local TV shows. Some of the networks too. Larry King wanted me, so did Geraldo – even Jane Pauley had called. Everybody was talking about me.

There was a picture that went out over the wires which showed me kissing Lisa moments after the charges against her were dropped. It had happened spontaneously. I was standing there, she ran over to me – and all the emotions I'd been holding in for so long suddenly came spilling out. So I kissed her. Right in front of all the other reporters and photographers and TV cameras. I didn't even care anymore if anyone knew about us. I didn't care about anything except Lisa.

'I can't believe it's finally over,' she said to me now as we lay in bed together.

'It's not,' I told her.

'What do you mean?'

'The real killer is still out there,' I reminded her. 'Now that everyone knows you didn't kill Franze, I still have to find out who did. Whoever that is probably is responsible for the deaths of all those other people on David Galvin's hit list. That story hasn't been told yet. I want to be the one who breaks it.'

Lisa looked worried.

'Maybe you should just walk away from it right now,' she said thoughtfully.

'Why would I do that?'

'It could be dangerous for you.'

'I'm not worried.'

'Well, maybe you should be.'

'Lisa, this is my job.'

'So get another job,' she said.

I wanted to tell Lisa about all the reasons I couldn't walk away from it. About how this was more than just another story for me. About Susan and Joe Jr. About how they died. And about how I needed to find the answer to what happened to them before I could ever hope to get on with living the rest of my own life. But I didn't say any of those things to her that night. It just didn't seem like the right time.

'So let's just forget about Felix the Cat or whatever his stupid name was,' Lisa was saying.

'I can't do that.'

'Bet I can make you forget,' she said.

And she was right too.

She kissed me on the lips. And I suddenly realized I was ready to make love again. Then I was lost in her perfume and her hair and the softness of her body. Everything else – David Galvin, my career at the *Banner*, even Susan and Joe Jr, – they all seemed very far away when I was in her arms.

Later, as I was drifting off to sleep, I heard Lisa get up and go into the next room. I lay there for awhile and waited for her to come back. When she didn't right away, I got up to see where she'd gone. I saw her sitting in her nightgown and a robe at a table. She was talking on the telephone.

'I don't want to do that,' she said into the phone.

I wondered who in the world she could be talking to at this hour of the morning.

'But, Dad . . .'

Her father?

'No, he's asleep in the other room,' she said.

I realized Lisa didn't know I was there. I moved back against the wall to make sure she didn't see me. I wasn't sure why I did, or even why I was listening to her conversation. It probably had nothing to do with me. I guess I was just curious.

'Yeah, I know,' Lisa was saying. 'I'll take care of it.'

Her face looked very grim.

'I said I'd take care of it,' she said impatiently.

Then she slammed the phone down.

I hurried back under the covers before she came into the bedroom. She started taking off her nightgown and robe next to the bed. I pretended that she had just woken me up.

'Where'd you go?' I asked sleepily.

'I had to make a phone call,' she said.

'To who?'

'It's not important.'

Lisa crawled into bed again. She was wearing only a skimpy pair of bikini panties now. God, she was so beautiful. She snuggled up close next to me, put her arms around me and rested her head gently on my chest. She looked up at me and smiled.

'Is everything all right?' I asked her.

'Everything's great,' she said.

That was the last really good time I remember with her.

Before everything started to go wrong . . .

thirty nine

• • • • • • • • • • •

I've always had a lot of trouble saying goodbye.

'You seem to have this need to hang onto something long after it's finished,' a psychiatrist once told me during the dark days of depression after my firing, Susan and my son Joe's death and my gambling problems. 'You're never willing to let go. You know, there comes a time when you have to just move on, turn the page and jump-start your life. But you don't want to do this. You prefer to live in the past. You fantasize that somehow things will go back to being the way they used to be. Or at least the way you remember them. That's your problem, Joe. Are you going to do something about it?'

I guess my parents had a lot to do with that.

Like I said earlier, when I was growing up, my father and mother fell out of love very quickly. My memories of childhood mostly consist of the two of them arguing and yelling and slamming doors all over our house. But they never got divorced. They stayed together because of me, my father told me once a long time later. The family is the most important thing, a boy needs two parents – blah, blah, blah. But I don't think that was the reason at all.

I think my father was just one of those people who could never admit he'd made a mistake. He didn't know how to say goodbye either. To just get up and walk away from the table when life dealt you a bad hand.

I guess I inherited that from him.

For a long time after my wife and son were gone, I couldn't say goodbye to them. I went to the funeral. I accepted people's condolences. I grieved for them. I cried for them. But I still didn't accept the fact that Susan and Joe were really dead.

On the night before they died, we'd gone out to dinner together at a seafood place near the ocean. All three of us. It was the first time we'd ever taken Joey anywhere like a restaurant. Susan drank Bombays and tonics, I had beer and Joey some milk. Over dinner, Susan and I talked about us and about our future. Of course, I had no idea at the time that it would be the last night we would ever spend together.

It was six months later that I finally got myself together enough to say goodbye to them – in my own way.

I went back to the same restaurant where we'd eaten that last night. I reserved a table for three – and sat in the same place, ordered the same drinks and the same meal we'd eaten together. Three drinks, three places. But just me, sitting there alone at the table. Of course, it was a very painful experience. The waiters and some of the other people in the restaurant thought I was crazy. But I didn't care. What really hurt was sitting there staring at those empty places across the table.

That's when finally I realized they were never coming back. They were gone forever. It was time for me to get on with my own life and put the the two of them behind me. That's what I did too.

Until David Galvin.

Now I had to call Carolyn to tell her it was over.

I had no choice.

On the day after the charges against Lisa were dropped, the picture of me kissing her appeared on the front pages of newspapers around the country. Carolyn didn't try to call me again. She simply packed up all my stuff and had it delivered to my hotel. I found it piled up in the lobby when I got back from work.

'Do you want this all delivered up to your room?' the guy behind the front desk asked me.

'I don't think I'm going to be here much longer,' I said. 'Can you keep it in storage for me?'

'No problem. Are you moving back to New Jersey?'

'No, I'm staying in New York.'

I figured I'd get my own apartment in Manhattan for the time being. Until Lisa and I moved in together. I had it all figured out. Except for what to do about Carolyn. I knew I had to talk to her one more time, but I was really dreading doing it. It turned out to be worse than I expected.

'I'm sorry,' I said when she came on the line. 'I know you deserve better. But things happen.'

There was a long silence on the other end.

'That's it?' she said finally.

'What do you mean?'

'I'm sorry? Things happen? That's the best you can do? I mean you can shovel the bullshit with the best of them, Joe. I really expected something more eloquent than that. Go ahead, try again. Say anything. It doesn't have to be true. Make it up. Like you did with that story the time you got fired. You're good at making stuff up, Joe.'

'Look, I know you're very hurt . . .'

'Don't flatter yourself. You're the one who's hurt, Joe. You've fucked up big time. Again. I gave you a life, a life you'd thrown away a long time ago. And now you're doing the same thing you did before. Do you really believe your rich girl friend is going to think you're so great once she doesn't need you anymore? I don't think so.'

'Lisa and I are in love,' I told her.

'You don't know what love is,' she said.

I didn't say anything.

'Let me ask you one question, hotshot. This story you did – the one that got Lisa Montero off the hook? Is it true?'

Carolyn was just flailing away in anger at me, of course. She didn't know anything. But it did make me uncomfortable.

'Of course it's true.'

'Really? Because you know what I think, Joe? I think the bitch really did do those murders.'

'Lisa Montero is innocent,' I said.

'And how do you know that? Did she tell you? While you were in bed together?'

'I knew, Carolyn. I always knew. I had a gut feeling about her right from the very start.'

'Yeah, well you once told me you had a gut feeling about us,' she said. 'You were wrong about that too.'

forty

Another big story was breaking.

'Arthur Dodson is dead,' Andy said. 'Shot to death in a hotel in Pennsylvania. The killer dressed the body up in a clown suit, then painted a smile on his face with makeup. It was a really weird scene. We're breaking the exclusive today on Page One.'

I remembered Bonnie going to a little town in Pennsylvania to check out the tip on him.

'Bonnie found Dodson's body?' I asked.

'Yeah.'

'Is she okay?'

'She's fine. She's the one who called the police. It was a big scoop for her.'

Good for Bonnie.

She told me the whole story herself later.

'It was friggin' unbelievable,' she said. 'Christ, I almost peed in my pants.

'I'm mean I'm standing there knocking on this motel room door, figuring the whole trip to Hilldale is going to be one big waste of time. The damned door will open up and I'll be face to face with an appliance salesman, or a guy from Nebraska on his vacation, or maybe just some local yahoo who's bedding down his secretary at the town's hot sheets palace. He'll ask me what I want. I'll say I'm looking for a missing person on a serial killer's hit list. He'll tell me to fuck off, slam the door shut in my face and I'll have to make the long trip back to New York City feeling really stupid.'

She took a deep breath. 'Only it didn't happen that way. There was no answer when I knocked. But somebody's car was parked in front of the door. Of course, it could have been anybody's car. The manager of the motel's. Another guest. But I had a really bad feeling about it. So I decided to let myself in.'

'How did you do that?'

'I used a credit card in my purse to pop open the lock on the door.'

I must have looked surprised.

'I learned how to do that once when I interviewed a professional burglar for a series I was doing on home security,' she explained. 'It's actually kinda easy. Although some credit cards do work better than others. They tell me it has something to do with the size of the plastic.'

'Which one did you use?'

I was just curious.

'American Express,' she smiled. 'Never leave home without it.'

I shook my head. 'The killer could have still been inside the room, Bonnie. You could have been the next victim.'

'Yeah, and the depleted ozone layer is killing me a little bit every day too. So what?

'Anyway, I see Dodson the minute I get inside. He looks like fuckin' Bozo the Clown. All done up in clown makeup and a clown suit. And he's tied down to the bed; his hands and feet bound are bound with really heavy rope and there's a gag in his mouth. It looked like he'd been like that for awhile. There was a bag from McDonald's next to him and a lot of empty hamburger wrappers. I don't know if Dodson's captor was feeding him to keep him alive or feeding himself while he did the dirty deed.

'And then there was the blood. Lots of blood. Blood all over the place. Christ, I'd hate to have to be the maid who cleaned up that room. The place would be a real challenge for Martha Stewart.'

The Dodson murder bothered me. That's why I had started pumping Bonnie for information on it as soon as I was back in the *Banner* office. How did the killer ever manage to track Arthur Dodson down to a little motel in Hilldale, Pa?

'I found him,' Bonnie pointed out.

'You got a tip.'

'Maybe the killer did too.'

'That seems like an awfully big coincidence.'

I suddenly had another thought.

'What if the killer was the one who called you?' I said.

'Why do that?'

'Why not? Felix the Cat liked publicity. This one seems to too. Look at the two new victims – the Hiller woman dressed up in a bridal gown store's window and Dodson made up to look like a clown. I don't know what the significance is. But the killer's crying for our attention. What better way to get it than to call up a reporter and lead her to the crime scene?'

'Jesus, I never thought of that.'

'You took the call from the anonymous tipster yourself, right?'

'Yes.'

'Do you remember what his voice sounded like?'

'Hers.'

'Hers?'

'Yeah. It was a woman.'

'Okay, do you remember anything about her voice?'

'It was a 20-second call, Joe. I didn't tape it or use a lie detector or do a stress analysis test on it. I get a million calls a day. I didn't know there was going to be anything special about this one.'

'Would you remember the voice if you heard it again?'

'I don't know. Maybe. I'm not sure.'

There was one other big question we didn't have the answer for either, of course. Why? Why did someone want the two of them – Linda Hiller and Arthur Dodson – dead?

'Look, I know you've probably thought about this a lot, but here's my theory,' Bonnie said.

'There were four Great Pretenders, according to Galvin. Him

and three others. Arthur Dodson and Linda Hiller went to NYU at the same time as Galvin. What if they were in The Great Pretenders? That leaves one. One Great Pretender who's trying to cover his – or her – trail. Cleaning up all the loose ends.'

'Yeah, I thought of that too,' I said.

'The question is who?'

'Someone who has a lot to lose,' I said.

forty one

It took me a long time to realize that Lisa Montero seemed to be avoiding me. At first, I thought I just kept missing her. I'd leave a message on her machine and not get any answer. So I'd call back a little later. Still nothing. I tried her place in the city, her office on Wall Street and her father's house. Sometimes I checked in with the operator at the *Banner* maybe a dozen times an hour to see if there had been any calls from Lisa that I'd missed. There never was. It was as if she had disappeared off the face of the earth.

Except she hadn't.

She was a real celebrity now, and a lot of people saw her around town. At Elaine's. LeCirque. Madison Square Garden. The hot clubs in town. Lisa was back in the fast life again, traveling in the same circles, running with the same crowd.

But where was I? I was on the outside looking in. I finally admitted that to myself about a week after the murder charges against Lisa were dropped – and there was still no sign of her.

'Any messages for me?' I asked one of the secretaries as I sat down at my desk in the *Banner* office.

She nodded toward a stack of memos in front of me. A lot of people wanted me for interviews or TV shows or to have lunch with me. 'You're a very popular guy,' she said.

I skimmed through them quickly.

'Nothing from Lisa Montero?' I asked her.

'No.'

'Are you sure?'

'I know how to answer the telephone, Joe.'

Bonnie gave me a funny look from the next desk after the secretary walked away.

'What's going on with you and the Montero woman anyway?' she asked. 'I thought you two were really tight.'

'We are.'

'Then why the long face?'

'I haven't heard from her in a day or two.'

'Maybe she's busy.'

'Yeah,' I said sarcastically.

'Exactly how many days are we talking about here, Joe?'

'Well, actually it's been a week.'

'Uh-oh,' Bonnie said.

Bonnie was right. Uh-oh. Something was definitely wrong. I needed to find out why.

So I went looking for Lisa. I tried everywhere. Her place. Her father's house. Both of their offices. All of her usual hangouts. I finally found her at the same place I did the first time. Elaine's. She was sitting at the same corner table in the front of the restaurant. There was a tall, good-looking blond haired guy with her. I didn't recognize him at first. Then I realized it was Michael Conroy, her lawyer. He had his arm around her and her head was resting on his shoulder. They didn't look like they were having a legal discussion.

I walked over to their table.

'Joe, what are you doing here?' Lisa asked.

'I've been looking for you.'

'Yeah, I know,' she said casually.

Conroy shook my hand. 'Listen, I want to thank you for that article,' he said. 'You saved her. It's all because of you she's not in jail.'

'I'm a newspaperman,' I said. 'I was just doing my job.'

Lisa rolled her eyes.

'For chrissakes, give it a rest, Joe,' she said. 'This whole Clark Kent routine of yours is really getting boring.'

I pulled Lisa away from Conroy and walked her over toward the bar. She was holding a drink in her hand. She swayed a bit as she stood there next to me and she had a glazed sort of look in her eyes. I realized she was probably drunk. I didn't want to talk to her when she was like this. But I had to. I didn't know when I might get another chance.

'You haven't returned any of my calls,' I told her.

'Gee, you're a bright boy.'

'Why?'

'Didn't feel like it,' she giggled.

She took a big gulp of her drink.

I grabbed Lisa by the shoulders and pulled her close to me, looking right into her eyes. For just a second, I thought I connected with her. I saw something there. A spark, a hint, a sign of the old Lisa. But then I saw something else too. Sadness.

'What did you think was going to happen between us, Joe?' she asked softly.

'I – I don't know . . . I thought we'd be together.'

She shook her head. 'Go back to your girlfriend in New Jersey, Joe. Marry her. Start a family. Live happily ever after – or whatever the fuck people do in New Jersey. You and me, we had a good time. We had some laughs. Now it's over.'

I didn't know what to say.

'I love you, Lisa,' I said impulsively.

She didn't answer me.

'The appropriate response is, "I love you too,"' I told her.

'Sorry.'

'But you said . . .'

'I'm fickle,' she shrugged.

Conroy came over now to bring her back to their table. I stood there helplessly, trying my best to think of something to do. Something to say. Something to make things go back to the way they were a week ago. So I decided to tell her the truth.

About what really happened that day in the Bronx with Connie Reyes.

About how I had stopped being a reporter and became a part of the story.

About what I had sacrificed for her.

'Lisa, there's something you don't know about that witness I found,' I called out to her. 'I didn't tell you everything about her. There were some problems . . .'

'Who cares?'

'It's important.'

'Not any more.'

She turned around and came back to me at the bar.

'You know, Joe, you really do need to lighten up about all this,' she said. 'You take all this newspaper crap much too seriously.'

Then she leaned over and gave me a kiss. It was a tiny peck on the cheek, which only lasted for a second or two. A perfunctory kiss. A decidedly unpassionate kiss. A goodbye kiss.

'The story's over, Joe,' she said.

forty two

• • • • • • • • • • •

'She dumped you?' Bonnie said.

'I wouldn't say dumped . . .'

'Let's recap here. Lisa Montero won't go out with you. She won't answer your phone calls. And the last time you saw her she was hanging onto another man's arm and told you – I believe this is a fairly accurate quote – "I'm sorry. I'm just fickle." Right?'

'Well, yeah. But . . .'

'That, my friend, is dumped.'

We were sitting on the floor of Bonnie's apartment, which was on West 12th Street in Greenwich Village near Sheridan Square. There was very little furniture in the place. Just a lot of books, stacks of newspapers, and posters of New York City and famous movies on the walls. There were also some sort of psychedelic lights that kept flashing off and on, which gave everything an eerie look. Bonnie's place was a lot like Bonnie. Funky, unpredictable, a little weird – but always interesting. It reminded me of the way I used to live when I was in college.

I'd told her what happened while she was driving me back to the hotel the next day after work. I needed to talk to somebody. Bonnie didn't seem very surprised when I told her about the encounter at Elaine's. But she decided I shouldn't be alone right now.

So there I was, sitting on her floor and smoking some marijuana with her, while we discussed my love life.

'Sorry about the way the apartment looks, but my decorator didn't show up today,' Bonnie said. 'As you can probably tell, I'm not exactly cut out to be a homemaker. I never seem to have time to worry about buying furniture and wallpaper and stuff like that. It might be some sort of serious character flaw on my part.'

She took a toke on her joint. 'This is one of my other vices,' she said, looking down at it. 'I know Nancy Reagan probably wouldn't approve. But I find it really helps me relax after a hard day at the office. Otherwise, I get sort of hyper and stressed out and start doing stuff at 100 mph. I mean I'm still hyper and stressed out. But I think it slows me down a bit.'

'Bonnie, you are a remarkable individual,' I told her.

'Yeah,' she shrugged, 'everybody tells me that.'

'Where are you from anyway?'

'The Midwest.'

'Ohio? Where you went to school.'

'Yeah.'

'You still got family back there?'

'No. My father died when I was young. My mother a few years after that. There were no brothers and sisters. I got raised by my grandmother. But she's dead now too. I've been on my own for awhile. How about you?'

'My mother and father are gone too. They got divorced, but not soon enough. I don't think they were ever very happy together.'

'Jeez, maybe that's why we're both so screwed up,' she said.

'Who said I was screwed up?' I asked her.

'You? C'mon!'

'What do you mean?'

'You've got a real act going for you there, Dougherty. That sincere face, those puppy dog eyes – a real sensitive, '90s kind of guy look. Except you dumped that woman in Jersey the minute

Lisa Montero batted an eyelash at you. And I don't think that's the first time it's happened either.'

'I don't know what you're talking about, Bonnie.'

'Sure you do. You know, I've been thinking about that whole story you told me one day in the car about gambling away all your severance money after you got fired. The way I figure it that was eight years ago. Your wife died sometime after that. So what in the hell were you doing in Atlantic City and Las Vegas with some bimbo blackjack dealer when you had this loving wife and this baby son back home? It kinda blows a hole in the whole grieving widower rap you like to use sometimes. You know what I mean?'

I nodded. She was right, of course.

'Anyway, I was curious. So I looked up the story of your wife and son's deaths in the clips. There was an article that said they died in a boating accident off the coast of Long Island, near Sag Harbor. You were in the boat too. You said you swam for shore to try to get help. But when the Coast Guard got to the scene, it was too late. They were already gone.

'That's what you told the cops anyway. But they had some questions about your story. It turns out that people at the house in Sag Harbor where you were staying had heard you and your wife having a big argument the night before. Some other people said she'd told them she was planning on taking the kid and leaving you. That made the cops suspicious. They began to wonder if it was really an accident, after all.

'They questioned you all night. For twelve hours or so, you were a suspect in a possible murder. Only no one could break your story. In the end, they just declared it an accident. Since then, you like to tell everybody about this wonderful marriage and wonderful family you tragically lost. Only it wasn't so wonderful. Am I right or am I right?'

I shook my head. 'Like you always say, Bonnie, you're a helluva reporter.'

I took a long toke on the joint in my hand. It was all coming back to me now. All the pain. The anger. The terror. And the questions too. The questions that I still didn't have the answers for. Not even after all this time.

No, it wasn't always so wonderful for Susan and me. I remembered the time I came home from work early one day. I never came home early. A lot of the time I didn't even come home. But I didn't have any big story to work on and I guess I was feeling guilty about the lack of time I spent with her. She was pretty much raising Joey on her own, with me as more of a drop-in visitor than a dutiful husband and father. So I decided to make this night special. I'd surprise her. We'd get a sitter for Joey, then we'd go out on the town and have a good time like the old days. She'd drink her Bombay and tonics, smoke her Marlboros and then we'd come home and make mad, passionate love just the way we used to.

But Susan wasn't home when I got there.

By the time she finally did come home, I'd worked myself up into a real state of anxiety. And I got another surprise when she walked in the door. She was all dressed up. She had on a short dress with a slit up the side, a sexy blouse, and her hair and makeup were done up like I hadn't seen her do for me for a long time. That made me mad.

'Where have you been?' I asked her.

'Out.'

'That covers a lot of territory.'

'Well, you should know,' she said.

'What's that supposed to mean?'

'I just think it's pretty funny that you're asking ME where I've been. You're the one that's never home, Joe. That's the problem.'

Then she told me that she'd been to see Jack Whittaker. Jack Whittaker was a lawyer that we knew. He was very successful and wealthy, owned a posh condo on Park Avenue, drove a flashy sports car and was a real womanizer. One of the women I always felt he had the hots for was Susan. I looked at the sexy outfit she was wearing again. Now it all started to make sense.

'Did you screw him?' I blurted out.

'No, I didn't screw him,' she replied calmly. 'It was a business appointment.'

'Oh, sure,' I said sarcastically. 'I can just guess what kind of business you were doing. Hell, Jack Whittaker's been dying to get into your pants for a long time.'

'Unlike you, I don't sleep with every person on the planet that's willing to sleep with me. But if I was interested, he'd be a good candidate for a new man in my life. He's charming, he's got plenty of money to take care of me and Joey because he doesn't lose it all in Atlantic City or Las Vegas, and he's there. He's there, Joe. That's a big thing for me. Someone who's there. But then you wouldn't know anything about that.'

'What in the hell were you doing with Jack Whittaker this afternoon?' I demanded to know.

'I was seeing him about getting a divorce from you,' Susan said.

She looked at me sadly.

'It's time we put this marriage out of its misery, Joe. You killed it a long time ago.'

I was shocked. But I was angry too. Maybe I had cheated on her. Maybe I had betrayed her. Maybe I had given her and Joey a raw deal. But, in the end, I wasn't the one saying goodbye. She was. That still seemed very important to me.

'I'm not divorcing you,' I reminded her. 'You're the one who's divorcing me.'

'Yeah,' she said, 'and it took a slow news day before you finally noticed.'

'So what really happened that day out on the water, Joe?' Bonnie wanted to know.

'Sure, Susan and I were having a lot of trouble,' I said, remembering those last troubled days of my marriage.

'And no, I wasn't the best husband in the world. I was going through a really rough time. I'd lost my job in New York. I was bouncing around from small paper to small paper, and getting more fucked up at every stop along the way. I was gambling heavily too. We had bills mounting up, loansharks at the door. It wasn't a pretty picture.

'Obviously something like that has a pretty detrimental effect on a marriage. Susan and I were going through a lot of troubles. She seemed unhappy, distant – that's why we took the trip to Long Island. It was supposed to be a chance to rekindle the romance, a second honeymoon. Only it didn't work out like that. We fought most of the time. Except for the last dinner we had together. We went to this restaurant with little Joey, and it was like nothing had ever been wrong. I really thought we were going to make it.

'Then the next day we rented this boat. I probably shouldn't have, I didn't know anything about boats. But I thought I could handle it. I always thought I could handle anything in those days. Well, the motor gives out on us somewhere a mile or so offshore and we just start drifting out to sea. At first, I figured someone would see us and pick us up. But there were no other boats around. We were alone. That's when we got really scared.

'I knew if we drifted out into the open ocean, we had no chance. So, before we got too far away from shore, I decided to try to swim for it. I've always been a pretty good swimmer. I didn't know what else to do. Susan begged me not to go, not to leave her and Joe Jr. But I thought I could save them. I really did.

'Instead I almost died too. The tides were really strong, and I had a lot of trouble keeping in the right direction toward shore. I don't know how long I was in the water, it felt like hours. But then, just when I felt like I couldn't go on anymore, I saw the shore. Finally, a big wave hit me, almost knocked me unconscious and the next thing I knew I was lying on the beach.

'There was no sign of Susan and Joey. The Coast Guard searched for days before giving up the search. A couple of weeks later, some debris washed up a shore nearby that looked like it was from the boat we'd rented. One of those big waves that gave me so much trouble while I was trying to swim for help must have broken it apart. So my wife and my son died out there that day. Alone. Without me. I couldn't save them.

'The cops? Yeah, I think they suspected at first there might be some kind of foul play. They could never figure out how I could have pulled it off without almost drowning myself though. And besides, my grief was very real. I think they realized that after questioning me for so long. In the end, it was declared a case of accidental drowning. No one blamed me for what happened. Except for one person. Me.'

'And that's what you've been living with for the past eight years?' Bonnie asked.

'Yeah.'

'Jeez, you've had a real run of bad luck, haven't you?'

'I guess you could say that.'

'Well, they always say there's one good thing about bad luck,' Bonnie said softly. 'It can only get better.'

forty three

• • • • • • • • • • •

I almost missed it in the morning papers. The story about two new murders was hidden away in a back section of the *Banner,* a very small item at the bottom of a page. No reason it shouldn't have been there. It seemed like a routine low-life, double shooting. There was no way for anyone to connect it to Lisa Montero or David Galvin's hit list. Except for me. I read it several times:

MAN AND WOMAN FOUND
SLAIN IN MIDTOWN GARAGE;
MOB HIT SUSPECTED

A man with a long criminal record and his girlfriend were found shot to death yesterday in their car.

The victims were identified as Joseph Corman, 45, and Karen Raphael, 28.

Police said their bodies were found inside a blood-splattered

1993 Pontiac that was parked in a garage at Eighth Avenue and 47th Street.

Both had extensive arrest records, and cops suspect underworld connections to the bloody crime . . .

There were pictures of Joseph Corman and Karen Raphael along with the article. Two grainy mug shots dug out of the files from some of their previous busts. I recognized them right away. Not as Joseph Corman and Karen Raphael, of course. I only knew the two of them by the names they'd used the time I'd met them.

Victor Granville.

And Connie Reyes.

I drove downtown to police headquarters to talk to my friend Capt. Righetti in his office.

'Joe Dougherty!' he boomed from behind his desk when I walked in. 'The man of the hour.'

'Right.'

'Hey, I saw you on CNN the other night. A couple of the local newscasts too. My kids were really impressed when I told them I knew you. How about giving me your autograph?'

'I need some help, Dennis,' I said.

I sat down in a chair across from him.

'Do you remember when I asked you a few days ago about a woman named Connie Reyes?'

'Yeah, I guess so. Why?'

'I want to see a picture of her.'

Righetti and I walked down the hall to another office, where a woman police officer sat behind a computer. We stood and watched while the woman punched Connie Reyes' name into the system. A few seconds later a file appeared on the screen. The woman at the keyboard pushed another button and then we saw Connie Reyes' face.

It was not the same woman I met in the Bronx.

'Dammit!' I muttered.

Righetti and the woman police officer both gave me a funny look.

'You got any idea how I'd find this Connie Reyes?' I asked her.

'Oh, she's easy to find. She's not going anywhere for awhile.'

'What do you mean?'

'Connie Reyes,' the woman said, pointing to one of the entries on the screen, 'has been an inmate at the State Prison for Women at Albion for the past six months.'

'You didn't tell me she was in jail,' I said to Righetti.

'You didn't ask,' he said, looking very confused. 'Why? Was it important?'

He was right.

I could have checked it easily, but I never did.

Because I was in too much of a hurry.

At one point, during the depths of my pre-Carolyn lost years, I started going to Gamblers Anonymous.

The people there were really screwed up.

There was one woman, a housewife and mother of two, who said she used to tell her family she was going shopping. Instead, she would drive to a gambling parlor to play poker. She'd stay there all day, and sometimes all night. She made up bizarre stories to tell her husband and kids when she got home. Once she said she had suffered a blackout. Another time she beat her hands on a wall until they bled, then claimed she'd been accidentally locked in a restroom in the store at closing time and banged on the door until morning. She was in charge of the family finances, but she gambled away all the money that was supposed to pay their bills. When medical insurance payments came in the mail, she cashed them and used the money to gamble instead of paying the doctor. Then she'd tell her father that she needed money to pay the doctor and use that to gamble too. 'I was sick,' she said. 'I didn't care about anything but gambling.'

Another hard-core bettor said that even winning was never enough. He told of winning $30,000 in Las Vegas early one Sunday morning, and then heading back to his hotel with his winnings. But, sitting there in his car at an intersection near the Las Vegas Strip, he turned right instead of left. He headed for the blackjack tables, where he lost the entire $30,000 before the sun was up. 'It wasn't about money,' he said. 'It was about action. I always had to have the action.'

And there were so many more. The people who thought they'd come up with systems to beat the odds at the track or the roulette table or for basketball games. A guy who spent hundreds of thousands of dollars on lottery tickets, dreaming that if he hit the numbers just once, he could repay all his debts. A compulsive sports bettor who kept it under control all year and then bet the house, car and life savings on Super Bowl Sunday. The ones who would bet on anything: the weather, numbers on car license plates or even whether one person would cross the street before another.

I wasn't like that. I had a little bit of a problem, but I basically had it under control. That's what I kept telling myself for a long time.

And then one day I was watching this movie called *Lost in America*. It's the one where Albert Brooks decides to quit his job as an advertising executive, sell his house and use his life savings to travel around the country with his wife in a mobile home. Their first stop is Las Vegas, where his wife turns out to be a secret compulsive gambler who loses all the money in one night at the roulette table trying to play the same number. The number is 22. Even after she's broke, she just keeps chanting '22 . . . 22 . . . 22.' She's convinced that if she can play it just one more time, she'll win big. Everybody who saw the movie thought that was really funny. Except for me. I got it. I understood exactly what she was talking about. I realized I was doing the same thing in my own life, I was always looking to play my own '22.' The big score. The one that would turn everything around for me.

A movie. A goddamned movie. That's what finally made me realize I'd hit rock bottom.

Now I was back at rock bottom again. Just like the day I was so broke I had to take a cross country bus home from Las Vegas.

This time I'd gambled everything I had on one more big story.

And I'd lost it all.

John Montero wasn't so nice to me this time. There was no talk about how much his daughter liked me. No cold beers. No questions about betting or baseball or the world of gambling. No fatherly advice. The man was all business. My standing in the Montero family had definitely fallen in the last couple of days.

'I don't have very much time,' Montero said impatiently, when I finally managed to track him down at his office in downtown Manhattan. 'What can I do for you?'

'You said I should come see you if I ever had a problem,' I reminded him. 'Well, I have a problem.'

'What's the problem?'

'You.'

I told him everything. About Connie Reyes. Joseph Corman and Karen Raphael. How I'd found out that they both listed a company called Bay Ridge Sand and Gravel as their place of occupation the last time they were arrested. I'd done a bit of checking and found out that Bay Ridge Sand and Gravel was owned by – surprise, surprise – the Montero Corp. I finished up by explaining to him the way his daughter, who I thought was in love with me, now was doing her best to discard me like I was yesterday's newspaper.

'What is it that you're trying to tell me?' he asked.

'I think you set me up,' I said.

'How did I do that?'

'The notes someone sent me. The girl I met in the Bronx. Your daughter whispering sweet nothings into my ear. Going to bed with me the night before her hearing started. The whole thing was a game. A very well-thought-out plan. A setup. You were betting that I'd fall for it and go after the story she was innocent. You were right. I did. You probably checked me out first. Found out I had a reputation as the kind of reporter who'd play a bit loose with the facts when I needed to. Bend the rules. Cut some corners to break a big story. I was just what you needed, huh?'

Looking back on it now, I'm not sure what I thought Montero's reaction was going to be. Would he deny it? Throw me out of his office? Or maybe I'd even wind up in the trunk of a car like Joseph Corman and Karen Raphael.

But Montero didn't do anything of those things. He didn't have to. He had me in a trap that I couldn't get out of – and we both knew it. I was caught just like a big fish at the end of one of his hooks. And he could play with me for a very long time before he decided whether to let me go or not.

'Of course, I knew all about you, Dougherty,' he said.

'So that's why you picked me?' I said.

'Sure, you were perfect.'

The perfect patsy.

'Why go to all that trouble?'

He shrugged. 'I love my daughter very much.'

'I want to know one thing,' I said. 'Did she really kill William Franze and the girl in bed with him?'

'No.'

'You're sure of that?'

'I've never been surer of anything in my life.'

'Then why not let a jury decide that?'

'Like I told you the other day,' he said, 'I always like to have an ace in the hole. An advantage on my opponent. You were my ace. I needed you. I just didn't like the odds. I figured they were stacked against Lisa.'

I thought about the two stories Greg Ackerman had told me that first day in his office. About how John Montero had beaten those criminal raps before. Ackerman had said that Montero was a very bad man. A liar. A cheat. And probably a killer too. Only I didn't listen to him. I thought I knew better.

Now Montero had done the same thing again. Only this time he'd used me to wriggle out from under the law.

I told him that. He smiled at me. A scary smile.

'I've made too many enemies over the years,' he said. 'Let's just say that I didn't want my daughter to have to pay the bill on some debts I ran up a long time ago.'

I stood up to leave.

'So what are you going to do now, Joe?'

'I can't do anything,' I said. 'The story was a phony. If I admit that, then I'm dead in the newspaper business.'

'Dead is a very permanent thing to be,' Montero said.

'Like the couple I met in the Bronx?'

Montero shrugged. 'I've lost my wife and my son in the past year,' he said. 'Lisa's all I got left. I'll do anything to protect her. Remember that. Just in case you think about doing anything stupid.'

'I think I've already used up my allotment of stupid,' I told him.

forty four

• • • • • • • • • • •

That night I went to Lanigan's. Bonnie was there. Andy. Even Spencer Blackwood. Everyone bought me drinks. Everyone patted me on the back. Everyone wanted to be my friend again.

There was a drunken discussion going on at one of the tables about what was the most important part of the *Banner*.

'Okay, here's my hypothetical question,' Spencer Blackwood said. 'You have to get rid of one section of the newspaper. Which one do you pick – the comics, the horoscope or the editorial page?'

'Editorial page,' someone said, without hesitation.

'Editorial page,' another one chimed in quickly.

'We have an editorial page?' Bonnie asked.

I finally managed to pull Blackwood away from the table and into a corner, so I could talk to him in private.

'What's so important?' he asked me when we were finally alone.

'I think I set some things in motion with my story, Spence,' I told him. 'Things I didn't know about . . .'

'Such as?'

I stared down at my drink.

'I'm not sure.'

'Then don't worry about it. You're not God, Joe. You're a reporter. All you do is report the facts.'

'Yeah . . . well, sometimes I wish I'd never heard of this story.'

'I felt that way about a story one time when I used to be a reporter,' he said.

'You?' I asked.

'Yeah, me. That's right, Dougherty, I used to be a reporter. For chrissakes, I wasn't born at the age of seventy and immediately named editor-in-chief.'

I smiled.

'Anyway, I set some things in motion a long time ago with a story too,' Blackwood said. 'It happened back in the '50s, during the McCarthy era. Everyone was looking for Communists in those days. People were being blacklisted, lives were being ruined.

'One of the biggest witch hunters was a guy named Joe Flaherty. Flaherty was a congressman and a bully and a pretty all around despicable person. The paper I worked for assigned me to do an in-depth profile on him. Well, I was young and ambitious and I figured this could be a big story for me.

'And it was. I discovered that Joe Flaherty was really Joseph Finkelstein. He'd changed his name and lied about his history because his parents were Communist agitators during the 1930s. Finkelstein himself had belonged to a Communist cell when he was a teenager.

'I confronted him with everything I knew. He begged me not to use it. He said his life would be ruined.'

'Did you run the story?' I asked.

Blackwood nodded. 'The day after it appeared Joe Flaherty walked out onto the streets of New York City with a rifle, shot five people to death and then blew off his own head.'

'My God!'

'Yeah, I've had to live with that one for more than forty years.

Sometimes I can still see the faces of those five innocent victims who died. One of them was a little baby in a stroller.

'Now I'm not sure what you're talking about when you say you set some things in motion with the Lisa Montero story. But I know that I set things in motion with my story too. I realized that if I hadn't done that story, those people would still be alive. And that bothered me. Hell, I even thought about quitting at the time.

'But, in the end, I realized I'd done the right thing. And you want to know why? Because I told the truth. That's what a reporter does. He tells the truth.'

He picked up the copy of the *Banner* that was lying on the bar in front of us. It was an old one. The one with my story about the secret witness on the front page.

'You told the truth on the Montero case, Joe,' Blackwood told me. 'As long as you've done that, you've done your job. No problem. Right?'

'No problem,' I said.

I eventually drifted away from the rest of the crowd and found a spot at the end of the bar where I could be alone. I ordered a double bourbon on the rocks. As I drank it, I remembered doing the exact same thing the day I lost the last of my severance money in Las Vegas eight years ago.

Yep, I here I was, basically in the same situation again. Which was totally fucked. I'd screwed up really badly. I'd lost everything that I worked so hard to get back over the last few years. Carolyn. My new life. My job too, if this ever got out. But even if it didn't, I wasn't sure I could live with the truth of what I had done.

There was another problem too. I still didn't have the slightest idea what happened to William Franze or the rest of the people on Galvin's list. Montero had admitted a lot of things to me. But when I asked him if his daughter really killed Franze and the callgirl, he said she didn't. Maybe she really didn't. Maybe Montero was just playing it safe by using me as her insurance policy against a conviction.

But I still believed that the Franze murders were connected to the others on Galvin's list. No way it was there just by accident.

If Lisa Montero did do it, then that meant she was responsible for all the other unsolved crimes too, including my wife and son.

If not, then the real killer was still out there.

John Montero had said there was nothing I could do. But he was wrong. I still had one more move in me.

There's a theory in gambling called the Martingale Maneuver. It first gained fame around the turn of the century when a gambler used it to win $100,000 in three days of play in Monte Carlo. The idea behind the Martingale Maneuver was a simple one; the more you lost, the more you upped the ante. In other words, every time the bet went against you you just increased the size of the next one. No matter how down and out you were, you played for the big score.

That's what I was going to do.

I just needed one more big score.

I needed to do this story.

Only the right way this time.

It was nearly 1 a.m. by the time I left the bar. I'd had a lot to drink by then, so I don't remember everything that happened next too clearly.

What I do remember is hearing a car engine start up just as I stepped off the curb to cross the street. Then, when I got to the middle of the crosswalk, there was a loud roar. I looked up just in time to see the car hurtling toward me at full speed. I leaped frantically out of the way, landing on the hood of a parked car. The other car sped past me without stopping. Another few seconds and I would have been dead.

I wasn't hurt, but I was pretty shaken up. And I was suddenly very sober.

I remembered something Bonnie had told me the other day in the newsroom: 'There were four Great Pretenders, according to Galvin. Him and three others. Arthur Dodson and Linda Hiller went to NYU at the same time as Galvin. What if they were in The Great Pretenders? That leaves one. One Great Pretender – someone who's made a whole new life and has a lot to lose if the truth ever comes out – who's trying to cover his – or her – trail. Cleaning up all the loose ends.'

Was that what was happening now?

Was someone out there trying to clean up the last of the loose ends in this story?

Joseph Corman.

Karen Raphael

And me.

PART FIVE

Catch Me If You Can

forty five

I needed to understand David Galvin better. I needed to understand his followers too, since at least one of them was still out there playing his deadly game. The bottom line was I had to understand what made all of The Great Pretenders tick if I wanted to stop them. So I decided to find someone who could help me.

Her name was Dr Christine Whalen, and she was a psychologist who had an office on Fifth Avenue, not far from the Empire State Building. Dr Whalen had written a book about the phenomenon of fantasy and role-playing games called 'Game or Obsession?' That's how I found her. I'd picked up the book on the shelves at the NYU Bookstore, where I'd gone looking for some help. Not that I expected her to know David Galvin. The book had been written only a year or so earlier, long after Galvin went to jail. But I figured she was the closest thing I could find to an expert on the subject.

'The world likes to put people in categories,' Dr Whalen said, as

I sat in her office. 'We usually take the most extreme example – or the worst case scenario – and assume that is the norm.

'Look at people who ride motorcycles, for instance. Most of them are decent, law-abiding citizens. But when we think about motorcycle riders, the popular image that comes to mind is Hell's Angels; scary people with tattoos and chains and knives who run in vicious gangs. Do you see what I'm saying, Mr Dougherty?'

I nodded.

'Anyway, it's the same thing with these fantasy types of games you're talking about. We all hear stories about the horrors they sometimes lead to. Obsession, suicide, violence, sometimes even murder. But there are many people who play the game for what it really is – a game – without ever losing touch with reality.'

'Is that what you found out when you were writing your book?' I asked.

'No, that's what I thought before I started it.'

'What about now?'

'I discovered it really was a worst case scenario,' she smiled.

I stared at her. 'You're kidding, right?'

'I'm afraid not. In this case, the worst is the norm. The horror stories aren't myths, after all. These really are very dangerous games for people to play. They are addictive, they're obsessive, and they sometimes separate you from reality. Put ideas like this into the minds of the wrong people – especially young people, the very bright and impressionable – and it can turn into a disaster. That's what I discovered in the process of doing my book.'

Christine Whalen was probably about forty or so. Her hair was short, she had on a pin-striped women's business suit and she wore a pair of half-glasses that made her look a little like Glenn Close as a lawyer in the movie *Jagged Edge*. No-nonsense was probably the best way to describe her.

'The lure of these fantasy games is tremendous,' she said. 'They are incredibly addictive. You become whoever you want, assume any role, do anything you choose kill, maim, injure people for no reason. There are rules, but many times no one bothers to follow them. That's one of the things people who play these games always say: the only real rule to remember is that there are no rules. You can cheat, lie, double cross other players – anything you want. It's all part of the game.

'Violence is a big part of it too. Everything in the game – the kills, the bloodshed, the victories – is predicated on violence. Of course, none of it is supposed to be real.

'Except that sometimes it does become real. The line between fantasy and reality gets very blurred. That happens more than anyone realizes. It happened with your David Galvin and his friends. Only in this case to a degree so unthinkable that it dwarfs any of the incidents I talk about in my book.'

Dr Whalen took off her glasses and rubbed her eyes wearily. She looked better without the glasses. She'd look even better if she let her hair fall down a bit around her shoulders and got out of that business suit into something sexier.

'You've read what I've written in the *Banner* about Galvin?' I asked her.

'Yes. I found it fascinating reading. David Galvin certainly seems to me to be a classic case of the Godhood Syndrome.'

'What's the Godhood Syndrome?' I asked.

'The people who create these fantasy games, the leaders, the one who make the rules – even if they don't always follow them themselves – are called Gods,' she said. 'Gods have the ultimate powers. They can create life, they can kill it, they can resurrect it. The power of Godhood is even more powerful than just playing the game. If I'm a God then . . . well, no matter how powerful you become, I can destroy you. I can reward my friends, punish my enemies, set deadly traps and create monsters to wreak havoc throughout my entire fantasy world. I am the ultimate power. But, as we all know, ultimate power ultimately corrupts. It sounds to me like that's what might have occurred with David Galvin. He began to believe he really was a God.'

I shook my head. 'I don't understand,' I said. 'This is just supposed to be a game, isn't it?'

'Not to the people who play it.'

'So you're telling me that David Galvin may have actually thought he was a God?'

'Yes, I think that's a distinct possibility.'

We talked about my interview with Galvin at the prison. Everything he'd told me that day. And the things he hadn't.

'He said he felt remorse for everything he'd done,' I told her. 'He discussed God and how religion was helping him as he battled the cancer that was killing him. He said he wanted to make peace with God before the end, get his life in order, settle all this unfinished business, before his own Judgement Day. That's why he told me everything he did. He wanted a clear conscience when he died.'

Dr Whalen threw her head back and laughed loudly. 'And you believed him?'

'He was dying,' I told her.

'I think he was still playing a game with you,' she said.

forty six

• • • • • • • • • • •

Janet Parsons remembered David Galvin very well. Even after eleven years, the nightmare had never gone away, she said.

She was his last victim. The one he was with when police burst into an apartment not far from the NYU campus and ended his reign of terror. Now she was in a wheelchair. A permanent reminder of the monster who claimed to be a man of God during his last days on this earth.

I'd already been to see Becky Spangler. She was the one in a mental hospital. Whatever happened between her and David Galvin would probably always remain a mystery. She had survived the horror by retreating into her private little world. Now the doctors said that she might never come out of it again.

Janet Parsons would never walk again. One of her vertebrae had been broken – and the nerves in her spinal cord severed – at a point just above the small of her back. This type of injury usually happens during some kind of accident. But this was no accident. Galvin had done it to her deliberately when she tried to escape.

He was a pre-med student at NYU, who'd read medical books about the spinal cord and nerve system. He knew exactly what to do to cause the damage that he wanted.

'I found out later that he'd been watching me for days,' she said now, as I talked to her in her apartment in the Park Slope section of Brooklyn. She was married now and she was the director of a school for handicapped children and she'd even adopted a handicapped child of her own a few years ago. She'd put her life back together again after David Galvin. Janet Parsons was a survivor. I don't know many people that could have done what she'd done. I know I couldn't. I admired her.

'That was his modus operandi,' she said. 'He watched women for hours, days, sometimes even weeks. He got off on it, I guess. I suppose it was some kind of power trip. Playing God and deciding how long he'd let us all live or something. That's what the cops and the shrinks and all the other people I talked to afterward told me. I don't think they understood though. The only person who knew why he did what he did was Galvin, and he's dead now. For the rest of us, we're trying to rationalize sane motives for the actions of an insane man. It can't be done.

'Anyway, I was living then in this place on West Fourth Street. A little brownstone in Greenwich Village, where I was working as a model/actress/waitress. I thought I was going to be the next Lauren Hutton or something. It might have worked out that way too. But now I'll never know.' She smiled sadly. 'There's not too much demand for a model or an actress in a wheelchair.

'One day I'm coming home from my job at the restaurant, and I see this guy in the hallway outside my apartment. He tells me he's just moved in down the hall and he's already locked himself out. Can he use my phone to call the super? Well, he looked kind of familiar. I realized later that was because he'd been hanging around the coffee shop where I was a waitress, checking me out. He was handsome too. And very polite. I remember even hoping that he'd ask me out. So I let him in.

'Once he was inside, he changed completely. Some of it is still a blur, but I remember that he hit me and I lost consciousness. When I woke up, I was tied to the bed. Then he . . . well, he started playing this game with me.'

'What kind of game?' I asked.

'He wanted me to beg for my life. To tell him what I'd promise to do if he let me live. He said many other people had played this game before me. So I better be imaginative and creative and come up with things that he'd never heard before.'

'Did you do it?'

'Of course I did. I would have done anything at that point to survive. So I told him what he wanted to hear. I told him I'd be his love slave for life. I'd worship him. I'd treat him like a God. I'd run naked through Times Square for him if he wanted. For the rest of my life, I'd do everything he wanted me to do. I'd belong to him.'

'And he believed you?'

'No. He was too smart for that. But I was playing the game with him. I knew that as long as I kept him talking and playing his game, he would let me live. When the game was over, my life was too.'

'When did he do that to you?' I asked Janet Parsons, looking over at her wheelchair.

'He left the apartment,' she said, a pained expression on her face as she recalled the moment. I hated to do this to her, but I had no choice. 'Somehow I managed to get free. I don't how I did it, but I did. I could barely move. My legs were cramped from my confinement and I'd had no sleep and, as you can imagine, I was in a pretty hysterical frame of mind. But I managed to get out the door and into the hall of my building. That's when he caught me. I screamed for help and I tried to fight back, but I was too weak. He dragged me back inside the apartment. Then he said he'd make sure I never ran away from him again. That's when he did this,' she said, looking down at her wheelchair. 'He began doing something to put this pressure on my back. It hurt terribly, and he gagged me so I wouldn't scream anymore. I didn't know exactly what he had done until later. But I was in so much pain that I wanted to die. Only he wasn't ready for that yet. He wanted me to suffer some more. And we were on his timetable now, not mine.'

'But you did survive,' I said. 'What happened?'

'My run for freedom – my last run of my life on these legs – worked after all. Someone had heard my screams and called the police. It took them awhile to get there. At first, they figured it was just another domestic argument or something. But eventually they arrived to check it out. After they found me, they arrested Galvin. They knew then they were dealing with a madman. But they didn't realize until later that this was the madman named Felix the Cat who had killed all those people in the past year.

'They'd never have caught him without me,' she said. 'I was the person who saved a lot of other women from a terrible fate. I guess I should feel good about that. Only it's hard to feel very good when you're spending your life looking at the rest of the world from a wheelchair.'

I wasn't sure what to say. When I'd talked to David Galvin in the prison hospital, none of the things he'd done back then seemed real to me. But Janet Parsons was real. This was Felix the Cat's legacy to the world he'd left behind. I thought about what he told me about wanting to get into Heaven. They say God is all-forgiving. Well, David Galvin was going to be a real test for him.

'What do you remember most about him?' I asked Janet Parsons at one point.

'The look in his eyes.'

'What was it you saw there?'

'Evil,' she said. 'Pure evil.'

The same thing Dennis Righetti had told me.

They'd both seen the real David Galvin. The one I'd met was sick and weak and old before his time. Janet Parsons had come face to face with the true monster. I was glad I hadn't. I don't think I've ever had the kind of courage that she did.

'I don't know if this matters,' I told her, 'but he changed in prison. He found God. He confessed his sins. I know he did a lot of terrible things, but he sought some kind of salvation at the end. He wanted God's forgiveness. That's what he told me.'

'That's bullshit!' she said.

I didn't want to get into an argument with her.

'He was dying,' I said. 'He was a changed man. That happens to people. Even to somebody like David Galvin.'

'He never would have changed,' she said.

'You don't know . . .'

'I know. Believe me, I know. I spent forty-eight hours with the man. I'll never forget a single second of any of it. I know him better than anyone else does. Except maybe Becky Spangler. And, from what you say, she'll never be able to tell anybody what she knows. David Galvin loved pain, he loved suffering, he loved snuffing out people's lives. All this talk about him and God is just more of his lies. The man was the Anti-Christ. He was Satan. I hope David Galvin burns in hell.'

'Well, anyway, he's dead now,' I said quietly.

'Are you sure about that?'

I was stunned by the question. 'What do you mean?'

'I've been reading about everything that's happened,' she said. 'His list. All the other murders. It's like . . . well, it's like he's still playing a game with us all.'

Just like Christine Whalen had said.

'Do you know for sure that he's dead?' Janet Parsons asked. 'I mean, what if it was all a ruse or something? What if somebody else is buried in his grave? And David Galvin is still out there. Killing people. Changing lives. Playing his sick games. He called his group The Great Pretenders. Nothing was real. It was all pretend. Maybe his death is pretend too. Maybe . . .'

Janet Parsons began to cry. She was a strong woman. But she wasn't that strong. My meeting with her had brought back too many bad memories.

Of course, she was just being paranoid. I knew that. David Galvin was dead. Definitely dead. He had to be. There was no doubt about that. But I checked anyway.

I guess her paranoia had gotten to me too.

The people at the prison thought I was crazy when I asked the question. So did the coroner. The cops. Everyone else too.

And, of course, it was all for nothing. It really was David Galvin who had died in the prison hospital. He was buried in an unmarked grave in New Jersey, not far from his parents' house. There was no question about it. The monster was gone.

Death remains the great equalizer.

No one can come back from it.

Not even David Galvin.

forty seven

The newspaper library at the *Banner* was a lot different now than when I worked there eight years ago. It used to be filled with tattered, yellowed newspaper clippings and photos, stuffed into bulging envelopes in old filing cabinets. Then they switched to microfilm, which you threaded through a projector to find the article you were looking for. Now everything was on computer. You just punched a few keys and . . . presto, there it was on your screen.

The newspaper business sure was changing awfully quickly. I had to hurry if I wanted to keep up.

I went through all the clips on the Felix the Cat case again. I was looking for some kind of clue or lead that might help me unravel everything that had happened. I read about his nine victims. The reign of terror he spread throughout the city eleven years ago. About the special elite police squad set up to catch him. The details of his arrest. And the whole account of his trial and sentencing, when he was sent away to jail for life with no possibility of parole.

None of it told me anything new. I was still left with the same version of the Felix the Cat story we'd always believed.

David Galvin was a monster who killed a lot of people, but he did it all by himself. There was nothing to support his story of a group of college friends who'd helped him carry out his bloody rampage.

Except for one thing.

People were still dying.

I looked up John Montero's file next. Somehow he seemed to be at the center of this case.

There were hundreds of articles listed under his name. I paged through them all. I read about Wall Street takeovers, market power plays, financial world double crosses and cuthroat political dealings. I wrote down all the names, all the incidents. I wasn't sure why. I still didn't know what I was looking for.

Then I thought again about the two stories Greg Ackerman had told me. I found them both in the clips.

The first one was about a federal prosecutor from the US Attorney General's office and a witness named Louis Archer. There was a list of articles about it. I pulled up one of them. It was pretty much the way Ackerman had described it:

DA DROPS FRAUD
CASE AGAINST
WALL ST BIGGIE

The key prosecution witness in the John Montero fraud and racketeering trial stunned a Manhattan courtroom yesterday when he suddenly recanted all his testimony.

Louis Archer had been expected to take the jury through a detailed account of the US Attorney's case against Montero, the Wall Street czar who is accused of laundering millions of dollars in illegal funds, evading taxes and engaging in a variety of other unfair business practices.

But Archer told Judge Thomas Hannigan that he had perjured himself in his earlier testimony during depositions in the landmark case. He said that he had made up many of his allegations against Montero at the insistence of federal prosecutors, who threatened him with jail unless he told them what they wanted to hear.

Judge Hannigan, after conferring with attorneys for both sides, said he had no choice but to drop all charges against Montero.

Montero's attorney, Jack Milton, at a tumultuous press conference held on the steps of the courthouse afterward, blasted the government's tactics.

'John Montero personifies the American dream,' Milton said. 'He is a hard-working, enterprising, law-abiding individual who has become very successful in his chosen field. If our government can harass someone like John Montero, then none of us is safe.'

Federal prosecutors called the judge's decision a 'travesty of justice.' But they made no comment when asked if they planned to bring new charges against Montero . . .

A few weeks later, I found another clip about the prosecutor in the case. The one who quit.

PROSECUTOR RESIGNS;
SEEN AS FALL GUY
FOR MONTERO MESS

The lead prosecutor in the abortive case against Wall Street czar John Montero resigned yesterday, saying he planned to take advantage of several job opportunities in private practice.

But Jonathan Ackerman, 51, gave no indication of any specific jobs offers he had received.

And sources in the prosecutor's office said that he had been forced out of his job as a result of the public embarrassment over the government's failed case against Montero.

'We screwed this up bigtime,' one prosecution source said. 'Someone had to take the blame for it. He was the fall guy.'

I almost missed it at first. I was reading the article for the whole story, trying to find something about it that linked it to Franze or one of the other deaths on Galvin's list. But then it hit me. The lead prosecutor was named Jonathan Ackerman. Ackerman, of course. The story had been told to me by Greg Ackerman. It could have just been a bizarre coincidence, I suppose, but I didn't think so.

Sure enough, the file under Jonathan Ackerman's name told me what I needed to know. It said he had a wife and three children. Two sons and a daughter. One of the sons was named Gregory. The age worked out right for Greg Ackerman.

I read through the rest of his father's file. He'd gotten a job with a small law firm in Brooklyn, but that only lasted for a year or so. Then he went into private practice for himself. It seemed like he had not been very successful. He died of a heart attack four years after the Montero case. The way I figured it, Greg Ackerman must have been just about ready to go off to college then.

What did all this mean?

Well, it told me why Greg Ackerman had such hatred for John Montero, his daughter and everything else related to the Montero family.

I called up the other story Ackerman had told me about. The one about the man who had disappeared after he refused to sell his company to John Montero.

NO CLUES IN
DISAPPEARANCE OF
QUEENS MAN

Police said they were baffled by the mysterious disappearance of Edward Findlay, a businessman who was last seen when he left his house in Kew Gardens to drive to work in Manhattan.

He never arrived.

The last people to see him were his wife and daughter, who said he kissed them goodbye – the way he always did – before setting out on the 30-minute drive into lower Manhattan.

Findlay's wife did say that her husband had seemed tense and worried for several days before he disappeared.

She said she believed his concern had something to do with business dealings he'd been involved with recently.

She said he'd been under tremendous pressure from Wall Street business tycoon John Montero to sell his share of the company – and told her he was afraid of Montero.

She said he had also believed he was being followed.

> But she could provide no concrete examples of any connection to Montero, one of the richest and most powerful men on Wall Street and in the New York City political world.
>
> Police said they had no evidence to connect the business dealings with Montero to Findlay's disappearance . . .

There was a picture of Edward Findlay with the article. One of him with his wife and little daughter too. Two days later, there was another story about Findlay's body turning up in the East River. There was no sign of foul play, and his death was ruled accidental. I looked, but couldn't find any more articles about him.

I shut off the computer. At least I knew one thing I didn't know before. One of the people whose lives John Montero had screwed up a long time ago was Greg Ackerman's father.

I decided to go to talk to Ackerman again. I had a feeling I was still missing something else really important. But I was getting used to that feeling.

forty eight

Greg Ackerman lived in a brownstone on East 88th Street. I got the address from Bonnie, who had a contact in the DA's office. It was late, after 11 p.m., when I pulled up my car in front of the building. I wondered if I should wait until morning. But I knew I wouldn't sleep. I'd been thinking about this all day, ever since I'd read about his father in Montero's newspaper file.

Okay, maybe Ackerman did have a personal grudge against the Montero family.

But there was something else bothering me. What if Ackerman was right? What if Lisa Montero really did murder Franze and the hooker?

And what if I was right about their deaths being connected to all the other killings?

That meant Lisa Montero was the last of the Great Pretenders – the person I was looking for.

* * *

I got out of the car, walked through the front door into the lobby and buzzed Ackerman's apartment.

To say he was surprised to see me when he opened the door would be an understatement.

'Hi,' I said. 'I was just in the neighborhood so . . .'

'What the hell do you want?' he snapped.

He was wearing a terrycloth bathrobe and looked very tired. Maybe I'd woken him up. Or else he was just about to go to bed.

'I need to talk to somebody,' I told him.

'Why me?'

'You're the only person I could think of.'

'We've got nothing to talk about.'

'Yes, we do.'

'What?'

'What if Lisa Montero really did it?' I said.

Ackerman stared at me in amazement. He couldn't believe what he was hearing.

'Jesus, Dougherty, it's a little late for that . . .'

'Do you still think she killed Franze and the hooker?' I asked.

'Hey, you're the one who found the goddamned witness who said she didn't do it.'

'Yeah, I did,' I said slowly. 'That's what we have to talk about.'

We sat at his dining-room table, drinking coffee and going over it all for a long time. The apartment was small, but comfortable; a one bedroom with a view of York Avenue. Assistant District Attorneys don't make a fortune. There were a number of awards on the walls that Ackerman had won. There was also a framed diploma from NYU Law School.

'I've found out some new information,' I told him. 'I think it could change things.'

'Change things how?'

'I'm not so sure anymore that Lisa Montero is innocent.'

'Tell me what you've got.'

'I can't.'

Ackerman shook his head in frustration. 'Just like you couldn't tell me the identity of your source, huh.'

'Look,' I said, 'you've got your rules, I've got mine. We both have to live by them.'

'So what do you want me to do?'

'Tell me everything you know about Lisa Montero and the Franze murders.'

'Why? What's in it for me?'

'When I find something out, I'll come to you. I'll work with you. I'll tell you everything I know.'

'Before you print it in the *Banner*?'

I took a deep breath. I was violating every rule of being a newspaper reporter here. But desperate times require desperate measures. And I was a desperate man.

'Yes,' I said.

'How do I know I can believe you?'

'You have my word on it,' I told him.

In the end, Ackerman agreed. We stayed up late into the night going over it again and again.

Lisa and William Franze had met for dinner at about 8 p.m. at a restaurant on Madison Avenue. People at the restaurant told police afterward that they both were drinking heavily. Franze even more than Lisa. The two of them also did not seem to be getting along very well; they exchanged angry words in loud voices on several occasions during the meal. But Franze was a regular at the restaurant, and this apparently was not terribly unusual. He brought lots of different women there, and he was often loud and obnoxious. Sometimes other customers complained, but the restaurant never said anything to him about his behavior. When you're rich, you can get away with a lot.

Sometime around 10:30 or so, they showed up at Elaine's, where the drinking and fighting continued. No one at either place knew what the argument was about. 'I don't think it mattered,' said one waiter at Elaine's. 'They always seemed to be fighting whenever I saw them together. They sure had lots of practice at it.'

They arrived at Franze's townhouse on 61st Street between 11:40 p.m. and midnight. According to Lisa, it was very soon after that that he called the escort service and proposed a three-way sex session to her. She says she refused, they argued some more and she stormed out. Lisa claims that before she left she heard him talking to someone on the phone about getting a second girl. She drove around aimlessly for a half hour or so, then went back to his house where she saw a woman going in. She insists it was not the same woman who was murdered. She says she was so embarrassed that she left, went home and fell right asleep.

There were a number of witnesses. Several neighbors had heard Lisa and Franze arguing in loud voices shortly before the murders. They had also seen Lisa storm out of the house. And – perhaps most damaging for her – one eyewitness, an old man walking his dog, saw everything that night. He saw the argument between Franze and Lisa. He saw the Martin girl going in – he says he even talked to her when she stopped to pet his dachshund. Then he saw Lisa coming back to the house later. He said he was sure of the times too because he always walked the dachshund at the same time.

The phone records were very specific too. Franze had made only one call, to the Elite Escort Agency at 11:54. He said he wanted a girl right away, so they sent Whitney Martin out to his house. Franze was, the agency pointed out, a regular customer. The agency said there was no second call from him and that only the one girl was assigned to the job. In fact, there were no other calls at all from Franze's phone that night. He'd made a total of fifteen calls from his home phone on the day he died: nine to business associates, one to the escort agency and five to the plumber he was trying to get over to fix the toilet in his bathroom. The plumber never arrived until the following morning.

'Everything points to Lisa Montero as the only person who could have pulled the trigger,' Ackerman said.

Most of this, of course, had already been in official police reports and media accounts of the murder.

What he told me next was not.

'Do you really think she could be a killer?' I asked him.

'Let me tell you about Lisa Montero,' he said. 'Her mother died six months ago. Did you know that?'

'Yeah, she told me. So what?'

'Did she tell you the death was listed as suspicious. Carbon monoxide poisoning. They found her in the garage.'

'What are you saying . . . ?'

'Lisa's brother died a year ago. He drowned. Or at least that's the official verdict.'

'You're saying it was murder?'

'Two accidental deaths like that? Hard to believe that it's just a coincidence.'

'And you think Lisa was responsible?'

'I think the lady's a psychopathic killer.'

'Why? What was her motive?'

'Ambition. Greed. The brother was supposed to take over the business after the father died. I hear Lisa didn't like that. She figured she should be next in line. All of a sudden, no more brother. The mother – who knows? Maybe she figured out what Lisa had done and was set to blow the whistle on her own daughter.'

'But what about her father, John Montero?' I said. 'Does he suspect that any of this is true?'

'I don't know.'

'I mean if he did, why would he still be trying to protect her?'

'She's all he has left,' Ackerman said.

I thought about everything he'd just told me. I still couldn't believe it.

'Why didn't any of this come out before?' I asked him.

'It probably would have. At Lisa Montero's murder trial.'

'But now there won't be any trial.'

'That's right,' Ackerman said. 'You made sure of that.'

forty nine

The forgotten woman in all this was Whitney Martin. The girl from the escort service found dead in bed with Franze. She'd been mentioned in every account of the murder, but no one ever really talked about her. She was just there. One more detail at the crime scene. Like a piece of furniture or the broken toilet or the blood on the walls.

Except Whitney Martin was once a living, breathing human being.

I decided to find out more about her.

The Elite Escort Agency, where she worked, was located in an expensive high-rise building on Lexington Avenue. There was a suite of offices, with an attractive, red-haired woman sitting behind a desk at the front door. It looked like the office of any big business or corporation. Except what they were selling was sex.

I'd read about places like this. They walked a fine line with the law. They were really just fronts for prostitution. But they dressed themselves up in all this glamour; advertised on TV and in glossy, high-brow publications; and talked about providing 'a sophisticated companion for an evening at the theater, ballet or dinner.' The theory was that whatever happened after that was a business transaction between the girl and her client. But the reality of it was no different than the girl in hot pants standing in the middle of Times Square and shouting: 'Hey, sailor!'

Me, I had no personal experience with this kind of operation. On the few times I'd been to prostitutes in my life, they'd turned out to be more of the Times Square variety. A couple of times in Atlantic City. Once at a bachelor party for a sports writer at the *Banner*. And another time when I was doing a piece on street prostitution in the city, and I decided to do some real investigative reporting. I was always willing to go that extra mile for a story.

But none of them looked anything like the red-haired woman sitting behind the desk at the Elite Escort Agency.

'Hi, I'm Stacy,' she smiled. 'Can I help you?'

'I'm not sure.'

'We cater to all tastes. Some of them very commonplace, some quite bizarre.'

Stacy stood up now. She was in her twenties, tall, with a nice figure and dressed very fashionably. Yep, no question about it. This was a class operation, and she was a classy woman.

'The woman I'm interested in is dead,' I said.

'That is bizarre.'

I smiled. 'I'm a reporter,' I said. 'I work for the *New York Banner*. Tell me about Whitney Martin.'

She did. Not there though. Stacy said she was due for a break anyway. She switched on the voice mail, and we went downstairs to an outdoor cafe next to her building. As we sat down at the table, I realized that if I saw her on the street I never would have guessed what she did for a living. She looked like a model or an actress.

'So why do you work for an escort service?' I asked.

'You mean how did a nice girl like me wind up at a place like this?'

'Something like that.'

'I go to City College. I'm majoring in economics. I need the money for tuition.'

'You're kidding?'

'Nope. Whitney went to City College too. That's where I met her.'

'So the two of you are sitting around the dorm room and just decide one day to become hookers?'

Stacy shook her head. 'I'm not a hooker,' she said. 'I don't go out on calls. I just work in the office. It's really very legit.'

'Sorry.'

'No problem. I just want to make that clear to you.'

'Whitney went out on calls though, didn't she?' I asked.

'Oh yeah, she loved it. She thought it was a real kick. She used to come back and tell me about all the guys she met. Stockbrokers. Oil barons. CEOs. They had all this money and power and big houses and cars and boats. But when they were with her, she said, she was the one in control. They'd do anything to have sex with her. She was calling all the shots. I think Whitney really liked that.'

I suddenly thought of something. 'Was she blackmailing any of them?' I asked.

'Of course not. Why would you say that?'

'You said the men she went out with had all this money and power and property. Maybe they'd lose it if she exposed them. Maybe she figured this out and figured it was an easy way to make some serious college money.' I saw the disbelieving look on Stacy's face. 'Look, it would make a good motive for murder.'

'I thought the motive was supposed to be William Franze, the guy she was with. A jealous girlfriend or something.'

'That's one theory.'

'You think it might have been somebody who was really after Whitney?' she asked.

'No one knows for sure what happened that night.'

'Whitney wasn't a blackmailer,' she said emphatically.

I nodded. I had no idea if she was or not. I was just fishing anyway. 'Where did Whitney come from?' I asked.

'Wayne, New Jersey. Her family had some decent money. They were sending her to college here and a younger sister to Boston

University, which is a pretty hefty fee. But Whitney had a falling out with them, so she was living off the money she made at the agency. She made a lot of money.'

'And the two of you were friends?'

'Whitney was neat. She was fun. We were almost even roommates.'

'What happened?'

'She couldn't get along with Oscar.'

'Who's Oscar? Your boyfriend?'

'Oscar's my dog.'

She took a picture out of her purse and showed it to me. A little white fluffy dog on a beach somewhere with her. She was dressed in a bikini, and throwing a rubber ball to the dog. Cute. Definitely cute. The dog wasn't too bad either.

'Whitney didn't like dogs?' I asked.

'She was scared of them. I think a dog bit her once when she was a kid or something, and she never got over that. She wouldn't even come into the house if Oscar was around.'

I handed her back the picture.

'So what's the deal with you?' she asked. 'Are you married? Engaged? In love with somebody? Gay?'

I laughed. 'What makes you think I'm one of those?'

'All the good ones are.'

'You think I'm a good one?'

'You've got possibilities,' she said.

'Well, I used to be married,' I said. 'I was engaged up to a few days ago. I was also in love. Unfortunately, the woman I was in love with was not the same woman that I was engaged to. As you might guess, that created a few complications in my love life. The bottom line is I no longer have a fiancée or a girlfriend. I haven't gone the gay route yet, but maybe I should try that next. My luck with women hasn't been very good.'

'Maybe you've just been with the wrong women.'

'I've been with a few of them,' I told her.

Wayne was about a forty-five minute drive from Manhattan. Stacy gave me the address of Whitney Martin's parents, and told me how to get there.

I didn't want to go see them. I always hated to talk to the family of a murder victim. Besides, I didn't really know what it would accomplish. But I didn't know what else to do.

I'd tried everything else on this story without any luck.

So I decided to follow the trail of Whitney Martin and take it wherever it led.

fifty

I could figure out right away where Whitney Martin got her good looks from. Her mother, Janet Martin, was a drop-dead beauty. A lot older, of course, somewhere around fifty, but the years had been kind to her. I remembered reading one of the accounts of the murder that described her as a former fashion model. She had high cheekbones and striking features; she still looked as if she could have just stepped out of the pages of *Vogue* magazine.

She was digging up a flower bed in the front lawn. She had on a crisp white blouse, a pair of freshly ironed jeans and expensive looking leather boots. There wasn't a speck of dirt on any of them.

'What do you think of my azaleas?' she asked.

She pointed to a long row of bright pink flowers in front of us.

'They're beautiful,' I said.

'I'll bet you've never seen azaleas like that before, have you?'

The truth was I hadn't thought that much about azaleas in my life, but I didn't tell her that.

'They're one of a kind,' I agreed.

'My azaleas have won first prize at the Wayne Garden and Flower Club for four years running,' she said proudly. 'A lot of people try to grow them. But most people can't do it well. No one's ever won the award five years in a row. I hope to be the first.'

She stood up now and surveyed them proudly. There was a small blade of grass sticking to the knee of her jeans, where she'd been bending down on the lawn. She saw it now and frowned. She reached down and flicked it off. Impeccable.

'I'm here to talk about your daughter, Mrs Martin,' I said.

'You mean Whitney?'

'Yes.'

There was a pained expression on her face. She looked back at her flowers. Like she could find some sort of comfort there.

'What Whitney did,' she said slowly, 'it was just unbelievable. She brought shame onto our family.'

'She died, Mrs Martin.'

'It was the way she died.'

'You mean because she was a prostitute?'

'Yes.'

'Things happen,' I said. 'It doesn't mean she was a bad person.'

'She brought shame onto this family,' Mrs Martin repeated, staring at her azaleas.

We went inside after awhile. The house was a lot like her. Beautiful, impeccably clean, everything in its proper place; so perfect that it almost seemed unreal. There was an old-fashioned quilted sign on the wall in the living room which said: 'God Bless Our Happy Home.' I hadn't seen one of those in a long time. Next to it was an award from the Wayne Garden and Flower Club. There were also family pictures. Janet Martin and a man I assumed was her husband, with two beautiful girls. One of the girls was Whitney.

'Did you know your daughter was working for an escort agency?' I asked her.

'No.'

'She never told you?'

'I said I didn't know.'

Of course, she did.

'What did you fight about with her?' I asked.

'What do you mean?'

'You had a big falling out. You cut off her money for college and she hadn't spoken to you in awhile before she died.'

'Who told you that?'

'One of her friends.'

She sighed. 'Do you have any children, Mr Dougherty?'

'I did. A son.'

'Did?'

'He died.'

'Oh, I'm sorry.'

'It was quite awhile ago. He was very young.'

Maybe that created some kind of bond between us. Maybe it helped her trust me. Or maybe she just wanted to talk to somebody about it.

'Sometimes we try too hard for our kids,' she said. 'We want so much to protect them from being hurt that we hurt them even more. And we don't know we're doing it until it's too late.'

'Is that what happened with you and Whitney?'

She nodded. 'A long time ago, when I was young and about Whitney's age, I wanted to be an actress. I came here to New York, went for auditions and kept looking for my big break. But I had to pay the rent, buy food, find nice clothes – and there was no money. So I found a way to make money. Just until I became a big star. That's what I told myself anyway.'

I suddenly realized what she was going to tell me.

'I became a prostitute. Oh, they didn't call it that. I worked for this big fancy spa; leisure consultants was the term they used for us. But we all knew what it was about. Men would pay us money, we'd do stuff for them and well, as they say, it's the world's oldest profession. Then one day I met a man I liked. Whitney's father. He took me away from all that. We moved here, we created this beautiful home, we raised our two daughters. I did everything I could to protect them, to make sure they would never have to suffer some of the pain that I had.'

Wow! I wondered what the Wayne Garden and Flower Club would say if they found out about this.

'Did Whitney know all about your background?'

'Yes, I told her one day.'

'Why?'

'I wanted to make sure she never did anything like that.'

'But it didn't work.'

'No. In fact, the exact opposite happened. She became fascinated by it. The whole thing really intrigued her. She wanted to see what it was like. Maybe if I hadn't told her the story, none of this would have happened. And Whitney would be alive today.'

I looked at a picture in the living room of a happy, smiling Whitney Martin. She had her arm around another girl. The second girl was very pretty too. The two of them looked a lot alike.

'Is that your other daughter?' I asked Mrs Martin, pointing at the picture.

She nodded. 'Elizabeth.'

'And she's in college too?'

'Yes. This was her freshman year at Boston University. She did really well too. Made the Dean's list. Her major is political science. She wants to work with the peace corps.'

She seemed very proud of Elizabeth.

'Where is Elizabeth now?' I asked.

'She's not here.'

'Is she at Boston University.'

'No.'

'Then she's living here for the summer?'

Mrs Martin didn't directly answer my question. 'Elizabeth was very close to her sister, Mr Dougherty. She's having a great deal of difficulty dealing with all this. They were only two years apart in age, and Elizabeth always looked up to Whitney as a role model. She just can't believe that she's now gone. None of us can.'

'Can I talk to her?' I said.

'I don't think that's a good idea.'

'Why not?'

'I don't want Elizabeth to get involved in this,' she said firmly. 'It's been too hard.'

I could have pushed it, but I didn't. I guess I didn't really think Elizabeth would have much to add anyway. So instead I just stood up, thanked Mrs Martin for her time and said goodbye.

I felt sorry for her.

She had worked for a long time to make this the perfect

American house. Perfect parents. Perfect daughters. Perfect furniture. Perfect flowers in the yard. But then one day tragedy came calling. And now this house would never be the same.

It was a long way between what happened to Whitney Martin and the strange games that David Galvin and The Great Pretenders started playing at New York University more than a decade ago.

But there was a connection.

There had to be.

fifty one

You never know about a story. Sometimes you dig and dig and come up with nothing. Other times the answers jump up and practically hit you over the head. That's what happened when I went back to William Franze's neighborhood to talk to the witnesses from the night of the murders.

Sure, the cops had already done that during the early days of the investigation. But cops – no matter how good they are – can sometimes miss an important clue. Or see it and not realize what it means. Or maybe I had some information or perspective or viewpoint on the case that the police didn't, which could help me find something that they had overlooked. I figured it was worth a try.

The first witness I saw was Blanche LaMotta. She lived in the building next door to Franze's. She said she remembered hearing a loud argument coming from the Franze building around midnight on the night of the murders. She remembered the time because she had just started watching a rerun of Murphy Brown, she said, which came on at twelve o'clock.

'What did you do then?' I asked.

'I went to the window to find out what was happening.'

'What did you see?'

'Nothing at first. But I could still hear the yelling.'

'What happened then?'

'I saw a woman come running out of the building. She seemed very agitated. She was still shouting as she ran away from the place. I wasn't sure who she was talking to. But then I saw Mr Franze. He was standing at the door of his place. He was yelling at her too.'

'William Franze was still alive at this point?'

'Yes. He even came part way down the walkway and tried to grab her. But she pulled away from him. They screamed some more and then she ran down the street. He went back inside. I figured it was all over so I went back to my TV program.'

'This is very important,' I said to her. 'Did you see the woman well enough to identify her?'

'No,' she said. 'I told the police that. It was too dark for me to see her face.'

'Well, can you remember what they were arguing about?'

'I never could make out most of it,' she said. 'Just the one name Mr Franze kept using.'

'What was that?'

'Lisa. He called the woman Lisa. I'm sure of that.'

Jack Graham lived across the street. He'd heard the argument too, he said.

'It was loud, definitely loud. Both of them were shouting at the top of their lungs. I had my windows closed and the air conditioner running. So it had to be really loud for me to hear it. I mean they were really going at each other bigtime. You know what I mean?'

'Did you see anything?'

'No, but I didn't really look. Hey, this is New York City. Stuff like this happens all the time out on the street, even in nice neighborhoods like this. I'll tell you the truth I didn't want to get involved. I wasn't looking to be any peacemaker or good samaritan. Good samaritans can get themselves killed in this town.'

'What did you hear then?'

'Just words. Snatches of conversation. Lots of profanity. Most of it didn't really mean anything to me . . .'

'Most of it?'

'Yeah, there was one thing. At the end. Something the guy said. I heard it really clearly too. Of course, he was probably standing out on the street now, yelling at her, which is why I could hear him so well. He said: "Go ahead, run back to daddy. Who needs you anyway? I'd rather fuck a whore than an ice-cold bitch like you anyway, Lisa."'

I canvassed the rest of the neighbors after that, ringing doorbells all the way up and down the block. It took a lot of time, but didn't produce any results. No one else heard anything. No one saw anything. No one remembered anything special about that night. There was always a lot of noise on a New York City street at night. Most New Yorkers just shut everything out. Even a murder.

There was one other person I needed to talk to. But he lived on the next block. The old man who was walking his dog in front of Franze's house on the night of the murders. His name was Albert Edelman. He said he'd seen Lisa coming back after the argument. And he saw Whitney Martin, the dead woman, go in too; in fact, he said she'd even talked to him.

I had an address for Edelman, but I decided to do it a different way. One of the clips quoted him as saying he always walked his dachshund dog at the same time – a little after midnight – and followed the same route which took him past Franze's townhouse. I figured it might be a good idea to try to recreate the exact events of that night. Maybe I'd see something that everyone else had missed.

So I went back to East 61st Street at midnight, parked my car in front of Franze's place and waited for Edelman and his dog.

Sure enough, at a little after twelve, he came down the street with the dog on a leash. The dog was a brown dachshund. If Edelman remembered that this was the spot where everything had happened the night of the murders, he didn't seem bothered by it. He stood waiting patiently as the dog sniffed along a patch of sidewalk right in front of the Franze townhouse.

I got out of my car, walked over to Edelman and told him why I was there. He shook my hand and said he'd be happy to help. He told me his dachshund's name was Gretchen. Gretchen wagged her tail at me. I kneeled down to pet her, and she licked my face. Then she rolled over on her back to let me scratch her stomach.

'She's very friendly,' Edelman smiled.

'I can see that.'

'Yeah, everyone likes Gretchen,' he said.

I asked him what he remembered about the night that William Franze and Whitney Martin had been murdered.

'I saw the girl. The one that got murdered.'

'Tell me what happened.'

'I was here walking Gretchen, just like I am here with you now, and a taxi pulled up at the curb. This young woman got out. She had to walk right past me. She saw Gretchen and smiled at her. Then Gretchen wagged her tail, so the woman stopped to pet her. Gretchen licked her face too. Like she did with you. Gretchen's shameless when she finds anyone who'll give her attention.'

'So if this woman stopped to pet your dog, you got a really good look at her, right?'

'Yes.'

'And you're sure it was the woman who was killed – Whitney Martin?'

'Absolutely. I saw her picture in the paper the next day. That was the same girl. She was very beautiful. She seemed very nice too. I mean she didn't look like a call girl or anything. She looked more like a college coed. What a shame that she had to die so young.'

'What did you do then?'

'I started walking Gretchen down the street. I saw the woman go toward the front door of that house.' He pointed to William Franze's place. 'Then as I was coming back down the street again later another woman walked right past me and turned into the same place. I saw this one face to face – we were only a few feet away. It was Lisa Montero. The one the police arrested.'

'Did she say anything to you?'

'No, I don't think she even noticed me. She seemed very agitated, very upset.'

'And you saw her go into Franze's house?'

'No. I said she was heading toward it. I remember thinking it was unusual; two such beautiful women showing up like that at the same place at the same time. But I didn't really think much more about it. Until I saw it on the TV news the next day. I mean it didn't have anything to do with me. I just finished giving Gretchen her walk and went home.'

'So you can't be sure that Lisa Montero ever actually went back inside Franze's house.'

'No, I never saw that.'

I took out a newspaper clip about the murder and showed it to him. There was a picture of Whitney Martin on the front page.

'That's the first woman you saw, right?' I said.

'Yes,' he said, squinting at the picture.

'And you're sure?'

'Oh yeah, she's got the same features. The same eyes. The same facial structure. Everything's the same . . .'

He looked at the picture again.

'Except . . .'

'Except what?'

'I don't know,' Edelman said. 'She just looked a little younger that night.'

There was something wrong here.

I knew that, but I just couldn't put my finger on what it was.

I'd gone over the same ground as the police did in the days right after the murders. I'd talked to the same eyewitnesses. I'd gotten all the same answers the police did. Nothing was different. So why did I have the nagging feeling there was a clue out there I was missing?

I thought about it all the way back to my hotel. I pulled up in front, got out and headed for the front door. There was a woman coming out of the hotel walking a large dog. She was tall, wearing tight designer jeans and high-heeled boots and looked like she was a model. But it wasn't her I was looking at. It was the dog.

That's when it hit me.

'The woman stopped to pet my dog,' Albert Edelman had said. 'Gretchen licked her face too.'

He'd told that to the police, of course. Only they didn't make anything of it. No reason to. Only now I knew something the cops didn't know. That story didn't make any sense.

Whitney Martin was terrified of dogs.

Her friend Stacy had told me so.

'I wanted Whitney to move in with me,' Stacy had said. 'But she couldn't, she didn't get along with Oscar. Oscar's my dog. Whitney was afraid of dogs.'

Why would Whitney Martin – who was afraid of dogs – stop to pet Albert Edelman's dachshund and even let it lick her face? There was only one possible answer. It was so easy I wondered why someone hadn't stumbled over it before.

The woman he saw was NOT Whitney Martin.

Of course, Edelman insisted that she looked just like the pictures of Whitney Martin that he saw. And he had no reason to lie. But he admitted to me that there was one thing that was different. The woman he had seen looked younger in person, he said.

Who looked just like Whitney Martin – only a little younger?

Her sister.

fifty two

I was back on a stakeout again.

They really are a miserable part of the newspaper business. You're always too hot, too cold, too wet or too dry. You get hungry, you get thirsty, you have to go to the bathroom. Worst of all, you get bored. Bored out of your mind. And, in the end, most of the time you don't even find out anything new anyway.

I once knew a reporter who spent a week staking out the apartment of a woman who was the key witness in a big New York City murder case. Morning, noon and night, he was parked right in front of the woman's door. Of course, nothing happened. On the eighth day, the reporter desperately had to go to the bathroom, so he decided to slip off to a gas station around the corner to take care of it. He was gone maybe ten minutes at the most. He came back to find out that the witness had walked out the front door, another reporter from the *Daily News* had spotted her and gotten an exclusive interview. It ran on Page One of the

News the next day. This guy wanted to kill himself. So did the editors at his paper. I didn't blame any of them.

Another reporter I knew solved the bathroom dilemma one time by simply refusing to leave. As the call of nature became too great to ignore, he simply dealt with it there. Literally. In his pants as he sat in the car. So now his pants were soaking wet and smelled horribly of urine. So when it came time to approach the person he'd been following, they fled in terror from this foul-smelling stranger in wet pants.

Then there was the reporter on a stakeout who figured out how to deal with his boredom by listening to the radio. He really got into it too. News. Sports. Music. Those long hours of waiting in the car for something to happen just flew by. The only problem came when he tried to start the car again to follow the subject of the stakeout. He couldn't. His battery had gone dead from all his radio playing.

The thing is though, sooner or later, every good reporter winds up having to do a long stakeout. Sometimes it's the only way to get information.

So there I was, sitting in front of the Martins' house in Wayne, and waiting for the sister to make an appearance.

It was just a hunch, of course. But the more I thought about it, the more excited I got.

Now all I had to do was talk to the little sister.

I'd gotten there at 7 a.m. and parked down the street from the Martin house; close enough so that I monitor their comings and goings, but far enough away to avoid attracting their attention. I ate Dunkin' Doughnuts for breakfast, a Big Mac and french fries for lunch and a couple of slices of cold pizza for dinner. I listened to the news, an afternoon Mets game and lots of classic rock and roll music on a Walkman I'd brought along. I played solitaire with a deck of cards left over in my glove compartment from my gambling days. I sang songs to myself. I recited Casey at the Bat and The Raven. I made lists of every woman I'd ever been with – or wanted to be with – since high school, then ranked them in their order of desirability. By 9 p.m., there was still no sign of Elizabeth Martin. I drove back to Manhattan.

The next day I did it all over again. The exact same procedure. Except this time I switched from pizza to Chinese food for dinner.

Still nothing. I was starting to get frustrated. Maybe she wasn't even at the house. Maybe she was back at Boston University. Maybe it really was Whitney that Albert Edelman had seen that night.

On the third day, something finally happened. It was a Saturday, about 11:30 a.m., when a woman came out the front door of the house, walked down the driveway and got into a Honda Accord parked by the curb. She was young, she was pretty, she looked almost like a dead ringer for Whitney Martin. Only younger. Her sister Elizabeth.

She started up the Honda and drove away down the street. I followed her in my car.

She took me through some local streets and then onto Route 17, which is a large highway that runs across much of New Jersey. We stayed on that for a half dozen exits. Then she got off at the sign for a large shopping mall. I followed her off the exit ramp and into the mall's parking lot. She parked the Honda near one of the big department stores. I pulled up alongside her, parked in the next spot and got out.

She was still totally unaware of me.

'Are you Elizabeth Martin?' I said to her.

She seemed stunned. 'Who are you?' she asked warily.

'My name is Joe Dougherty. I'm a reporter. I work for the *New York Banner*.'

'Is this about Whitney?'

'Yes.'

'I don't know anything about it.'

She turned her back and started to walk away from me.

'I know you were at Billy Franze's house on the night that she died,' I said.

That's when she began to cry . . .

fifty three

• • • • • • • • • • •

We sat on a bench inside the mall and talked.

She wanted to tell the story. She'd kept it bottled up inside her for weeks, ever since the murders happened. It was eating her up, I could see that. Reading about it in the newspapers every day. Seeing Lisa Montero arrested. Hearing about the search for a mystery witness. Her mother had made her keep quiet all this time, she said, but she knew that was wrong. All she needed was someone to come along and help her make it right.

That was me.

'I called Whitney that night at her apartment in the city,' she said. 'I'd just finished taking my spring finals at Boston University, and I came home to New Jersey to see my parents. They talked about how bad things had gotten between them and Whitney. They didn't say what the fighting was all about, of course, but I knew. Whitney had already told me what she was doing to make money. She was my big sister. We were always very close.

'Anyway, I wanted to see how she was doing. I was in Manhattan that night, so I called her. I got her on the phone just as she was about to walk out the door. When I asked her where she was going, she just laughed. She said she had to go to work. Now, like I said, I knew exactly what kind of work she was talking about. So I told her I wanted to hear all about it.

'I said it was because I was worried about her. Mom and dad were worried too, I said, and I wanted to assure them that she was going to be all right. But do you want to know the truth? That wasn't the reason I wanted her to talk about it. I was curious. No, more than curious. I was fascinated. I wanted to hear all the steamy details.

'You see, I really idolized my sister. She was two years older than me, and she always did everything first. I thought she was so cool. She had cooler friends than I did. She wore cool clothes. She did cool things. I just couldn't imagine her ever doing anything wrong. So when I heard all the stuff about her and the escort agency, I never thought any of it was wrong, I just thought it was really cool.

'Whitney told me on the phone she'd just called this client to get his exact address and that he asked for another girl to come with her. He wanted a three-some. He said this girlfriend of his who was supposed to be the other girl had freaked out and left when he suggested the idea. So he told Whitney to call the agency and make the arrangements for somebody else.'

Whitney Martin called him! Of course. That's how it happened. That's why there was no record of another call to the Elite Escort Agency on Franze's phone.

'Well, then my sister got this idea,' Elizabeth said. 'She said I should come along with her. I would be the second girl. That the client would probably really love it if he got a sister act. Especially two sisters who looked so much alike. Men really got off on that sort of thing, Whitney told me. And I could pocket all the extra money, we wouldn't have to share it with the escort agency. They'd never even know.'

'Had you ever done anything like this before?' I asked.

'No. But Whitney said it would be a kick. How it would totally blow our parents' mind if they ever found out. Especially our mother. She'd freak out big time if we ever got up the nerve someday to tell her. I think Whitney really got off on that idea. She told me to meet her at the client's place. Then she gave me the address of the townhouse on East 61st Street.'

'But I still don't understand why . . .'

'She was my sister,' Elizabeth Martin said. 'I trusted her.'

It was getting later, almost lunch time now, and the mall was beginning to fill up with more people. Mothers holding on to young children. Teenagers shopping for clothes and new CDs. Families out for a leisurely Saturday afternoon of shopping. They talked and laughed and pointed in store windows. But Elizabeth Martin wasn't paying attention to any of them.

She was a long way away now.

Back at William Franze's townhouse on the night of the murders.

'What happened when you got there?' I asked softly.

'It was horrible,' she said. 'That man – Franze – he was so repulsive. He asked me to do things. Unnatural things. I'm no prude, but this was different. He was so perverted. I didn't even want him to touch me. And when he did, I could feel my skin crawl.'

'What about your sister?'

'She was used to it. She dealt with a lot of weirdos. But she was worried about me. I knew that. I think she realized she made a big mistake by bringing me there. She told Franze the deal was off, that it was just going to be him and her. But he kept saying how he paid for two girls and he wanted two girls. I think he was pretty drunk.'

'Did you have sex with him?'

'No. I got sick right after I got there.'

'Sick?'

'Literally. The man actually made me nauseous. At some point, I just ran out of the bedroom and found a bathroom. Then I threw up in the toilet. I stayed in there for a long time. My head hanging over the bowl, throwing up, flushing it all down and then throwing up some more. I finally decided I was going to leave. He could have the money back. I was just about ready to go back out and tell him that when . . .'

She shuddered now as she relived those nighmarish last moments with her sister.

'. . . when the shooting started.'

'You were still in the bathroom?' I asked.

'Yes.'

'So the killer never knew you were there?'

Elizabeth Martin nodded solemnly. 'That's what saved my life,' she told me.

'But you know what happened?'

'That's right.'

'Tell me everything,' I said.

Later, I walked Elizabeth Martin back to her car in the parking lot of the mall. She got behind the wheel of the Honda, rolled down the windows, put her key in the ignition and then just sat there for a long time without saying anything. She looked drained. But I still had one question to ask her. One very big question.

'You told me you used the bathroom at William Franze's house that night,' I said. 'You said you felt nauseous and went in the bathroom and got sick. You said you just kept throwing up, flushing the toilet and then throwing up some more.'

'Yes.'

'Are you sure that's exactly what happened?'

'What do you mean?'

'Don't you remember anything unusual at all about William Franze's bathroom?'

'No.'

Wrong answer. It couldn't have happened that way. If Elizabeth Martin was telling the truth, she would know about the bathroom. She would know that the toilet was broken. She would know that she never would have been able to flush it. Because the plumber never showed up to fix it until the next day.

Was she lying?

Was this whole story of hers all part of another setup?

Just like Connie Reyes?

'So you're telling me that you left Franze's bedroom before the murders,' I said, 'went into the bathroom next to the bedroom, but you don't remember anything being wrong there?'

She shook her head.

'I didn't use the bathroom next to his bedroom,' Elizabeth Martin said. 'I used the one downstairs. The bathroom next to his bedroom was broken. The toilet didn't flush.'

Sonavagun!

fifty four

It took me awhile, but I finally was able to get Lisa Montero on the phone.

'Stop calling me, Joe,' she said. 'I told you before – we have nothing more to talk about.'

But she didn't sound angry when she was said it. More like she was sad. Just like the last time.

'I have some news about your case,' I said.

'The case is over.'

'Not quite,' I told her.

I wanted to ask her about the speeding car that almost hit me outside Lanigan's. I wanted to ask her about Joseph Corman and Karen Raphael. I wanted to ask her if I was supposed to wind up with them in the morgue or if it was just a warning to keep my mouth shut.

'I found the missing witness,' I told her.

She sounded stunned. 'You – you mean the woman you told me about from the Bronx?'

'No, she was a phony,' I said. 'Someone set me up.'

There was a long silence on the other end of the line. I had her off balance. She wasn't in control anymore. I liked that.

'What are you talking about, Joe?' she asked finally.

'C'mon, Lisa, I'm not that stupid. Oh, I was stupid. Really stupid. But I've gotten a lot smarter in the last few days. In fact, I know something you don't know. There really WAS a witness there on the night of the murders. Franze did ask for a second girl to come along. Of course, you just made that part up about seeing her go in the house to convince me to chase your phony witness. You had no idea it was true. But someone did see what happened.' I started to laugh. 'It's kind of funny when you think about it.'

'I don't know what you mean.'

'Sure you do. C'mon, Lisa, it's just you and me here. I'm not taping this phone call or anything. Let's be honest with each other. Be honest with me for one goddamned time since I've known you, okay?'

She didn't say anything.

'So how did it work anyway? Was it your idea or your father's? You needed an alibi, a witness who could nullify any evidence the DA's office threw at you. Only you didn't have one. So you decided to make one up. But you couldn't find the phony witness yourself – you needed someone else to do that. I was perfect. A newspaperman. A hungry newspaperman. A desperate one. A newspaperman who would do anything to get a story. The kind of guy who was willing to cut corners, take chances and break rules. Well, meet Joe Dougherty. He'll do all that for you – and fall in love with you too. No problem. All you have to do is hop in bed with him a few times, whisper some sweet nothings in his ear and he'll do anything to make sure you're innocent of murder. Even make up a phony story. Why not? He's good at it. He's done it before. Is that how you picked me for the job? Did somebody tell you about me? Or did you just keep looking until you found the ultimate patsy?'

'It wasn't exactly like that,' she said.

'Okay, but I'm pretty close. Right?'

'Yes,' she said softly. 'Pretty close.'

She started to cry.

'So don't you want me to tell you?' I said to her.

'Tell me what?'

But she knew what I was talking about.

'What the real witness saw that night,' I said.

'Yes.'

I thought about everything Elizabeth Martin had told me. How she saw the killer after the murders of Franze and her sister. How the killer was wearing a black ski mask and body outfit that masked his or her identity. How Elizabeth Martin saw Lisa OUTSIDE the house when she looked out a window – while Elizabeth was desperately trying to decide whether to run outside or keep hiding from the killer. How she watched as Lisa, still looking upset from the argument with Franze, started walking back toward the front door, then thought better of it and left for good. Lisa had been telling the truth about that part of it. Elizabeth Martin was convinced that Lisa had nothing to do with the murders.

Of course, I still didn't know who killed Franze and Whitney Martin.

I didn't know any more about the other deaths on the hit list Galvin had left for me.

And I didn't know if Ackerman was right when he suspected that Lisa might have something to do with the mysterious deaths of her mother and her brother.

But now I knew one thing for sure. She didn't kill William Franze and Whitney Martin.

I'd finally done something right on this story.

'Joe, what did the witness tell you about me?' Lisa asked anxiously.

'Are you sure you really want to know?'

'Yes!'

'Fuck you,' I said. 'Go read it in the newspaper like everybody else.'

Then I hung up on her.

That wasn't true, of course. I could never print this story. I'd already printed that Lisa was innocent once before. The difference this time was that it was true. But it gave me real satisfaction to end it with her like that. I felt good when I slammed the phone down in her ear.

I told myself that was the last time I would ever talk to Lisa Montero.

I told myself she was out of my life forever now.

I told myself a lot of things.

Most of them were wrong.

PART SIX

Let's Play Dead

fifty five

'So where are we on this story?' Andy wanted to know.

'Back to square one,' I said.

'Oh, that's terrific,' Jack Rollins snorted. 'After all this time – not to mention all the money we've paid you – that's the best you can tell us? You're back to square one?'

'It's a very confusing story,' I said calmly. 'Everyone else seems to be about ten steps behind square one. So the way I see it I've really made some progress.'

'Maybe you'd make more progress if you'd look in some new places.'

'Such as?'

'Well, I don't think you're going to find too many answers in Lisa Montero's bedroom.'

There was a long silence in the room.

Rollins, of course, was a bit behind the story. As usual. He didn't know that Lisa and I were history. And I sure wasn't going to tell him.

'Gee, maybe you can help me brush up on my journalistic techniques, Jack,' I said. 'I mean you've made such a success out of your career. There's not a restaurant in town you haven't made a personal investigation of. Nose to the grindstone. Back to the wheel. You're a real pro, Jack. A newspaperman's newspaperman.'

There was no Spencer Blackwood this time to referee the argument. Just me, Rollins, Andy and Bonnie. Andy and Bonnie didn't look like they wanted to get involved either. So no one said anything for a long time.

'I think we're missing something important about this story,' I finally volunteered.

'That's brilliant,' Rollins said.

'What do you mean, Joe?' Andy asked.

'We've been all over the story, backward and forward. But we still don't have a real clue about what's going on here. So maybe we're going in the wrong direction. Maybe we need to back off and start over again. Maybe we need some new ideas on how . . .'

'Maybe we need a different reporter on it,' Rollins said.

'Go to hell,' I told him.

'I think Jack's right,' Andy said suddenly.

I looked at him with surprise.

'Look,' Andy said, 'you and Bonnie split this up when we started. You concentrated on the William Franze murders and Bonnie did the footwork on all the other victims. The six new cases on Galvin's list, plus the new ones; Dodson and the Hiller woman. Why not switch? Bonnie works on Franze and the call girl and we see what she comes up with – you go back over everything she did again.'

Now it was Bonnie's turn to get upset.

'Are you saying I don't know how to cover an assignment?' she asked Andy.

'This isn't personal,' he told her.

'Yes, it is. You're questioning my abilities. I checked all those names out, I investigated everything, I didn't miss a thing . . .'

'Nobody's perfect, Bonnie.'

She sat there glumly. I was a little surprised by her reaction. I'm generally protective about my stories too. And I sure didn't much like the idea of somebody else – even Bonnie – digging too deeply into everything I'd done on the Franze case. But Andy was right. It made sense to switch assignments. One of us might just stumble across something the other one had missed.

'Anyone got any other thoughts?' Andy asked.

'What about the list?' I said.

'Galvin's list?'

'Yeah, there's something wrong with it.'

'Like what?'

'Franze and Whitney Martin, for one thing. It's like they don't belong on the list. What's the connection to Galvin or NYU or any of his Great Pretender friends? And what happens now? All the names on Galvin's list are answered for. Everyone's dead. So it should be over. But I don't think it is. I think there's going to be more murders. Unless we can stop them. But I don't know who or how or why.'

I looked over at Bonnie for a second. She was staring down at the floor. Still sulking.

'You sure do have a lot of questions,' Rollins said.

'It's called being a reporter, Jack.'

'Maybe you should get off your ass and go find some answers, huh?'

A few minutes later, as we were walking out of the office and back into the city room, Rollins caught up with me. He wasn't finished yet.

'I just want you to know, Dougherty,' he said, 'that if I ever become editor of this paper, you're finished. My first order of business will be to get you fired. Again.'

'Well, then we should all hope that day never comes,' I told him.

He shook his head. 'You fucked up a big story eight years ago. Since then, you've fucked up your career, you fucked up your marriage, you fucked up your new engagement to this woman in New Jersey – let's face it, you fucked up your whole life. And now you're fucking up this story too. The bottom line here is you're just a total fuck-up.'

I realized as he was walking away that what I'd told Lisa about him that first night in bed together was probably the truth. Jack Rollins had forgotten the real Walter Billings story. His role in it had been buried away deep in his subconscious a long time ago. It was easier to blame me for the whole thing. Maybe that's why it made him so uncomfortable to have me around again.

Bonnie came up behind me.

'Nice conversation?' she asked.

'Yeah,' I said, 'Jack said he was thinking of nominating me for employee of the month.'

'Watch out for him, Joe,' she said. 'He's out to get you.'

He'll have to wait in line, I thought.

'How about you?' I asked her. 'Are you okay with everything that happened in there?'

'No, I'm not,' she said. 'I did a good job checking out Dodson and Linda Hiller and all the other victims. I don't know why they want you to go back again now.'

'Sometimes a fresh perspective can . . .'

But Bonnie wasn't listening. 'I'm a good reporter, Joe. I'm just as good a reporter as you are. Maybe better. You're not going to find anything I didn't find out from those people. Believe me.'

'I'm sure I won't,' I said.

fifty six

Except I did.

I went into it figuring that I wouldn't uncover a single thing that Bonnie hadn't. That she really was as great a reporter as she said she was. That she'd left no stone unturned. That I'd know no more at the end than I did when I started out.

But, by the time I was finished, I had a lot more information.

I also decided I had a problem.

Margaret Dodson was not in good shape. That wasn't surprising. A few weeks ago, she'd been living a happy life with her husband and their two children. Then he suddenly disappeared. After that, he was found brutally murdered in a motel room hundreds of miles away. And now there were a lot of questions about what he might have done sometime in his life to wind up on David Galvin's death list.

'Did your husband seem worried or anxious at all before he disappeared?' I asked her.

'No, he was the same as always,' she said. 'We didn't always see a lot of each other, what with Arthur's job and the kids. He worked long hours, and he also coached our son's soccer team. But he seemed fine.'

'Tell me about the last time you saw him.'

'Gosh, I don't know what to say. It was all so normal. We had breakfast, he said goodbye and then he caught the 8:11 train to New York City. He worked for an accounting firm on Park Avenue, Kelly, Strachnan and Dodson. He'd been named a full partner last year.'

I nodded.

'Then, somewhere in the middle of the day, I got a phone call from the people at work. They wondered where he was. He'd never shown up at all.'

'Do you remember what day that was?'

She gave me the date.

It was the same day my article about David Galvin had appeared in the *Banner* – along with Arthur Dodson's name included on Galvin's list of targeted victims.

'After that, the police came to my door. And people kept calling me up and telling me about Arthur's name being in the paper. On some serial killer's list. They asked me what was going on. I didn't know what to make of any of it. I still don't.'

It seemed pretty obvious what had happened. Arthur Dodson had read the newspaper sometime that morning, probably on the train on his way to work. The *Banner* with my article about Felix the Cat. When he saw his name, he panicked and decided to run. He didn't tell anyone where he was going. His wife. His kids. The people he worked with. He just ran. What would scare somebody so badly that they would do that? David Galvin, I guess.

I talked to Margaret Dodson about her husband's days at NYU. That was before she knew him, she said, but she told me proudly that he'd graduated Magna Cum Laude and been president of his fraternity. She said he still kept in touch with some of the fraternity members. Had she ever heard him mention David Galvin's name? No, she said, he never did.

Then I asked her some more questions about his job.

Their neighbors.

Friends.

I wasn't sure where I was going, but I felt like I had to ask her as many questions as I could. Maybe I'd get lucky. Maybe I'd stumble across something that was important.

And that's exactly what happened.

'Why Hilldale?' I asked her at one point. 'Do you have any idea why your husband wound up dying in this little town in the middle of Pennsylvania? Any connections he had there? Friends, family, business trips?'

'It's funny you mention that,' Mrs Dodson said. 'We did go to Hilldale once. Spent a night there on our way to visit my family in Chicago. Anyway, Arthur just fell in love with Hilldale. He thought it was a quaint little town. He said he'd love to retire there someday. In fact, whenever things got really crazy or hectic around here, he would joke about how we should move to Hilldale and get away from all our troubles. Trouble could never find us there, he said.'

I stared at her. 'Did you tell this to anyone else?'

'I didn't remember until it was too late.'

'What do you mean?'

'Well, the police asked me if I had any ideas where Arthur might have gone. I said I didn't. I just didn't think about Hilldale then. I guess I was too upset. It wasn't until later, when someone else asked the same question, that I told them about he sometimes talked about going there.'

'Who was that?'

'The other reporter from the *Banner* that was here.'

'Bonnie Kerns?'

'Yes, the red-headed one.'

'When did you tell her about Hilldale?'

'The day before my husband was found dead.' Mrs Dodson shook her head sadly. 'I guess she never had time to do anything about it either until it was too late.'

There was something wrong here.

Bonnie had said that she got the tip about Dodson from an anonymous phone call. But Margaret Dodson said she'd told her about his love for the town a day before he died. So why hadn't Bonnie mentioned that to anyone? If it was a phone call AND a tip from Dodson's wife, that was more than just the wild goose chase Bonnie claimed she'd gone to Hilldale on.

There couldn't be that many motels in Hilldale. A half dozen or so at most. What if Bonnie had gone there looking for Dodson on her own after the conversation with his wife? What if there never was any phone tip about him being there? She could have canvassed all the motels in the area in a few hours. An out-of-town visitor like Arthur Dodson wouldn't be hard to find, even if he had changed his name.

But why would Bonnie do that and not tell anyone?

Well, there was one answer.

An unthinkable one.

But I thought about it anyway.

fifty seven

• • • • • • • • • • •

'We need to talk,' I said to Bonnie.

'About what?'

'Clarion State College.'

Bonnie and I were sitting in Bryant Park, which is in the middle of Times Square and a few blocks away from the *Banner* building. Bryant Park used to be a home for drug dealers and derelicts. But, a few years ago, they cleaned the place up and turned it into a real garden spot of New York City. Now it was filled with mothers pushing baby strollers, yuppies on their bikes and roller skates and midtown office workers taking a long lunch hour.

But I wasn't there for lunch. I was working.

'You checked?' Bonnie asked.

'Yeah. Clarion State said you never went there.'

'They must be mistaken. Maybe you talked to the wrong person. Maybe . . .'

'What town is Clarion State in?' I asked her.

'What?'

'You went there for four years, Bonnie. A little place in southern Ohio called Clarion State College. That's what you told me. So you must know what town you were in. That's pretty basic. What town in Ohio is Clarion State located in?'

'Clarion is the name of the town too,' she said, but not with a lot of conviction.

I made a loud buzzing sound like the host of a TV game show. 'Wrong answer,' I said.

'I'm sorry,' she stammered. 'I meant Clarion was the name of the county. The town is . . . Oh, Christ, what was it called again? Look, Joe, I'm just drawing a blank here. It's more than ten years ago and . . .'

'There is no town of Clarion in Ohio,' I said. 'No county either, for that matter. There is a Clarion State College though. It was named after James Clarion, who led a Union Army regiment that defeated the Confederates in a key battle at Gettysburg during the Civil War. The school is located in the town of Loganville, which is in Hocking County. That's in Southeastern Ohio, about twenty miles from the Ohio River and the borders with Pennsylvania and West Virginia. I checked. You should have too. If you're going to make up a story like that, it's important to get your facts straight.'

Bonnie sighed deeply. 'What made you check?'

'I didn't, not for a long time. There was really no reason to. Which, I guess, is why you volunteered the information. A pre-emptive strike. Tell me what I want to know before I ask it. That way I won't dig too deeply into your past. It worked too; caught me off guard and bought you time. But then I began to wonder about you.

'Like the way you found Arthur Dodson, for instance. I always had a problem with the fact that the killer tracked him down to that little out of the way motel in Pennsylvania just about the same time you did. It just seemed to be too much of a coincidence. Sure, he could have gotten the information from the same tipster you did, but that didn't make much sense. I began to think maybe there wasn't a tipster. Maybe you found him on your own and then paid him a visit. I wasn't sure how you found him though. Until I talked to Margaret Dodson.'

I went through everything the dead man's wife had told me.

'So I decided to do some more checking. Linda Hiller, for instance. I found out that you were at the bridal shop where her body was found a week before the murder. One of the clerks there remembers you asking questions about wedding gowns and stuff. I figure you were doing some research on the place.

'Then I discovered that you went to see David Galvin too – about a year before I did. Your name's in the records at the prison. But you never did a story about it. So what were you and Galvin talking about? Old times? When the two of you went to NYU together?'

'My God, you think I'm the killer, don't you?' Bonnie said.

'Did you go to NYU?' I asked

'No.'

'Well, you didn't go to Clarion either.'

'That's right. I went to Penn State.'

'Oh, so now it's Penn State?'

'Yes.'

'Bonnie, if you really went to Penn State, why wouldn't you just tell me that in the first place?'

'Because I didn't want you digging into my past.'

'Why? What was I going to find?'

She looked at me sadly.

'When I was in high school, I wasn't very popular,' she said. 'I know you probably think I'm kinda weird now, but I was really weird in high school. I never had one date, never had a boyfriend and spent the night of my senior prom watching Lawrence Welk on TV by myself.

'I thought it would all change when I went to college. Different place, different people. But it was just the same. No, that's not true. It was worse. All the other kids at Penn State seemed to have more money than I did and be better looking and have more friends. I was still the weirdo on the outside looking in.

'But I was smart. I was always smart. So I figured out a way to get guys to like me. I'd be easy. You wonder why I don't like sex now? Well, I guess that's the reason. Back then, I was the easiest girl in the freshman class. You went out on a date with Bonnie Kerns, you got laid, no problem. Because I was so fuckin' desperate to be liked. And it worked too. Suddenly guys were interested in me. Of course, most of them were dorks, perverts and creeps. And they all wanted to be with me for the wrong reason. But I didn't care. At least I didn't think I did.

'Until the night of this big fraternity pledge party. I got invited by a really good-looking freshman guy, this jock who was at school on a football scholarship. I was surprised he wanted to go with me. But excited too. Really excited. I bought a new dress, I spent hours trying to fix myself up in front of the mirror. I wanted so much to make him proud he'd invited me. Only when I got to the party, I found out I wasn't his date at all.'

'I don't understand,' I said.

'I was supposed to be the date for the fraternity's entire freshman pledge class.'

'You mean . . . ?'

'I was the party entertainment.'

'They had sex with you?' I asked.

'They raped me.'

'How many . . .'

'All of them.'

'Did you go to the police?'

Bonnie shook her head. 'I never pressed any charges. I never even told anyone else what happened. I was too embarrassed. Instead, I just went back to my dorm room and cried all night. The next morning, I realized I could never face seeing any of them again. I could never face seeing anyone on campus. I figured everyone would know about me. So I got on a bus, left college and never looked back. I came here to New York City, got a job for awhile as a waitress, then did temporary office work and finally wound up at the *Banner*. Anyway, that's why there's no record of me at Clarion State College or whatever the hell the name of that place is.'

'Why didn't you just tell me that in the first place?'

'Like I said, I've never told anyone. You're the only one who knows.'

'But that was such a long time ago . . .'

'When I filled out my application to work at the *Banner*, I said I'd graduated from Clarion State with a degree in journalism. That's how I got this job. I lied. I figured that no one would ever bother to check it. And they didn't. Until now.'

'So you never went to college at all after Penn State?'

'No.'

'And if Andy or Rollins found out . . . ?'

'Who knows? They might just laugh about it. But I lied on my application. I was hired under false pretenses. They could fire me if they wanted to. I love this job, Joe. It's my whole life. That's why I didn't want you poking around into my background. I couldn't take the chance.'

'What about the rest of it?' I asked. 'Arthur Dodson. Linda Hiller. Your visit to David Galvin.'

'The reason I went to the bridal shop where they found Linda Hiller was that I'm going to be in a wedding. One of the women in personnel, Kathy Neeland, is getting married next month. I'm supposed to be a bridesmaid. I've never done anything like that before so I guess that's why they remember me asking a lot of questions. You can check with Kathy, if you want.

'As for the phone tip on Dodson, they log all incoming calls at the *Banner* switchboard. Check that out too. The stuff about Hilldale from his wife I didn't connect to the phone call until after I went to the motel. After that, it didn't seem worth mentioning since I'd already found him.

'The interview with Galvin was assigned by Andy Kramer. He thought it would make a good "Whatever Happened to?" feature for a slow news day. Only Galvin wouldn't talk to me, so it never came off. Maybe he remembered though. Maybe that's why he came to the *Banner* when he decided to tell his story at the end.'

I wasn't sure what to say. I'd convinced myself on the way over to meet Bonnie that all these things somehow added up to a smoking gun – a pattern of devious deception on her part that she'd never be able to explain. Now I realized I'd just been jumping to conclusions. I felt bad.

I looked out at the people in the park. There was a young guy near us now in a tank top T-shirt and cutoff jeans throwing a frisbee to his dog. Each time he threw it, the dog happily chased it, then brought it back and started all over again. I felt a little bit like the dog. Constantly chasing something for no reason. I'd uncovered a lot of facts in this case. But I wasn't sure what any of them meant.

'Look, I'm sorry,' I said to Bonnie.

'I guess I should be flattered, huh?' She smiled. 'Being a suspect right along with Lisa Montero. That puts me in pretty good company.'

'I've been under a lot of pressure,' I told her.

'Yeah, I've noticed. Accusing me of being a murderer seems to be the act of a pretty desperate man. I once heard you'd do anything to get a story, but this is ridiculous. Look, I'm going to say something very personal to you, Joe. OK?'

I shrugged. 'Sure, go ahead.'

'I know you like to think that life dealt you a bad hand,' she said. 'But it seems to me that the cards you've gotten were pretty good. You just played them badly. By my count, you've had at least two good women who loved you; your wife Susan and Carolyn. But you treated both of them like shit. Then you fall head over heels in love with someone like Lisa Montero, who's guaranteed to break your heart. Now you wonder why you're unhappy. Well, no one's doing these things to you, Joe. You're doing them to yourself. You self-destructed your marriage. You self-destructed your engagement to Carolyn. You self-destructed your newspaper career. And now it looks to me like you're doing it all over again.'

She was right, of course.

Especially about me and Susan.

I remembered again how much Susan used to love Christmas. The excitement in her voice when she talked about it. The sparkle in her eyes when she put up decorations. The joy in her on Christmas morning when she opened her presents.

Then I thought about the one Christmas she and Joey and I spent together before they were taken away from me. Or almost spent together.

It was right after I'd lost my job at the *Banner*, and I was gambling pretty heavily. I'd gone through most of our savings and the money Susan had put away to pay bills. But I'd opened a special Christmas account at the bank the year before, and there was still enough money in that to buy presents for her and Joey. Which was what I intended to do when I withdrew it on the day before Christmas.

I never wanted to lose the money.

I really thought I could parlay it in a poker game into enough to buy them something really special.

By the time I left the game, I was broke. I called up every friend I knew – some of whom I hadn't seen in years – and begged them for money to buy my family gifts for Christmas. It was already Christmas Eve, so many people weren't home. The ones that were took pity on me and gave me money. But when I finally made it to the stores, it was too late. They were all closed. Everyone had gone home to be with their families. So did I.

I'll never forget the look of sadness on Susan's face the next morning when there were no presents under the tree. Joey was too young to understand what was going on, but I knew I had let him down too. On the day after Christmas, when the stores were open again, I used the money I'd borrowed to buy them some wonderful gifts. But it wasn't the same. It was never the same between Susan and I after that.

Until the very end.

That last night, the night before she and Joey died, I thought I'd gotten through to her again. That we'd rekindled the love we once had. That we were going to be okay.

But then they were gone.

And now I'll never know for sure . . .

'I can still do this story,' I told Bonnie.

'And you think that's going to make everything better?'

'Yes.'

I really did think that. I figured that if I could just figure out the riddle of David Galvin and The Great Pretenders, then everything else would fall into place. The William Franze murders. The deaths of my wife and son. My job at the *Banner*. Maybe even my life.

Looking back on it all now, I was really naive. I was like a poker player betting big on a pair of twos, while everyone else in the game was holding full houses and flushes and four-of-a-kind. Only I didn't know that until it was too late.

'Do you have any real leads?' Bonnie asked.

'Just one,' I said.

'What's that?'

'Someone who still seems to be at the center of everything that's happened.'

'Who?'

'John Montero.'

fifty eight

John Montero was a creature of habit. Every morning he got up at the same time, 6 a.m. Then he jogged for thirty minutes on a treadmill, while he watched the morning news on TV. After that, he always ate the same breakfast: a glass of grapefruit juice, bowl of oat bran and decaffinated coffee, as he read the *Wall Street Journal, New York Times* and overseas market listings from Europe and Japan. Then he got into his car and drove to his office on Wall Street, arriving exactly at 10 a.m. every day.

The point is that he was easy to catch up with if you really wanted to do it. I did.

But someone beat me to it.

John Montero had been shot to death.

They found him in his parked car in the garage of his office building. He was slumped over the steering wheel with two bullets in the head. Both shots were fired from very close range. Police theorized that he must have known his killer or at least not been frightened by the assailant. There was no sign of forced entry into his car or a violent encounter beforehand. Whoever did it had apparently been sitting in the passenger seat next to him.

By the time I got to the murder scene, the place was a real circus. The police were there, of course. So were a lot of press.

Dennis Righetti was one of the cops standing near Montero's bloodied car. I walked over to him.

'Is there any possibility at all that this could have just been a random killing?' I asked. 'A carjacking? Or a robbery? I mean maybe it had nothing at all to do with all the other murders.'

'The car is a $60,000 Mercedes, and no one even tried to take it,' Righetti said. 'Montero's got a couple of thousand dollars in cash in his wallet, not to mention credit cards and the like. Also untouched. Now what do you think the motive was?'

'Somebody wanted to get rid of him.'

'That's pretty obvious.'

But I still didn't understand why.

I'd pretty much convinced myself that Montero was somehow behind everything. He was the bad guy. The bogeyman. The man I had to put behind bars. But now he was dead too. So none of it made any sense to me anymore.

'You're gonna love this,' Righetti said. He gestured toward Montero's car. 'You know what we found in there? A scrapbook with newspaper clips of the new murders on Galvin's list. Dodson. Linda Hiller. Like he was keeping track of the killings. Oh, there was something else too. A gun. A Smith and Wesson semi-automatic. 40 caliber gun. We have to wait until the ballistics tests come back, but I'm betting it's the same gun that was used on Dodson and Hiller.'

'You think he killed both of them?'

'Maybe.'

'But what was the motive?'

'One scenario goes like this. His daughter gets herself into a real jam with the Franze murders. Maybe she really was innocent, like you say. But Montero didn't want to take that chance. He figures there's too many enemies out there who want to make a member of his family pay for his past crimes. He needs a way to get her off the hook. And he's willing to do anything to beat a criminal rap. We've seen that in the past with him. Suddenly this list of

Galvin's appears with Franze's name on it and you start writing stories about some wacko ex-college students out there still killing people. It's like a gift from Heaven for Montero and his daughter. All they have to do is convince everybody that your story is true and she gets off free. Only, to make it convincing, there has to be more murders. Otherwise people might think Galvin is just making it up. But, after Dodson and Hiller die, everyone believes it.'

'Then who killed Montero?' I asked.

'I don't know,' Righetti said.

Greg Ackerman was there too. I figured he'd be happy the man he wanted to nail so badly was now dead. But he didn't look very happy.

We talked about the scrapbook and gun that had been found in Montero's car.

'It still seems thin to me,' I said, when he was finished.

'You think so, huh?'

'Yeah. Why would a busy guy like Montero care enough to keep a scrapbook of the killings? And why carry it around in the car with him? For that matter, why would he keep the gun in the car with him? What if he got stopped by a cop or something? I don't buy any of it.'

'You think maybe someone set him up to take the fall?'

'That's right. The same person who really did the killings.'

'Well, that's scenario No. 2 that we're working on,' Ackerman said.

'You got any idea who it could be?'

'How about your ex-girlfriend?'

I stared at him. 'You mean Lisa?'

'Sure. First she does the brother. Then the mother. And now the father. She's the only one left. All the money now belongs to her.'

He was right, of course. I didn't want to admit it. But I'd thought of the same scenario.

Maybe Lisa hadn't killed William Franze and Whitney Martin that night in the East Side townhouse.

But that didn't mean she couldn't be responsible for any of the other killings.

'Are you going to arrest her?' I asked Ackerman.

'I can't.'

'Why?'

'Because of you. You made sure that I looked stupid the last time I arrested her for murder. I can't do it again. No one would take it seriously, they'd think I was just harassing her. I could never get a conviction. Because of you, Lisa Montero may just get away with murder.'

fifty nine

Christine Whalen was wearing her hair long this time when I went to see her at her office. The half-glasses were gone too. Probably using contacts. She had on a pale blue silk blouse with the top two buttons open, a grey blazer and a pair of blue jeans. She sat on the edge of her desk and crossed her legs. The jeans were tight against her thighs.

'I need your help again,' I said.

'Professionally?'

I looked at the open buttons on the blouse. I wondered if she greeted all her patients like that.

'Is there an option?' I asked.

'My fee is $100 an hour,' she told me. 'I didn't charge you the first time. But people do pay me for my advice. That's how I make a living. And my time is money. So . . .'

'How about I buy you dinner, charm you with my witty repartee, dazzle you with my unerring ability to always choose just the right little bottle of wine and we call it even?'

She laughed. 'You're very charming, Mr Dougherty,' she smiled. 'I'm sure that many women would jump at the chance to go out with you. It's just that I'm not one of them.'

'Not your type?' I asked.

'Not my sex.'

It took me awhile to understand what she was saying. I guess I'm just not a '90s kind of politically correct guy. Finally, it dawned on me.

'You're gay?'

'Yes, I'm a lesbian.'

'Are you fanatical about it?'

She laughed again. 'Let's just say I'm involved in a very serious relationship right now.'

'Maybe you haven't met the right guy,' I said brightly.

'Gee, that's an original line.'

'You've heard it before?'

'Every man in the world thinks he's the one who can turn a gay woman straight. They never do.'

'Maybe we can break some new ground here.'

'Doubtful,' she said.

In the end, she agreed to talk with me more about David Galvin. No charge. Maybe she did have a secret crush on me.

I told her everything that had happened so far. About Galvin. The Great Pretenders. Arthur Dodson and Linda Hiller. Me and Lisa Montero. Carolyn. Bonnie. My gambling. The way I got fired at the *Banner* eight years ago. Once I started talking, I couldn't stop. I'd held a lot inside me for a long time. She was the only shrink I knew, and I felt a need to unburden myself.

'Let me get this straight,' she said when I was finished. 'You broke up with your fiancée, got dumped by the woman you left her for and now you come here and make a pass at me?'

'Well, it wasn't technically a pass . . .'

'It was a pass.'

'So what do you think, doc?'

'You are totally fucked up.'

I smiled. 'Stop talking in that technical medical jargon and give it to me straight.'

She said it would be easier if we just concentrated on the story.

'The key to this is still David Galvin,' she said.

'But he's dead.'

'Whatever,' she shrugged. 'Let me tell you something about serial killers. They always want to leave something behind for us to remember them by. They say the Boston Strangler always left the head of his victims tilted at a certain angle as his own personal signature. Another man in Florida, who killed thirty-two women, wrote short stories about all his murders. Son of Sam wrote letters boasting of his bloody deeds. Charles Manson left messages in blood. These are very vain, egotistical people we're talking about here. They always leave clues for us to follow. Not because they're sloppy, because they want us to know everything they've done. They think they're smarter than us. They think we'll never be able to catch them. So we have to prove they're wrong.'

'But how do I chase after a dead man?'

'If you really want to understand everything David Galvin has done, then you have to think like him,' she said.

'I thought I was.'

She shook her head.

'I checked out everything he said in his last letter,' I said stubbornly. 'He said there were three Great Pretenders besides him. I'm pretty sure that Arthur Dodson and Linda Hiller were two of them. So that leaves one person unaccounted for. That's the person who's doing the killing now. Probably to cover up their own involvement. So all I have to do is find the last Great Pretender. The one he didn't put in the note.'

'Why do you think he wrote that note and gave you that last interview?'

'He felt remorse for everything he'd done,' I said. 'He talked about God and how religion was helping him as he battled the cancer that was killing him. He said he wanted to make peace with God before the end. Get his life in order, settle all this unfinished business before his own Judgement Day. That's why he told me all these things. He wanted a clear conscience when he died.'

Dr Whalen laughed. 'You really don't have a clue,' she said. 'Why didn't Galvin tell you in the note who The Great Pretenders were? Why is the name of the third Great Pretender not in the note? How do you know there were only three of them?'

'Galvin said . . .'

'This is a fantasy game,' she said impatiently. 'Everything is make believe. It's all pretend. Nothing is as it seems. You always have to remember that.'

'But why would Galvin lie to me?' I asked. 'He had nothing to gain from it. He was dying.'

'Like I told you before, I think Galvin was still playing a game with you.'

'What game?' I asked impatiently. 'The game he was playing ended a long time ago. For chrissakes, the man's been in prison for the past eleven years.'

'You just haven't been listening, Dougherty. You're still playing by the rules. But there are no rules in this game. Galvin made the rules. He can change them without telling anybody. He can do anything he wants. He is God. Remember?'

'But he's dead. I checked.'

'I never said he was alive. But anything is possible in a fantasy player's world. Even death isn't permanent. Do you understand?'

I nodded.

'All the bizarre events that happened since the day you met with him,' she said. 'The murders, the intrigue, the unanswered questions; it's almost as if he's out there choreographing the whole thing, isn't it? Now I'm not sure exactly how, but I think Galvin figured out a way to accomplish that. Do I really think he's still alive? No, I don't. But I also don't believe he was being totally truthful with you.'

'He said he'd found peace with God,' I said again.

'Galvin thought he WAS God. When he talked about God, he was talking about himself.'

I suddenly realized the full magnitude – and the horror – of what it was she was telling me.

'Here's a man who killed nine people – horribly and without a trace of human compassion,' she continued. 'Why would he change so much in prison? It doesn't make sense. From what you say, he was truly evil and totally brilliant and operated for most of his life without the slightest hint of remorse. Maybe he was dying of cancer, but I don't believe he suddenly developed a conscience overnight.'

'So what do you think happened?' I asked her.

'I think David Galvin decided to play God, right to the very end. That's what he's doing now.'

'But Galvin's dead,' I repeated.

It seemed important to keep saying that.

'Okay, he's dead.'

'Then what are you trying to say . . . ?'

'Somehow,' Dr Christine Whalen told me, 'David Galvin is still playing the game. A deadly game. A game with no rules. And someone out there is playing it with him. So are you. That's what he was trying to tell you that last day you saw him.'

'But who . . . ?'

'David Galvin is still The Great Pretender,' she said. 'You just never understood.'

sixty

Okay, David Galvin was dead, and now someone else was helping him play out the end of his deadly game.

I sat at my desk in the *Banner* city room, took out a yellow legal pad and began writing down the names of all the potential suspects.

The first name I wrote down was Lisa Montero. Only I'd already eliminated her. Elizabeth Martin had told me she didn't do the Franze killing. It was on Galvin's list of victims. And I still believed all of those murders were connected. So, if Lisa was innocent of that one, it was logical to assume she was innocent of the others too. Of course, if you believed Greg Ackerman, she was a prime suspect in the deaths of her father, mother and brother. He said she wanted control of the entire Montero business empire for herself. But that was a different story. I had trouble enough dealing with one story at a time.

Then there was Ackerman and Andy Kramer. Both of them went to NYU at the same time as Galvin. Other than that, I didn't have a whole lot of evidence linking either of them to the murders. I'd been suspicious of Ackerman at first because of his zeal to prosecute Lisa. But, after seeing the old newspaper clipping about his father, I understood why he was bitter about the Montero family. That didn't make him a murderer.

As for Andy, he was my boss. He was ambitious, he was two-faced and he was the one who put me on this story in the first place. Did he have some ulterior motive for doing that? Probably not. And I wasn't exactly going to help my career at the *Banner* by making wild accusations against my boss. I'd already made wild accusations about my best friend at the *Banner*, Bonnie. If I kept doing it, people there might begin to suspect there was something wrong with me. Or, as Dr Whalen so aptly put, they'd start to think I was totally fucked up.

Another late entry in the suspect sweepstakes was Jimmy Richmond. The son of the *Banner*'s owner and the new publisher. He'd gone to NYU in the mid-'80s too and he asked me a lot of questions about Lisa Montero. Wow, lock him up and throw away the key, huh? I had no reason to suspect him of anything but curiousity about my love life.

I wrote down Linda Hiller and Arthur Dodson too.

They were dead, but I remembered what Christine Whalen had told me. Assume nothing. There are no rules in this game. Just for the hell of it, I checked on both of them. Just like I did before with Galvin. When I was finished, I was satisfied. The bodies that were taken to the morgue were Arthur Dodson and Linda Hiller. They were definitely dead.

That was all.

I'd run out of suspects.

Of course, the killer might be someone not on my list. Someone who'd gone to school with Galvin, but I didn't know about yet. There were 20,000 students there with him. That was a lot of suspects. But I had a gut feeling the answers I was looking for were right in front of me. I just couldn't see them.

I went through all the names on the list again. They all had some connection to NYU when Galvin was there. For most of them, it was a very tenuous connection. Except for one. One person's fingerprints were all over this case. A student at NYU. A friend of David Galvin there. And a connection to at least one of the victims on his list.

I looked at the name and drew a big circle around it.

The key to my entire story.

Been there right from the very beginning.

Lisa Montero.

sixty one

The Montero estate on Shelter Island, where I found Lisa this time, was under incredible security.

There were guards at the gate, all over the grounds and in the house. Those were only the ones that were visible. I figured that there were more hidden away out of sight. Out on the water, the cabin cruiser that John Montero and I had fished from that day patrolled the shore line. I saw men on the deck with guns.

'Someone murdered my father,' Lisa told me. 'They may be responsible for the deaths of my mother and brother too. I'm not taking any chances.'

We were sitting on a deck behind the house, which had a view of Long Island Sound and the jagged coastline across the bay. Lisa was wearing a two-piece blue bikini with a short white robe over it. Her dark black hair hung down over the back of the robe, making it look even whiter than it was. She looked sexy, but I didn't care about that anymore. I was there on business.

'I don't think it's just what happened to your father and family that's got you scared,' I said. 'I think it's Arthur Dodson and Linda Hiller too. You want to make sure you don't wind up like them.'

'What are you talking about?' she asked innocently.

But her heart wasn't in the lie anymore.

She knew that I knew.

'You see, I keep coming back to William Franze's death,' I said. 'It just doesn't fit the pattern of any of the rest of them on Galvin's list. Why now? Why him? What was the connection? I could never find one. It just doesn't make sense unless you murdered him in a jealous rage. Now that makes sense. But you didn't kill him, I know that now. So that leaves only one possibility.'

I took a deep breath. 'It was supposed to be you that died that night. You were the target. Always have been. I don't know why I didn't see that before. You'd been out on a date with Franze. Someone followed you back to his place and decided to kill both of you. Franze was just in the way. Only you had a fight with him and left before the shooting started. In all the confusion, the killer might not have even known that at first. But, even after the killer knew the mistake, it didn't really matter. You were the obvious suspect for the murders. You'd go to jail for the rest of your life. Either way, the killer got you. It was a no-lose situation. Until I came along and cleared you.'

'My hero,' Lisa smiled.

'Tell me the truth about what really happened at NYU,' I said.

Lisa sat there, staring out at the boat on the water for a long time.

'How much do you already know?' she finally asked.

'I know for sure that you knew Galvin in college. The rest is mostly speculation. But logical speculation. There has to have been a connection between your relationship with him and what's happening now.'

'Yeah, you're right,' she sighed. 'We did have a relationship. But it's not like you think.'

She said they had met early during her freshman year, just like she'd told me before. At first, she was really interested in him. He was handsome, smart and fascinating to talk to. There was something more too, she told me. She said. he had this piercing quality in his eyes. When he talked to her, she said, it was like he could see right inside of her. He was incredibly mesmerizing. He probably could have had any girl he wanted.

But he made it clear that sex wasn't what he wanted from her.

'He said he was looking for a spiritual mate,' Lisa recalled. 'Someone he could spend eternity with. Real weird stuff like that. If some guy told me that today, I'd get away from him as fast as I could. But I was young, nineteen years old. I'd had guys hitting on me all through high school, who just wanted to get into my pants. He was different. I bought his whole brooding genius act; at least for awhile. I figured sooner or later we'd wind up in bed. Especially after he introduced me to his parents and everything. But we never did. He just wasn't into sex. At least not the conventional type of sex.

'One morning he was really excited. He told me how he had spent the whole night watching some girl in the dormitory next to his through binoculars. He watched her get dressed for a date. He watched her get undressed after the date. He watched her and her boyfriend make love together. He even watched her sleep at night. He said he felt so close to her that it was like he was in the bed next to her.

'Okay, he was weird, but I still thought he was harmless. And I got a kick out of the fact that he was so different. He told me he liked to play something called The Pretend Game and he showed me how to do it. We'd pick out a couple of people – a girl for him, a guy for me – and come up with a whole fantasy about what we'd do with them. Sometimes we'd watch people for hours, following them around campus all day without them having a clue we'd entered their private little world. It was fun. Kind of like our little secret. And, like I said, it still seemed really harmless.

'After awhile, David's fantasies started getting violent. He started talking about kidnapping people and torturing them and making them plead for their lives. And then one day – I remember we were sitting right in the middle of Washington Square Park – he said we should do it for real. Kidnap someone, torture them and then murder them. He said that would be the ultimate fantasy. And no one would ever know we did it, he said. Because there'd be no motive. Nothing to ever connect it with us. We'd murder just for the thrill of the kill.

'Well, I got really scared. Even though I still never believed he was serious. Yet he was so intense about it. I told him I'd play the game with him. I was afraid to do anything else. But I vowed that I'd never see him again. And that's what happened. That day was the last time we ever talked.

'Then, maybe a year or so later – after he was arrested for all those murders – I checked the date of the killings. The first one was right after our conversation in the park. He'd been planning it all along.'

'What did you do?'

'Nothing.'

'You didn't go to the police?'

'No. I was afraid. I didn't want to get involved. I thought they might think I had something to do with the murders. I had my whole life ahead of me, my career, my future, I didn't want to get dragged into a murder scandal. Besides, Galvin was already caught and behind bars. He'd confessed to all the murders. There was no reason I had to tell my story.'

'And that day in the park – it was the last time you ever talked to him?' I asked.

'No, there was one more meeting. I ran into Galvin in the library a month or two later. I said hello to him and asked how he was doing. But he was very cold and unfriendly. He said he'd found some new friends – and he didn't need me anymore. Then he just walked away. I never saw him again.'

'He didn't mention Arthur Dodson and Linda Hiller's name to you, did he?'

'No.'

'And you never heard of either one before?'

'No, I never knew them.'

It wasn't hard to figure out what happened. Galvin had befriended Hiller and Dodson with the same mesmerizing charm he had used on Lisa earlier. They'd probably played along with his little games for awhile too. Until they realized how insane he really was. Then they had stopped seeing him and probably forgot all about him for a long time. Until he was arrested for the murders. And they realized the enormity of his evil. And that they had played a small part in helping him plan his deadly spree.

Just like Lisa, they didn't want to get involved, so they put it out of their minds. They got on with their lives.

I remembered what David Galvin had told me that day I'd visited him. 'The rest of The Great Pretenders, they're all happy, they're successful, they have new lives. They've forgotten all about me. But I've never forgotten about them. Tell them that.'

Except there never were any Great Pretenders. They only existed in David Galvin's mind. Arthur Dodson. Linda Hiller. Lisa Montero. In the end, David Galvin decided to seek revenge against them all because he thought they had failed him.

They had to die.

David Galvin's final game.

But who was killing them?

And who had killed the people on his list – including my own wife and daughter – that died after Galvin was safely behind bars?

If it wasn't Lisa, then there was someone else still out there.

'I think I've figured out most of the Connie Reyes business,' I said to Lisa.

We were sitting inside now. In the same living room where I'd talked with John Montero. The giant projection screen TV was on again too. There was a newscast on. The woman reading the news looked like she was about ten feet tall.

'Your father set up everything, didn't he?' I said. 'Sent me the notes, in the same style poetry that Felix the Cat used to use. Pointed me in the direction of Corman and the Raphael woman, so they could play their parts. Then, after their performance was over, someone killed them. To keep them quiet, I suppose. Just like someone tried to keep me quiet by trying to run me down.'

'My father had nothing to do with their deaths,' she said. 'He was as upset as anybody when he heard about it.'

'How do you know that?'

'He told me so.'

'And you believed him?'

'He was my father.'

She said it like she was talking about Ward Cleaver or somebody.

'Of course, you had the star performance, Lisa,' I said. 'You had to bat your eyes at me and whisper sweet nothings in my ear and even take me to bed. It must have been really disgusting for you. But I guess it was better than the alternative; a life behind bars.'

She shook her head. 'It wasn't like that, Joe. I know it started out that way. You see, my father said he'd dealt with the justice system before, and just being innocent wasn't enough. He said you always had to have an edge. I was scared. So I did what he told me to do. But then, after I was with you, I wasn't acting anymore. I realized that I . . .'

I made a face. 'Don't tell me,' I said with, with as much sarcasm and derision as I could put into my voice. 'You fell in love with me . . .'

'Something like that,' she said.

She reached over and put her hand on mine. I took it away immediately. No way I was going to get fooled by this woman again.

'I didn't know what else to do,' she said. 'I didn't mind lying to you in the beginning. But then . . . after we . . . well, things changed. I wanted to tell you the truth. But I couldn't.'

'Oh, you could have. You just didn't.'

'Those things we did together, Joe,' she said, 'I couldn't have done them . . . I couldn't have been like that with you in bed unless I really meant it. We were good together. I really liked being with you. I liked you. I couldn't fake it that much. I'm not that good an actress.'

'So why did you cut me out of your life after the court decision?'

'My father made me do that.'

'How?'

'How? He told me to stop seeing you. He said I should have nothing to do with you anymore.'

'And you agreed?'

'I had to. You really didn't know my father, Joe. He was a very powerful man and a very scary one. Most of the people he worked with were frightened to death of him. That's one of the reasons he was so successful. He built his business empire on fear just as much as he did on business smarts. He even terrified me when he got angry. I never was able to stand up to him. But it wasn't just me. I was afraid if I didn't do what he wanted, he wouldn't just take it out on me. He might go after . . .'

'Me?'

'Yes,' she said.

I thought about the bodies of Corman and Raphael lying in that bloody car in a parking garage in midtown Manhattan.

About Greg Ackerman's father and the federal witness who had suddenly changed his story the day he was supposed to testify against William Franze a long time ago.

About the guy who didn't want to sell his business to Montero that turned up in the East River a few days later.

But now John Montero was dead too.

So was Lisa's brother and her mother. Three deaths in one family within the past year. And it would have been four – except Lisa got into an argument with William Franze and left early the night he was murdered.

But who was doing all the killing? And why? Lisa was the only one left, but I really couldn't believe it was her. There was still one more player in this game that I had to find.

The newscaster on the giant TV screen began to deliver an item about police searching for leads in the murder of Wall Street mogul John Montero. Lisa reached over to the remote and shut it off.

'I hate that big television,' she muttered.

'Why do you have it?'

'My father loved it.'

'You could get a smaller one now.'

'No, I could never get rid of this.'

'Why?'

'Too many memories.'

I knew what she meant. Her father loved that TV. Now her father was gone. But when she looked at it, it reminded her of him. I did the same thing with Susan and Joe. I never cleaned their closets out until six months after they were dead. We always hold onto our memories. Clothes. Pictures. Letters. It's our last link to people we love who are dead.

Even bad people.

Like David Galvin.

sixty two

Barbara Galvin looked as if she'd been expecting me when I showed up at her door. Eleven years ago, her world turned upside down when she discovered that her son was a monster. She tried to forget about him, to wipe out all the memories and get on with her life. But she could never do that. It wasn't over yet.

David Galvin was still her son, no matter how hard she tried to deny that.

'We need to talk,' I said.

'I've told you everything I know.'

'I don't think so, Mrs Galvin.'

We went into the living room where we'd been before. Just the two of us this time. Her husband was at work, she told me. I looked over at the picture of him with his family on the wall next to her. Him and his wife. Their two daughters. No pictures of David though. Those had been taken down a long time ago.

Outside, through the picture window in the living room, I saw the quiet suburban neighborhood where a little boy had grown up to become a terrifying killer like Felix the Cat.

Expensive houses. Nicely manicured lawns. Good people. Next door, two kids were throwing a baseball back and forth. The Galvins' dog was sitting in the driveway, barking at the kids and at cars that drove by. Above him I saw the basketball hoop still on the front of their garage. An old, rusted basketball hoop.

'Do your daughters play basketball?' I asked Barbara Galvin.

'No.'

'How about your husband?'

Another no.

'David did though, didn't he? You told me that the last time I was here. You said he was just like any normal kid growing up – liked to spend hours shooting baskets outside in the driveway.'

She didn't answer me.

'When people die or go away, we like to try to hold onto a piece of them,' I said. 'I knew a woman once whose son died and she never threw away any of his clothes or changed a thing in his bedroom. Left everything the way it was, just like he was coming back someday. Sometimes it's hard to let go of the memories. We like to remember the way it used to be.'

I looked outside again at the basketball hoop, the one where David Galvin used to play, before he started playing fantasy games and murdering people and writing letters to the media about his bloody exploits. The basketball hoop that no one used anymore. But it was still there.

'What is your point?' she asked.

'I don't think you really threw away David's last letter, Mrs Galvin,' I said.

She sat there for a long time without answering. At first, I thought maybe she hadn't heard what I said. But then I realized she was going over it all in her mind, thinking about her options. Except she had no options. And she knew that.

She got up and left the room. When she came back, she was holding an envelope in her hand. She handed it to me. It was still sealed.

'You never opened it?' I asked.

'No.'

'Why not?'

'I was afraid to find out what was inside.'

I nodded.

'But you didn't throw it away either.'

'No. I lied and told my husband I had. But I never did.'

'How come?'

'Like you said,' she told me with a sad smile, 'sometimes it's hard to let go.'

sixty three

There were two letters inside the envelope.

The first one was addressed by David Galvin to his mother and father. I read through it quickly. Galvin said he was sorry for all the pain he had caused them. He talked about finding God. He begged them to find it in their hearts to someday forgive him. The whole thing had an unreal quality about it. Like he was telling them what they wanted to hear, not what he really believed. ('He's still playing a game with everyone,' Dr Whalen had said.) There were no clues in the letter that I could see.

I folded it back up again, put it inside the envelope it came in and handed it to Mrs Galvin. I wasn't sure if she'd read it or not. I think I hoped that she never did. That she would put it back where she kept it unopened. Maybe she was better off with her old memories of the creature named Felix the Cat that had once been her son.

The second letter was for me.

This was the real deal:

Dear Joe:

Congratulations on getting this far!

By the time you read this, I assume that a lot will have happened since my departure. I'm not sure exactly what that will be. But I've put all the pieces in motion, all the balls in the air, so it should be interesting. One last game for old times sake.

It's a funny thing about death. Mankind has gained so much knowledge over the years about so many things medicine, technology, the environment. But death remains our great mystery. We know no more about it today than the caveman did. It is still the ultimate unknown adventure. I'm looking forward to it.

In the world of fantasy, those of us who are Gods never die.

We are resurrected, reborn. We are indestructible.

I truly believe I can blur the line between fantasy and reality — and live on even after my physical death through my deeds.

There were five of us who played the game — me and four others. (Yes, I know I said there only three, but I lied. Ha-ha! Welcome to the game!)

We were supposed to be noble warriors. Crusaders. The best of the best. We took an oath to the death to remain as one powerful force. But only I kept my word.

The rest were weak. They failed me. All of them, while I sat in this jail cell, went on with their lives. They made money, they became successful, they thought they could forget about me. But they were wrong. They know that now. I must have my revenge.

Vengeance is mine, saith the Lord.

And I am the Lord.

You and me, Joe, we really are a lot alike. I felt your passion, your intensity, your energy when you came to see me in the hospital. That wasn't why you were chosen, as you will soon see. But you were an excellent choice. I know you will do me proud.

It's funny the way things have worked out so well. Something — maybe luck, maybe fate or maybe there really is another God out there somewhere — brought everything together for me like this at the end. I know you don't understand everything right now. But you will. Very soon.

And now one last poem before I depart for eternity:
One for the money (Dodson, the accountant.
Two for the show (Hiller, the theaterical agent.
Three to get ready (Franze and the girl, who was supposed to be Lisa as you've probably already figured out.)
And four . . .
Well, four . . . well, four you'll know.
Make sure to say hello for me.

There were five pictures attached that Galvin must have cut out of an old NYU yearbook.

Himself.

Arthur Dodson.

Linda Hiller.

Lisa Montero.

And one more.

There was also a newspaper clipping which contained pictures of an exclusive social event that had taken place a few months ago. He had drawn a circle around the face of one of the prominent guests.

The fifth person I was looking for.

The final answer.

The last of The Great Pretenders.

sixty four

The house was big and expensive looking. It was on the water in an exclusive section of Greenwich, Connecticut, where many rich, famous and powerful people lived. The occupant of this house had done very well.

I sat in my car looking at it, thinking about all the things that had happened to me since that phone call out of the blue from Andy Kramer. When this all started, I had a new career, a new woman, a new life. I had security. I had stability.

Now I was back to being a newspaperman again, constantly living on the edge and putting myself on the line each and every day. For better or worse, that phone call had changed my life.

Of course, I thought all along that it had all just been an accident that I was the reporter David Galvin picked for this story. But now I knew the truth.

I got out of the car and walked up to the house.

We always think that we have choices in life. That we control our own destiny. That no matter what happens – like Robert Frost believed – we can still choose the path we want to follow.

But it doesn't always work out that way. Sometimes our decisions have been made for us a long time before. And, when that happens, we find ourselves out of options. All we can do then is hold on and try to survive, like a sailor in the eye of a storm who is trying to get home again.

We are always doomed to keep repeating our own failures, someone once said.

I rang the front doorbell.

The person who answered had changed a lot over the years. The hair was a different color and length, there were a few more pounds and some wrinkles and aging on the face too. Maybe some plastic surgery too. A lot of people who knew the occupant of this house eight years ago might walk by her on the street today, never recognizing her at all.

I knew her right away though.

I should.

I used to be married to her.

'Hello, Susan,' I said.

PART SEVEN

The Great Pretender

sixty five

'I knew you would show up here sooner or later,' Susan said.
She had a gun in her hand and was pointing it at me.
'How could you be sure?'
'You always were a great reporter, Joe.'
'And after you heard about Arthur Dodson, Linda Hiller and Lisa Montero, you figured you were next on the list. Right?'
Susan nodded. 'That's why I'm carrying this.'
She looked at the gun in her hand, put it down at her side and then we went into the house.

It all seemed like a terrible dream. A nightmare I was going to wake up from any second.
'Where is Joey?' is the first question I asked.
'He's at school.'
'Is he all right?'
'He's fine.'
'How much does he know?'

'Nothing.'

'He thinks I'm dead?'

'He doesn't even remember you. My husband Charles is the only father he knows.'

We were sitting in the living room of her house. Me and the woman that used to be my wife a million years ago. The mother of the child I had never seen grow up. Their deaths had turned my whole world upside down. Now it was happening again.

I looked at a picture on the coffee table in front of me of the three of them. Susan. Her husband, whose name was Charles Matheson and was the CEO of a big corporation. And Joey. Joey was almost ten now. In the picture, Matheson had his arm around him. Father and son. They looked like a happy family.

'I guess I'm looking for an explanation from you,' I said to Susan.

'It's a long story, Joe.'

'You went to NYU with David Galvin?'

'Yes, I did.'

I never really knew her, she said.

Everything had always been a lie until her marriage to Charles. Her years at NYU. The time with me. Her entire life.

When she was seventeen she had run away from home and gone to New Orleans. She supported herself first by waitressing. Then dancing in a topless bar. Later, she started dealing drugs along Bourbon Street and in the French Quarter. She was arrested on a drug rap when she was twenty, skipped bail and ran off to marry one of the men she was dealing to. He was a mob guy, and he always kept a lot of cash. So when things went bad in the relationship, she simply took off, along with his money. She used it to enroll herself under a new name at NYU, where she decided she'd get an education and maybe make some money on the side dealing drugs to students.

'I've always been able to do that,' she said. 'Just get up and leave. Switch identities. Start a new life. Different name, different city. I had to do it first when I jumped bail, then again when the mob was looking for their money. It got to be a habit, I guess. When things start to go wrong, I just go. How did you find me?'

I showed her the newspaper article that Galvin had left for me.

The picture from the *New York Times* of Mr and Mrs Charles Matheson of Greenwich, who were being honored at a dinner by a local hospital for their generous charitable contributions.

'I guess he's followed what happened to you from jail,' I told her. 'Probably kept tabs on all four of you. Then, when he saw this picture in the *Times*, he made the connection to me as the reporter who'd covered his arrest. That's why he asked for me in the letter to the *Banner*. He wanted me to find you. It was his sick joke.'

I remembered the day we'd first met. She'd been tending bar at a place on East 34th Street, and I'd just had a big day at the track. I told her about it, and she said maybe she could help me celebrate. We had, I guess, what you'd call a whirlwind romance. We were married a month later. I didn't think much about it then, I just thought we were madly in love. Now I realized I was just part of her pattern. Meet a guy, run off with him, and then leave him.

'What happened that day on the boat after I went for help?' I asked her.

'A fishing boat picked us up. When I got to shore, I realized that they'd found the overturned boat and thought we'd drowned. It seemed easier to leave it that way. I was ready to leave anyway. So I just left.'

'It didn't bother you at all how it might affect me,' I said angrily.

'I figured you'd survive.'

'I loved you, Susan.'

'No, you didn't. You were just in love with the idea of being in love. Hell, you were never even around. Always at the paper or in some bar drinking with your newspaper friends or out gambling away your paycheck. I'm sorry, Joe, but that's the truth. You're a nice guy. But you were a lousy husband and a lousy father.'

'And Charles?' I asked, looking down at the picture on the coffee table.

'He's everything you weren't as a family man.'

'So when do you leave him?'

'I don't.'

'Why not?'

'Because I love him.'

I looked around at the big house she lived in,

'Are you sure you're not in love with the money?' I said.

'The money's nice. But there's more. Charles has given me the stability I always needed – always really wanted – in my life. I have him. I have Joey. I'm happy. He's a good man, Joe. He's the one I was waiting for all of my life.'

I had a lot of other questions I wanted to ask her. About her past. About us. About Joey.

But was there no time for that now.

I needed to know about NYU.

'The thing you have to understand about David Galvin,' she said slowly, 'is that back then I thought he was the most fascinating person I'd ever met. He was simply mesmerizing. Good looking. Charming. Brilliant. But it was more than that. If there was one thing I remember about him, it was his eyes. He had these incredible eyes.'

Lisa had talked about how fascinating Galvin was at NYU too, and talked about his eyes in the same way.

By the time I'd met him, Galvin was frail and sick and dying. But the truth is I'd found him fascinating too. Even at the end, he still had some of that mesmerizing quality. And maybe he'd touched my soul a little bit too. I remembered lying in bed with Carolyn after that last interview and thinking about his passion and his intensity. Thinking about how it scared me. And wondering if maybe there was a bit of David Galvin buried deep inside of me too.

'I've thought about it a lot over the years,' Susan said. 'About how I could fall under the spell of someone like that. I guess the closest comparison I can make is what happened to Charles Manson and the girls around him. I've read a lot about Manson since then. The whole helter-skelter thing. Susan Atkins, Squeaky Fromme and the rest. People who met Manson said they were almost hypnotized by the man. Some of them still are – even after all this time he's been in jail. I guess I was a little bit like that for awhile. Until I realized what kind of a person he really was. And then I got out.'

I had a million questions to ask her. But there was one thing I had to know first.

'The other three – Dodson, Hiller and Lisa – I think I know their stories,' I told her. 'They became friendly with Galvin, got caught up in his pretend games and didn't realize until too late how crazy he really was. Then, after his arrest, the three of them went on with their lives as if nothing had happened. They hadn't killed anyone, but they felt somehow responsible for not stopping him in time. That's what they've had to live with for the past eleven years. Is that what happened to you too?'

I knew what she was going to answer. Of course, that was the way it was. Just like with the other three.

Except I'd been wrong about so many other things in this case.

I was wrong this time too.

Susan had already told me a lot. She'd told me about the boating accident. Her marriage. Her secret past as a drug dealer, stripper and mobster's girlfriend. She said she was a changed person now, and maybe she was. She wanted to tell the truth. About everything.

Sometimes confession really is good for the soul.

'Is that what happened, Susan?' I repeated.

'Not exactly,' she said.

sixty six

The first time was easy, she said.

His name was Thomas Macklin, and he was an attorney for some big Park Avenue law firm. Had a wife and kids, but he was known around the NYU campus as a player. He liked to come to down to Greenwich Village and hit on college girls. He dressed well, he had a lot of money, he wasn't too old – only twenty-eight when he died – so he found some takers.

He'd made a pass one night at Susan while she was working as a waitress at a restaurant near Washington Square. She mentioned it to Galvin, who said he had an idea. They'd play a game with Thomas Macklin. A pretend game. She didn't know it then, but this time they were playing for keeps.

The idea was for Susan to agree to go out with Macklin, giving him lots of reasons as she did so to think he was in for a really good time. She told him the name of a bar they'd meet at. Only the bar was a notorious gay hangout in the middle of a rough area by the Hudson River. And Susan had no intention of being there. Galvin went instead.

Galvin watched in fascination as the notorious ladies man, looking extremely uncomfortable, sat at the bar surrounded by gay men. He kept searching for Susan. In order to make sure he didn't leave, Susan called him several times from a pay phone to say that she was on the way. Each time, she made more lewd suggestions to keep him interested. So Macklin kept sitting at the bar, desperately wanting to get out of there, but desperately not wanting to miss out on Susan either. As time went by, several guys hit on the good-looking guy waiting there by himself. He managed to brush them off. But he didn't look like he could take much more.

Then, after the last phone call from Susan, the beer finally took its toll on his bladder. He had to use the men's room. Galvin followed him in. The two of them were alone.

At first, when he saw the knife, Macklin thought it was a homosexual rape attempt.

He pleaded for his life.

He offered Galvin money.

He even said he'd have sex with him.

She never knew how long the scene went on for. But, when it was over, Macklin was dead. The police found him stabbed to death – with his pants left around his ankles – in the bathroom of a rough homosexual hangout. It looked like an open and shut case. As far as they were concerned, the victim had just gone looking for a different kind of sexual adventure, and gotten more than he bargained for.

Susan never found any of this out until later.

When Galvin told her the story the next day, he left out the part about the murder. She thought Macklin had just had an extremely embarrassing night. The story didn't get much publicity in the papers. Both Macklin's family and his law firm had done everything they could to keep the circumstances of his death private. And Susan had no reason to ever see him again.

The same thing happened with the next two. Marilyn Dupree and Judith Curran. Marilyn Dupree was an exotic dancer and Judith Curran a young black woman trying to work her way through Queens College to become a teacher. In a city like New

York where a dozen murders happen every day, neither of them drew a great deal of attention. If there was much coverage of their deaths, Susan never knew about it.

But the fourth time was different.

That was the one that changed everything.

Her name was Toni Aiello, and she was a popular, pretty eighteen-year-old high school student from Long Island. She was murdered the morning after her senior prom. Toni Aiello and her friends had come into the city to party after the dance, still wearing their formal attire, and Susan had waited on them at the restaurant. Galvin was there too, and was fascinated by the idea of having some fun with a prom queen. Susan lured her into the park late at night with the promise of meeting someone who could sell her drugs. She left her there standing alone in her prom dress. She never knew what happened next.

But later they found Toni Aiello's murdered body behind some bushes near the archway at the entrance to the park.

This murder did not go unnoticed.

A high school girl killed in her prom dress in the middle of Washington Square Park was big news, and the story was splashed over the front page of every newspaper in town.

When Susan read about it, she thought at first the whole thing was just some sort of horrible coincidence. She found Galvin and told him what had happened. She thought he'd be shocked too. But he just laughed. Then he told her. He told her everything. About Aiello. About Macklin. And about all the rest of them too.

'He said they were my murders,' she remembered. 'He'd done the actual killing, but he said he'd give me credit for these four. He said it was just the beginning. He said there'd be a lot more too. He said I was the only one that had lived up to his expectations. He said he was proud of me.'

Susan never went back to NYU. She changed her name, her address, even the way she looked. She never talked to David Galvin again. She was afraid of him. Eventually she got a job tending bar at a place on East 34th Street, which is where I met her.

She agonized over what to do. If she went to the police, she'd have to confess her part in the murders and she'd go to jail too. But if she did nothing, Galvin would carry on with his murder spree. And no one would know the horrible truth except her.

Finally she sent an anonymous letter to the authorities telling them about Galvin. She never knew for sure whether they had taken it seriously or not. But soon after that Galvin was captured. So maybe his arrest wasn't just a lucky break after all. After he was in jail, there was no reason for her to ever admit what she had done. Galvin could never hurt anyone again. So she tried to put it out of her mind. To get on with her life.

She married me.

She had Joey.

Then she married Charles Matheson and became a wealthy Connecticut socialite.

And until this had all exploded around her again most of the time she'd managed to forget all about David Galvin and the games they'd played at college eleven years ago.

Most of the time.

'Sometimes at night,' she said, 'I wake up and I can still see their faces. All four of them. Macklin. Dupree. Curran. Aiello. It's like I could almost reach out and touch them. I want to say I'm sorry. I want to say I didn't mean it. I want to say a lot of things to those people. But it's too late. So instead I get up, send my son off to school, kiss my husband goodbye as he goes off to work and try to pretend like it never happened.'

Then she talked about the night that we met.

'When you told me your name, I knew who you were,' she said. 'I remembered it from the story about Galvin being arrested. I'd kept a copy of that article and looked at it every once in awhile just to tell myself that he really was in jail and couldn't come looking for me anymore. I couldn't believe the man who wrote that newspaper article was asking me out. I took it as a sign. A sign of hope. A sign that I could somehow turn my life around by being with you.

'That was why it was so important to me to have Joey too. I wanted to bring something good and wonderful and hopeful into this world. I knew I could never make up for the four lives that were gone. But I could do this. I could have a son and I could raise him to be a good person. It became the most important thing in my life. When I look at Joey, when I think about him, well, that's the one thing that makes the nightmares go away.'

I wasn't sure what to say.

We all go through life thinking we're making our own choices about which direction to go. Then sometimes, like now, we find that the choices were made a long time ago.

'If Joey was so damn important to you, then why did you leave me?' I asked angrily.

'That's why I left you, Joe.'

'I – I don't understand . . .'

'You weren't the one for me,' she said. 'I thought you were, but you weren't. Your life was falling apart just like my mine had been back then before I met you. I had to move on. For myself. And for Joey. That's when I met Charles. And I knew he was a good man and a kind man and the man I wanted to spend the rest of my life with. I'm sorry.'

I nodded. There wasn't much else to do. I had a million things I wanted to say to her, but I didn't.

'And you've never told anybody else about all this?' I asked.

'No.'

'Not even your new husband.'

'That's right.'

'So why are you telling me now?'

'I figured it was time,' she said.

I looked down at the gun that was lying next to her down on an end table. 'And you're afraid.'

'Yes. He's coming after me. Just like he came after the others. I know that's what's happening here.'

'David Galvin is dead,' I reminded her.

'You don't know him,' she said. 'He's evil. He's the devil. Somehow he's found a way.'

A few minutes later, Susan walked me to the front door. I put out my hand to say goodbye. She hugged me instead. I hugged her back. I thought I'd feel nothing for her. This woman who had once been my wife and the mother of my child. Who I now knew had been alive for the past eight years while I grieved for her. Who had married another man. And who once played deadly games with a cold-blooded murderer. But I was wrong. I felt her touch, I smelled the scent in her hair and I was under her spell again. I missed her. I'd always miss her. I loved her. God, help me.

'What are you going to do now, Joe?' she asked.

'I don't know,' I said.

sixty seven

I needed to talk to someone. Someone I could trust.

For the first time in my life, I wasn't sure what to do about a story. If I printed it, I'd have the scoop of a lifetime. But I'd also be sending Susan – the mother of my son – to prison.

There was something else bothering me too. I wasn't convinced I had the whole story yet. Susan had given me the answers to a lot of my questions. But not all of them.

I went through the possibilities of people I could go to for advice. Jack Rollins was obviously out. Andy too, he was too ambitious to think about anything but what an exclusive like this would do for his own career. Spencer Blackwood? Maybe, maybe not. He was a nice enough old guy and he seemed to like me, but he was a newspaper editor too. I didn't know which way he would go. I remembered Christine Whalen and tried to get her on the phone, but there was no answer. Maybe she'd be back soon, but I didn't want to wait. I needed someone now. There was only one other person I could think of.

'Bonnie, do you want to get some coffee?' I said.

'I've already had about eleven cups of coffee this morning,' she answered. 'Do you really want to be responsible for pouring more caffeine into me? It could get ugly.'

'I'll take the gamble,' I told her.

We sat at a small table in the corner of the *Banner* cafeteria.

Bonnie, as usual, was doing most of the talking.

'I really shouldn't be drinking coffee. Coffee is supposed to get you up. Well, I'm so up I feel I should have a parachute on my back. I mean I am flying. Maybe I should try decaf instead, huh? Hey, what is decaf anyway? Did you ever see that bit on Seinfeld? What's the deal with decaf; do they cut open the coffee beans and pour out the caffeine or something? I think about stuff like that all the time . . .'

'My wife and son are alive,' I told her.

I didn't think there was anything that could stop Bonnie from talking when she was on a roll, but that did it.

'And she told me she was a murderer.'

Bonnie took a deep breath. 'Well, there's a real conversation stopper if I ever heard one,' she said slowly.

I told her about everything that had happened in Greenwich.

'So what do you think I should do?' I asked her when I was finished.

'Run the story,' she said without any hesitation.

'But if I do that, I'll ruin Susan's life. And my son's too. She could go to jail, and he'll be without a mother. She did a terrible thing eleven years ago. And she did a terrible thing to me when she faked her death and ran off with Joey. But now she seems to have pulled her life together. She's an upstanding citizen. She's happy. Joey's happy. What the point of changing all that?'

'Then don't do the story,' Bonnie said.

'She's the key. The missing person I've been looking for. The whole story hinges on her. I've been working on this for weeks. My whole newspaper career depends on it. I can't just walk away from it.'

'Jesus Christ, Joe, I don't know what to tell you. You've got to make the decision. Not me.'

'You could do the story yourself,' I pointed out to her.

'No, I couldn't. I have no proof.'

'I just gave it to you.'

She shook her head. 'It doesn't work like that,' she said. 'We're a team. We started out on this story as a team, we're going to finish it as a team. Whatever we decide, we decide together. Okay?'

'Okay,' I said.

There was something else we hadn't talked about yet. Bonnie brought it up before I did.

'What about the new murders? Dodson, Hiller, Franze and Montero? She confessed to helping Galvin kill four people eleven years ago. Maybe she murdered these people . . .'

'She told me she didn't know anything about them,' I said.

'You believed her?'

'Yes.'

'Why?'

'I just think she was telling the truth.'

'She's a liar, Joe. She told you that. A very good liar. Her whole life has been built on lies.'

'I believe her,' I said.

Bonnie started to say something, then just shrugged. 'Okay, so where does that leave us, partner?'

'Still looking for a killer.'

'You got any ideas?'

'John Montero.'

'What about him?'

'He doesn't fit the pattern,' I said.

sixty eight

• • • • • • • • • • •

The Montero killing had been bothering me ever since it happened. It was different from the rest. Dodson, Hiller and Lisa had been members of Galvin's secret group. There was a reason for a surviving member to want to kill them to keep the story quiet.

But why Lisa's father? The circumstances of his killing were different too.

Dodson and Hiller had been murdered with all the trappings of one of Galvin's fantasy games. The wedding dress. The clown suit. But there was nothing like that with Montero. It was a hit. Plain and simple. Whoever killed him wasn't there to play games. They just wanted him dead.

So what did that mean?

Well, maybe there were two killers at work here. One for Dodson, Hiller, Franze and Whitney Martin – thinking Martin was Lisa. Another who simply wanted to get rid of John Montero.

Or maybe the killer was really after Montero all along and just killed the rest of them to cover up his real motive. Someone who had a motive for wanting Montero dead.

Someone who hated him.

Who hated John Montero?

Well, Greg Ackerman did.

I went over the stories about Ackerman's father and Montero in the library again. Looking for something I might have missed the first time around.

Greg Ackerman's father died five years after the case fell apart, a broken man. Then Ackerman went to NYU, where one of his classmates turned out to be Lisa Montero. The daughter of the man who ruined his father's life.

Did Greg Ackerman know she was there? He said he didn't, but I had to consider the possibility. I also had to consider the possibility that maybe something else had happened between him and Lisa. She was very attractive. Even he had admitted that to me. ('On a scale of one to ten, I'd make her a fifteen,' he said to me.)

What if he asked her out and she turned him down? Or they had a relationship that went bad? Would that be enough to push him over the edge to murder? First, her father destroys his father's life, then she breaks his heart. So he carries a grudge around with him all these years until he finally gets a chance for revenge. And when I mess up his murder case against Lisa, he goes right after the father.

I shook my head. This was all speculation. I needed some facts.

The man who had changed his testimony in the case against Montero all those years ago, Louis Archer, moved to Arizona afterward, according to one clipping I found. Maybe that was a lead. If I tracked him down, maybe he'd tell me the truth about what really happened. Maybe that would lead me to the evidence I needed on Greg Ackerman.

I managed to follow Archer's trail to a retirement home in Tucson, where he had died several years ago. Natural causes. Nothing suspicious about it, they said. He was an old man.

Another dead end.

Just for the hell of it, I looked up the other story Ackerman had told me. The man who had died mysteriously after refusing to sell his company to Montero. Edward Findlay. I read about his disappearance, the discovery of his body in the East River, the police refusing to bring any charges against Montero and the sad story of Findlay's wife and little daughter. There was a picture of the two of them taken at his funeral. I found a later clip that said his wife had committed suicide. They said she had never recovered from the pain of losing her husband.

I knew that same pain.

I'd felt it when I lost Susan and Joe Jr.

Now I felt it again knowing they were alive all this time, but realizing they could never be a part of my life anymore.

I read the Edward Findlay file again. The first time I'd looked at the clipping a few weeks ago I'd been bothered by a nagging feeling that I was missing something. I still had that feeling.

One of the later stories said that his little girl had been sent to a foster home after the mother died. It said she was having a lot of adjustment problems. I looked at the picture of her again at the funeral. A little girl who'd just lost her father.

The vague uneasy feeling I had suddenly got a lot stronger.

I walked over to the head of the library and asked if she had a magnifying glass. She gave me one from her desk. I took it back to where I was sitting and looked at the picture again. The little girl's face jumped out at me now.

People change a lot over the years. A little girl doesn't always look the way she's going to when she grows up.

But some things are the same.

I must have sensed some of it the first time I looked at the picture, but it didn't click until now.

Now I knew.

I knew who the little girl was.

And I suddenly knew who had a reason for killing John Montero.

sixty nine

It took me only about half an hour to get back up to Greenwich. The afternoon commuter jamups hadn't started yet, and I drove very fast. I did 70 mph on the East River Drive, weaving in and out of traffic like a crazed race car driver. Then, once I was over the Triborough Bridge and headed north on the New England Thruway, I pretty much floored the accelerator on the open stretch of road until I got to Connecticut.

I was furious with myself.

I've always been a sucker for a woman's sob story. All my life, a woman bats her eyes at me and I believe everything she says. I keep looking for the truth, and expecting I will find it. But I never do. They'd all lied to me. Susan. Lisa. All of them.

The big house loomed in front of me now.

The house of Mrs Charles Matheson, who used to be my wife Susan Dougherty. Susan had lived a lie for a long time, and now it was finally going to all end.

I squealed to a stop in front of the house, jumped out of the car and ran up across the lawn to the front door. Susan must have heard me coming. She opened the door before I got there.

'What's going on?' she asked.

'The police will be here soon,' I said.

'You called them?'

'Dennis Righetti. He's an old friend of mine.'

'Why?'

'Because I don't want anyone else killed.'

'I didn't kill any of those people,' she said. 'I told you that.'

'I know what you told me.'

'But . . .'

'We better go inside,' I said.

I went over it all in the living room. Everything I'd found out that day. She didn't ask me any questions. She didn't interrupt. She seemed to be in a state of shock.

'The thing is,' I explained, 'David Galvin has a disciple. Someone he convinced to finish the job for him before he died. This person has become a killing machine just like Galvin was. Murdered Dodson, Hiller, Franze, Whitney Martin, John Montero, and probably Montero's two accomplices in his little scam with me too. There's two names left for the killer – you and Lisa. Lisa's got more protection than money can buy. I figure you're an easier target right now.'

'Do you think someone like that would be able to find me?'

'I found you.'

A frightening thought suddenly came to me. 'The killer doesn't have to find you,' I said.

'What do you mean?'

'I may have already led the killer right to you.' I got up and looked out the window. Everything on the street was quiet. No sign of anyone there.

'We've got to get out of here,' I said. 'Before it's too late.'

'It already is,' a woman's voice said.

But it wasn't Susan. The speaker was in the living room with us. I don't know how long she'd been in the house. I realized that she'd probably followed me on my whirlwind trip up from the city. She wouldn't have had any trouble keeping up with me. Because she drove even faster than I did.

She looked manic and jittery and kind of crazy, but then she always did.

I just never knew why.

Now she was standing there pointing a gun at me.

Bonnie.

seventy

'You were right about me the first time, Joe,' Bonnie said. 'But you let me talk you out of it. I really had to think fast to come up with all the answers on Hiller and Dodson. The wedding I was supposed to be in. That anonymous phone call about Hilldale I said they had a record of at the switchboard. If you'd checked, you'd have found none of it was true. But you never did. Not very good reporting, partner.'

'I believed you,' I said.

'That was your big mistake.'

'You killed them all, didn't you?'

'That I did.'

'Why?'

'Haven't you figured that out yet?'

'John Montero,' I said.

She nodded. 'He ruined my life.'

Bonnie was the little girl in the story. The one about the man who was found in the East River after he refused to sell his company to the Montero Corporation. I finally realized it when I'd looked closely at that old picture of Edward Findlay's family.

'My mother committed suicide about six months later because she just couldn't go on anymore,' Bonnie said. 'I was sent to live with some foster family named Kerns, which is where I picked up this name. My foster father sexually abused me all through high school. I hated him, I hated them, I hated their name. I kept using it though because it was a reminder of what John Montero had done to my family. Then one day I decided to do the same thing to him. Take away his family. One by one. First I killed the brother. Then the mother. Lisa was supposed to be next, but that got screwed up. It still would have worked if she'd gone to jail. Then, after you got her off, I decided to go right after Montero. That just leaves Lisa. I'll go see her after I've finished here with you two.'

'Why us?' I asked. 'Why the others like Hiller and Dodson? We didn't have anything to do with your father's death.'

'You're talking too much,' she said. 'Sit down over there. Next to your wife. Or your ex-wife.'

I sat. As I did, I looked over at Susan. I thought she'd be scared. She was, but not just by the gun pointed at the two of us. She kept staring at the front door. At first I didn't know why, but then I remembered about Joey. It was close to four o'clock, and Joey would be coming home from school soon. He'd come bouncing in through the front door, yell out a greeting to his mother and then . . .

'The police are on their way,' I said to Bonnie.

'Nice try,' she smiled.

'I called them before I left.'

'You're bluffing.'

She didn't seem worried.

'Okay, here's the deal,' Bonnie said. 'You turn up here, find your ex-wife – who you thought was dead all these years – and discover she's married to another man. So you go crazy, shoot her, and then shoot yourself with the same gun. Which just happens to be the same gun that killed all the rest of them.' She smiled. 'Or maybe we'll just do it as another David Galvin murder. They'll find you dead in each other's arms. Two last victims for Felix the Cat. A final fantasy from beyond the grave.

That's got front page headline written all over it, doesn't it, Joe? Hell, I could even write the story.'

Susan just sat there silently. I knew she was still thinking about Joey walking in on this.

'Let us go,' I begged, 'we won't tell anyone.'

'Jesus Christ, Joe, don't insult my intelligence. Of course, you'd tell people. It's the fuckin' story of a lifetime. Only you're never going to get a chance to write it.'

I tried to keep her talking. I didn't have a plan. It was the only thing I could think of to do.

'What about the rape story at Penn State?' I asked. 'Was that all a lie too?'

'As a matter of fact, that one was true. Yeah, that was pretty traumatic. Just like it was pretty traumatic to lose my mother and father within six months of each other, and have to go live with some family from hell. I was really messed up as a kid. Sexually and a lot of other ways too. I have John Montero to thank for it. I promised myself that someday I would make him pay for what he had done. Except I never knew how. Until I met David Galvin.'

'How does Galvin fit into this?' I asked.

'I went to see him in prison about a year ago. For an interview, just like you found out. That part was true. I lied though when I said he wouldn't talk to me. He talked to me, all right. God, did we talk. David was the most fascinating person I've ever met. He opened up my life in a way no one had ever done before.

'I told him about John Montero, and he said he'd known the daughter in college. That set something off between us. Something special. Something inspired.

'He'd just been diagnosed with cancer a few weeks earlier. I guess he knew he was going to die. He wanted to do something spectacular before he left this world. One last game.

'So he gave me this idea. A way to get back at John Montero. He said killing was fun, it was easy, it was the greatest high, the biggest thrill, a person could ever experience. Once he put the idea in my head, I couldn't get rid of it. I thought about it constantly. I became obsessed by it. It was my only reason for living.

'I decided to take John Montero's family away from him, just the way he'd taken away mine. Slowly. One by one. Galvin helped me. He took me through it. He helped me plan everything. He was my mentor. He was my inspiration.

'We started with the brother. I made friends with him at this lake house he was staying at in upstate New York. Then one day, when we were alone, I knocked him unconcious with a hammer and threw him into the deep water. I figured if anyone saw the bruise on his head, they'd figure it happened when he hit a rock at the bottom of the lake. But no one ever did. Everyone just assumed it was a case of accidental drowning.

'Mrs Montero was next. She was a lot tougher. But I waited until no one was home, snuck in and knocked her out with some chloroform. Then I dragged her into the garage, put her in her car, closed all the doors and windows and started the engine. Pretty soon she was on her way to eternity.

'And then there was Lisa. Dear, sweet Lisa. That was supposed to be her under the covers with Franze, when I shot them. I started firing as soon as I walked into the bedroom, so I didn't realize my mistake until after they were both dead. It should have been Lisa. But, when she became the chief suspect in the murder, I liked it even better. She'd go to jail for the rest of her life. Montero would be devastated. And I even got to cover the story for the *Banner*. It was perfect. Until you came along and messed everything up. I was so mad after the charges were dropped that I wanted to kill you right then.'

I remembered the speeding car that almost hit me outside Lanigan's.

'That was you, wasn't it?' I said. 'You tried to run me down.'

'Yeah, that's right. A few inches the other way and it would have been over right there. We wouldn't be sitting here right now. But then I decided it would be better to let you live for awhile. That way you could lead me to my last victim.'

She pointed over toward Susan. She still hadn't said anything. She looked like she was in a trance.

'And Joseph Corman and Karen Raphael?'

'Your detective and mystery witness?' Bonnie laughed. 'Oh yeah, I did them too. I followed you that day you told me about going to meet them. Once I knew who they were, it was easy. I just waited for them in the parking garage. I said I worked with you on the *Banner*. They were very surprised at the end.'

'Why them?'

'They helped Montero.'

'But they were just acting out a role . . .'

'They were the enemy. They had to die. All our enemies have to die.'

Our enemies.

'You mean you and Galvin?' I asked.

'David and I made a pact,' she said. 'He taught me how to get revenge on John Montero and his family. In return, I'd help him get revenge against his enemies. He said all the others had failed him. I was the only one worthy of him. The one he needed for his last game. We took an oath to be allies forever. A blood oath. And we sealed it with a kiss.'

I stared at her.

'We had sex, Joe. One time in his cell. They left us alone because I was a reporter, and we did it right there. My experience with sex has never been very good. I told you that. After everything that happened to me, I'd pretty much given up on it. Until David Galvin. I suddenly realized he was the one I'd been waiting for. It was like . . . like having sex with a god.

'Afterward, he told me his idea. He knew he had only about a year to live. But he said it was fate that had brought us together. Just like fate was bringing everything together for him in one last burst of passion at the end of his life on this planet. Lisa Montero. The Great Pretenders. You and your wife. It's strange how something like that happens. All the planets are in alignment or something, I guess. But it's a sign. A sign from God. Or in this case a sign to God.

'You see, that was our deal – David and me. He taught me how to get rid of the Monteros. He turned my life around. So I agreed to finish his last job for him. To close the book on The Great Pretenders. They'd all let him down, he said. They were all unworthy. If he was dying, he wanted to take them all with him.'

I remembered she said she'd followed me to get to Susan. So Galvin hadn't given her all the answers.

'He didn't tell you who the last Great Pretender was?' I asked.

Bonnie shook her head. 'No. I was as surprised when I found out who it was as you were,' she said, looking over at Susan. 'But that was part of the game, I guess. And I was playing it, just like you. Only I knew it.'

'Galvin was using you too, Bonnie.

'David loves me,' she said proudly.

'He's dead.'

'Not really.'

'But . . .'

'I still talk to him every day,' she said.

I wondered how it would end up for Bonnie. Would she kill herself to be with the man she loved? Or would she spend the rest of her life in some fantasy world pretending that Galvin was still alive? I thought about that cult in San Diego who committed mass suicide because their leader convinced them that a space ship was coming to take them to a new world. About all the people who died in Jonestown because they listened to the wrong person. About the Manson girls who savagely murdered actress Sharon Tate and others because Manson ordered them to do it. We're all looking for something in this life. Some of us just find it in the darkest places.

'That's enough talking,' Bonnie said. 'I know you probably have a lot more questions. Reporter's curiosity and all that. But we're out of time. Besides, it's not your story anymore. It's my story. It's always been my story.'

There was a sense of serenity that settled in on me when I realized that I was going to die with Susan.

I'd always felt that I should have been with her and Joey in that boating accident I'd thought they died in eight years ago.

Now, at least, she and I would be together again.

Suddenly there was a knock on the front door. Susan looked over at me in terror. Bonnie seemed confused at first too, but then she realized who it must be.

Joey.

'Well, well,' Bonnie laughed. 'The whole family is going to get to be together one last time. Isn't that nice?'

There was another knock. Then the door started to open.

Bonnie turned in that direction with the gun.

'N -o -o-o!' Susan screamed. She hurtled herself at Bonnie and the gun like a human projectile.

Bonnie started firing. The first shot hit Susan in the shoulder.

There was a bright red splotch of blood on her blouse. Susan hesitated for just a second, then kept coming at Bonnie. She leaped on top of her and the two women went down in a heap. I ran over and desperately tried to get the gun away from Bonnie, but I couldn't get at it in time. There was another gunshot. And then I felt Susan's body go limp.

That's when Righetti and a half dozen other cops came bursting in through the front door.

A lot of what happened after that is very hazy. I remember them pulling Bonnie to her feet, getting the gun away from her and putting handcuffs on her. I remember someone calling for an ambulance. I remember the blood all over Susan's clothes. There was so much blood. I tried to stop it, but I couldn't. No one could.

When the ambulance finally came, I got in and rode with her to the hospital.

She had enough strength left to reach out and hold my hand. She squeezed it tightly. She tried to say something, but I couldn't make out the words.

I leaned down closer to try and hear. So close my lips were almost touching hers.

'I love you,' she whispered. 'You were the one. You've always been the one. I've always loved you. That's why I had to leave. It hurt so much that you could never love me back.'

I kissed her gently.

'Joey . . . ?' she asked.

'He's fine.'

'Take care of our son.'

'Everything's going to be all right.'

I cradled her in my arms again and kissed her. I held onto her like that until we got to the hospital where they told me she was dead.

seventy one

'I've decided to quit,' I told Spencer Blackwood.

'You mean the *Banner*?' Blackwood asked. He didn't seem as surprised as I thought he would be.

'Being a newspaperman.'

'Now why would you want to do that?'

'I screwed up, Spence.'

'How?'

'Lisa Montero.'

'Oh, you mean that phony story about the witness,' he said.

I stared at him. 'You knew?'

'I figured it out somewhere along the line. Like I told you once before, I just didn't wake up one day at seventy and become the editor. I used to be a pretty damned good reporter myself.'

We were sitting at the bar in Lanigan's on a hot June afternoon, a few weeks after Bonnie had been arrested. When I had told Blackwood I needed to see him, he suggested we meet here instead of his office. He'd done the same thing eight years ago after Rollins had fired me. That time he told me that I'd be back someday. That all bad things do eventually pass.

So now here we were again.

'If you know, how come you didn't fire me?'

'I never had any proof.'

'You do now.'

'Okay, you're fired,' he smiled.

Blackwood took a drink of the beer on the bar in front of him.

'So what are you going to do next?' he asked. 'I guess that fancy public relations job with your ex-fiancée's daddy is out, huh? Let's see, you're forty-one years old, you've never really been anything but a newspaperman in your whole life and – to be perfectly candid – you're pretty much damaged goods if you leave here again under a cloud. But there's still probably plenty of opportunities out there for you. Hey, maybe you can apply to one of those correspondence courses for hotel management. Or go to truck driving school, you know, like those ads on late-night TV. And then there's the food services industry. I hear that's a really interesting field. I can picture you right now as the up-and-coming assistant manager of some McDonald's in a place like Peekskill. Or maybe even Poughkeepsie . . .'

'This isn't a joke,' I said quietly. 'I'm serious.'

'So am I.'

'I fucked up.'

'So what? Do you think you're the first person that ever fucked up? Look, you made a mistake on this story. But you also did a lot of things right. I've got reporters upstairs who go their entire careers without doing as many things right as you did on this story. You're not perfect, Joe. You're flawed. We all are.'

He drank some more of his beer.

I realized now why we had met here instead of his office. If I'd admitted to him up there that I lied about the story: he was the editor, and he'd have to do something about it. Down here it was just two guys talking at a bar. Just like we did after Walter Billings died.

'You got a bad break on Billings eight years ago,' Blackwood said to me now. 'You wound up being the fall guy for something that probably really wasn't your fault. I figure we owe you one.

So, as far as I'm concerned, you get a free ride on Lisa Montero. Then we're even.'

I stared at him. He knew it was Jack Rollins who had screwed up the Billings story. He probably knew it eight years ago too.

'I don't know, Spence,' I said, shaking my head. 'It just doesn't make sense . . .'

'A lot of things don't make sense, Joe. Hell, I'm going to have to retire soon and one of those two jackasses – Jack Rollins or Andy Kramer – is going to wind up being the editor. That sure doesn't make sense to me. And what about Bonnie Kerns? They'll probably make a TV movie about her, she'll get interviewed by Diane Sawyer and some hotshot lawyer will convince a jury she's really not responsible for any of the murders. In a couple of years she could be out and gunning for you again.

'The whole world doesn't make sense,' Spencer Blackwood said to me. 'You want to quit that too?'

seventy two

In September, three months after Susan died, I talked to my son for the first time. Sort of.

It was the first day of school, and I watched him come out the front door of the big house in Greenwich. Charles Matheson was there too. He gave Joe Jr a big hug before he got on the school bus. I watched Matheson go back into the house. Then I followed the bus to school.

I watched as he milled around with other students in front of the school until the bell rang. It would be easy to approach him. All I had to do was climb out of the car and introduce myself. I had a million things I wanted to tell him. I didn't say any of them.

After school was over, he went to a park and played baseball with some friends. There was a bench next to the field. I sat on it and watched the game. Lost in my thoughts. Then a batter hit a foul ball that rolled a few feet away from me.

'Hey, mister,' someone yelled.

I looked over toward the field.

It was Joey.

'Mister, can you throw me the ball?'

I leaned down and picked up the baseball. I'd always wanted to play catch with my son. Ever since he was born. Now I had the chance. I picked up the baseball. I threw it back to him on the fly.

'Wow,' he said, 'you've got some arm.'

'Thanks.'

'Do you play baseball?'

'A long time ago. I'm a little too old now.' I smiled at him. 'But my son does.'

'My dad's taking me to see the Yankees on Saturday,' he told me.

'Your dad sounds like a great guy,' I said.

Then he went back to the ball game.

Thirty minutes later, Charles Matheson came along to pick him up and take him home. Joe Jr ran over and gave him another big hug. Then he started talking excitedly to him. Probably about what he'd done on the ballfield that day. Matheson beamed proudly as he listened.

Charles is a good man, Susan had told me just before she died. He's the only father Joe has ever known.

Take care of our son.

I felt like an outsider watching the scene. A voyeur. Just like David Galvin used to be. Looking at other people, intruding on their private world, without them ever knowing until it was too late.

I remembered what Galvin had said to me in that final note. You and me, we're a lot alike, Dougherty. I'd had that same feeling when I met him. I felt his passion. I felt his intensity. I somehow understood what he was looking for. It scared me. And here I was now acting just like him.

Except I wasn't.

I wasn't like David Galvin at all.

We were both searching for passion in our lives. But not in the same places. Galvin liked to hurt people. He enjoyed causing pain and suffering. I'd hurt some people too, but not in the same way. And I never meant to hurt anybody. I always wanted to do the right thing. I wanted to be a good person.

That was the difference.

For whatever it's worth, I'd never told anyone about Susan and Joe Jr being my wife and son. Bonnie hadn't said anything in jail either. And no one else had ever made the connection.

As far as everyone knew, Susan was simply Mrs Charles Matheson, the last name on Galvin and Bonnie's list of targets.

Someday, someone probably will figure it out.

Someone who knew Susan, and recognizes her picture in the paper as the same woman who died in Greenwich.

Or Bonnie might spill the beans if she ever really does do that TV-movie or book.

Or maybe I'll decide to tell the story myself. Maybe I'll tell the whole truth to my son someday too.

But for now it would just be my secret.

I'd told too many secrets already.

I decided to let this one be.

seventy three

I used to pretend that I had all the answers. I thought I knew it all. Now I'm not sure about anything anymore.

Lisa called me one day after everything had calmed down. She said she still thought about me a lot. She suggested we get together for a drink sometime. We did. After that, we met for dinner. Eventually we started sleeping together again.

I do not know what will happen between us.

When I'm with Lisa, I still feel that same passion I felt the very first time I saw her. She excites me. She thrills me. She makes me come alive again. I feel her fire, I feel her pain and I feel what I desperately try to convince myself is her undying love.

But then there's other times, mostly late at night after she's gone home again, that I'm uncertain.

I tell myself that too much has happened between us for me to have any realistic hope about our future. She lied to me. She used me. She kept secrets from me. I understand why she did it, but I can't ever forget that it happened. I wonder if I will ever be able to trust her completely again.

I think about Susan too.

Not the Susan who died as I held her hand in a speeding ambulance. Not the one who was married to Charles Matheson. No, when I think about Susan now, she's my wife again. We're both young, we're in love and we're filled with hope for the future. Sometimes the fantasy is so real that I feel I can almost reach out and touch her. But then she's gone again.

And I wonder if we only get one chance at happiness in this life.

A long time ago, I found the woman I loved. I married her. I had a son with her. Then I threw it all away. And now she's dead. 'I love you, Joe,' Susan told me at the end. 'You were the one. You've always been the one. I've always loved you.'

Maybe that's all we get. Maybe there is no second time around. Maybe what I have now with Lisa – those brief moments of excitement and exultation and ecstasy – is the best that it will ever be for me again.

And so that's how I live my life now.

I live for the ecstasy.

I live for the thrill.

I live for the passion.

And I pretend that it will never end.